OBELISTS
AT SEA

C. DALY KING (1895-1963) was an American psychologist and detective story writer. He was born in New York City and educated at Yale University. After fighting in World War I, he worked in textiles and in advertising before returning to school at Columbia to study psychology, with a particular focus on sleep and consciousness. In the 1930s, King published nine books that quickly established him as a master of the Golden Age mystery, but ceased writing fiction with the advent of World War II.

MARTIN EDWARDS is the author of numerous mystery novels and short stories, including those in the Lake District Mysteries and Rachel Savernake Golden Age Mysteries series. His nonfiction work has won Edgar, Agatha, H.R.F. Keating and Macavity awards, and he was the recipient of the 2020 Diamond Dagger award for lifetime achievement. A renowned expert in the genre, Edwards is the series consultant for the British Library's Crime Classics series, the archivist for the Crime Writers Association and the Detection Club, and the editor of 37 anthologies. He lives in Lymm.

OBELISTS
AT SEA

C. DALY
KING

Introduction by
MARTIN
EDWARDS

AMERICAN
MYSTERY
CLASSICS

Penzler Publishers
New York

Published in 2023 by Penzler Publishers
58 Warren Street, New York, NY 10007
penzlerpublishers.com

Distributed by W. W. Norton

Cover image: Andy Ross
Cover design: Mauricio Diaz

Paperback ISBN 978-1-61316-416-7
Hardcover ISBN 978-1-61316-415-0
eBook ISBN 978-1-61316-417-4

Library of Congress Control Number: 2023902485

Printed in the United States of America

9 8 7 6 5 4 3 2 1

INTRODUCTION

OBELISTS AT SEA is a striking example of American Golden Age
detective fiction at its most convoluted and self-confident. This
novel launched the brief and remarkable career of Charles Daly
King, whose contributions to the crime genre were as outland-
ish as they were intriguing. The book has an odd literary history which somehow typifies the unorthodox nature of King's
writing.

King's stories exert a special appeal for connoisseurs of the
curious, partly because the scarcity of his books has made them
highly collectable, but also because at his best he was admirably ingenious and inventive. No author skilled enough to win
the praise of such discerning novelists as E.C. Bentley, Dorothy
L. Sayers, Anthony Boucher, Julian Symons, and (perhaps more
surprisingly) Storm Jameson can sensibly be dismissed as a mere
eccentric. King's fiction has a distinctive and sometimes pun-
gent flavor and anyone who enjoys an intricately plotted whodunit may well develop a taste for it. Until the appearance of
this edition, however, copies of his debut novel have been van-
ishingly scarce.

King summarizes the key distinguishing feature of the story
in a prefatory note: "four psychologists, representing different
schools within their science, apply their particular theories to-

ward the solution of the mystery." The four men are passengers on the *S.S. Meganaut*, one of the most luxurious of the North Atlantic liners, and are travelling from New York, their ultimate destination a convention in London.

Victor Timothy Smith, a millionaire accompanied by his glamorous mistress, is killed after the lights suddenly go out in the *Meganaut*'s crowded smoking-room. When emergency lighting illuminates the scene, a still smoking revolver falls from the hand of a shady lawyer called de Brasto, Not surprisingly, the lawyer is seized, but it soon becomes evident that the case against him is far from watertight.

As complication piles on complication, Captain Horace Mansfield decides that he cannot simply rely on the ship's detectives to solve such an unconventional puzzle. Desperate for enlightenment and having recently read "a tale of mystery in which a noted psychologist had successfully baffled the more ordinary agents of justice and had produced, at the conclusion, a brilliant train of reasoning through which the villain had been seized," he consults the psychologists.

As in so many Golden Age whodunits, the main characters are listed at the beginning of the book. The four amateur sleuths in the ship's company are: Dr Frank B. Hayvier, "a popular psychologist"; Dr Malcolm Plechs, "a fashionable psychologist"; Dr Love Rees Pons, "an earnest psychologist"; and Prof. Knott Coe Mittle, "a cautious psychologist." The jokey names reflect the men's specialisms and King's lack of interest in the realistic characterization of his puppets. They also illustrate his satiric approach to crime writing, as do the headings of the sections into which the book is divided. They include "Behaviour," "Conditioning," "Inferiorities," and "Dominance"—only for the final section to be headed: "The Criminal: Trial and Error."

There is fun to be had in the way each of the four men, in turn, approaches the task of explaining the apparently inexplicable, although some of the humor and theorizing is dated, while King's enthusiasm for psychology causes him to linger over the detail. The most appealing member of the quartet is Pons, whose interests reflects those of his creator. In one scene he seeks to elicit the truth from de Brasto through a technological gizmo called the "Marston-Troland voice-key" and by applying a "free association" test he reaches a "diagnosis of an unstable type with a serious organic inferiority, centering around the digestive system."

Each psychologist arrives at a distinct interpretation of events, but I hope it is not an unforgivable spoiler to reveal that they are all "at sea" in more than one sense. None of them comes too close to identifying the true culprit or the motive for the crime. King was playing a game with the detective form in a way that calls to mind Anthony Berkeley's legendary whodunit *The Poisoned Chocolates Case*, first published in 1929. Berkeley—like E.C. Bentley in *Trent's Last Case* sixteen years earlier—aimed to satirize the notion of the omniscient detective by demonstrating that a particular set of facts might have a range of different interpretations. In his novel, the six members of the Crimes Circle come up with half a dozen contrasting explanations for a baffling murder. Berkeley's writing was highly influential and "multiple solutions" to cerebral whodunits soon came into vogue. A gifted exponent of this type of mystification was Ellery Queen, and an especially notable example is his *The Greek Coffin Mystery*.

Queen's novel appeared in 1932, the same year that saw publication of the first edition of *Obelists at Sea*—in Britain. Surprisingly, the book was not published in the US until the following year; what is even stranger is that there were significant differences between the two editions.

The UK edition was published by John Heritage, a small firm whose list in the early 1930s also included early detective novels by the British author Cecil M. Wills. This edition also included a definition of "Obelist." Since I have never found a dictionary which includes that word, I assume that King made it up; he doesn't explain it in the text of the story. According to a note at the front of the John Heritage edition: "An Obelist is a person who has little or no value" However, when inscribing a copy to a friend, King amended this wording to read: "An Obelist is one who harbours suspicion." For good measure he added a further comment: "It's not my fault that the English don't know their own language." What explains this mysterious contradiction? Did King change his mind about what he meant, or did the UK publishers simply invent their own definition? We will probably never solve this bibliographic puzzle.

British reviewers were kind to the book. E.C. Bentley described it as "a most unusual and commendable story," and there were also rave reviews in *The Times Literary Supplement*, *The Sunday Times*, *The New Statesman*, and *The Spectator*. It is unclear whether this enthusiastic reaction prompted Alfred A. Knopf to acquire the right to publish the novel in the United States, or whether he had already done so and John Heritage were simply quicker off the mark in bringing it to print.

What is undeniable is that there were several differences in the American edition. The prefatory note and the cast of characters, absent in the British version, were included. There were also some minor changes of character names: the British version featured John B. Hayvier, Rudolf Plechs, and Prof. Knott Mittle, suggesting that King made emendations of his own to the text. The American edition also included King's preferred definition of an "Obelist."

On the dust jacket blurb, Knopf proclaimed that the book "has everything the hardened detective story fan seeks—a good murder, a novel setting, an exciting running down of legitimate clues, an author who plays fair with the reader, and a fair and completely satisfying solution."

This emphasis on fair play is reflected in the inclusion of an especially significant ingredient that was missing from the John Heritage edition—"The Clue Finder" at the end of the book. This is accompanied by the instruction "Do not open until you have finished the story." King, who seldom resisted the temptation to hammer a point home, adds: "Personable readers, even though they cheat at solitaire, never cheat at this." There follows a list of no fewer than thirty-six page references to hints within the text on such matters as "the opportunity to commit the crime" and the killer's "attempt to implicate the innocent."

King wasn't the first detective novelist to offer readers a clue finder. The earliest example that I have traced is to be found in J.J. Connington's *The Eye in the Museum*, published in 1929. The clue finder was no mere gimmick; its value as a means of demonstrating the author's commitment to fair play," while teasing the reader at the same time, was quickly recognized. The concept was borrowed—in varying forms - by writers on both sides of the Atlantic, including Freeman Wills Crofts, Elspeth Huxley, Rupert Penny, John Dickson Carr, and Anthony Boucher. The last example in the twentieth century that I know of featured on the dustjacket of Kingsley Amis's *The Riverside Villas Murder* in 1973, which offers a paltry three clues. Almost half a century on, I revived the clue finder myself in *Mortmain Hall* and *Blackstone Fell*, but there is no doubt that King is the supreme exponent of this particular device.

The British and American first editions of the book both included five diagrams—plans of different parts of the *Meganaut*—but the prefatory note, cast of characters, and clue finder were again absent from the Penguin paperback edition of 1938. This was presumably because the text was based on the John Heritage edition; as a result the "erroneous" definition of an "Obelist" was retained, no doubt to the author's chagrin.

Charles Daly King (1895-1963) was born in New York City and graduated from Yale before serving as a lieutenant in the field artillery during the First World War. After working in textiles and in advertising, he turned to psychology and received his M.A. from Columbia University in 1928. He produced several books about psychology, including *Integrative Psychology*, co-written with his mentor William Moulton Marston and Marston's wife Elizabeth. Marston was a pioneer of the systolic blood pressure test, which became an element in the polygraph or "lie detector," while his wife was said to be the inspiration for his famous comic book creation "Wonder Woman."

King dedicated his second novel, *Obelists En Route* (1934), to Marston. In the UK, it appeared under the prestigious imprint of Collins Crime Club, as did his next five books. Surprisingly, however, the novel failed to find an American publisher, although *Obelists Fly High* (1935), an outrageously ingenious story, was published by Smith in the US. *Obelists Fly High* became his most famous novel, mainly thanks to the praise accorded to it decades later by Julian Symons in *Bloody Murder* aka *Mortal Consequences*.

As a detective novelist, King was plainly influenced by

the success of S.S. Van Dine and Ellery Queen. Like Berkeley he was an innovator with a sharp sense of humor and mischief but my impression is that his novels were not rigorously edited. Sometimes he tested his readers' patience; those weird character names start to grate after a while. *Obelists En Route* is weighed down not only by seven diagrams and a clue finder but also by copious footnotes and a long and irrelevant conversation about economics between his series characters, Pons and the New York cop Michael Lord, that takes self-indulgence to an extreme.

King was promoted by Collins as an author of "the intelligent man's thrillers," while the writer and occasional detective novelist C.E. Bechhofer Roberts described him as "the Aldous Huxley of the detective story." Sayers—often an acerbic reviewer - was complimentary, calling him "the highbrow of highbrows." In addition to six novels, he was the author of the short story collection *The Curious Mr Tarrant* (1935). The 'episodes' in the book feature the enigmatic Trevis Tarrant, a specialist in impossible crimes. This is said to be the rarest and most sought-after of all the two-thousand-plus Collins Crime Club titles. In the US, it remained unpublished until a paperback edition appeared in 1977.

The domestic neglect that King suffered reflected declining enthusiasm among American publishers for cerebral whodunits at a time when hardboiled detective novelists such as Dashiell Hammett and James M. Cain were rising to prominence. Like Berkeley, King seems to have lost his zest for the detective game. Although psychology became, in a variety of ways, central to post-war crime fiction, King proved unable to adapt to changing fashions in the genre.

Careless Corpse (1937), a novel whose structure resembles musical movements, did not appear in the US, and for the American edition of his penultimate title, *Arrogant Alibi* (1938), King moved yet again, to the publishing house of Appleton. He published no more novels after the underwhelming *Bermuda Burial*, a Crime Club title of 1940. In the US, *Bermuda Burial* appeared under the imprint of yet another American firm, Funk; in other words, astonishingly, he had a different publisher for each of the four novels that came out in the US while he was alive.

Frederic Dannay encouraged him to write two more Tarrant stories for *Ellery Queen's Mystery Magazine*; a third was published in *EQMM* after being found among King's papers after his death, while another appeared elsewhere as by Jeremiah Phelan (the name of Tarrant's narrator). These uncollected mysteries, along with those in the original collection, were ultimately gathered in *The Complete Curious Mr Tarrant*, published in 2003.

In 1946, Dannay tantalizingly mentioned the existence of an unpublished novel featuring Trevis Tarrant, with the characteristically quirky title of *The Episode of the Demoiselle d'Ys*. Since then, nothing further has been heard of it and I don't know of anyone who has read the manuscript. Nevertheless, I dare to hope that it still exists and that the book may eventually see the light of day.

In the meantime, it's a genuine pleasure to welcome back to print the first mystery of one of America's most extraordinary detective novelists. Enjoy your trip aboard the *Meganaut*—and then test your crime-solving prowess with that clue finder...

—MARTIN EDWARDS

OBELISTS
AT SEA

All the events in this story are fictitious.

Note. An Obelist is one who harbours suspicions.

NOTE

IN THE following story four psychologists, representing different schools within that science, apply their particular theories toward the solution of the mystery. Lest any misconception should arise, I wish to state that the characters of Drs. Hayvier, Plechs and Pons and Professor Mittle are in no way intended as portrayals of any actual and living psychologists. I would beg the reader to consider these characters as, in reality, the embodiments of their own theories, but scarcely as the flesh-and-blood people of real life.

In certain quarters, I suspect, such a tale as the one I have concocted, may be charged with serving a propagandist purpose—namely, that of destructively criticizing the course of modern psychology. Such a purpose I would deny at once . . . propaganda seems both ridiculous and hopeless to

THE AUTHOR

CONTENTS

DIAGRAMS

OF THE SHIP'S COMPANY

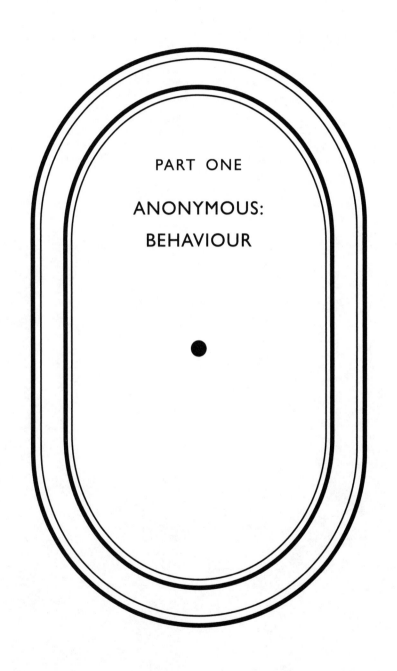

PART ONE

ANONYMOUS:

BEHAVIOUR

PART ONE

ANONYMOUS: BEHAVIOUR

Abruptly a lightning flash lit up the sea. Where the watch officer paced slowly up and down there sprang up about him the standards supporting the control mechanisms, the instrument housings, switchboards, all the complicated apparatus by which the great vessel was temporarily under his command. The fore decks and hull, the towering mast and cluttered deck machinery stood clearly etched for an instant against the waves that stretched to port, to starboard and forward, an empty desert of tossing, hurrying rollers.

At once the scene vanished, and the officer closed his eyes for a few seconds to adapt them to the dark. Then he turned again to the blackness ahead. It was black; near at hand an occasional gleam of white declared the crest of a huge wave, beyond that—nothing. Only the officer's accustomed imagination could suggest, through the continually spattered windows, the slight difference between the dark sea and the greater blackness of the *Meganaut's* bow. Even his imagination failed to construct an horizon. Here there was only the constant whistling of the wind, the swish of spray thrown across the bridge a hundred feet above the sea, the dull glowing of shaded instrument lights, and the slow roll and recovery of the mighty ship, as it yielded to the combined assault of waves and wind.

In the smoking-room the curtains had been drawn across the windows, but the doors to the enclosed promenade deck were open. The room, large as it was, was crowded; all the tables were filled and extra chairs had been brought in to accommodate the surplus. Everywhere was the chaotic noise of people talking, the frequent burst of laughter as some table responded to a witticism or unusual toast. Stewards flitted about deftly, like large cats, bearing trays of drinks, and behind the bar, stretching entirely across the forward side of the apartment, the bar-tender and his assistants were busy pouring and mixing for the replenishment of these trays and the service of the half-dozen passengers perched on the high stools along the bar itself. Near the service end of the bar the ship's doctor in his neat uniform leaned negligently against the tall counter.

Immediately before the bar a small space had been cleared. Here, at his table, the secretary of the ship's pool was rearranging his papers, while beside him his assistant, the chief steward of the smoking-room, pointed out to the evening's auctioneer the next number to be sold and the name of its owner.

For many of the voyagers the ship's pool constituted perhaps the most entertaining feature of their passage; it was this that accounted for the crowded condition of the room. Every evening they gathered, the majority of the ship's passengers, to observe or perchance to participate in the auctioning off of the numbers, one of which would correspond to the count of sea miles traversed by the boat from noon of the previous day to noon of the next.

There is a peculiar isolation about a sea trip that clings even to the short, swift ferries across the North Atlantic. The land, with its familiar sights, sounds, activities, slips away. These things can still be talked of but no longer experienced; within twenty-four hours they become scarcely more real than one's childhood, as new faces, new voices, totally different activities replace those left behind. There is an interim, a definite hiatus. For a time the traveller is suspended, as if on a foreign planet; never again, perhaps, will he see his fellow passengers, and the bars of convention (such as are left to us) are dropped by common consent. All are companions, for a period, on a holiday from life. Thus it happens, since most of us are gamblers at heart, that even those who scorn to wager at home, find themselves prepared to try their luck at sea. It has frequently been noticed that courage rather than scruple usually determines whether they do so or not.

Although the auctioning of the ship's pool held an attraction for most of the passengers, by no means all of them were in attendance. In the great lounge amidships more than two hundred persons still lingered over their coffee and liqueurs, while a large orchestra played the newest dance music for those who preferred this form of exercise immediately after dinner. In the Ritz restaurant on the highest deck the lights were being lowered as the last party of strikingly clothed women and dress suited men strolled out to take part in the events of the evening.

Already a few couples and larger groups were invading the pink and gold ballroom aft, where the terraced tables and polished floor gleamed brilliantly under the lights and the curtains had been drawn across the tall windows to the promenade deck and the french doors leading to the Veranda Cafe over the stern. No noise of the tempest without penetrated to these precincts; here the only sounds were those of careless gaiety, of melody and modulated laughter, and the only reminder of the sea was the slight list of the ship before the wind and the occasional slow slanting of the floors to the roll.

Mr. Victor Timothy Smith was a very wealthy man; he was either a copper king or a western railroad magnate, no one seemed to be sure which. At all events he was rich enough to have had a table reserved for him in the smoking-room; yet when he entered with his three companions, he attracted little attention. Making their way slowly into the room, they grouped themselves about the table indicated by a steward who, for the past forty minutes, had been dividing his efforts equally between his proper duties and watching for Mr. Smith.

Just as they were settling down, the auctioneer straightened up from an inspection of his records, and called for the attention of the room. His eye fell upon the new arrivals.

'Just in time, Mr. Smith,' he called. 'Your number is next. Will you open the bidding?'

This request Mr. Smith acknowledged with a short nod. 'Fifty dollars,' he responded, and turned back to his companions, apparently dismissing the matter from his mind.

More or less perfunctorily the bidding progressed; not until it had reached the hundred and fifty dollar mark and all of the bidders except one had been eliminated, did the owner seem to take any interest in the sale of his number. Then, however, he looked up calmly and mentioned, 'One hundred and sixty dollars.'

At once the general interest began to mount. It was appreciated that the auction of this number had settled down to a contest between two of the passengers. Heads were turned in the direction of the two contestants, and the auctioneer, unable to resist the belief that his own efforts were responsible for the rising bids, redoubled his exertions.

'That,' he acknowledged, 'is a bid.' He did not rub his hands together, but no one could have noticed his involuntary smile and thought of anything else. 'One hundred and eighty dollars for number 634; from Mr. de Brasto, I think?'

From the far end of the room the pale, dark-haired, semitic-looking gentleman nodded assent.

'One hundred and ninety.'

The bid came in a low, almost careless voice from Smith's table, the one on de Brasto's left. The passengers, now silently curious, saw a stocky man in correct evening dress, of ruddy complexion, his hair slightly greyed at the temples. It is doubtful, however, if, in the presence of his daughter's astonishingly blonde beauty, anyone especially remarked these distinguishing features.

'One hundred and ninety dollars,' repeated the auctioneer, his smile perceptibly broadening. 'The highest bid this evening, ladies and gentlemen. Now this is better, decidedly better. In my opinion not one of the very best numbers, but these gentlemen seem to like it. Will anyone join the competition? One hundred and ninety dollars for number 634.'

Apparently no one would.

'Two hundred,' snapped de Brasto.

'Two ten.'

'Mr. Smith bids two hundred and ten dollars,' the auctioneer replied. 'Come, gentlemen, the winner of to-day's pool bids two hundred and ten dollars. This must really be a very good number. I am changing my opinion and I advise you not to let it slip away.'

'Two hundred and twenty dollars!' De Brasto's voice conveyed a certain vehemence.

'Three hundred and fifty,' commented Smith negligently.

'Three hundred and fifty; three hundred and fifty dollars for number 634. There can be no doubt that this is a very excellent number indeed! An opportunity, gentlemen, an opportunity. Am I offered three hundred and seventy-five? No. Well, three hundred and sixty. If it's worth three fifty, it's worth three sixty. Come, three fifty bid, three fifty?'

The auctioneer paused and looked around the room. 'Steward,' he called, 'just move to one side, please. Mr. Mortimer? Would you care to bid for 634? Sir Henry? Mr. Duller? Mr. de Brasto?'

He paused again, as the *Meganaut* slowly heeled and recovered. 'Come, come, gentlemen, am I bid no more? I'll knock it down. Going once to Mr. Smith for three hundred and fifty dollars.

'Going twice, number 634, one of the best numbers on the list!' Inquiringly he looked towards de Brasto, who was looking elsewhere.

The auctioneer paused and looked around the room. 'Mr. Smith, for three hundred and fifty dollars!'

As the auctioneer turned away to see that the sale was properly entered on the sheets, the talking rose again throughout the room. The stewards serving the tables sprang into activity, hur-

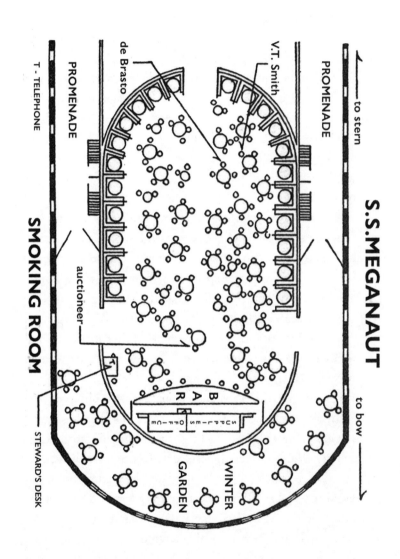

S.S.MEGANAUT

← to stern   to bow →

PROMENADE

V.T. Smith

de Brasto

PROMENADE

auctioneer

T - TELEPHONE

SMOKING ROOM

STEWARD'S DESK

WINTER GARDEN

B A R

SPRATT'S COLUMN

rying back and forth to the corner of the long bar. The hubbub became general.

'Oh, Steward, two scotch and sodas and a side-car.' . . . 'My dear, it's a Paquin, I'm certain.' . . . '—and a poor number, too. Throwin' his money away, it seems to me.'

'Smith? Oh, he could buy them all, old chap, and never know the difference. Int'restin', isn't it? Only bids against the Jews, d'you notice? Fancy he intends to keep that fellow, de Brasto, out altogether. He wouldn't have got a number last night, but that Smith came in late. Amusin' show, not?' . . . 'Beers all around, Steward. Dark, please.' . . . 'Must be quite a blow outside; do you feel her rolling a bit now?' . . .

The stewards picked their way with difficulty among the crowded chairs. In the port doorway to the promenade a group of men stood talking; through the empty entrance opposite them could be seen the rain-splashed windows on deck, whose blankness was now and then illuminated by the lightning. The dark woodwork and fittings of the saloon reflected the gleams from the side lights, and the concealed lighting in the ceiling made brilliant flashes where it struck the jewels of the women and the white shirt-fronts of the men.

During the interlude many persons covertly observed the adjacent tables occupied by the recent rivals. De Brasto's party, it was evident, were discussing the situation with scarcely concealed anger. They numbered, besides de Brasto himself, a strikingly handsome Jewess, a small, animated brunette who might also have been Hebraic, and a portly, heavy featured man of indeterminate race. At Smith's table there was likewise a party of four, himself and next him his daughter, while opposite sat two younger men, one of whom was leaning forward to enforce some observation he had just made. They appeared entirely unconscious of the incident that was attracting so much actual, if unobtrusive, attention; as a matter of fact they were altogether absorbed in their discussion of the coming international polo matches on Long Island.

At the other end of the room the auctioneer still bent over the shoulder of the pool's secretary. While consulting the lists he wiped away the perspiration from his forehead and refreshed himself from a glass of cool champagne which, indeed, was not his at all, but belonged to his seated friend.

Then he turned away, and lifting his gavel, rapped sharply for attention. 'Ladies and gentlemen,' he began, and waited for the talking to die away.

'Ladies and gentlemen, we have now to consider perhaps the best number of the evening. Sir Henry Merton's number, 640. Let me read to you once more the last six runs on the third day east. They were 637, 638, 648, 634, 641, 645. The average was 640.5 This evening we are nearing the middle of the Atlantic Ocean, and, as you have doubtless noticed, the sea is not very congested hereabouts. We have every reason to expect an average run.'

'How about the storm?' murmured someone close at hand.

'I am reminded by somebody,' continued the auctioneer, 'that we have run into a storm, but I am told,' glancing toward the chief steward for confirmation, 'that our speed has not been reduced, not yet, at any rate. Therefore I should say that the present number is the best chance of the whole evening. What am I bid for number 640? Sir Henry, would you care to open the bidding for your number?'

Sir Henry, from his large table in the centre of the room, where he was entertaining his own party as well as several shipboard acquaintances, made his perfunctory bid of fifty dollars.

'Fifty dollars is bid, ladies and gentlemen, fifty—'

'Fifty-five.'

'Sixty.'

'Sixty-five dollars, from the lady on the left. Sir Henry?'

'Seventy dollars.'

'Seventy-five.'

'Seventy-five from Mr. Mortimer. Seventy-five dollars for number 640, the best number on the list. Who will bid me eighty?'

'Eighty.'

'Eighty dollars I'm bid. Eighty-five, Mr. Mortimer. Ninety, Mr. Hughes. Ninety-five from the gentleman in the far corner. How about my friend at the bar,' said the auctioneer, turning suddenly about. 'Would you care to make it one hundred, sir? For our best number?'

The stout gentleman on the high stool, thus appealed to, nodded slowly.

'One hundred dollars,' cried the auctioneer. 'Splendid, gentlemen, but still much too low for this number. Sir Henry? Surely you won't lose this fine number?'

'One hundred and ten,' said Sir Henry.

'One hundred and twenty,' said the stout gentleman.

And there it stayed. In spite of all the urging the auctioneer could summon up, no one was found to advance the bidding higher. 'But gentlemen,' he pleaded, 'three hundred and fifty was paid for 634, a much poorer number, and you are allowing the best one of all to go for a hundred and twenty.' At this a general smile went round the smoking-room; it seemed well understood that number 634 had scarcely been sold on its merits.

'Very well,' the auctioneer acknowledged defeat. 'Once,

twice, and sold! For one hundred and twenty dollars, to the gentleman at the bar. Your name, sir? Thornton? Thank you. . . .'

'And now, ladies and gentlemen, we have 648, Mr. de Brasto's number. May I remind you that three trips ago the *Meganaut* made six hundred and forty-eight miles for this run? What am I bid for number 648?'

Not a few glanced with amusement toward Smith. It was easy enough, so the general opinion ran, for him to outbid de Brasto for his own (Smith's) number, since the owner had only to pay into the pool half the price at which he bought it in. But now the number was de Brasto's and the shoe was on the other foot.

'Fifty dollars.'

'Fifty dollars from Mr. de Brasto. Will someone kindly advance the bid for this very good number? Ah, fifty-five dollars from Mr. Fields.'

'Sixty dollars.'

'Sixty-five.'

'Seventy.'

'Mr. de Brasto bids seventy dollars. He likes his number, ladies and gentlemen, and I don't blame him. It's a good number, a fine—'

'Seventy-five dollars.'

'Seventy-five from Mr. Mortimer.'

'Eighty.'

'Eighty-five.'

'Thank you, Mr. Fields. Eighty-five dollars I'm bid.'

'Ninety.'

'Ninety dollars. Mr. de Brasto bids ninety dollars for his own number. Are there no more bids, gentlemen? Surely you won't see number 648 go for ninety dollars. Three trips ago this boat made six hundred and forty-eight miles, don't forget that. Ninety I'm bid. Who'll say one hundred? Mr. Smith, are you interested? Will you bid me one hundred for 648?'

Smith interrupted the conversation at his table long enough to nod briefly to the auctioneer.

'One hundred dollars I am bid,' came the prompt response.

'One hundred and five dollars.'

'One hundred and twenty,' said Smith.

'A hundred and thirty.'

'One forty.'

The bids came rapidly, one tripping over the heels of its forerunner. At the three hundred mark they stopped.

'Three hundred,' urged the auctioneer, obviously enjoying his success. 'Mr. Smith bids three hundred dollars. You won't let him have your number at three hundred dollars, Mr. de Brasto. Three ten? Will you bid me three ten?' He paused. 'We still have several numbers to auction off. Three hundred I'm bid; will you make it three ten? Going once at three hundred dollars to Mr. Smith. Going twice. . . .'

Disappointment was written on many faces in the room. Smith's determination to keep his opponent out of the pool was an unusual incident and the other passengers possessed the ordinary liking for a good fight. The many eyes turned curiously toward the two men saw a certain disturbance at de Brasto's table. His companions were evidently urging him to continue. With a characteristic disregard for appearances the taller Jewess slapped a packet of express cheques on the table and looked angrily at her neighbours. The auctioneer also observed these proceedings and delayed his sale of the number.

His set face paler than usual, de Brasto turned back to the

auctioneer. The room pricked up its ears; there was no concealing the renewed interest now.

'Three ten, Mr. de Brasto?'

'Yes!'

Not the slightest difference could be discerned between Smith's voice now and when he made his first bid. 'Three fifty,' he said.

'Three sixty!'

'Four hundred.'

There was a slight pause, during which a steward made his way to Smith's table. The darker of the two young men helped him unload his tray and distribute the drinks. He did so rather clumsily, or perhaps he was excited, for he used both hands to convey each of the glasses to the table. Then de Brasto's voice, slightly strained, 'Four hundred and ten.'

Still almost negligently, Smith said, 'Five hundred.'

De Brasto's air was that of a man who has thrown caution to the winds and proposes to win at any cost. 'Five hundred and fifty.'

'Six hundred and fifty.'

At last the auctioneer had controlled his delighted surprise. 'Six hundred and fifty dollars,' he interjected.

'Seven hundred dollars!'

'Eight hundred.'

It was just then that the lights in the smoking-room began to dim. Involuntarily everyone glanced up at them. Gradually they were growing fainter; like a curtain, gauzy and transparent at first, then steadily heavier, darkness seemed to descend from the ceiling. The entire assemblage sat as if struck dumb by surprise. In the face of the totally unexpected phenomenon all activity was suspended; everyone waited. . . . Only Smith and his dainty daughter seemed unaffected. The first intimation of the change had found her sipping from her glass; she finished calmly and set it down before her. Equally unruffled, her father lifted his own goblet, drained it thirstily and replaced it on the table.

Now there was only a weak glow in the room; the features, then the figures of the occupants faded into obscurity. Even the bar-tender stood motionless while an astonished silence reigned.

Just as total darkness came, a new voice, that of a woman, spoke from the port doorway. 'One thousand dollars,' it said; and was followed by a silence as complete as before.

When Pons afterward tried to remember exactly what had happened during those, probably few, seconds of darkness, he seemed to recall several things definitely. First of all, there always rose in his mind the picture of that last undisturbed action of Smith's. Then came the blackness—and the noise of a chair overturned. Almost simultaneously there was a subdued hiss, from somewhere, and the crash of a falling body, the tinkling of broken glass, from the neighbourhood of the Smith table. At the same instant a bright flash and the loud report of a revolver. The only other sound was that of the bar-tender groping for a telephone behind him and starting to speak into it.

With a dazzling abruptness the powerful emergency light, hidden in the ceiling, lit up the saloon. In the sudden blaze the tableau sprang out, sharply defined.

De Brasto was on his feet beside his table; his still smoking revolver was falling from his hand onto the floor. The two young men at Smith's table were half out of their chairs. Smith himself was lying face downward across the table, his chair overturned behind him, while the contents of a wine glass, splintered by his fall, spread across and began dripping over the edge.

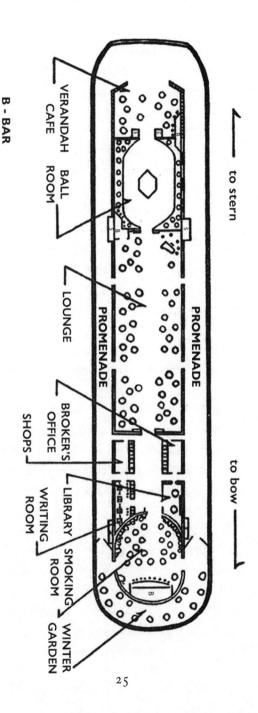

S.S.MEGANAUT

← to stern

to bow →

VERANDAH
CAFE

BALL ROOM

LOUNGE

PROMENADE

PROMENADE

BROKER'S OFFICE

SHOPS

LIBRARY

WRITING ROOM

SMOKING ROOM

WINTER GARDEN

B - BAR
E - ELEVATOR
S - STAIRWAY

PROMENADE DECK

25

For a moment, under the shock of the sudden illumination, the tableau held. Then a woman screamed, 'He's been shot!'

As if it were a signal, her cry released confusion throughout the room. Most of the people were on their feet; some shouted, others besought calmness in voices equally loud, a chair crashed over in the central aisle. Many crowded toward the scene of excitement, while their neighbours endeavoured to push past them in the directions of the exits. Now the chief steward had clambered up onto the auctioneer's table; his loud, remonstrating shouts, 'Ladies and gentlemen, there is no danger. Ladies and gentlemen,' began to be heard above the tumult. Frantically he gesticulated toward his under-stewards, pointing them to the exits.

And then the moment of near-panic elapsed. At first here and there, then rapidly throughout the room the poise of the passengers reasserted itself. A chatter of questions, of surprise and bewilderment, replaced the clamour, and the volume of noise, though still large, was being reduced to lesser proportions. It became apparent that several ladies had fainted and at various tables their escorts were attempting to minister to them with the means at their disposal. In the forward part of the room the head bar-tender's voice became audible, as he stood at the telephone, '—the whole squad. The doctor's here. You'd better hurry!'

During the first rush the two men at Smith's table had jumped upon de Brasto and seized him. He made no resistance, but stood perfectly still for some seconds as if stupefied. Then his knees began to tremble violently, and but for the grasp of his two assailants he would have collapsed. They pushed him back into his chair; the younger of his captors, suddenly realizing the impossibility of escape, relinquished his hold and turned back to the girl beside Smith. His companion, however, continued to maintain a firm grip upon de Brasto's shoulder and arm.

The girl lay back in her chair, her face deathly pale; from the side of her neck a tiny stream of red trickled down over her white shoulder and was lost beneath the low-cut front of her evening dress. The young man looked dazedly at his stricken companions and while he was hesitating, a grey-haired gentleman struggled through the press and came up to his side.

'I am a doctor,' said the newcomer shortly. 'Let me see what's wrong here.'

As the young man fell back to make room for him, the physician bent over the girl and, whipping out his handkerchief, wiped the trickle of blood from her neck. A small cut, scarcely more than a scratch, was revealed. Lifting her inert hand, his trained fingers pressed her wrist for a few moments. He nodded as if satisfied and turned to the young man again.

'She's only fainted,' he announced. 'Now help me with this gentleman.'

Together they placed Smith's overturned chair on its feet and, one on each side, lifted his body into it off the table. His shirt-front and vest were stained a vivid crimson, and on the left side of the stiff bosom, where it was still white, a tiny black hole stood clearly defined. The strong hands of the medical man quickly ripped apart the evening shirt and tore the silk under-vest which appeared beneath it. In the pallid flesh over the region of the heart was a red-rimmed puncture as large as a small nut. The doctor knelt quickly and pressed his ear against the chest of the recumbent man; then turned back, first one, then the other, of the closed eyelids. As he rose and faced the young man who still stood next him, his somewhat puzzled expression gave way to one of certainty.

'This man is dead,' he said. 'He has been shot either through his heart, or near enough to it to be fatal.'

During the brief examination a quiet man, clad unobtrusively in a well-worn dinner jacket, had been forcing a determined path through the crowd. As the announcement was made, he appeared at de Brasto's table. He flicked back the lapel of his coat, displaying a small badge. 'I am one of the ship's detectives,' he said, addressing the man who was still guarding de Brasto. 'I shall take charge of this man, and I should like your name, as well as those of the persons at this table.'

'My name is Younghusband. I was at the next table with Mr. Smith when this fellow shot him and I—'

De Brasto was galvanized into sudden activity. He jerked himself up, crying excitedly, 'I didn't kill him, I didn't! I wasn't looking at him.' With one hand he caught feverishly at the detective's coat, stabbing rapidly with the other toward the starboard entrance. 'I—I—he was going to kill me. He had a gun—he was drawing it! I—I—he—'

'Never mind all that,' the detective interrupted. 'You'll have plenty of time to talk later. We all saw you fire and we saw you drop the gun. Here,' he said, turning to the woman next to de Brasto, 'give me that revolver, please. Pick it up by the barrel.'

The woman looked down at the floor where the weapon had fallen. She started to reach down for it, then shrank back. Younghusband bent over quickly and retrieved it, handing it grip foremost to the detective, who took it by the muzzle, set its safety catch and dropped it into his pocket. At that moment his attention was attracted by a scuffle at the main entrance, where two men were grappling with each other.

'You stay right here until I come back,' he said sharply to de Brasto. 'The rest of you, too,' he added, and began to push his way toward the new disturbance. Before he could reach the contestants, however, four sailors, led by a petty officer, came rapidly up the main alleyway leading from the lounge, and separated them. The larger man they held, while his opponent searched him quickly but thoroughly. The searcher then turned his captive over to two of the sailors, who marched him away, while the petty officer and the remaining pair posted themselves at the doorway. The man whom they had assisted made his way within to join his fellow detective.

Other sailors were now guarding the remaining exits. A smart young officer in immaculate uniform, at whose side swung a business-like automatic, mounted one of the stools before the bar. His voice rang clearly through the room, commanding attention. Everyone turned toward him, and the immediate silence was a measure of the relief now felt in the presence of authority.

'Ladies and gentlemen,' he began, 'the Line regrets extremely the present unfortunate incident. As you know, the captain is completely responsible for this vessel. While we are at sea, his authority is absolute. At his direction I am in command of this room. I am here to see that no further disorder occurs; I have plenty of men with me and you need have no apprehension on that score. I must also reassure you respecting the lights. A temporary accident has occurred to our main dynamo, but the emergency motors are in perfect condition and there is no cause to fear that the lights will fail again. No harm whatsoever has been done the ship.' He paused and from several parts of the room came scattering applause.

'I must now ask you, ladies and gentlemen, for your co-operation. I do not know as yet just what has happened here, but I am told that there has been violence of a serious nature. On behalf of the captain and of the Line I assure you that the circumstances will be carefully sifted and those responsible will be dealt with by proper authority. We regret extremely the disagreeableness to which you have been subjected; I can promise you that there will be no recurrence. It is now necessary for me to clear this room, so that we may make our investigation. My men are stationed at all the exits and if you will please assist me by giving them your names, and if possible by identifying yourselves as you pass out, it will be greatly appreciated. We will inconvenience you no more than is absolutely necessary. This room will be closed for the remainder of to-night, but the other services of the ship are at your disposal exactly as usual.'

He paused again and looked down the room to the tables where the two detectives stood. 'Mr. Bone,' he called, 'will you designate who is to remain?'

'Only the people at these two tables, sir. We will want no one else just now.'

'Our detectives are in charge where the accident has occurred,' the officer continued. 'They will keep those whom we need. Will the rest of you ladies and gentlemen please leave now? Kindly don't crowd at the doorways, as it will take a little time to get your names. Oh, and one thing more. Naturally we cannot expect that you will not talk about this very unfortunate excitement. But we would ask you kindly not to exaggerate what has happened. Perhaps it is not as bad as it seems and rumours will easily go to undue lengths. Once more I assure you that the Line very greatly regrets the inconvenience to which you have been put. I wish to thank you for your attention and assistance.'

As the officer finished, the applause—intermingled with several 'Bravos' and a loud 'Hear, hear,' from Sir Henry's table—broke out again, and there was a general movement toward the doorways. While there were undoubtedly a few who would have been glad to remain and acquaint themselves with the forthcoming details, the majority, now that the crisis had passed, seemed anxious only to quit the scene and, in more comfortable surroundings, to recover themselves at leisure. In a shorter time than would have appeared possible, they had filed through the exits, leaving behind them only the officer, the stewards and the group about the two tables far down the room.

The officer descended from the bar, whence he had superintended the evacuation of the smoking-room.

'Schmidt,' he called to the petty officer at the port entrance, 'you'd better see that the winter garden outside here is cleared also. Be easy about it, though. My God, there's going to be enough hell to pay about this, as it is.'

He hurried down the room to where two men were bending over the quiet figure of the girl. 'What about it Pell?' he asked, sharply. 'Can anything be done?'

The ship's doctor, a bearded, professional-looking man of about fifty, left the girl to his colleague and straightened up.

'Nothing for this gentleman,' he answered at once. 'He seems to have been killed instantly. Shot through the heart. The young lady, however—. I don't understand it. This doctor, Dr. Schall is it? Yes. Dr. Schall says he examined her as soon as the lights went on; she had fainted. But she doesn't respond. We must get her up to the hospital at once.

The officer was staring down at the girl. He was struck by her extraordinary beauty. Then his glance fell upon the red trickle over her shoulder, and for the first time he felt a wave of anger sweep over his body. 'She's been shot, too,' he cried, 'Look there—'

'It's nothing,' Dr. Schall reassured him. 'A little scratch on her neck; you can see it's stopped bleeding already. We can find no signs of any other wound.'

Younghusband suddenly caught the officer's arm. 'Her necklace!' he ejaculated. 'She was wearing a pearl necklace. It's gone. It must have been worth thousands! That's what scratched her neck, don't you see? It's been stolen. It's gone.'

'Here, Heddes,' the officer turned to the detectives. 'He says a valuable necklace has disappeared. Take a look about, right away, will you? Better help him, Bone. We must find that at once.'

As the two men began a hurried search under the nearby chairs and tables, Dr. Pell spoke again. 'We must get her out of here immediately, where I can attend her properly. Her pulse has almost ceased.' He motioned to a pair of attendants standing by the now closed main entrance with a collapsible stretcher.

'Go ahead. Can you take her through the winter garden? It's been cleared. We don't want any more attention than we can help.'

They were lifting the girl's body gently on to the stretcher when the second young man who had been at the Smith table found his voice for the first time since the lights had gone up. 'Doctor!' he implored excitedly, 'you must do something for her. My God, don't let her die! There must be something, there *must.*' He sat down abruptly and began to mop his face with a handkerchief.

Surprised, the doctor turned to him briefly and spoke in professional tones. 'She will be all right,' he said soothingly. 'She has only fainted. A bad shock. She couldn't come to here. No use taking chances; perhaps her heart is not too strong. We'll take care of her.' He turned to the officer. 'You won't need me now? I had better attend this lady myself.'

'I shall stay,' spoke up the other doctor. 'I can tell them anything they wish to know, as I was here when it happened.'

As the two attendants started out with their burden, 'You'll send back?' asked the officer, indicating the second still body, slumped in its chair. The doctor nodded and motioned his men ahead. Half-way up the room, the second young man sprang up from his seat and started uncertainly after them. Dr. Pell, glancing around, stopped, walked back and took him decisively by the shoulders. But his voice, when he spoke, was kind.

'Now see here, young man,' he said firmly, 'you are only delaying matters. I shall take care of this lady. Don't worry; she'll be perfectly all right. Get one of the stewards to give you a brandy. You've had a shock yourself. You can inquire at the hospital after they have finished here.'

The executive officer met them at the door. A brief word with the doctor, and he walked rapidly in. As he approached, the junior officer drew himself up and saluted smartly. 'Sir, this is a very serious matter. This man has been shot.'

The executive officer stopped short. 'Shot?' he repeated incredulously. 'Killed?'

In an instant he had recovered himself. 'Mr. Lane,' he said sternly, 'tell me what has happened here.'

In a few sentences he was acquainted with the occurrences since Lane's arrival. 'That's all I know, sir,' concluded the officer. 'Of course, the shooting took place before I got here.'

'I see. Very good, Mr. Lane.' The executive officer turned to the people grouped behind his lieutenant. 'Now who can—'

Both the women at de Brasto's table had risen to their feet.

They broke out volubly, 'It's a mistake, officer.' . . . 'He didn't mean to—' . . . 'He didn't shoot—' . . . 'This man was acting very—' Younghusband was also trying to make his voice heard above those of the women. 'Don't you believe what they say, sir, they are all in it together. We have plenty of witnesses.'

'Mr. Drake, sir,' began one of the detectives.

'Just a moment now,' interrupted the executive officer. His voice held the sharpness of command. 'One at a time. You'll all have every opportunity to speak. First of all let me hear what our detectives have to say. You were in the room when this— this assault took place?'

'I was here, sir,' said Bone, stepping forward.

'Ah, go ahead, Bone. Kindly do not interrupt him,' he added, glancing meaningly at the rest.

'I was sitting near the centre of the room when the lights went out. These two men had been bidding against each other in the pool. Quite nasty it got, sir, at one time.'

'Which two men, Bone?'

'This man, sir; he says his name is de Brasto. And the man who has been shot. His name is Smith, V. T. Smith.'

The executive officer nodded.

'Then the lights went out. While they were out, a shot was fired from his table,' indicating de Brasto. 'Then they went up again—'

The officer cut in. 'How do you know the shot came from that table?'

'Because, as soon as the lights went out, sir, I got to my feet. There was some noise down this end of the room and I was looking that way. I saw the flash of the gun. When the lights came on, this de Brasto was standing beside his table. His revolver was still in his hand. Then he dropped it and this gentleman, Mr. Younghusband, who had been sitting with Mr. Smith, grabbed him. Of course, there was plenty of pushing and crowding; as soon as I could, I got here and took him in charge. I have his gun; there'll be no doubt about the prints on it.'

'Heddes, can you confirm this? Just a minute, sir, Mr. Younghusband, is it? Just let me hear what Mr. Heddes has to say.'

'No sir, I can't,' spoke Heddes, replying to the first question. 'I wasn't here. Except I saw Bone get the gun from the floor. When the lights went, I was in the lounge. I got up, of course. Then I heard the shot in here. Before I'd got out of the door of the lounge and past the elevators, the lights went up again. I saw Stym—, er, one of the men we're watching, just going into the smoking-room here. I jumped along and said, 'I'd like to have at look at you.' Thought it had sounded like a shot, you know, sir, though I wasn't sure. Well, he resisted, tried to break away.'

'Just a moment, Heddes.' The two hospital attendants had reappeared, and the detective stepped back a pace or two. In complete silence they lifted Smith's corpse, lowered it on to their stretcher, which they had placed across two chairs, and departed once more through the port doorway forward. The silence was maintained for some seconds. The young man who had pled with Dr. Pell, sitting now with clenched hands and white face in a chair to one side, looked up for an instant as the bearers passed him. He said, 'Ugh,' in a grating voice, and resumed his set posture.

Heddes stepped forward again. He continued in the same tone. 'We struggled for quite a bit, until part of the emergency squad came up and held him. I found two holsters on him, one under his arm and the other in a gun-pocket in his trousers. No gats in 'em. I didn't want to make a show there, so I sent him down to the brig with two of the men, to hold him there until

I get a chance to get down and give him a good go-over. Then I came on in and saw Bone getting the gun from the floor, as I said. Then someone said there was a pearl necklace missing and we've been looking around for it since. It's nowhere around the floor or these tables. We ought to search these people right now, sir.' As he completed his speech, he cast an ominous look at de Brasto's party.

'What's this about a necklace?' began the executive officer, when Younghusband broke in imperatively. 'Yes, sir, that's perfectly right. Miss Smith was wearing a very valuable pearl necklace; had been all evening. I saw it just before the lights went out. Later it was gone; and her neck was scratched where it had been jerked off. There,' he cried suddenly, pointing to the wreckage on the table at which he had sat, 'there's one of the pearls now!' He leaned over and rescued the small globe from where it lay imprisoned between the fragments of a glass.

The officer took it and looked at it curiously. 'Perhaps it only broke when she fainted,' he said. 'The rest of it may be here somewhere, too.'

Heddes was peering around his side. 'No, sir,' he insisted, 'there's no more of those around here at all. We've been looking for ten minutes or so. Absolutely not, sir. Only place we haven't looked was on top of that very table.'

'Of course not,' clamoured Younghusband. 'Pearls like that have knots between each of them. That's a valuable stone, Officer. When the necklace was broken, that one fell off, but none of the others. I insist on being searched. Everyone here *should* want to be. Furthermore,' he hurried on, 'I want to confirm what your man has already told you. That Jew there shot Mr. Smith. We all saw him. They had been having a little brush over the bidding, and when the lights went out, he saw a chance to shoot and throw his gun away. But they came up too soon. Everyone in the room saw him with the gun in his hand. I was right next to him here; he shot right past my face. I charge him with murder, Officer. I demand that he be arrested. And I want those people searched; you'll find the necklace on one of them.'

'Those are serious words, Mr. Younghusband.'

'I repeat, sir,' said Younghusband. 'I charge that man with murder. And I want these people searched.'

'Does anyone object to a search?' The officer, though impressed, still seemed somewhat in doubt.

The larger of the two women raised a shrill voice. 'Certainly we object, Officer. No one at this table took any necklace. We were nowhere near that girl. You won't search me, I can tell you.'

The voice of the large, red-faced man who still sat next her and, so far, had taken no part in the proceedings, boomed forth deeply. 'Yes, we object to being searched. I am Stander, Bering Y. Stander, and Mr. de Brasto is my law partner in New York. The lady who has just spoken is his wife, and the other lady is mine. I do not believe Mr. de Brasto shot the man at all. I was sitting at the same table, and my evidence is as good as anyone else's. In the excitement his revolver was discharged accidentally, that's all. He wasn't even facing toward the man. And most certainly we know nothing of a necklace. I protest most vigorously against the indignity of a search.'

The officer was plainly perplexed. 'What do you say about this, Mr. de Brasto? In the face of the evidence you cannot deny you fired a shot. What explanation have you to offer?'

'Don't you say anything, Saul,' counselled his partner. 'This man is not the captain and this is only a preliminary investigation. You wait until the real hearing. Meantime, I will consult with you.'

'What about it, Brasto?'

The man was still badly shaken. At his first attempt no sound came from his lips. Then, 'I have nothing to say,' he managed.

'That attitude will get you nowhere, sir. If you persist in it, I shall have to order you confined.'

'I have nothing to say,' repeated de Brasto.

'Very well. You are under arrest; when we are through here, you will be taken below. Now, let's see; do you think a search necessary, Mr. Bone?'

'I demand—' began Younghusband.

'One moment, one moment. Well, Bone?'

'We'll have to search them, sir. If one of them has it, and we let them go, they might hide it anywhere. It's a pity we didn't know before everyone else got away. But there's no use letting these birds fly.'

'That's right, sir. We ought to search 'em now,' confirmed the other detective.

Stander growled, 'You'll hear more of this—'

The executive officer cut him short. 'I'm in charge here. I'll take the responsibility. You will all be searched. Heddes, you have a man in confinement now. You'd better go down and get through with him; you can't keep him there all night. On the way, send us a stewardess and a couple of screens. We'll get through with this at once. Tell them to make it right away, please.'

With Heddes' departure an uncomfortable silence fell. No one seemed inclined to make the next move. It was not until a competent-looking stewardess arrived, followed by two sailors bearing a pair of large screens, that the executive officer recollected a witness hitherto unheard.

After directing the setting-up of the screens in opposite corners of the room, 'I suppose, Doctor, you will not object to the formality of a search,' he ventured. 'In your case, I scarcely feel able to insist, but you can help us greatly if you are willing. It will be much better if everyone is treated alike.'

Dr. Schall made a wry face. 'I can't say I like it,' he answered. 'But yes, of course, I can see it would be better.'

'Thank you, Doctor. Then will you go first? Over there, on the right. Detective Bone will search the men, while the stewardess is attending to the ladies. I'd like a few words with you while the others are,' he smiled, 'undergoing what I hope is a useless ordeal.'

In a few moments the doctor again presented himself. 'Now, Doctor, what can you tell me of this affair?'

'Nothing, I am afraid, that you have not already heard. I was sitting with a friend at one of the alcove tables behind these. During the darkness I heard and saw the shot, and when the lights came back, I saw the man whom your detective accused, drop the gun. There can be no doubt that it was he who fired the shot.'

'What about the incident of the bidding? Was there a serious fracas?'

Dr. Schall appeared to consider. Then he said slowly: 'Well, no; I should not have thought so at the time. Certainly the man who was shot seemed to have decided to keep the other fellow definitely out of the pool. He overbid him drastically whenever it seemed likely he might get a number. But I must say he did it well, almost impersonally. I never even saw him look across at the other table.'

'And Brasto, or whatever his name is, how did he take it?'

The doctor shrugged. 'Not so well. But you know the man's an excitable type. And, so far as I could see, it was the women who became really disagreeable about it. On these boats, you know, sir, you have many people who, how shall I say, are a trifle lacking in background.'

The officer nodded. 'Yes, I know what you mean, but after all, we can't help that.' He dismissed the side topic. 'Now just what did you find when you came over to these tables? And, by the way, how soon did you get here?'

'Oh, I got here right away. I saw at once that someone had been injured, and for a few moments everyone sat in their chairs, quite stunned. I found the man they call Smith dead. He must have died instantly. His daughter—I believe it was his daughter—was in a faint, or at least it seemed at the moment that she had fainted. I can't understand why she is so long coming out of it. A weak heart, no doubt. And, well, I guess that's about all I can tell you.'

The doctor stopped speaking. Then he seemed to recollect another point, and continued. 'Oh, yes, about this necklace you are looking for. Of course I don't know whether she really was wearing it; I hadn't noticed it, but I can see no reason to doubt the statement. What I want to mention is the small wound on the young lady's neck. It was only a scratch, but it might very easily have been made if a necklace had been snatched away from her. Just a bit of corroboration, for what it's worth. Naturally the cut could have been caused by many other means, a broken glass, for instance, if she had fallen across the table. But she hadn't.'

By this time both the women had been searched and most of the men. De Brasto's party had defiantly resumed their seats; their attitudes spoke plainly of their vindication. The detective came round the corner of his screen and approached the pale young man who continued to sit in an almost crouching position to one side. 'Will you come with me?' he asked quietly. 'You're the last.'

The young man struggled to his feet. He was white as a ghost and seemed scarcely to know where he was. The executive officer looked at him not unkindly.

'Just a moment, young man. I don't believe I've heard yet what your name is.'

'Oh—ah—Gnosens, sir. John I. Gnosens. Ah—'

'How was that? Nuisance, did you say?'

'No-sens, sir. You spell it G-n-o-s-e-n-s. I was with Miss— that is I was at Mr. Smith's table.'

'All right, my boy. Go ahead now. We'll be through in a few minutes. That lad needs a bracer,' he added to the doctor, as Gnosens stumbled after the detective. 'He's all in.'

'He certainly does,' agreed Schall. 'I'll give him one when he comes back.'

The officer turned to the rest of the party. 'We have practically finished to-night,' he said; 'unless anyone of you has something to add that I have not heard. Come, Mr. Brasto, I don't want to arrest you. Can't you give us some explanation of your behaviour?'

De Brasto seemed now to have composed himself completely. In a decided voice he repeated his former decision. 'I have nothing to say at present.'

'Very well,' snapped the executive officer with some heat. 'You are under arrest. Detective Bone will take you below and confine you until morning. There will be a hearing in the captain's office at nine-thirty. Everyone now present will be there promptly. Ah, Heddes, you have finished with your prisoner and turned him loose?'

Heddes had just re-entered the room and his face broke into

a broad grin. 'I guess not, sir. But I've found the necklace! It was in a little pocket at the back of his vest. He'd had no time to get rid of it. Lucky I grabbed him when I did.' From his own pocket he produced a magnificent string of rose-touched pearls, practically intact, and triumphantly offered it for inspection. As everyone bent forward to see the exhibit, Dr. Pell entered hurriedly through the main entrance. He came up to the group around the two tables with a grave expression and addressed himself at once to the executive officer. 'I have some further information for you, Mr. Drake. I have found, not one, but two bullets in Mr. Smith's body, both entering at the same spot! I must also tell you that, despite all I could do, the young lady we took above has died.'

Returning to the group, Gnosens was coming up behind the doctor. As he heard the latter's words, he came to an abrupt stop. The last vestige of colour drained from his face, and he fell forward at full length on the floor.

The suite of the *Meganaut's* captain would have been unbelievable to a commander of thirty, or even twenty, years ago. It comprises a bedroom, a large bath and dressing-room with a built-in shower and wardrobes, a dining-room and service pantry, a commodious office and a comfortable living-room containing a brick fire-place. From such surroundings Captain Horace Mansfield superintended the operation of his ship, maintaining among his officers and men an almost military discipline. Hardly ever did he appear in the public rooms of his vessel during a voyage, and never in the dining saloons, except when inspecting; occasionally he took a meal with his officers in their own mess room just aft of his quarters, but usually he dined alone

S.S.MEGANAUT

BOAT DECK

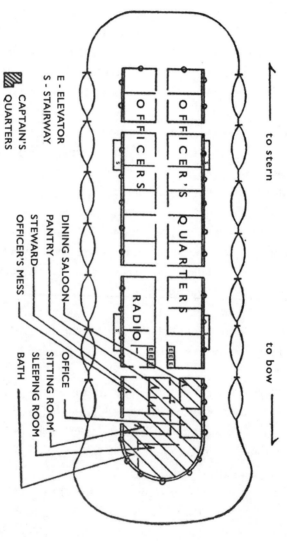

to stern

to bow

E - ELEVATOR
S - STAIRWAY

CAPTAIN'S
QUARTERS

DINING SALOON
PANTRY
STEWARD
OFFICER'S MESS

OFFICE
SITTING ROOM
SLEEPING ROOM
BATH

or with his executive officer. Of all his subordinates it was only to the latter that he allowed himself, upon occasion, to unbend.

The present morning was to be one of those occasions. Seated at breakfast with his trusted junior, the captain attacked an ice-cold grapefruit with vigour. 'Have the repairs been completed yet, Mr. Drake?' he inquired, between mouthfuls.

Hastily swallowing a piece of his own fruit, the executive officer replied that they had not. 'The men have been working all night,' he continued, 'but I am afraid the damage was more extensive than we thought. The two main dynamos were practically ruined. The armatures were simply melted together, and every fuse in the main circuit was blown. The fuses, of course, were replaced immediately, but the dynamos are another matter. The chief electrician tells me, sir, that we shall have to lay to during the final adjustments; the armatures naturally have to be adjusted in very true balance, and he maintains that the ordinary vibration makes this impossible.'

'How long does he want?'

'Several hours, sir, I believe, at the least. He says the job is too important to be hurried. I'm afraid there's no doubt he's right.'

'I suppose so,' growled the captain. 'I must say, though, that I've never heard of such a thing happening before. How lightning could ever reach those dynamos down in the engine-room is beyond me. You're certain it had nothing to do with that trouble in the smoking-room?'

'I've been into it thoroughly with the chief electrician, sir. We have examined the whole system for any signs of tampering and there are absolutely none. The electrician happened to be there himself when it occurred. He is certain that the lightning struck one of the funnels instead of grounding through a mast, and was carried through the walls and floors to the dynamos, where its force was sufficient to pass through their insulations. Incidentally the insulated bases were burnt through; of course they were never designed to hold anything like a million volts. I think we must conclude that the lightning did it, sir. No one in the smoking-room, even if he had an accomplice somewhere else, could possibly have effected it.'

'Apparently not,' the captain concluded. 'Unless his accomplice was God.'

During the recital the steward had cleared away the grapefruit and brought in a substantial repast of bacon and eggs, jams, marmalade, toast and muffins, and coffee.

'You can go now, Mann,' the captain directed him, as he finished pouring the hot coffee into their cups. 'Close the door and see that I am not disturbed. I will ring when I want you again.'

For a while they ate in silence. The captain's appetite was always hearty, and the executive officer, having remained on duty all night, was easily prepared to equal him. At length the captain wiped his mouth, took a deep draught of water and turned to the other. His formality fell from him like a cloak and he presented a frankly worried countenance.

'Tell me, Drake,' he said, 'have you made anything further of this damnable situation since you left me at two o'clock this morning?'

'To tell you the truth, sir,' replied his executive, 'I haven't had much time to think about it. But it has certainly occurred to me that this affair is perhaps not quite as simple as I thought at first. There's the man who got away with the necklace; what is his relation to the mix-up? Then Bone told me that in the first excitement this de Brasto accused Smith of firing at him, or attempting to. Everyone seems to have thought that they were strangers to each other, but after all what do we know of them? There may have been some connection that we know nothing about.'

'We know this much about Smith,' asserted the captain gloomily. 'He was one of the richest men in America. And one of the best known. His death will be a sensation, probably is already. To have had him shot in one of our saloons is a terrible blow to the boat. It is a very serious thing under any circumstances; and the only way we can save any face for the Line is to have the whole thing completely cleared up. Everything having the slightest bearing on this horrible situation must be brought to light. We must establish the culprit without any doubt whatsoever, and we must collect sufficient evidence to make certain of his conviction. My God,' the captain exclaimed bitterly, 'to think of a murder being committed on my boat, *my* boat!'

Drake, who understood that to his superior the honour of the ship was as precious as that of their daughters is to most men, attempted consolation. 'Well, sir, so far as the shooting itself is concerned, there should be no difficulty. Although it took place in the dark, there seems to be no doubt at all as to who did it. The flash and noise could not be missed; and we have a score of witnesses who saw the gun in de Brasto's hand when the lights went up a few seconds later. No matter what else comes out, I don't see how that can be got round. It's as plain as if it had happened in broad daylight that de Brasto shot him. By the way, sir, have you had the report on him yet?'

'Yes. Came in this morning. It wasn't very full, but as much as we could hope for in the middle of the night, I suppose. Stander and de Brasto are in the law; the firm is poorly thought of, in fact they have a rather shady reputation, but they seem to have always kept on the safe side. They have never actually been charged, although it appears that some investigation or other skirted pretty close to them no longer ago than last year.'

'He seemed rather a slimy specimen last night. And he was certainly in a funk. Was there anything in the report on Smith that might connect them?'

'Not a thing. Of course there was much more on Smith than on de Brasto. He was the regular American self-made millionaire. Started from nothing and made his first fortune in lead mines; then he branched out and now he is credited with having his finger in the pie in a dozen different lines. No one knows what he's worth, but the estimates range from two hundred to six hundred millions. Seems to have been a rough customer but well enough liked by those who didn't happen to be on the opposite side of the fence. Of course he had plenty of enemies too, must have had with that sort of career. For all we know de Brasto may have been one of them. Well, there's no use our guessing about it.'

'We'll get something out of him this morning, sir. Although it may be hard to get him to talk. That partner of his advised him not to, last night. They may stick to that programme.'

'He will talk, all right,' promised the captain. 'They're not on land now, with a paid judge to back them up. And they'll damn soon find it out, if they try any monkey business here.' He straightened up and poured out another cup of coffee. 'Have one, Drake?' Receiving a negative answer, he went on, 'We can't do much here talking. I'll see if they're ready yet.'

Mann appeared at the door immediately, in response to the bell. 'Mann,' the captain addressed him, 'you can take those people into the sitting-room; the office will be too small. How many of them are here?'

'They are all here, sir,' answered the steward. 'Except Dr. Pell and the—ah, the prisoner, sir. Mr. Bone has not brought him in yet, sir.'

The steward disappeared, and Drake got up from his seat, crushing out his cigarette. The captain also stood up and smoothed out the full dress uniform he had chosen for the occasion. His informality vanished and his face set itself in stern lines.

'Let us go, Mr. Drake,' he said.

'That is the second time you have interrupted, Mr. Stander,' said the captain. He spoke with some heat. 'I want you to understand that this investigation is not to be obstructed with interruptions or otherwise. I will not allow it for a moment. Proceed, Mr. Bone, if you please.'

The captain stood at the end of the long table that occupied the centre of his sitting-room. As he resumed his seat, he shot a quick glance around the comfortably furnished apartment. On the divan at his left were de Brasto and his party of the night before. Gnosens and Younghusband, with the two doctors, sat in leather upholstered chairs near the foot of the table, and on the captain's right were the two detectives and his executive officer. The side lights and the handsome lamp in the middle of the table furnished the illumination, for although the morning was gloriously bright outside, all the curtains had been drawn over the windows to shut out the gaze of any of the curious who might be walking the boat deck. At each of the doors, one to the deck, the other to the captain's office and dining-room, a pair of sailors stood stiffly to attention. The detective continued his interrupted evidence.

'As I said, sir, the two men had been fighting over the bidding. Mr. de Brasto had got himself quite worked up; his people became very angry because Mr. Smith was always overbidding him. Then the lights went out and he fired. I saw the shot and I saw him drop his gun when the lights came up. I took the gun and it is in evidence, sir. It is a .38, the same calibre as the bullet that killed Mr. Smith. As there were so many witnesses, we have not bothered to take any prints from the grip. There is no question about it, sir; the man is guilty. He got so mad at his opponent that he shot him.'

The detective sat down and the captain called upon Younghusband, who corroborated Bone's testimony in every particular. Dr. Schall came next, his evidence being to the same effect. The captain then turned to the ship's doctor.

'Dr. Pell, what is the medical finding? Have you made any autopsy?'

'I have not had an opportunity to make a detailed autopsy, sir, as yet; in fact, I can see no reason why one should be necessary. The cause of death is perfectly obvious; Mr. Smith was shot and his heart was punctured. In such a case death must supervene immediately. To be sure, there appear to be certain features, of a purely technical nature, which I should like to discuss with Dr. Schall and which I should very much like to clear up by means of an autopsy, if possible. But in view of the nature of the wound, they can have no bearing on the present investigation. I have no hesitation in saying that Mr. Smith died as a result of these bullet wounds.'

'Wounds, Dr. Pell? Was there more than one?'

'To be strictly accurate, there was only one wound, sir. But I discovered two bullets in the body. They had entered at the same place, one very slightly above the other, and both had ruptured the heart. I have recovered these bullets and they are in evidence. They are both of .38 calibre.'

'Is that all, Doctor?'

'That is all, sir.'

'I will recall Mr. Bone,' said the captain. 'Mr. Bone, how many shots had been discharged from Mr. de Brasto's revolver when you took charge of it?'

The detective got to his feet once more. 'I have been puzzled about that, sir,' he admitted grudgingly. 'Only one shot had been fired and all the other chambers were filled. There was only one shot that I heard, sir. I don't know where the second bullet could have come from, but I know who fired the first one.' He pointed across the table at de Brasto. 'That man fired it,' he insisted; 'I saw him do it.'

The captain's face wore a frown of perplexity. 'If there were two bullets,' he considered, 'there must have been two shots.' He looked around the room. 'Is there anyone here who heard the second shot? Did Mr. Smith have a gun of his own?'

De Brasto's party said nothing, but Dr. Schall, Younghusband and the detective were certain that they had heard no more than one shot fired. That shot had been so loud in the darkened and momentarily quiet smoking-room, that it would have been utterly impossible for them to have missed a second explosion. Gnosens sat forward in his chair with his hands tightly clenched; he stared ahead of him and made no remark. Both Bone and Dr. Pell were positive in their assurances that the victim had been unarmed.

The executive officer leaned over and touched Captain Mansfield's arm. 'May I ask a question, sir?'

'Certainly, Mr. Drake.'

Drake addressed the doctor. 'Is it possible, Dr. Pell, that Mr.

Smith had carried one of these bullets in his body, having been wounded on some previous occasion? We understand that Mr. Smith came from the western part of the United States. Is it possible that he might have received this bullet in his younger days—'

'It is entirely out of the question, Mr. Drake,' the doctor answered. 'Absolutely impossible. Mr. Smith could not have carried either of those bullets for ten seconds without dying. Also, on medical grounds, neither of them could have been in his body for any period when I removed them. Their appearance before I had them cleaned, established at once that they had recently entered.'

'I see,' said Drake. 'Thank you, Doctor.'

'It is time we heard from Mr. de Brasto,' the captain announced, turning to the man who up to now had sat perfectly still on the end of the couch. 'You have heard the evidence, sir, as to the shot which you fired last night. What have you to say in your defence?'

Before de Brasto could speak, his partner leaned across from the other end of the divan and said in a clearly audible undertone, 'Don't say a word until we land, Saul. Remember what I told you.'

'Mr. Stander,' cried the captain sharply, 'I have warned you before. I will not tolerate your interference in this matter. Leave the room at once, sir. Mr. Drake, have one of your men take him out.'

'I have a perfect right—' began the portly lawyer. Before he could complete the sentence, one of the sailors was at his side and attempted to take his arm. With a sudden movement Stander threw the man away from him against the table.

The captain rose abruptly from his chair. His face had paled slightly with anger and his voice was deadly quiet. He motioned to the remaining sailor.

'Take this man below. He is to be kept in confinement for two days,' he directed. 'I shall teach you, sir,' he continued to the astonished lawyer, 'who is in command of this vessel. I don't know what you can do at home, and I don't care. According to international convention this ship, while at sea, is entirely under my jurisdiction. My investigation of this murder will take place while we are at sea, not after we have landed. You have obstructed my hearing in spite of repeated warnings, and you have assaulted one of my men in the performance of his duty. For that you will be confined as I have directed. Do you intend to go peaceably, or shall I have you handcuffed and carried? Kindly make up your mind at once.'

'Why, I— This is the most high-handed— When I reach—'

'When you reach wherever you are going, you can do as you please. While you are on my ship, sir, you will obey my regulations. That is all; take him below.'

When the two sailors had escorted the still protesting Stander from the room, the captain turned to those who were left. 'You have seen, ladies and gentlemen, that I will stand no nonsense. The matter we are engaged upon, is by far the most serious that has ever come under my hand, and I am determined to make a final disposition of it. Any further obstruction will not only meet with immediate punishment here, but I shall prefer the most serious charges against the culprit the moment we reach port. I am in earnest, I assure you. Let us proceed with the investigation. Mr. de Brasto?'

No one had failed to be impressed by the captain's action; de Brasto, in particular, had quickly decided that silence was no longer the better part of caution. Small beads of perspiration gleamed on his pale forehead as he addressed himself to the task of explaining his position.

'There is no doubt, Captain,' he began in a subdued voice, 'that I could stand on my rights and refuse to testify, if I were guilty of this crime.'

'That is so, Mr. de Brasto. Do you wish to plead guilty to this murder?'

'I do not!' de Brasto cried, suddenly vehement. 'I do not even care to claim immunity on the ground that I might incriminate myself. I never had the slightest intention of shooting Mr. Smith, and I did not shoot him!'

'How can you deny that you did so, in the face of all these witnesses?'

'I do not deny firing a shot, nor do I know where it went. But I do know that it went nowhere near Mr. Smith, because I shot it in an entirely different direction.'

'That is a strange statement, Mr. de Brasto. Why did you fire at all, may I ask?'

'I fired at a man who was drawing a gun to kill me in the dark. I saw him in the right hand door of the smoking-room just as the lights went out. He was pulling his gun when I saw him. I had no time to do anything but get out my own revolver and shoot.'

'Who was this man?'

'I don't know. That is, I don't know his name, or the name he is travelling under. He has been following me about ever since I got on board. I've caught him several times spying on me. And last night he found the chance he had been waiting for. I tell you I didn't dare not defend myself.'

'Why had you not reported this before, Mr. de Brasto? You know well enough that such behaviour would not be allowed to continue for an hour aboard this ship. Why did you not appeal to my officers?'

'I didn't care to, Captain. There would have been notoriety; I didn't want it. And I wasn't sure about him until I saw him drawing a gun.'

'It comes to this, then. You say a mysterious man has been following you about. He was in the starboard entrance to the smoking-room when the lights went out last night and you saw him drawing a gun. You then fired at him. No, I'm afraid that won't hold, Mr. de Brasto; that is a pretty thin yarn, if you will permit me to say so. And where did your shot go? No one was found wounded by that door. In fact, no one, so far as we know, has been wounded on the boat, except Mr. Smith.'

'How do I know where it went? I shot as quickly as I could, and in the dark. Perhaps I missed him. Maybe the bullet is in the door or on the deck. I don't know, but I swear that's the truth, Captain, so help me God!'

'Surely, sir, you cannot expect us to take this as an explanation. Who is this strange man? Do you expect us to believe that you fired at some stranger because you thought he had been spying upon you and you saw him reaching into his pocket, probably for a handkerchief?'

'But he *did* fire at me. I saw the flash of his gun!'

'What? Why, everyone is agreed that there was only one shot. You have heard that brought out.'

'There was only one in my neighbourhood. But no one was paying any attention to the opposite end of the room. His shot came from there; it was just a little ahead of mine and—'

'We shall have to look into this, of course,' said the captain. 'Mr. Drake, will you kindly go below and see if there are any signs of Mr. de Brasto's bullet where he claims it should be? Look very carefully around the starboard doorway; also out on deck where it should have struck, had it gone out through the door. And find out from the stewards if there was any trace of blood on deck when they cleaned up the winter garden last night.'

The executive officer had already started to leave when the captain called him back again. 'Also, Mr. Drake,' he added, 'I believe you have a list of all the passengers who were in the smoking-room last evening. See if you can locate any who were near the starboard doorway. Let us be sure about this shot that Mr. de Brasto says was fired at him. Detective Bone, you should know most of the passengers by sight now. Do you recall anyone in particular who was near there?'

'Well,' the detective considered, 'yes, sir. I remember a large party in that part of the room; I think the name is van Ness. De Witt van Ness, I think. Shall I see if I can find him, sir?'

'Do so, Mr. Bone. All right, Mr. Drake, you may go. Now,' when the two men had departed, 'I want to be perfectly fair to you, Mr. de Brasto; that's why I am having this search made. But to be frank, I think it is probably a wild goose chase. Your story is a very weak one.'

The appearance of the accused man was one of complete sincerity. 'But, don't you see, Captain,' he urged, 'that's where the bullets came from that killed Smith? He missed me and hit Smith, who was at the next table to mine. I missed him, too, apparently. I know I shouldn't have let off a gun in that crowded room, but what was I to do?'

'Your whole story, sir,' repeated the captain, 'including the mysterious stranger, is very hard for me to credit.'

'It's true all the same, Captain,' de Brasto insisted. 'Can I see you alone for a few moments? I can soon convince you that I have not made it up on the spur of the moment.'

'You certainly may not see me alone, sir. Everyone here is under oath. If you wish to make a confidential communication, I will exact a statement under oath, remember, from all present that what you say will not be repeated outside this room, unless it becomes necessary in the proceedings growing out of this investigation. If you are innocent in this matter, Mr. de Brasto, such a statement should be all that you require. May I have your assurance, ladies and gentlemen?' The captain looked keenly around the room.

A chorus of agreement greeted his request. Captain Mansfield made sure that everyone had definitely and verbally declared himself, then turned his attention once again to de Brasto. 'You may feel perfectly secure on this point; I shall deal personally with any infringement of the promises that have just been given. I may add that you will be well advised to make entirely clear anything whatsoever that has a bearing on the shooting.'

It was plainly apparent that de Brasto's reluctance had been overcome in part only. For some moments he continued to hesitate, before a full appreciation of the captain's cold and unconvinced attitude turned the scales in favour of frankness. After a short, inward struggle the suspected passenger straightened up in his seat and began to speak.

'Well, it's like this, Captain. Mr. Stander and myself are in the business of law; and part of our business is to defend criminals, that is,' he hastily amended, 'men accused of crime. We have been moderately successful.' He favoured the company with a deprecating smile. 'But of course some of our customers, clients, have been a pretty hard lot. Last year we undertook to defend some men who had been charged with murder in connection with a beer racket, and unfortunately we lost our case. Two of the men were convicted and electrocuted, and a third is in prison with a life sentence. In spite of all our efforts, and how Stander and I worked on that case, the other members of the gang accuse us of letting their pals down. It's crazy, of course, but they believe, or say they do, that a rival mob got to us and bribed us to connive at a conviction. Most unfortunately they have obtained some evidence, I need not say it is entirely misleading, which has confirmed them in their false belief. They have threatened us, they have shot at Stander on the street, and they have wrecked our offices.' De Brasto paused and shrugged his slim shoulders.

'What was there for us to do? We decided to come abroad for a few months and let the storm blow over. Then on the boat I thought I recognized one of the mob that is trying to get us. I became suspicious. Twice I caught this man following me, trying to get me alone in a deserted passageway, but each time I found a steward or another passenger in time. Then last night he came in that door just as the lights were going out. I looked up and saw him. He drew his gun and fired, and so did I. My God, Captain,' de Brasto concluded, wiping away the sudden perspiration, 'I don't see yet how he missed me. All that gang are crack shots.'

For some minutes the captain sat attempting to digest this tale of modern adventure. His astonishment was reflected in his features when he finally said, 'But my good man, do you mean to tell me that such lawlessness goes on unchecked in New York

City? And how could some member of this gang of toughs possibly pass himself off as a first-class passenger on board my boat? Why, it's unbelievable!'

'Oh, no it isn't,' he was assured. 'This particular mob makes three, four hundred thousand a year. The beer isn't the only racket they have, they have strong connections and influence and go about wherever they want to. And one of them is certainly on this ship!'

Despite his doubts the captain could not avoid being impressed by the urgency of the man's avowal. He was still frowning over this new affront to his boat when there came a knock at the door and an elderly, smooth-shaven gentleman entered, accompanied by Detective Bone.

'Mr. van Ness, sir,' announced the detective, as he entered on the heels of his quarry. 'This is the captain, Mr. van Ness; he wants to see you for a few minutes, as I explained.'

The newcomer's glance went rapidly around the room, as he advanced with a slightly pompous air. 'Ah, Captain Mansfield, I'm sure this is an honour,' he said.

'Not so much an honour as a duty,' the captain replied grimly. 'I am obliged to you for your prompt appearance, Mr. van Ness. We are investigating last night's unfortunate mishap, and we believe you can be of some assistance.'

'Ah, a shocking affair, Captain, shocking, I'm sure. And how can I be of help? I shall be only too glad—'

'Yes, yes, Mr. van Ness, we appreciate your offer. Now I believe you were sitting near the starboard, that is, the right hand door of the smoking-room last evening when the excitement occurred. Is that right? Yes. Well, now will you please cast your mind back to those few minutes when the room was dark, and see if you can help us determine just what happened.'

'I shall be most pleased, Captain. Yes, I have cast my mind back, as you suggest.'

'Now think most carefully, Mr. van Ness, and tell us how many shots were fired during that period of darkness.'

'But, my dear sir, I don't have to think about that. There was only one; everybody in the room must have heard it. It was enough to shatter one's ear drums, Captain. Why—'

'You are perfectly sure?' the captain insisted. 'Think well, Mr. van Ness. We have no idea of doubting your evidence, but it is more important than you may imagine. It has been claimed that a gun was discharged from the doorway, very near where you were sitting, while the room was dark, or just as it became dark.'

De Brasto leaned forward, his face paler than ever. 'Think, sir,' he pleaded. 'If you didn't hear that shot from behind you, did you hear anything at all at that time. *Anything?*'

The elderly gentleman looked somewhat bewildered. 'Well, well,' he ruminated, 'if it is as vital as this. . . . No . . . no, I certainly heard only one shot. . . . Of course, there were other noises. . . . A scuffle of some kind, but not near me; and I think a chair fell over. . . . No, I wouldn't say that, either; I couldn't be sure what it was. . . . And yes, ah yes, indeed,' he brightened and smiled as everyone's attention became focused on him, 'I do remember something that I thought most extraordinary at the time. After the lights had gone out, somebody opened a bottle of soda just behind me. I couldn't understand it at all, somebody opening a bottle like that in the dark,' he finished triumphantly, and looked from one to another of his hearers for approbation.

Approbation did not seem to be forthcoming. Everyone's expression appeared to be covered by the shadow of anti-climax.

De Brasto's face especially was the picture of despondency. Then all at once it was lit up vividly. In his haste he sprang to his feet.

'That's it!' he cried. 'Don't you see, Captain? It was a silencer! The hiss was a silencer. No one could have opened a bottle then. That accounts for it. That's why no one heard the shot.'

'Well,' the captain considered, 'I suppose it *might* be so. But I don't know. I've never heard a silencer. Do you think it sounds like a bottle of soda?'

'But I have; that's just—'

'Captain,' a voice interrupted from the opposite end of the table.

'Yes. What is it? Yes, Mr. Younghusband.'

'I don't believe there was any silencer, sir, or any of the rest of it. Why shouldn't someone have opened a bottle in the dark. We were all surprised and no one knew quite what he was doing for a moment. In my opinion, Captain, this whole cock and bull story is being just cooked up for the occasion.'

'But it is not!' de Brasto cried. 'A silencer also hides the flash. I saw a glare when the shot was fired, but I don't remember any noise. I thought it was because I was so excited that I didn't remember it, but now I see that there really wasn't any noise to hear.'

The captain shook his head slightly, as if to accommodate the new aspect of the situation. 'Your case is certainly strengthened considerably, Mr. de Brasto,' he admitted. 'Upon this basis we have now accounted for both bullets, at least. Accidental manslaughter is the gravest charge that can be brought against you, if your story is true. If so, it would appear that both you and this gangster fired at each other, and that both of you hit the wrong man.'

'But I couldn't have hit him, sir. Mr. Smith was behind me

to my left. I was almost in a line between him and the door. My back was to him when I fired. Both of the bullets that killed him were meant for me.'

Once more all eyes were turned upon van Ness. The captain immediately demanded: 'Did you hear two of these hisses, Mr. van Ness?'

'No, I did not.' The latest witness was positive. 'I am sure there was only one, and I am sure I am not mistaken. It was a long hiss, as if the top were being pried off a bottle slowly, but I know it was not repeated.'

'No, I'm afraid we can't allow you two shots from the doorway, Mr. de Brasto,' was the captain's conclusion. 'Still, I don't quite see how you could both manage to hit the same man by mistake. Dr. Pell, will you kindly describe the wounds for us again?'

Pell's face evidenced his astonishment at the turn affairs had taken. In a surprised voice, he replied: 'But there was only one wound, sir. You will understand my amazement when I tell you that the second bullet entered through the aperture made by the first. You will bear me out, Dr. Schall?' He turned perplexedly to his colleague.

'That is so,' the latter confirmed. 'The wound was no doubt enlarged by whichever bullet entered last, but very slightly so. The trajectories could not have been more than half an inch apart, at the most. I suppose there is a chance in some billions that it might happen, but—well, it's incredible.' The two doctors shook their heads solemnly at each other.

It was perhaps fortunate that at this juncture a hurried step was heard outside and the executive officer re-entered the room without knocking. As he burst in, the captain looked up sharply. Somewhat breathless with his haste, Drake pressed a small object into his superior's hand, at the same time beginning to speak.

'I am sorry to interrupt you, sir, but I feel you should have this new evidence at once. We could find no signs of anything near the door, but before I left I went over to refresh my memory as to the exact location of Mr. Smith's and Mr. de Brasto's tables. As we were arranging the chairs approximately as they were last night. the chief steward leaned over and noticed a mark in the central leg of Mr. de Brasto's table. We investigated and found the bullet that I have just given you, sir. I was delayed because we had to break up the table to get it out. It was up near the top of the leg, just below the under side of the table. It was directly in front of where Mr. de Brasto had been sitting and in a line between his position and the starboard entrance. He must have fired too quickly, before his gun had come up level. But I don't think, sir, in view of this discovery, that we can any longer doubt that he fired as he claimed.'

The captain had been comparing the new bullet with the other two which had found a living target and were now lying on the table before him. 'Yes,' he said. 'They are all of the same calibre. This bullet you have just given me, could have come from Mr. de Brasto's gun.'

'Might not the table have been turned around since last night, Captain?' queried Younghusband. 'Perhaps this is the bullet fired from the doorway.'

'No, that can't be,' Drake answered him. 'All the tables in the smoking-room are bolted down. They can't be moved or turned in any way.'

'If you will look at the side of that bullet, please, Captain,' suggested de Brasto quickly, 'I mean the one you have in your hand, you will find a small star cut in the jacket. You will find these stars on the other bullets taken from my revolver, but I don't think you will find them on the bullets that struck Mr. Smith. The concern that sells me my ammunition, mark their products that way; I've just remembered it. All the time I've known there was some little point that would clear me. Thank God I've got it at last.'

An immediate examination bore out the assertion. 'Well, Mr. de Brasto,' the captain said thoughtfully, 'I guess that settles the matter. I have no option but to consider the charge against you dismissed. Nevertheless, it is fully established that you let off your gun in my smoking-room; and I intend to hold you to account for that inexcusable action. When we reach port, you will not leave this boat without my permission. Meanwhile you are free to go where you will on the ship. You have no more firearms in your possession, have you?'

'No, sir,' answered de Brasto. His voice was both relieved and subdued.

'In view of what has happened, I think I am justified in having Detective Bone search the cabins occupied both by you and by Mr. Stander for other weapons. You will give him every assistance in his duty.' There was a slight pause. 'Now furthermore, I am led to believe by your story that there is a dangerous criminal at large on this ship. By the way, it's not by any chance the man who was arrested last night?'

'If it is, sir,' spoke up Bone, 'he didn't give any sign of it this morning. They both had breakfast together below.' He indicated de Brasto by a jerk of his head. 'I still think this man had something to do with the murder, sir. It stands to reason no one could get as mad as—'

'That is finished, Mr. Bone,' replied the captain decidedly. 'There is quite sufficient proof as to where Mr. de Brasto's bullet went.' He turned to the latter. 'You say you know what the man who shot at you looks like. He is not the prisoner we have below?'

'No, sir. He is not at all like that man, Captain. And now that you have disarmed me, how am I to protect myself? That man is still after me; he won't stop until he gets me, either.'

'If you are nervous, I will speak to the chief steward about having your cabin changed quietly. Also I intend to detail one of my officers to be near you constantly until we have captured that man and put him where he can do no more harm. If you will wait in your cabin, he will report to you in mufti in a short time. I am afraid your opponent may be on the look-out for our detective. I want you to agree upon a sign with my officer, who will be armed, and at your first glimpse of him I want that man taken. I am very serious about this, Mr. de Brasto; don't you try to incriminate him, leave that to me. I'll have no gangsters shooting off their guns on my boat, that's final.'

The captain rose from his chair and made a general survey of the room. He continued in a different tone: 'The hearing will be adjourned for the present, ladies and gentlemen. It would seem that the man responsible for Mr. Smith's death, is the criminal of whom Mr. de Brasto has told us. Our first task must now be to effect his capture. Of course I shall expect you to hold yourselves in readiness to assist us, but on the other hand it may not be necessary for us to trouble you further. At all events I wish you would accept my thanks for the cooperation you have offered this morning. That is all, ladies and gentlemen. Thank you again.'

As they all rose to file out, Younghusband broke the silence with: 'Anything I can do, Captain? I wish you would call upon me. I am very anxious to see the man responsible for Mr.

Smith's death brought to justice. I'm sure you understand, Captain, and will let me help.'

'You are no more anxious than I am, Mr. Younghusband. I shall be very glad of your assistance. After luncheon I shall meet with our detectives in my office to discuss the situation. If you care to attend as a friend of Mr. Smith, I shall be pleased to have you.'

'Thank you, sir. I shall be there,' said Younghusband. He bowed slightly and left the room. The others also walked to the door held open by the sailor guard; the last to pass out were the two women and young Gnosens, none of whom had said a word during the hearing, beyond giving their names when they first entered the room. Gnosens looked pale and ill; it could be seen that he had passed a sleepless night despite the doctor's tonic. He stumbled out, and the captain and his executive officer were left alone.

'Well, sir,' said Drake more cheerfully than he had spoken since the previous evening, 'we seem to have located the culprit. He can't lie hidden long aboard ship. We should have him locked up by to-night or to-morrow morning.'

The captain shook his head doubtfully. 'I'm not so sure of that, Drake. We can't hold de Brasto after the evidence of the bullet you found. But I am not so greatly taken by the story of the hypothetical gangster he saw in the doorway. Although of course it may be true.

'Even so,' he added, as he reached for a cigarette, 'don't forget that we still have one extra bullet to account for.'

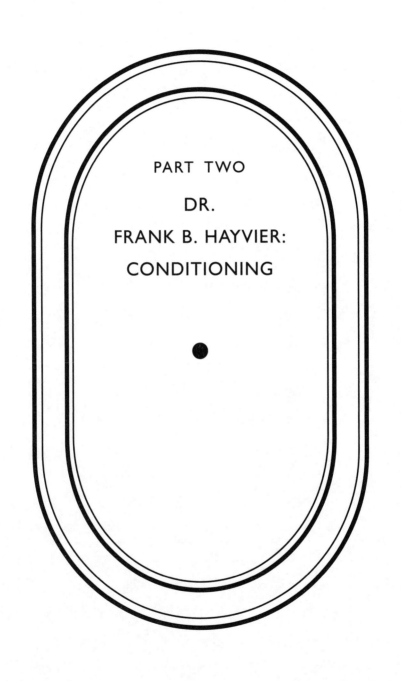

PART TWO

DR.

FRANK B. HAYVIER:

CONDITIONING

PART TWO

DR. FRANK B. HAYVIER: CONDITIONING

THE SUN was setting in mid-Atlantic. Behind the *Meganaut* it burst forth from beneath a bank of low clouds far to the westward, flooding the sun deck and the stern in golden brilliance.

Already the covered deck spaces forward were darkening; in the winter garden with its thick windows and towering palms the early arrivals for the cocktail hour found it gloomy until a steward switched on the ceiling lights and their diffuse glow spread downward. A few of the wiser passengers, already arrayed for the evening, found their way to the Veranda Cafe which still basked in sunset glory. In comfortable wicker chairs, behind small, glass-topped tables, they prepared to enjoy Martinis and salted nuts while gazing out into the orange and purple splendour of the west. Far beneath them the boat's wake trailed out from its white point under the stern to a broad, flat plume that finally intermingled with the green, following swells and was lost. A few points to the north the glaring, molten path of the sun spread a blinding carpet from their feet to the horizon.

At the moment not more than half a dozen passengers were

enjoying the advantages of this corner of the ship. They glanced curiously, and most of them with something approaching pity, at the haggard, nervous youth who for five hours or longer had sat alone in the farthest corner. His long legs, still clad in plus-fours, were stretched out before him, his head with its light, rumpled hair drooped forward between his hunched shoulders. Occasionally he fingered his face with a twitching hand, but for the most part he sat motionless and stared at nothing.

Younghusband, himself sleek and dinner-jacketed for the coming night, rounded the corner. Interrupting his walk, he made his way at once to the side of his acquaintance.

'My dear fellow,' he said solicitously, seating himself at the table. 'Whatever is the matter? You look like a ghost. Do you know it's past six-thirty? Time you went down and dressed.'

The other looked up slowly, and presently succeeded in focusing his gaze upon his companion.

'It's late,' Younghusband repeated. 'It's time you got dressed.'

Gnosens responded hollowly: 'Dressed? What the hell is there to get dressed for?'

'Dinner, I should say.'

'Dinner. . . . Christ.'

'Say, look here, what's the matter with you? Of course, it's been a shocking business. But after all, we hardly knew him. And from what they said this morning, it can't be long before they have the man who fired the shots. Although I'm still rather suspicious about that de Brasto, myself.'

'It's lucky for him,' said Gnosens suddenly, 'that they found his bullet. I'd have torn his heart out. If I had to kill his jailer first.'

'But why are you so excited about it? You didn't know them;

I introduced you to Miss Smith myself, not more than three days ago.'

An involuntary shudder ran down Gnosens's long frame. 'Oh, my God,' he groaned.

'Ah!' Younghusband's bewilderment was illuminated by a ray of comprehension. 'You had fallen for her?'

'If that's what you call it,' said Gnosens, hopelessly. 'I was going to ask her to marry me, last night.'

Younghusband's face was the picture of sincere astonishment. 'But, but—. After knowing her two days? Do you seriously mean to tell me that you were going to propose? I didn't know her very well myself,' he continued, surprised into indiscretion, 'but I think you might have made a serious mistake. It is possible that she was not just the kind of girl you thought.'

The words did not penetrate Gnosens's consciousness for some seconds. When they did, his long body jerked itself up in one swift movement. His pose was tensely minatory. Behind his eyes a fire burned redly. His voice was low, clear, ominous.

'Get . . . out . . . while . . . you . . . can.'

For an instant Younghusband regarded him questioningly. Then he got quickly to his feet.

'You're out of your mind,' he said coldly. 'I advise you to go to bed and get some sleep.' He turned abruptly on his heel and walked off. Gnosens, as if exhausted by the brief outburst, half rose and then slumped back into his former position.

Another figure, a paunchy little man in a dress suit, got up quietly from a nearby table and came over.

'Will you excuse me?' he asked with a slight, foreign accent. 'I could not help overhearing. You are in trouble; perhaps I can assist.'

Gnosens had not paid the slightest attention to his remark, and the newcomer continued. 'I am Dr. Malcolm Plechs of Budapest. I am a psychoanalyst. I can see that you have suffered a severe trauma.'

Gnosens looked up.

'Can you?' he asked, in no way flippantly.

'Of course you have, my boy,' said Dr. Plechs kindly. 'It will do you good to talk a little, if you find it possible. Almost everybody has left; we are quite secluded. Can you bring yourself to tell me a little of this unfortunate young woman who has—gone?'

'I love her,' said Gnosens simply, as if she had not gone at all.

'I see. . . . I see. . . . Yes. She was very beautiful, I am told. Now my boy'—with a change of tone—'you must pull yourself together. She has died and she will not come back; you must face the situation. You must not allow it to sink into the unconscious, whence it will trouble and upset the rest of your life. I will help you. I will be glad to help you. Let us face the fact. After all, you have known her but a very short time.'

'Five years,' said Gnosens with a painful grimace, '. . . five years.'

'But I thought—'

Under the analyst's sympathetic attitude Gnosens's pent-up speech burst forth.

'It was five years ago last week that first I saw Coralie. On my twenty-first birthday. I was at a night club with some friends. She was there with a large party. No one knew her. I cut in, and she danced with me. Five minutes, maybe. I haven't seen her since until this trip. I couldn't find out who she was but I swore I'd find her. I know a hundred girls, but they're not like her. She's—she's sort of a goddess. . . .

'And then I found her. I came up the gangplank right behind her. And next day I scraped an acquaintance with that skunk Younghusband and got him to introduce me. I've waited and searched—and I found her. Coralie Smith. And now— Oh, my God!' he cried suddenly. His expression crinkled into a tortured mask and he hid his face in his hands, sobbing violently.

The disturbance attracted the attention of two men who were just passing the open rear of the café. Commander Drake and his companion hesitated; the latter peered uncertainly into the darkening room, then turned back and said a few words inaudible at the distance. They approached.

'What's this, Doctor?' asked the man in the business suit. 'Something gone wrong?'

'Ah, it's you, Pons,' Plechs answered, his mien troubled. 'Alas, this poor young man, he has a breakdown.'

The young man shrank back, wriggled, finally lifted a tearstained countenance. He spoke in a rather smothered voice.

'I—I don't want to make a disturbance. Let me go, go away from here.'

'Why, man, you're sick!' Pons exclaimed. He looked at the haggard face, the deep circles under the eyes, the crooked mouth. 'Come, will you let me take you down to your cabin?'

Gnosens's grunt was unintelligible, but taking it for assent, Drake helped him to his feet. Pons took his arm and started through the ballroom toward the after stairways, Dr. Plechs and the executive officer bringing up the rear. 'Where is your stateroom?' asked Pons casually.

'Eh, oh, it's A101.'

They made their way the whole length of the boat without meeting anyone. Before the door Gnosens, after some fumbling, produced his key.

During the walk Pons had been covertly observing the young man at his side. As they entered, he inquired: 'By the way, how long is it since you've had any sleep?'

'Don't know,' said Gnosens vaguely. 'Oh, well, night before last maybe.'

'And food?'

'Can't eat.' Gnosens stood uncertainly in the middle of the floor, as Drake and the analyst closed the cabin door. 'How the hell can I eat!'

Pons regarded him searchingly and spoke with decision. 'You get undressed and into bed. You're going to have a double eggnog and then you're going to sleep. We're psychologists, not doctors, but I don't think you need a doctor. You're worn out and exhausted; things will look different when you wake up. Dr. Plechs or I will look in on you in the morning. If we can help you get straightened out, we'd like to. What you need first of all is rest. Now don't be foolish; go ahead and get undressed, there's a good fellow.'

Gnosens had already removed his shoes and stockings, when suddenly he stopped.

'But I can't. They haven't found the murderer yet.' He looked at Drake, who shook his head in confirmation. 'I must help find him. I can't go to bed until he's caught!'

Dr. Plechs looked surprised. 'I was told the assailant had been apprehended. Is it not true?'

'Wasn't the right man,' Gnosens answered, retrieving a stocking from the floor.

'But I don't understand that,' said Pons, puzzled. 'I was in the smoking-room last night. I saw the whole thing. The man was arrested on the spot.'

'No,' Drake explained. 'We found that man's bullet in his own table. There was another man who is supposed to have fired from the doorway. With a silencer,' he added, replying to Pons's puzzled look. 'We are looking for him. Perhaps I should not say this, but I feel sure you gentlemen are to be trusted.'

'By George, that's right,' exclaimed Pons. 'There was a hiss; I remember it distinctly. I've seen experiments with silencers, and it could have been one, certainly.'

'But no one except the man we arrested knows what this other man looks like,' the executive officer continued. 'He is looking for him, with a guard, but he hasn't found him yet.'

'Now you see,' Dr. Plechs admonished his charge, 'there is nothing you can do at this minute. I agree altogether with Dr. Pons that you should rest. And later you may be able to give better assistance.'

Pons added his persuasion. 'That's right,' he urged. 'Please be a good fellow and do as we ask. You can do nothing now. When you're fresh again, you can help.'

Gnosens, exhausted as he was, could oppose them no longer. 'Well—', he capitulated. 'But look here, you men are pretty clever chaps, I'd say. If I go to bed, will you try to help straighten it out? I can't think now; it seems all crazy to me, all mixed up. Will you see if you can help discover who did it? Mr. Drake, sir, surely the captain will let them?'

'Why, I suppose so. Of course. I'll be glad to speak to him about it.'

'Will you do it?'

'Yes, yes, of course we will. Now do get into bed. We will help if we can; and we will let you know in the morning everything that has happened.'

A few minutes later Pons, quietly opening the door, heard his deep, regular breathing. Fatigue had accomplished what advice could not.

The chief electrician stood very stiffly at attention. The captain had just returned his salute.

'Will you please inform me, Mr. Holt,' asked the latter, 'as to the exact condition of your repairs at the moment?'

'I had hoped to be finished long before this, sir. We have been working all the afternoon, and the dynamos are now installed. But as soon as we resumed full speed, it became clear that the bases will not hold in their present condition. They have been too badly burnt out, sir.'

'I suppose that means you will have to dismantle them again? How long will the job take?'

'Six hours, at the least. Maybe longer.'

'Then it's too late to begin it now. Eight bells went long ago. You'll have to start in the morning.'

'But we can't run more than half speed, sir, if you want the regular dynamos to-night. Won't the emergency ones do for this evening? In that case we can go right ahead; we'll have it done before midnight surely.'

'No, Mr. Holt.' Captain Mansfield was decided. 'I can't have any more disturbance among my passengers. There has been a great deal too much already. The lights must be in correct order as soon as it becomes dark. Can you guarantee their performance, if we proceed at half speed?'

'Yes, sir. I can guarantee that. I can brace the bases temporarily.'

With another salute the electrician departed.

As Captain Mansfield re-entered the office, his steward, a privileged character, duly noted the scowl that darkened his face. When something was seriously amiss, there were no scowls. Nevertheless, 'Is something wrong, sir?' he inquired.

'Nothing serious,' responded the captain. 'But it's annoying. Already we've lost a quarter-day. And it looks as if we would lose the third of another one.'

He sat down abruptly and began to go over the log.

Four friends sat late in the smoking-room. The attendance had been even larger than usual, the prevalent and recurring topic of conversation being the astounding occurrence of the evening before. But now all had departed to dance or retire, except two couples who still lingered at tables near the main entrance. To all purposes the four in the centre of the room had the saloon to themselves.

These four gentlemen were by no means nobodies; on the contrary they were all 'authorities' and all of them were 'eminent'. Reading from right to left (rather than in the usual manner), there was Dr. Frank B. Hayvier, the well-known behaviourist; Dr. Malcolm Plechs, the equally well-known psychoanalyst; there was Dr. L. Rees Pons (whose first name was Love, and who never allowed this parental oversight to be pronounced in his presence), the noted inventor of Integrative Psychology, and finally there was Professor Knott Coe Mittle, whose opinions had, scientifically, perhaps more weight than those of any of the others, since, not without care and agility, he had escaped the fate of becoming identified with any of the special, contending cliques in his science.

For some time they sat smoking in silence, Pons, whose enormous measurements suggested a limitless capacity, occasionally raising his tall glass, or calling a steward for its replenishment.

Professor Mittle broke the interlude. 'Of course,' he remarked, 'as you describe it, it is a very usual case.'

Dr. Plechs nodded. 'And so it is. A most severe psychic trauma. But it needs careful handling. Many abnormalities could be prevented if someone were at hand to offer treatment when such traumata occur. I am most interested to see what can be done.'

'I have no doubt,' the professor replied. 'Perhaps you can report the case to the Convention when we reach London.'

'I shall perhaps make mention of it in my address. If it turns out as I foresee.'

Pons spoke up. 'While I cannot agree with you at all upon the terms you use, I do think you may be able to help the young fellow. I should like to see you do it.' Dr. Plechs bowed slightly.

'Too bad,' said Dr. Hayvier, the fourth member of the quartette, 'that Pons has no chance to use his lie detector on your subject. You've got all the gadgets with you, haven't you, Pons?'

'Yes. They want me to demonstrate it. In my view it's the least important thing I've ever done, but no one seems to forget it. The publicity value, I suppose. They can see it work.'

Dr. Plechs felt impelled to return Pons's compliment. 'But perhaps you will have the opportunity. I hope so. The young man has urged us to assist in the investigation. Dr. Pons may be able to test the criminal.'

'Oh, that was just to get him to bed. I don't think the officer took it seriously. I rather wish he had; it's an interesting puzzle and I'd like to see how it comes out. But I guess we won't have any chance of that.'

'What officer is that?' asked Mittle.

'Oh, trust Pons,' smiled Hayvier. 'I'll bet he's picked up everyone on board by now. Probably be having dinner with the captain to-morrow.'

Pons grinned.

A steward approached and stopped before the table.

'Is Mr. Pons here? Or Mr. Plechs? I present the captain's compliments, sir; if convenient, he would like to see you two gentlemen in his office. . . . Yes, sir, right away. I will conduct you, if you can come.'

Pons rose with alacrity. 'Come on with us,' he said.

'But we're not invited—'

'Oh, that's all right. He wants to see us about this crime. We're to be detectives; might as well all be in on it. Come along, I'll get you in, don't fear.'

Hayvier was persuaded without further argument, but the professor said he would walk to the elevators with them and then go below.

'All right,' said Pons. 'But I think you're making a mistake. Well, let's go. We mustn't keep his nibs waiting too long for us.' From which it may be seen that Dr. Pons was not a person of natural reverence.

The captain carefully counted out all the bills.

'There it is, Dr. Hayvier. Seventeen hundred and thirty-five dollars, just the amount of last night's pool. Five ten-pound notes, five twenties, seven hundred and thirty dollars in travellers' cheques, all signed, sixteen dollars in miscellaneous coins, thirty in marks and two hundred and nine in francs. Will you count it, please?'

'Thanks. . . . Yes, I guess that's right. I don't know about some of this foreign money; take your word for it. Where shall I sign?'

'Oh, that won't be necessary. I'll just keep this memorandum, so we can check it later.'

'No, I'd rather, really. Habit I've got into, maybe; with laboratory equipment.' Hayvier smiled and reaching over, signed the memorandum. 'I'm sorry I had to trouble you for it, but you know, we psychologists don't usually have a thousand dollars lying loose in our pockets.'

'No trouble at all, Dr. Hayvier. I only hope you are successful. It will be a great weight off my mind. Good luck.'

'Thanks. Of course, you understand I can't promise a thing.' Stuffing the large wad of currency into a side pocket of his suit, the psychologist left.

'Good luck,' called Drake after him. At the doorway Hayvier waved his hand in a gesture of acknowledgement, and was gone.

'Have you had breakfast, Mr. Drake?' the captain asked. 'Well, come in and have a cup of coffee with me, anyhow. I only hope this new scheme will produce some results.'

Captain Mansfield knew little of technical psychology. He had heard of Freud, although not of Dr. Plechs. During his last voyage he had found time to read a tale of mystery in which a noted psychologist had successfully baffled the more ordinary agents of justice and had produced, at the conclusion, a brilliant train of reasoning through which the villain had been seized.

Yet Horace Mansfield was a hard-headed and self-reliant man. He was not accustomed to seeking help from others for his own problems. Only his present discouragement had caused him to grasp at the straw in Drake's suggestion. Twenty-four hours had passed with nothing accomplished, while a murderer was at large on his ship. The first suspect had been released and the second continued to be viewless. He had come to the reluctant conclusion that his detectives, while qualified to handle the innocuous crooks and professional gamblers of whom no boat can remain free, were not adequate to the solution of a major crime. He was becoming desperate and any suggestion was welcome.

But when they had answered his invitation of the night before, the psychologists did not remind him of those illustrious Corinthians of fiction who always get their man. Dr. Plechs in his fashionable dress suit did, indeed, look the part of a professional consultant; but Hayvier and Pons, the latter of whom scorned to dress for dinner, struck him simply as two very pleasant gentlemen. They all looked capable, and he had no doubt that in their particular field they were capable; but when all was said and done, he had failed to detect the searching eye, the inscrutable expression promising inevitable disclosure and punishment, possessed by all master minds.

Nevertheless, he had taken these gentlemen into his confidence; if by any chance they should be able to assist him, it would be foolish not to avail himself of their aid. He promised them his fullest co-operation.

Now he was becoming dubious.

'I don't know, Drake,' he complained, after the coffee was poured. 'I don't know.' He shook his head doubtfully. 'I'm afraid we won't get anywhere this way. What do you suppose he wanted all that money for? He wouldn't tell me a thing about it.'

'I don't know, I'm sure. Damned meticulous he was about it, too, sir. Must have the exact amount paid into the pool last night; nothing short, nothing over.'

'I can't imagine,' echoed the captain. 'Somehow I'm afraid it won't come to anything. By the way, what is this convention they are going to, do you know?'

'I believe, sir,' said Drake, 'that it's the International Convention of the Psychological Association. Or the Convention of the International Psychological Association. So the purser told me when I asked him. There's one every ten years, he said. This year it's in London.'

'They'll have a fine time when they get there,' the captain smiled, reminiscently. 'Did you ever hear anything like that argument they got into about the Bedido or whatever they called it? I was greatly surprised. I had no idea that there was any such disagreement among scientists.'

'Nor did I. But what got me was what Dr. Hayvier had to say about consciousness. Apparently he doesn't believe there is any such thing.'

With a final swallow the captain finished his coffee.

'Well,' he concluded, 'I don't know what they were talking about. But if Hayvier can find our man for us, I'll agree with him about his consciousness or anything else.'

Dr. Hayvier looked about him curiously.

He had taken an elevator to the swimming pool on G deck; thence, by a small stairway hidden behind the suite of apartments devoted to the therapeutic baths, he had descended yet farther into the apparently limitless depths of the ship. Now he stood at the end of a brightly lit, white painted passage directly before a small desk from which an armed sailor had just risen. In a wall bracket beside the man's chair stood a polished rifle and a few feet further along a steel grill stretched from wall to wall completely across the passageway.

Dr. Hayvier presented his pass and the note he had received from the captain. Looking up from a brief perusal of the note, the glance of the sailor fell upon the large wad of bills protruding carelessly from the passenger's left-hand jacket pocket.

'You're going to lose that money, sir. Hadn't you best leave it in my desk, until you're through here, anyway?'

'No, I think I'll keep it with me,' smiled the psychologist. 'Are you ready to help me?'

'Yes, sir. This note says I am to do whatever you direct, sir.'

'Good.' For the next few minutes Hayvier was occupied in giving the man his instructions and in making sure that they were fully understood. 'By the way,' he asked as he concluded, 'have you many prisoners here now?'

'No, sir,' answered the guard. 'Only one passenger. The crew is behaving themselves pretty well these days,' he added with a grin, as he proceeded to unlock a small door in the steel barrier and to lead the way to one of the "cells" down the passage. Producing a second key, he unlocked the door to this room, allowed the doctor to enter, then closed and locked it again.

It was a small, bare chamber, painted entirely in white and containing only an iron berth, a wash basin, a table and a small, straight chair. There was no porthole, since this deck was below the water-line, but a low, insistent purring evidenced the presence of a small ventilator above the wash basin. In the corner stood the prisoner's steamer trunk, hastily removed from his more luxurious quarters above.

'What the hell?' said the latter, looking up from behind the table, where, to judge by the amount of writing paper scattered over its surface, he was engaged upon a voluminous letter.

'Good morning,' responded Hayvier pleasantly. 'I am F. A. Kerr. I have received permission to come down and see if I can assist you in regard to the charge on which you are held. Your own lawyer, I suppose, is not on board. Mr. Stymond, I believe?'

'That's me,' acknowledged the prisoner. 'Though I don't know how them dicks found it out. I got a passport for Desmond Gize. This damn radio, I suppose. I was just writing my lawyer; hell of a lot of good he is to me now.' He waved to the cluttered sheets.

'Are you on a vacation trip, Mr. Stymond, may I ask?'

'Yeah—for my health.' The prisoner grinned, not pleasantly.

Kerr nodded, as one man of the world to another.

'A little unhealthy at home, eh? Something go wrong with your drag?'

'Naw.' Stymond looked surprised and contemptuous. 'I ain't worried about the cops, if you mean them. There ain't nothing the matter with things there. But I got competitors, see? They been getting nasty. And I don't think the weather looks like it's going to be too good in the city this summer; too hot.'

'Yeah, I see.' Kerr's attempt was not too successful. Stymond experienced the beginnings of a suspicion.

'Say, what's your racket, mister?' he demanded. 'Trying to string me along? That ain't very healthy either.'

'Certainly not, my friend. I came down here to help you. If you're going up in the air, I might as well leave. I can't do anything for you that way.' The psychologist turned toward the door.

'Well, well, keep your shirt on,' grumbled the gangster. 'I ain't turning down no helping hand. These dicks has got me with the goods and I haven't any in with this judge.'

Stymond got up from his table and crossed over to the bed. 'Sit down over here, fella, away from that door and let's hear what you got to offer.'

'Well, I don't know.' The psychologist seemed to hesitate.

'Come on, come on. What's biting you? I ain't going to.'

As Kerr turned back, two of his pound notes fluttered out of his pocket to the floor. Retrieving them and pushing them back with the others, he chuckled. 'Looks as if I'd had a break when you didn't,' he observed. 'Just won the pool.'

'Yeah? I thought they didn't pay it till noon.' Stymond was apparently uninterested.

'They don't usually. But we've been lying to, this morning. They're making some repairs and we won't start up again till about noon—'

'That's right. I noticed.'

'Well, the Low Field is sure to win. I was lucky enough to buy it last night. The steward said he might as well pay me after breakfast.'

'You sure got a break, bo. That's a bale you got there. How much did you pull down?'

'Why, I don't really know; haven't bothered to count it yet. About a thousand, I guess.'

'Yeah? One grand, eh? Sit here. What do you say we get down to business.'

'Sure.' Kerr seated himself beside the prisoner on the bed. 'But say, you haven't got a pal on board here, have you?'

Stymond looked up sharply. 'Not that I know of. What put that in your head?'

'Well, the other man they arrested said there was a gunman after him. Tried to nick him that night, he said.'

'I don't know anything about it,' Stymond asserted. 'There's none of my mob on board. If there's a rodman around, he's like to be after me, not that other mug.'

'You haven't a grudge against him yourself?'

'Me?' the gangster asked indignantly. 'I never saw the guy before yesterday. Why, he wasn't touched that I could notice. When I puts a guy on the spot, he stays there, see. He don't say nothing about it afterward. Anyhow, I ain't taking no rods with me this trip.'

For the third time since he had entered, Hayvier covertly observed his wrist watch. 'Well, let's get down to business,' he began. 'Now you say that you were caught with the—'

Without warning the single light in the ceiling of the tiny cabin went out. The room was plunged immediately in complete darkness.

After a moment, 'Hell, that's the second time it's happened,' said Kerr testily. 'What's the matter now?'

In the darkness Stymond leaned back to stretch his left arm toward the light switch on the wall beside the berth, while his right stole out in the opposite direction. Just as he clicked the switch impotently back and forth, Hayvier turned and grasped the hand that was withdrawing quickly. In the hand was a crisp note. It crinkled sharply as Hayvier seized it.

Stymond wrenched himself free and struck out as Hayvier jumped to his feet. The blow glanced off his shoulder, and then Stymond also was up. He struck again. The psychologist felt a terrific pain start at his eye and shoot over his whole body; he staggered back. There followed grunts, shufflings, a crash. . . .

Then the lights came on as abruptly as they had snapped off. A few seconds later the door opened and the guard looked in inquiringly. His mouth dropped open and he stared in astonishment.

The table and chair had been thrown over and into opposite corners of the cabin. Where they had been, Stymond lay groaning, doubled up over a broken arm, while Hayvier his eye already swelling to large dimensions, crouched above him still maintaining his simple ju-jitsu grip. None too gently, he gave the fallen gangster's head a final bump against the hard floor, and rose, dusting himself off, with a grin of triumph.

'My word, Doctor, what has happened to your eye?' Captain Mansfield surveyed Hayvier's face, with its court plaster and black eye-shield, with some concern.

'Don't worry, Captain; it's nothing serious,' the psychologist reassured him, his naturally good-natured expression breaking into a smile. 'The experiment was successful, but a little rough on the experimenter. Still,' he considered, 'it was rougher on the subject. I'm afraid I've given your doctor some work.'

'Well. . . . Let's go into my office and be comfortable while we hear about it. Come along, Drake. You too, Mr. Younghusband, if you'd like to hear.'

No second invitation was necessary. The four men walked into the captain's sanctum and the latter seated himself before his big, roll-top desk, a relic of earlier days.

'Now,' said Captain Mansfield, when they were seated, 'let us hear all about it. You said the experiment was successful? Have you found the criminal?'

Hayvier became serious. 'Yes, I've found him all right. No doubt about it at all. But the evidence to convict him is another matter. I'll have to leave that to you.'

'Oh.' The captain's face fell. 'Well, if you're sure of the man, perhaps we can get the rest. At any rate, it's something to know who did it. But, without evidence, how can you be so sure?'

'When I said evidence, I mean the sort of evidence that you'll want to produce in court. We haven't reached the point yet, unfortunately, where scientific proof is admitted in law; those fellows still spend their time talking.'

At heart the captain was quite in agreement with the statement. He said so. 'I don't know exactly what you mean by scientific proof, but lawyers certainly talk too much. That man Stander, for instance. But first, how were you injured? Had you a fight?'

'Short and sweet. He hit me, and I broke his arm with a little trick I once learned from a gymnasium instructor. I am sorry to say I also bumped his head—afterwards.'

'But who was the man?' Younghusband put in.

Drake answered. 'Why, Stymond, the man they arrested in the hallway the other night. Didn't you know?'

'Ah,' said Younghusband profoundly. 'So he's the man, is he? By George!'

'I hope,' said Drake, 'that we can convict him. He probably doesn't love you particularly, Hayvier. And from all accounts he's a bad actor. Might try to get his own back again later on, if he's free. Our detectives say they were warned by radio the day after we sailed that he's a dangerous gunman.'

'Yes, I've heard of him,' the doctor admitted. 'But I'm willing to take my chance. Where will we be if we let these gangsters terrorize us? There isn't much danger in my profession, but if I happen to come across some, it's my duty to face it.'

'I admire your attitude, sir,' the captain asserted warmly. 'And certainly I cannot thank you enough for what you have done. But we have yet to hear exactly what you *have* done,' he went on to remind the psychologist.

'I suppose I'd better begin at the beginning,' Hayvier responded. The others settled back in their seats. 'I wasn't in the smoking-room when the shooting took place, you know, so I had no means of knowing whether the vital actor had perhaps escaped altogether the attention of our witnesses. I had to rely entirely upon the characters you supplied me with.

'There were, however, quite a few. I made a survey of them all, but only, of course, from what I had been told or could gather by observing them casually. I had no facilities for taking them all into a laboratory and watching them under test conditions.

'I probably should not have done so anyhow. Science does not make tests the results of which had been ruled out in advance. De Brasto's innocence had been established before I took part; he had fired only one bullet and it had been found and identified, not in the victim but in his own table. Then had some other member of his party fired the shots? I did not take very seriously the assertion that there had been but one shot heard. The value of testimony under the unusual and exciting conditions that obtained, is practically nil. There might easily have been several shots fired. What really surprised me was that the witnesses agreed at all as to what had happened.

'But there was a much better reason that excused almost everyone on my list. All these people had been searched soon after the crime, and none of them possessed a firearm. Moreover the detective had searched on the floor and among the tables for a missing necklace, so that an incriminating gun had not been hastily disposed of by any of them. This same train of reasoning disposed of the possibility of Smith's having committed suicide. It also let out Dr. Schall and those who had been at the victim's table. Of all my cast only two had not been searched, Detective Bone and Detective Heddes. Frankly, I could not find it credible that they had had a hand in the murder. Commander Drake tells me that such an outcome is a favourite device with the writers of mystery stories. I do not read them myself, but if he is correct, then I must say that these stories resemble practically all our literature both past and present. It has been devised by persons entirely ignorant of the fundamental principles of psychology. That men who have been consistently conditioned to oppose crime should suddenly, for the benefit of a harassed author, turn into criminals themselves, is an extremely remote possibility.

'So now I was left with only two candidates, the phantom gunman of de Brasto's and the man arrested in the hall. At first glance the former looked much the best. But was there such a man? I understand that he is still being searched for in vain. Out of scores of people only one man saw him, de Brasto; and de Brasto looks to me, on casual observation to be sure, like a viscerally controlled person, what used to be called an emotional type. I should not be at all surprised to find that he suffered from sensory hallucination. Of course I use the term, hallucination, because it is popularly understood; it has nothing to do with those ghosts of sensations, the so-called images that still bewilder some of my colleagues.

'When I got at last to the man found just outside the smoking-room when the lights went up, I discovered someone well worth thinking about. Here was none other than Stymond, a notorious gunman, sailing under a false name and already watched by your detectives. There had been shooting and here was a real gunman, not an imaginary one. Where had he been when the murder occurred? At first he claimed to have been walking the decks; and then *the necklace belonging to the victim's daughter was found upon him.* He was a killer and a liar, a fully conditioned criminal. And at the very moment of the crime he had demonstrably been close enough to touch the murdered man!

'It occurred to me that de Brasto's shot might have been just a confusing coincidence due to his unbalanced reflexes and originating primarily from the unstriped musculature of the viscera. It is possible that, hearing Stymond's gun right in his ear as it were, a swift reflex caused him to pull out and discharge his own revolver. It all happened so quickly that he scarcely knew it; the fact that his bullet was fired downward before his gun was fully raised, shows the reflex nature of the act. And afterwards he imagined a totally different gunman, in order to account for his behaviour.

'The events, as I reconstructed them, were these: Stymond was sitting somewhere near Smith's table, with his eye upon the jewellery worn by the daughter of the famous millionaire. His "racket" was not robbery, but we must remember that he was as completely conditioned a criminal as we would be likely to find anywhere. The human body is a very complicated mechanism, and it is conditioned not only segmentally but as a whole. Present this man with a striking stimulus to crime of any sort and he cannot refuse to react. His first stimulus was the necklace; it was followed by a second equally strong one, the sudden darkness. His response was not difficult to predict. He got up and seized the necklace.

'Now came a series of further reactions. Smith, who had his wits about him, seized the man who had attacked his daughter, a practically universal response to that particular stimulus. Stymond reacted entirely in accord with his previous training, or conditioning. He tried to break loose, and failing that, shot and killed his opponent. Then he rapidly made his way out and threw his guns overboard. He was returning to brazen it out, as his former experiences with the police had taught him to do, when the lights went up and he was caught.

'Now what is against this theory? In the first place, was there time? Well, no one knows exactly how long the lights were off; indefinitely, it is said to have been a short time, and that might be anywhere from thirty seconds to two or three minutes. There was plenty of time, I think; you gentlemen probably have no idea how long and complicated a series of reactions can take place well within a minute.

'In the second place, only one shot was heard. I have already spoken of the reliance we can place upon such testimony. As a matter of fact, there were three shots fired, not theoretically but actually. Three bullets have been found. It is possible that two of them were fired with silencers; I am told that a Mr. van Ness reported a hissing sound and, under the suggestion of a man in the doorway, thought it came from behind him. Pons would have made no such mistake; he knows perfectly well that the human ear is not so constructed as to be able to place the direction of any sound in the dark. The hisses, I submit, came from Smith's table.

'I have spoken to Dr. Pell about Smith's wound. You all know its peculiarity. Stymond had been carrying two guns; the two empty holsters were found on him when he was arrested. My idea is that as he pulled the guns, Stymond's hands were knocked together in the struggle, and the two shots came simultaneously from muzzles that were at the moment in contact with each other. I asked Dr. Pell if there were powder stains upon Smith's clothing and he said not. That is to be accounted for by the use of the silencers, with which I assume both the guns were equipped.

'Well, I constructed my theory so. And then it became necessary to verify it. That is the method of science, and,' he smiled, 'I also am conditioned to a special mode of procedure, you see. In fact,' he added, 'I am so conditioned to giving lectures, either in class-rooms or publicly, that I'm afraid I have forgotten that I am not just now on the lecture platform. I have been talking for some time; you are being bored. I'll just hurry over the rest.'

The captain straightened up from his slightly tensed attitude. 'As for me,' he said, 'I find it very interesting. You put it so simply that I can't imagine why we hadn't thought of all this ourselves. I'm sure everyone else feels the same.' He too looked around the room.

'I do,' echoed Younghusband. 'I'm convinced that Stymond did the trick. Nothing could be plainer than the man's guilt.'

Hayvier smiled, a little mournfully. 'Ah, but we can't accept theories so readily in science. It is just because I have now to tell you of the somewhat technical experiment I made, that I am hesitating. If you wish, I will just say that I verified my hypothesis and leave it at that.'

'By no means,' said Captain Mansfield hastily. 'As to the technicalities, I wish to assure you that, entirely apart from this murder, I find your general ideas extremely sensible, Dr. Hayvier.'

Hayvier smiled with pleasure. 'I am glad to hear you say so, Captain. When behaviourism has superseded the former religious psychology, there will be a great many more people interested in our work. In the profession itself our success is nearly complete; we have been innovators and to some extent rebels. I mustn't lecture you on that subject, though. But I must tell you a little about the processes by which human beings become conditioned, if you are to understand my experiment.

'To begin with, the human infant starts out in life with a few reflexes, simple in comparison with what they later become. Typical stimuli call out these reactions. Already the baby is equipped to respond to the nipple with sucking, and so on. A loud noise or loss of support stimulates him to the more complicated response we call fear, restraint results in rage behaviour, and tickling or gentle stroking calls out the love responses, gurgling, cooing, smiling. This is our original equipment. And this has been discovered, not by arm-chair theorizing, but by actual experiments with babies in hospitals and nurseries.

'How then does it happen that we later find in humans all those tremendously complicated reactions involved in holding a job, getting married, having children, attending banquets, making speeches, the whole life behaviour in modern society? A relatively simple thing accounts for it all; the conditioned reflex. Even consciousness we have discovered to be a mere substitute for the soul of earlier times; it is a useless term and really has no definite and legitimate meaning that can be accepted by a true science.'

'But my dear Hayvier!' It was the executive officer who again broke in, and his intonation expressed an evident determination to pin the other down. 'Do you seriously mean to tell me that I am not conscious when I ask you this question and that you are not conscious when you hear it?'

'Oh,' said Hayvier with another of his frank smiles, 'I see that this statement about "consciousness" upsets you. It needn't; it only means that we have finished fooling around with imaginary "souls", that we're not preachers, but scientists.

'Now how does all this apply to our problem? The point is just this: a human being has been conditioned so that certain stimuli call out certain responses, in the absence of an uncondi-

tioning process those stimuli will *always* call out just those responses. That much is certain; neither the "person" nor his "soul"
nor his "will" can change the inevitable series of reactions.

'Very well. Now, I had theoretically deduced that Stymond,
when successively stimulated by an object of value, then sudden
darkness, was conditioned to try to possess the object and, if opposed, to do what injury he could to an opponent. Of course, I
am making it all as simple as possible; it is not just the sight of
the object and the ensuing darkness that cause his response, it
is the entire and very complicated stimulus situation. My theory
was that a certain situation stimulated him to a particular series
of responses. My next step was to reproduce the situation and
make a scientific test of this hypothesis.

'For this purpose I made my laboratory his place of confinement, appearing in the guise of a friend and having instructed
the guard to extinguish the lights after I had been closeted with
him for ten minutes. I took with me a large amount of money,
the supposed proceeds of last night's pool, and I made this both
noticeable and easily accessible by stuffing it carelessly in my
coat pocket so that several of the bills stuck out in plain view.
In my conversation I explained the presence of this money and
admitted that I had not counted it and was not sure of the exact
amount. Naturally most of my conversation was concerned with
far different topics.

'When the lights went out as arranged, Stymond took a
twenty-pound note from my pocket. I was waiting for this and
seized his arm, whereupon he attacked me and we had a bit of a
set-to until the guard had switched on the lights again and appeared in the door. Incidentally the note was badly torn in our
struggles; but I am relieved to say that the purser has accepted it
and pasted it together. As a result of this experiment, however, I

take it that my theory regarding Stymond and his reactions has been fully confirmed. I should be glad to hear if you gentlemen agree with me.'

He looked around the room and caught Captain Mansfield's eye; the latter took the opportunity to speak first. 'Well,' he said, 'I have followed your story as closely as possible, Dr. Hayvier. I find it very convincing. I am forced to agree with you further, I regret to say, that we cannot take your evidence into a court and hope for a conviction.'

Said Drake, 'That being the case, and I also think you are right about the crime, what are we to do? We must see that Stymond is brought to justice.'

'Would it be possible,' suggested Younghusband, 'to frame him in some way. If he is actually guilty, I do not see any harm in it. Naturally,' he added, as the captain favoured him with a sharp glance, 'as a friend of Mr. Smith's I am anxious that his death be avenged. He was a fine and very able man; it is unendurable that his murderer should go free.'

'I am as anxious as you are, Mr. Younghusband, have no doubt about that,' replied the captain. 'And while I have no intention of fabricating false testimony, nevertheless, some way must be found to secure the proper evidence. Let us all put our minds on the problem for a few minutes.'

Some moments passed in silence. Finally the captain turned again to the psychologist. 'Can you think of nothing, Dr. Hayvier, no means at all? By God, we *shall* have this criminal!' His fist banged upon the desk with a gesture of impotent determination.

'I see how you feel, Captain,' acknowledged the psychologist, 'although I find it hard to share your indignation. From my viewpoint, you know, this man is only the mechanical product of his environment. Of course, though, I should like to help you convict him.' He paused.

'I don't know, Captain; I can't think of anything now.' Hayvier smiled rather hopelessly. 'There are so many devious technicalities in the law; they seem to have been arranged entirely for the benefit of the criminals. Dr. Pons, for example, has invented an excellent device for the detection of lying on the witness stand which has been highly successful in convicting offenders and has often secured their confessions. And would you believe that it has been outlawed on the ground that the criminal is thus forced to give evidence against himself, although he never has to say a word directly? The evidence comes from such things as the changes in his heartbeat.'

The captain spoke decidedly. 'I have no use for nambypamby methods for hardened criminals. I've never had a crime of this nature on any boat I've commanded before, and I am not exactly sure of the precedents. But my authority runs quite far enough for me to put this man on the stand and have him crossexamined. Do you suppose we could persuade Dr. Pons to help us with this invention of his? I'll take the responsibility for it; and if we obtain a confession, Stymond can appeal later if he wants to.'

Hayvier considered the matter and yet again he smiled. 'Oh, I think you will have no difficulty with Pons. He'll be glad to help. Fortunately he has all his apparatus with him; he is taking it over to give a demonstration at the Psychological Convention. I'll speak to him, if you want. But I'm sure there won't be any trouble there. If you like I'll examine, while Pons does his tests. I've never worked with the lie detector before, but the reports of it are excellent. We might get a confession, after all.'

'Very good. You gentlemen are certainly coming to my assistance nobly. I can only tell you how greatly I appreciate your help.'

'That's perfectly all right, Captain. You owe me no thanks, for I've found it interesting myself. Shall I go take a look for Pons now, and get things arranged?'

'The sooner the better, as far as I'm concerned,' answered Captain Mansfield.

Hayvier went.

The captain's sitting-room had been transformed.

A heavy curtain of canvas had been stretched directly across the centre of the room, dividing it into two equal cubes. To one side of this canvas the long centre table had been moved, now completely cleared of its lamp and the other objects that were wont to adorn its surface. Several chairs had been placed along the table, facing the large, single armchair before the curtain. Two appliances lay on this chair, a rubber bulb with an attached tube, and a large band that looked as if it might also be of rubber, from which led a second tube. Hidden from view on the opposite side of the barrier were three small tables, accompanied by chairs. The small tables bore various pieces of apparatus; and on all lay ruled forms and several sharpened pencils.

The door opened and a small crowd came in. There were Captain Mansfield, Commander Drake, and Younghusband, Pons and Hayvier, Plechs and Mittle. Behind them two sailors brought in the prisoner, who already looked ill at ease. Last of all Dr. Pell hurried in with a stenographer and shut the door, closing it upon a third sailor, who was to stand guard outside.

Dr. Pons looked around; everything seemed just as he had

left it. 'Now, Dr. Plechs,' he suggested, 'if you will take the galvanometer and you, Professor, the hand bulb and the pneumograph, we will go behind and see that everything on the recording end is in order.' Leading the way for his fellow scientists, he disappeared behind the curtain.

'Say, what the hell,' Stymond began, eyeing with distaste the lone chair and the apparatus now on its seat. 'You ain't going to put me through no hanky-panky with all this junk. I won't do it, see.' He halted, and the sailors on each side of him, uncertain what to do, stopped also.

'You will sit in that chair,' Drake directed him, 'and you will answer the questions that Dr. Hayvier puts to you.'

'I will, hey? That's the guy that tried to double-cross me this morning. The hell I will!' said Stymond positively.

'Leave him to me, Mr. Drake,' spoke Captain Mansfield. There was an angry light in his eye but his voice was low. He was remembering the unforgivable insult of the murder of one of his passengers. 'Now see here, my man, you can make up your mind that you are going to do exactly what my executive officer has told you. You may not know that the penalty for serious breaches of discipline on this ship is fifty strokes with a cat-o-nine tails. I don't threaten, I don't have to; I am telling you what will happen.'

'Why, you wouldn't dare, you God damned—.' Stymond started forward toward the captain, his face flushed an angry red. One of the sailors caught his shoulder and impeded his progress.

'Hit him,' said Captain Mansfield.

The second sailor drew the short club, like a policeman's nightstick, with which they were both armed, and struck the prisoner a sharp blow over the head. Stymond staggered and would have fallen. The two guards lowered him into a nearby chair, where he bent over groaning and holding his head with the arm that was not in a sling.

The captain waited a few moments. 'I hope you see,' he said, 'that I mean business. It's time you thugs learned a lesson in discipline from the authorities, and you will certainly learn one from me. I meant every word literally that I said about that whipping. Give him a drink of water, seaman.' He pulled out his watch. 'You have exactly three minutes, my man, to decide whether you will answer these questions before or after a beating.'

Stymond looked up groggily. He drank the water that was offered him and shiftily tried to take stock of the unusual situation. He was forcibly reminded of an early adventure when, before he had risen to the heights from which he now dispensed gold with one hand and paid assassination with the other, the police of Philadelphia had put him through the third degree. He had never forgotten that experience and he never would. His head was dizzy and his confidence waning, but he decided upon one further attempt.

'When I, ugh, when I get back, you guys had better, ugh, say your prayers.'

Hayvier regarded him coldly. 'In that case,' he offered, playing up, 'perhaps it will be just as well if he doesn't get back.'

Captain Mansfield said nothing; he continued to look steadily at the gangster in grim silence.

It was borne in upon Stymond that he was in distinctly hostile company. The easy contempt in which he held the law-abiding abruptly vanished; for one thing these men did not appear to be quite as law-abiding as he had supposed. It occurred to him that this captain was himself the head of a well organized mob; it also occurred to him that an inconvenient body would not make any noticeable splash if dropped over the stern early some morning. Without another word he swayed to his feet and groped toward the chair he had never doubted was being reserved for him.

The stenographer took a seat at one end of the long table and opened his note-book. From around the corner of the curtain Pons approached the gunman and, having seen him seated, proceeded to adjust the instruments upon his body. Next he pushed back the chair until it touched the canvas and directed Stymond to thrust his uninjured arm through a slit in the curtain just behind him. Arranging the chair in the most comfortable position possible in relation to the slit, he left and disappeared behind the curtain. When Pons reappeared before the curtain, the stethoscope was dangling from his ears.

He addressed Stymond in calmly professional tones. 'Let me tell you something. Calm down. Oh, I know you look calm enough, but these instruments don't lie; inside you're all upset right now. You needn't be afraid; nothing will hurt you if you behave yourself and answer the questions. But don't make any mistake about this: the apparatus you are connected with always tells the truth; we don't have to guess about what you say or what you think you will let us know. You might be able to fool us, but you won't fool the sphygmomanometer; so don't try.'

'Say what the hell is all this hop about, anyway?' Stymond grumbled. But his voice was nervous. 'You got the goods on me, didn't yeh? Sure I took the doll's neckpiece. The dick found it in my vest, didn't he? Well, what the hell do you need all this junk for, then?'

Dr. Hayvier had seated himself at the table, facing the prisoner. Now he leaned forward and addressed him sharply. 'Go ahead; tell us the rest of it.'

'What rest of it are you talking about?' Stymond appeared plainly surprised. 'Haven't I just spilled the beans? What do you mean?'

'All right, we'll get the rest in a minute. Captain, can we have the stenographer type out the theft confession and get that signed?' Rapidly the clerk opened a small portable typewriter, wrote off a short statement and handed it up to the prisoner. Pons disconnected the galvanometer and Stymond's arm, still bearing the blood pressure bandage, was withdrawn through the slit. He read the prepared statement through quickly and signed it as if glad to get the ordeal over.

'There it is,' he said. 'Now take this harness off me and let me get out of here. I can't see as it did anything, at that.'

'Not quite so quick,' Hayvier hastened to interpose. 'I have a few questions to put to you. Let me know when you're ready, Dr. Pons, will you please?'

In a few minutes Pons's head reappeared around the end of the canvas. 'All set,' he called; and disappeared again to take charge of his instruments.

Hayvier addressed himself to the gunman.

'What did you do with your guns just before you were arrested outside the smoking-room the other night?'

'I didn't do anything with them; I didn't have any guns.'

'Come on now, we know better than that. We know you had two guns, and we know you jumped out to get rid of them. What did you do, throw them overboard?'

'How could I throw anything overboard? The windows were

all closed and there was a dandy little storm going. I tell you I didn't bring no rods with me.'

'Oh, so you did go out on deck; you knew that the promenade windows had been put up against the rain. If you couldn't throw them overboard, how did you dispose of the guns?'

'If you don't believe me, go and look for them. You won't find no rods, none of mine, anyway. I didn't have any.'

'Then why did you go out on deck in the dark?'

'Because I wanted to get away, that's why.'

'Then why did you come back?'

'Because that was the safest thing to do. Any boob'd know that.'

'On the contrary, you went out on deck to get rid of the guns with which you had just killed Smith! You might as well come clean. We've got the goods on you and we've got the apparatus on you that will prove it.'

For a moment Stymond went pale. 'Say, for Christ's sake,' he cried, 'what are you trying to do? Frame a murder on me?'

'We know all about it, Stymond,' Hayvier said steadily. 'You might as well admit it now and be done with it.'

'I will not! I won't admit anything. I don't know anything about it. I tell you I didn't even know he'd been shot until the next day.'

'Is that so? Well, we know all about it. We know you grabbed Miss Smith's necklace and cut her neck wrenching it off. She cried out and her father caught hold of you. You struggled, pulled your guns and shot him dead. Then you made your way outside, got rid of your guns and were captured on your way back.'

For some seconds Stymond appeared to consider. Then he

said earnestly: 'Say, look here, I don't know why you guys are trying to frame this on me, but it ain't true. I didn't bump him off and I didn't do any shooting at all.'

It was plain that none of his audience believed him, and after hesitating another few moments, he continued:

'This is what happened and it's God's truth, see. When the lights went out, I did go over and grab the necklace; I've admitted it, ain't I? But when I took it, the doll made no noise at all; she didn't yell out to her old man and there wasn't a peep out of him, either. When I got to the table, she was lying back in her chair with the beads around her neck all right. I thought she had fainted; it was a lucky break. No one at the table noticed me taking it at all. There wasn't a sound from the old boy next the girl. I was careful to come up on the side away from him, and as soon as I got the beads, I beat it. Just as I had got away from the table, there was a crash behind me and someone let off a rod right next door. I was afraid the lights would come on before I got out; my first hunch was that that shot was meant for me. But I made it all right. And then I figured to be coming in when they lit up, so as no one would think I'd been in there in the dark. That's what happened, and that's everything I know about it. It's God's truth and I'll swear to it on all the Bibles you got on the boat.' He finished and stared at his accuser.

'Humph,' said Hayvier, 'that's a fine story. You're mixed up in it yourself. Why, you have just said you heard the shot *after* the crash of the body. Does that make sense?'

The gunman paused, as if struck by the point for the first time. 'Well,' he answered finally, 'I can't help it. That's the way I remember it; and I'm perfectly sure of it. I can't explain it. I heard it that way, but I couldn't see it.'

'Is that all you've got to say, Stymond?' Hayvier's voice was cold and unimpressed. 'I told you before you might as well come clean and tell us the truth. We've got the records on these instruments to prove that that story of yours is a lie. You won't say anything more?'

'Of course I won't. Ain't I spilled you the whole thing? Every last thing I know about it. That guy next door shot him, didn't he?'

'He did not. You shot him. And we know it. We'll take the records now and find out just how much you've been lying. Unless someone else has some questions?' Dr. Hayvier turned inquiringly to the captain.

Captain Mansfield in turn looked around, but no one offered any further interrogation. 'You stay where you are, Stymond; I suggest we have Dr. Pons tell us the results so far.'

Pons had already removed the prisoner's arm from the slit for the second time. Now he drew back the curtain and the instruments behind it were exposed to view. The professor and Dr. Plechs were bending over their respective tables, jotting down their last records.

Dr. Pons addressed the room. 'It will take us a little time, gentlemen, to co-ordinate and interpret these results. However, we will do so as quickly as possible. Take a look, Stymond. There's some apparatus you can't beat. Think it over before we hook you up again for some more questions.'

He stepped back to his own table, the centre one of the three, and collected his sheaf of ruled and filled-in forms. Dr. Plechs removed the recording roll of the galvanometer and Professor Mittle disconnected the smoked paper on the drums of his instruments, upon whose murky surfaces there now appeared a series of wavy lines traced in the soot by the recording needles. All these informative papers and charts were transferred to the long table in front of the prisoner, where the scientists proceeded to pore over them and elicit the story they told.

It seemed a long time while they were matching the various records together and co-ordinating their time elements with that of the stenographic report which the clerk was rapidly typing out. As the work progressed, a puzzled frown appeared upon Pons's ample brow, and he rematched several of the long strips and checked them again. He questioned his colleagues closely and they appeared to give him renewed assurances. Once more he set about checking off the recorded sequences and they, not sufficiently familiar with the technique to take an active part, bent over his shoulders with interest. Elsewhere in the room the other spectators had gradually entered into desultory and low-voiced conversations. The prisoner still sat disconsolately solitary in his chair, an outcast from the central activity of the room, but watched attentively by the two guards.

With a final gesture Dr. Pons produced a huge handkerchief and mopped the perspiration from his face. He rose and with his back to the table, faced the gathering. At once the talking ceased.

'Gentlemen,' he began, 'the outcome of these tests is very different indeed from what I had expected. In view of its surprising nature, I should like to explain to you briefly the kind of measurements we have been taking and the theory, that is, the already verified theory of these tests. Of course with your permission, Captain.'

'Indeed, yes,' Captain Mansfield responded. 'I can promise you a close attention at any rate.'

'Thank you, Captain; I will be as brief as possible. And first of all I must tell you that these tests have been thoroughly verified not only by myself, but by other qualified psychologists.

Both Larson and Landis, for example, have investigated them. Larson found them 90 per cent. accurate, even in the hands of police officials, and Landis confirmed the original claim that they were "highly diagnostic". Were this not so, I would not presume to recommend their results to you.

'The accurate measurement of emotional states or experiences on the part of the subject,' he went on, 'is a very difficult problem at the present time. Personally I believe that the *consciousness* of emotion occurs in human beings at the central synapses of the motor system and we have as yet no instruments that are able to report directly the complicated and delicate energy changes there present. I know that Dr. Hayvier will not agree with me as to this use of the term, consciousness, but as all the measurements I make are purely objective, I do not think he will quarrel with the procedure or the results. After all, in these tests we are measuring the responses to certain stimuli, and if I firmly believe that these responses are much more complex than Dr. Hayvier's theory would seem to indicate, nevertheless we remain agreed upon the principle underlying the present method.

'With the techniques now perfected, I feel confident that the most reliable of all is the measurement of the consciousness of deception experienced by the subject, the tests of which we have just made. I regret again that I must use that word, consciousness, but it is what I mean. Naturally these records show nothing as to the objective truth or falsehood of the subject's story. But what they do unquestionably show is whether or not the subject himself *believes* that he is telling the truth; in many cases, as in the present one, this amounts practically to the same thing. We all feel sure that Stymond, if he wanted to, could tell us whether or not he killed the murdered man; our measurements indicate, with an extremely minute possibility of error, whether he himself believes his denial to be true or false.

'Just a few words about the instruments and what they measure. First we have the Tycos sphygmomanometer that was on the subject's arm behind the curtain. The stethoscope is placed on the arm next to the bandage and when the blood is heard rushing into the vessels, a reading of the sphygmomanometer is taken. We take five readings to the minute.

'The fingers of the subject's same arm are dipped into an electrolytic solution connected with a galvanometer which measures the variations in the action current of his body. The band which you have seen around the subject's chest is part of a pneumograph. This records the periods of inspiration and expiration of the breath.

'The bulb under his elbow is ordinarily used for measuring the unconscious variations in hand-grip, on the principle of a dynamometer. In the present case, since the subject's arm was broken, I had to place it under his elbow. The resulting inaccuracies were about what I had expected, and I think we shall have to throw out this part of the record. All these instruments measure what are called "non-voluntary" or unconscious reactions over which the subject has no control, thus obviating the possibility of any misrepresentation.'

Dr. Pons paused and again mopped his face. Then he put away his handkerchief and looked slowly and impressively around the room.

'Gentlemen,' he said, 'with the exception of the hand-grip just noted, the results of the test agree remarkably well. I have checked and rechecked the results, and I can only say that personally I have the most complete confidence in them. They show in the first place that Stymond's story about his guns was false. He did have the guns or gun, and he did either throw them overboard and secrete them somewhere outside the smoking-room when he left it.

'The records also show with entire unanimity that he sincerely believes what he told us of his theft of the necklace to be true. His story as to what happened to him at the Smith table in the dark was not false. *He did not kill Smith!'*

A dead silence followed, while the expressions of all those present registered astonishment in their various ways. Pons's surprise was that of the others, while Stymond could scarcely believe that the apparatus which he had supposed was being used to frame him, had actually established his innocence!

Drake was the first to speak. 'But, but,' he broke out, as if he could hardly credit his ears, 'how can it be so? Dr. Hayvier's theory, his reconstruction, was perfect. He accounted for everything. He gave us the motive—'

Hayvier himself interrupted. 'No, Mr. Drake, you are wrong there. I said nothing whatever about motives. Motive is an old word, handed down from subjective psychology. I know no more about motives than I do about instincts, or "consciousness", or "sensations". I must say that I am as much astonished as the rest of you, but there are the results.'

'Do you mean, Dr. Hayvier,' asked the captain, 'that you agree with Dr. Pons? You are convinced by his findings?'

'Yes,' Hayvier admitted, 'strange as it may seem, I am convinced. I understand your surprise, but I think you fail to fully understand how rigorous a mistress Science really is. We who follow her, acknowledge her decrees even when a pet theory is knocked in the head. Let me say at once that I do not agree with Dr. Pons about this "consciousness" of his, but that does not affect the question. What he was measuring was not a "consciousness" of deception or anything else; it was a belief, and that is thinking. Thinking is largely sub-vocal talking, it all comes under behaviour. So I believe he was measuring very definite behaviour, regarding which it is not necessary to mention "consciousness" at all.

'I have read of these tests in the literature, of course, although I have not hitherto seen them made. I can see no objection to be raised against them. They are natural science tests and we must bow to their results, whatever our private prejudices happened to be in advance.'

Captain Mansfield, who had listened somewhat abstractedly, looked up. 'I will say this for you gentlemen; if that is the method of science, in my opinion it is also the method of good sportsmanship. Naturally I am disappointed. I hoped we had the criminal, and I may say I was practically sure of it; I merely expected confirmation. But the same theories that cast suspicion upon this man, have now exonerated him.'

'I am sorry,' began Hayvier. 'I'm afraid I have led you on a wild goose chase. I can only say that I was sincerely convinced, and I am only sorry I have wasted your time.'

'Not at all,' replied the captain. 'As far as I am concerned, I was fully convinced by your idea. It appears we were both wrong, and there is nothing more to be done about him. Of course, he will have to answer to the theft charge when we reach England.' He motioned to the sailors. 'All right, men, you can take the prisoner below.'

The others stood about silently, offering no comment. Stymond got down from his chair and the sailors prepared to take him from the room. As he was led past, he turned to the two scientists.

'I'll say this for you guys,' he pronounced. 'You're square

shooters, if I did think different. You won't have to worry about my mob when I get back.'

The others watched his going in silence, hardly appreciating as yet the full breakdown of the case against him and that the real slayer was still at large in their small, floating community.

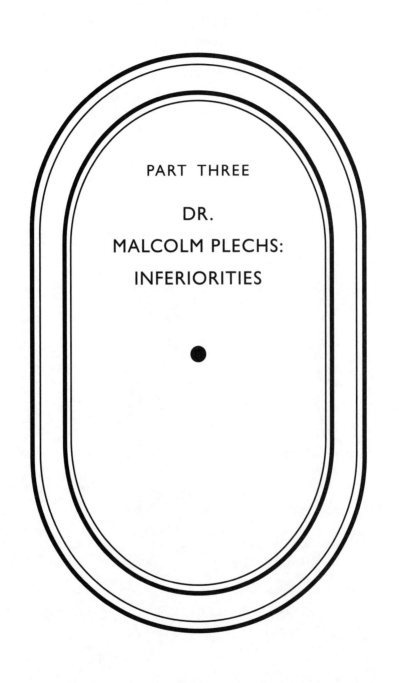

PART THREE

DR.
MALCOLM PLECHS:
INFERIORITIES

PART THREE

DR. MALCOLM PLECHS: INFERIORITIES

SCHALL AND Pell walked the sun deck outside the ship's hospital; it was shortly after luncheon but already the players of shuffle board and deck tennis were at their games, between which the two doctors strolled in and out. It was a glorious day with blue sky and fleecy clouds, just the time for a quiet constitutional.

'Nevertheless, Doctor,' said Dr. Schall, 'I am sorry it can't be done. I admit to a great curiosity about that matter and, short of an autopsy, I'm afraid we can do no more than guess. However, if the regulations forbid, I don't see what we can do.'

'I feel as you do, Doctor. But you know, on shipboard—' Pell shrugged and let the sentence go unfinished. 'I have suggested it to the captain but I suppose he doesn't want to let himself in for any extra complaints later.'

'I suppose so.' Schall walked in silence for a few minutes, then continued irrelevantly: 'I'm still surprised you don't remember me, do you know? With the beard you have grown I will say I scarcely recognized you at first, but of course as soon as I heard your name, I remembered you perfectly. I don't think

I'll ever forget those long discussions we had on that awful crossing on the *Panther*, or for that matter how you used to show up my game of chess. By the way, do you still play?'

'Occasionally, yes. But I'm afraid my game has fallen off a good deal lately. With these bigger boats there has been considerably more work for us doctors, and then I find it takes more time nowadays to keep up with the medical literature. We must try a match, though, some evening.'

'With pleasure.'

'I hope,' Pell went on, 'that you don't feel offended at my not remembering you. The truth is that I haven't a very good memory. And of course I meet so many new people each trip that what happened ten years ago on the old *Panther* has pretty well gone out of my mind.'

'Yes,' Schall admitted, 'I can well understand it. As for me, though, I make so few trips abroad that I am not likely to forget much about them.'

'My first trip on the *Meganaut*, you know,' the other added. 'I only joined her in New York last week. It was quite a decision for me to make, after being with another Line for so many years. And the more I see of the gentlemen here, the more satisfied I feel. Our officers are really very fine men, I find.'

'My impression is the same,' Schall agreed. 'To get back to that question of the autopsies, do you really think we cannot persuade Captain Mansfield? I was surprised at the lack of bleeding when I examined the body. There should have been a good deal of bleeding, certainly; especially as the possibility of the blood draining off into the pleural cavity was obviated.'

'You are undoubtedly right, Doctor. But there it is; I have not succeeded as yet, and we can't wait much longer.'

'There's the captain now,' said Schall suddenly. 'Up forward. Let us speak to him together.'

'Why, I don't think—. I wouldn't bother him now about it.' But Dr. Schall was already hurrying toward Captain Mansfield's figure at the forward end of the deck and his companion had no choice but to follow him.

'But you see,' Mansfield said, when Dr. Schall had succeeded in accosting him, 'I cannot appreciate the necessity for an autopsy. We know how Mr. Smith died; what more remains to be found out? Dr. Pell has suggested it, but I do not recall that he was especially anxious. Just why do you ask this, Dr. Schall? Do you suspect that something important might be discovered?'

'I'm afraid not in the sense you mean, Captain,' was the reply. 'From a medical point of view, though, there are several puzzling features that both I and Dr. Pell are curious about. I am very curious about the strange lack of bleeding, and when I examined the body in the smoking-room, it struck me as unusually cold for that of a man who had died no more than a minute or so before. And the eyes were curiously dilated, too.'

'This is all true,' Pell put in. 'As to the eyes, however, I think that the effect may have been due simply to the sudden darkness, possibly in combination with fear. The daughter's eyes were somewhat dilated also.'

'Her case seems remarkable to me, too,' Dr. Schall went on. 'I was amazed to hear that she had died. You know, Captain Mansfield, that in many places a thorough autopsy is obligatory in all cases of death by violence. While I do not wish to appear as if I were attending to what is not my business, I am supporting Dr. Pell's request in this case.'

Captain Mansfield, despite his courteous attention, was in

a hurry and he came to a quick decision. 'You've no objection, Pell?' he asked.

'None at all. On the contrary, Captain.'

'Very well, then,' said Mansfield. 'There's nothing to prevent it, that I know of. You gentlemen may make your autopsies whenever you wish. If you will excuse me now, gentlemen, I must go to the bridge.'

'Not so difficult after all,' was Schall's comment, when the captain had gone. 'From what you said, I hardly thought we would succeed so easily.'

'No more did I,' Pell admitted. 'He certainly seemed to me to throw cold water over it when I first suggested it. Anyhow, we have our permission now.'

'When shall we make use of it, Doctor?'

'Oh, I don't think we need worry about that. Say, nine o'clock to-morrow morning? I suppose our permission included the girl? Or do you think not? No, on the whole I don't think it did.'

Schall was surprised. He pulled at his beard and considered the matter. 'Yes,' he said finally, 'I think so. I think it did. And I am anxious to get a look at that heart. I think we can assume that both autopsies were included in the permission. And speaking of the time, I must get down below if I want to see the races. I'm greatly obliged to you, Doctor, I assure you; it is very courteous of you to permit me to assist to-morrow.'

'Not at all,' Pell assured him. 'And I think I'll come down with you. I'm scarcely familiar at all with this boat as yet and I've never seen their races. I shall have to stop at the hospital a moment, but you go right ahead down and I'll join you in a few minutes.'

Schall considered. 'All right, I'll see you a little later. And

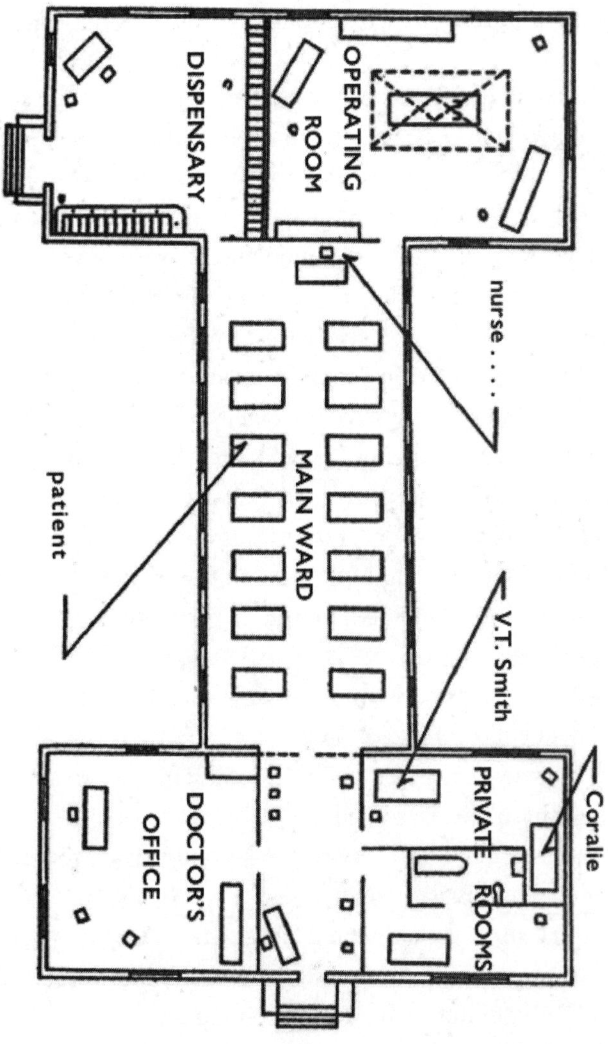

HOSPITAL

S.S.MEGANAUT

DISPENSARY

OPERATING ROOM

nurse . . . . .

patient

MAIN WARD

V.T. Smith

DOCTOR'S OFFICE

PRIVATE ROOMS

Coralie

119

thank you again, Doctor.' He held out his hand, shook that of the ship's doctor with a touch of formality, and turned away.

'Don't mention it.' Pell started aft. 'I'll be with you presently.' He walked away rapidly toward the hospital.

Dr. Pell entered the hospital on the after-end of the sun deck and looked down its neat interior with approbation.

As he came in, a trim nurse rose and walked down the ward to meet him. While awaiting her, he noticed that his single patient lay sound asleep half way down the ward. The nurse produced her chart and glancing over it, Dr. Pell assured himself that everything was progressing nicely. He nodded and turned toward the first door on his right, behind which lay the bodies of the victims of the mysterious tragedy.

As soon as he had gone in and closed the door he knew that something was wrong. But it was so very wrong that for a few seconds he quite failed to grasp the significance of what he saw. When he did, he sprang back through the door with alacrity.

Wildly he gesticulated to the nurse, who came hurrying down the aisle to him.

'Nurse,' he cried, with great difficulty lowering his voice. 'Has anyone moved one of the bodies from that room?'

'Why, why, no, Doctor. Not since I came on this morning. The door hasn't been opened. Is—'

Dr. Pell looked hastily into the second private room. It was empty of any human form.

'But it's gone!' he ejaculated. 'Miss Smith's body is not in the room. It isn't there,' he repeated in complete bewilderment.

Dr. Pell attempted to pull himself together.

'Telephone the night nurse at once, Miss Jenkins,' he directed, 'I want to see her just as soon as she can get here.' The nurse ran lightly down the ward to the telephone at the far end. 'But I know it's no good,' Pell mumbled to himself. 'I saw her when she went off duty this morning.'

Left to himself, the doctor gazed about him in a dazed fashion, as if expecting to discover what he sought on the floor or under an adjacent bed. Once more he strode to the room where the body of Victor Timothy Smith lay still and rigid, just as he himself had placed it. Again he came out and stood in the centre of the general ward. The nurse had finished telephoning and from the distance nodded to him in confirmation that his instructions had been conveyed.

Exactly three minutes after he had entered his model hospital, Dr. Pell rushed out on deck.

Once more the sun slanted down from the west upon the *Meganaut*, now pushing steadily ahead through the Atlantic rollers. The cocktail hour approached, and down the length of the broad promenade deck, stewards were folding up the two outer rows of deck chairs, leaving a single line for the accommodation of evening strollers.

In the winter garden small plates of salty pretzels and nuts were being set out upon the wicker tables in anticipation of the coming gathering. Around and around the deck marched several passengers, arrived from dressing a little too soon for their appetizers. Among them Dr. Plechs trudged forward with uniform pace, apparently deep in thought. Occasionally he raised his head and looked abstractedly out over the immense expanse of waves, shading now to a deep purple, above which hung three tenuous, rose-tinted clouds in the east.

As he approached the starboard companionway, a new idea

seemed to occur to him; he entered the enclosed stairs and mounted to the boat deck above. Here, after circling for some minutes, his ambition rose to yet higher levels, and he climbed to the sun deck.

Coming out upon this yet sunlit space, he arrived eventually near the hospital entrance, just as Dr. Pell rushed out in haste for the second time that day.

The face of the ship's doctor was a study in pent-up emotion; he appeared to be on the point of bursting with ill-suppressed excitement. The psychoanalyst, deep in his own thoughts, failed at first to notice these symptoms, and as Pell hurriedly approached, he greeted the physician in precise accents. 'Ah, good evening, Doctor. I have been thinking over the problem of these mysterious—'

'How are you, Plechs,' cried the physician, speedily. 'Mysterious—my God, yes, mysterious—I've just finished an autopsy.' He dashed on, abandoning Dr. Plechs to solitude and a considerable amazement.

Somewhat more leisurely, though still quite evidently in a hurry, Dr. Schall appeared at the hospital doorway, struggling into his coat. As he emerged, Plechs walked up to him in a determined fashion.

'What is all this, my friend?' he demanded. 'Dr. Pell has just passed in a state of high excitement. He states that he has completed an autopsy. But what autopsy? And why is he so distraught? Surely,' Plechs added, with a sly attempt at humour, 'it is not his first experience.'

'Yes, yes,' answered Schall, who also seemed unduly upset. 'We have made an autopsy upon the body of Mr. Smith. We made a most remarkable discovery, astounding. If you care to hear about it you can come with me. I am going to join Pell in the captain's office. As you have been invited before, I'm sure he won't object.'

'I shall come, certainly,' Plechs said at once, falling in with the hasty steps of the somewhat taller doctor. 'I have been thinking about this problem all the afternoon. I perceive now that a new development has arisen.'

'And I should say it has!' Dr. Schall added. They reached the forward companionway and descended rapidly.

Rather unceremoniously they opened the door to the captain's office and went in. They found Captain Mansfield seated at his desk, having turned his ancient swivel chair toward Pell, who stood beside him and had apparently only finished imparting his news.

The captain appeared calmer than any of the others. 'But Pell,' he was observing, 'I can hardly credit what you say. Naturally I don't doubt your findings, but how could the man possibly have died of poisoning when he was shot? I can't see yet that it's reasonable.'

'Reasonable!' the doctor exclaimed. 'Why, there's been nothing reasonable about the whole thing. We have a man shot and arrest the man whom everybody practically saw shoot him. But he didn't do it. We arrest a gunman who was robbing his daughter at the very moment; and he didn't do it, either. And now the fellow wasn't killed by gunshot at all, but by poison! And you ask me to be reasonable!'

'Yes, I know,' Captain Mansfield answered soothingly. 'But I still don't see why you now attribute his death to the poison when he was shot through the heart.'

Schall now stepped forward from the background where he and Dr. Plechs had remained since entering the room. When he spoke, it was in much quieter tones than his colleague's. 'Captain,' he asserted, 'Dr. Pell was kind enough to allow me to assist at the autopsy, and I can confirm everything he says. Strange as it may seem, and *is*, for that matter, we are convinced that Mr. Smith was dead of poisoning before either of the bullets entered what was not his body, but his corpse.'

'But he was alive when the lights went out, Doctor. And it was during the darkness that he was shot.'

'Even so, sir, the lights were out for some time. I don't know how long, but it must have been a minute at least, if not longer. It may have been anything up to three or four minutes. They came on almost immediately after Mr. de Brasto's shot; but at some moment before that, the poison must have entered Mr. Smith's body and caused practically instantaneous death.'

'What poison was found, Doctor? And how was it administered?'

Dr. Pell again took up the report. 'It was hydrocyanic acid, sir,' he said; 'I guess I forgot to tell you, I was so upset about the fact of the poisoning itself. It is sometimes called prussic acid, and it is one of the deadliest and speediest poisons known. A very small amount is sufficient to cause immediate death. It is absorbed at once through the tissues into the blood; a few drops of the pure acid on the tongue are quite enough to be fatal to anyone. The action is primarily on the central nervous system, paralysing the respiratory and heart actions. In the present case I have found, even to-day, a considerable amount of the toxin still in the stomach, so in all probability it was taken in through the mouth. It might, of course, have been in the form of a capsule, but I think it practically certain that it was introduced into some of the drinks at Mr. Smith's table.'

'Well, this is certainly most astonishing,' considered the captain. 'I should have thought that the results of so drastic a poison as you describe, Dr. Pell, would have been evident at once. And yet there appears to have been no suspicion until this moment. Had you some suspicion of this when you made your request of me, Dr. Schall?'

'Absolutely none, Captain. Our interest was just what we told you, and it is not really so remarkable as it sounds,' Dr. Schall hastened to come to his fellow physician's assistance. 'You see, in the case of this poison there are no convulsions, and the circumstances were such that everything conspired to conceal the true cause of death. If Mr. Smith had been visible when he died, the symptoms would have been unmistakable. But after he had died and the lights went on again, he was found with two bullet wounds in his heart, quite enough surely to render the cause of death so obvious that it would not occur to anyone to look beyond those wounds. Moreover, the smell of alcohol on his breath was sufficiently strong to cover the distinctive odour of bitter almonds, due to the hydrocyanic acid, which in any event does not persist long. Both Dr. Pell and myself did notice that his skin was peculiarly cold and his eyes dilated, but such minor symptoms were not enough to alter our opinions in view of the heart lesions.'

'It is true,' Pell contributed, 'that the post-mortem symptoms of the poison were present, but as Dr. Schall says, they were so overshadowed by the gunshot wounds that at the time I had no definite suspicions at all. You will recall though, Captain, that I was considerably puzzled by the lack of bleeding, which was the real reason I wished to make an autopsy. If the heart had been perforated while beating, there must have been a considerable discharge somewhere; as the man had fallen forward, I could not imagine where this discharge had gone, and I wanted to find out. Naturally, as soon as I began my autopsy, it became evident that this bleeding simply had not taken place, and there could be but one adequate cause for that; the heart could not have been beating when punctured. In short, the body must already have been dead when the bullets entered. Of course, the question arose immediately as to what had caused death if the gunshot wounds had not, and in prosecuting the autopsy further, we soon discovered the presence of hydrocyanic acid in the stomach, in quantity sufficient to kill half a dozen men.

'And the girl must have died of the same thing,' Pell continued. 'An extremely minute dose, however; it must have been too small to be measured. That is one reason for our thinking it may have been in the drinks. If she had taken just a mere sip of it in solution, she might have had so little that her death was delayed. Her symptoms were those of hydrocyanic acid poisoning, much modified, so modified, in fact, that they resembled those of a severe heart attack.'

'I suppose that explains the disappearance of her body?' the captain suggested.

'Of course. The criminal feared an autopsy upon her because there was no adequate cause of death, rather than upon her father. In some way he has stolen and either hidden or disposed of the body.'

'Have you ascertained anything further, Dr. Pell?'

'No, sir, I have not.' The ship's doctor was obviously distressed. 'I can get no light upon it at all. The night nurse assures me that she was in the ward all night and that she did not leave it at all. Her midnight supper was brought in by a steward and she ate it at her desk.'

'Is she reliable?'

'She is a very reliable young woman in my opinion, sir. Miss Jenkins, the day nurse, is also dependable; and she says that nothing out of the way has occurred since she came on in the morning. I am certain that neither of them could be influenced or bribed to so serious an offence. That accounts for the entire time since I was last in the private room, when both bodies were there. To be sure, there is a window in that room, through which a daring man could have removed the body at some time during the night. But not unless he had an accomplice.'

'Hum—well—supposing all this, what do you think they could then have done with the body, Dr. Pell?' asked Captain Mansfield.

'My God, Captain, I don't know. I can only suppose that they managed to convey it unobserved to the boat deck and then to drop it overboard. They must, of course, have chosen their opportunity carefully, and in addition been aided by luck. Any member of the crew or any passenger, seeing a body fall past the lower decks, would have raised the alarm immediately.'

'Would the body float?'

'Possibly. But of course it would have been weighted.'

The captain waited some moments but Dr. Pell had nothing further to offer. 'Well,' he summed up, 'I suppose for the time being we must take such happenings for granted. Of course, I have already instructed the detectives and the ship's police to be on the look-out for anything suspicious.

'Now about this other matter,' he continued, observing the two physicians, 'you are both agreed that Mr. Smith's death was caused by this poison and not by the bullet wounds? As I understand it, you feel sure that the poison acted first because of the lack of bleeding from the heart? Am I right in that?'

'That is correct,' Dr. Schall answered. 'Of course, there are other and more technical reasons for this conclusion, to which we would both be willing to swear.'

'Then whoever fired the bullets which entered Smith's body cannot be charged with his actual murder? Only the poisoner can be charged?'

'That is so,' echoed the doctors.

'But that opens up again the possibility of suicide, or of a suicide pact. No, it doesn't either,' the captain contradicted himself. 'I have taken possession of all the belongings of Mr. Smith and his daughter and there is no sign of any poison or means of administering it among them. Nor in the garments they were wearing when they died. Also, the vicinity of their table was thoroughly searched at the time, although for a different reason. I do not think they themselves could have disposed of all evidence of such a plot, even in the unlikely event that suicides would care anything about the point. We must conclude, then, that someone deliberately poisoned them. That is the person we must find. I must admit, gentlemen, that your news is very discouraging indeed.'

'Captain Mansfield!'

Dr. Plechs had spoken for the first time since coming in. Everyone turned to look at him where he still stood near the door.

Plechs launched forth with animation. 'I do not think that the situation is so bad, Captain. To me it seems that the light is breaking at last. All this afternoon I am thinking and thinking about this problem; and always I come up against the final argument that the murder is committed by shooting. It is out of key with the other factors; it will not fit in with the picture I have of the real criminal. But, now, now we find that the case is poisoning! It is the missing factor; now at last I think I see my way clear.'

Captain Mansfield looked surprised and interested. 'I am

glad to hear you say so, Dr. Plechs. And I should be very glad to hear your view, if you can give it to us now,' he said.

'I shall be pleased. But again, I cannot offer you the police proof. That you must obtain somewhere else. I can only point to the criminal, who is revealed by the psychological elements of the crime.'

'Ah! you have a definite suspect in mind, then?'

'Oh, yes; very definite. But if I am to tell you how I came to my conclusion, I must first say something about psychology, because I have come to it through psychology. You have heard of psychology from Dr. Hayvier. But Dr. Hayvier, highly as I regard him both personally and in his scientific work, is not a psychologist. He is a most advanced physiologist, being interested in what he calls highly complicated reflex actions; really responses of the muscles. The whole rich field of the mind he leaves unexplored; he even denies that it exists, a denial which all true psychologists will hardly think worthy of refutation or argument. People do have thoughts and feelings quite apart from their bodily accompaniment, and the laws governing thoughts and feelings are the true subject-matter of psychology. Even if they are not "apart from" bodily reactions, we can still study them as if they were.'

'Do you mean to say,' Pell asked, 'that a thought has no relation to what goes on in the brain? I have always taken it for granted that the two were simply different aspects of an identical happening.'

Dr. Plechs fingered his tiny moustache for a moment, and then went on. 'It may be,' he acknowledged, 'as the medical profession in general takes it for granted that when we think, there are certain occurrences in the brain. It may even be that such occurrences take place, not in the brain, but in the larynx, as Dr. Hayvier supposes. But those occurrences, wherever they may be, are not in themselves the act of thinking, they are only the accompaniments of that act. Psychic life, gentlemen, is not a mere reflection of these mechanical movements; no, psychic life is always and everywhere purposive. It seeks some goal, it has a will. The will to power, ever seeking the goal of superiority. That gentlemen, is the real key to psychic life. The psyche strives, and not for nothing; the psyche strives to attain the goal of superiority. So I find it, always.

'But we must get back to the present crime. Now as to this, who could have poisoned Mr. Smith's drink? Anyone at his table, presumably, the steward who served him or someone at an adjoining table. I dismiss the steward, I dismiss Miss Smith, who was also poisoned as we hear, and I dismiss the two young men sitting with him. Mr. Younghusband I have not analysed of course, but I believe him to be a normal young man; all of his actions since the tragedy have been those of a well-adjusted personality. Mr. Gnosens is abnormal just now, in fact is informally under my care, but his abnormality is well accounted for by the fact that he was greatly in love with Miss Smith. I am sure he is not of the unbalanced type of sadist who would have seriously considered poisoning his beloved.

'What have we then? First of all I think of Mr. de Brasto. And I do not think we have farther to go. Here we find—'

'But de Brasto has been acquitted,' interjected Schall.

'Of the shooting, but not of the poisoning,' Dr. Plechs reminded them. 'In other respects Mr. de Brasto was indicated as the man, but these indications also showed that he could not have killed with a gun. Then why did he ever fire at all? Perhaps

I can show you why, now that we know the real weapon was poison, a weapon he would be much more likely to choose.

'What do we find of Mr. de Brasto?' Dr. Plechs asked again. 'He suffers from an organic inferiority,' he asserted, answering his own question. 'I would not hesitate to say that he has a weak stomach.

'It is well known that those who suffer from a defective digestive apparatus develop great psychic capabilities in nutritional directions; they frequently exhibit gourmandism on the physical side, together with stinginess and greed for money on the psychic side. We do not know if Mr. de Brasto is stingy, but we may believe that he has an inordinate desire for money, if only from his occupation as a dubious lawyer. He is even willing to give up a portion of social respect in his efforts to acquire money.

'In such unfortunate people, when they discover or suppose that they are organically inferior, a psychic compensation arises. They strive in distorted ways to become the Perfect Man; we call this the "masculine protest". But they do not do so normally; they devise a guiding fiction in which they become more and more enmeshed, until they hang suspended in a world of unreality.

'I have thought much of Mr. de Brasto, and I have, even this afternoon, made inquiries about him. I find that he eats only in the Ritz restaurant and that he insists upon "kosher" food, prepared for him according to special recipes which he has given to the chef personally. Here, in one action, he compensates in three ways at once. He patronizes an exclusive restaurant instead of the ordinary dining-room; he sets himself off from many of those, even of his own faith, by eating nothing but "kosher" food on all occasions; and he sets himself off from most of mankind by being a delicate gourmand, with his dishes further specially prepared. By these abnormal means he attempts to re-assure himself as to his superiority when in fact he really feels inferior. He is a very bad case of the ego-centricity which so often finds the antithetical inferior-superior expression.

'And all this in addition to the fact that he is a Hebrew, one of those who, because of racial prejudice, frequently suffer from a feeling of inferiority in the absence of a true organic cause.'

At this point Captain Mansfield interrupted him. 'Won't you sit down, Dr. Plechs? Take this chair over here. You will be more comfortable.'

'No,' said Plechs. 'I speak better on my feet.' He continued to walk up and down the office, the heads of his listeners turning rhythmically to follow his progress.

'I have ascertained further that he was being actively per-secuted by Mr. Smith. In every auction pool of the voyage Mr. Smith, who possessed far greater resources, tried to keep him from acquiring a number, and of course succeeded. Can you imagine, gentlemen, the effect of this upon a man already suf-fering from de Brasto's feeling? In Smith he saw the actual per-sonification of that brutal, unreal world of his fiction, which scorned and humiliated him. With what greater gesture could he seek the goal of superiority, could he reassure himself of his own suspected manhood than the destruction, the death, of this enemy who stood for all his enemies?

'I should like to know,' said Dr. Plechs, 'if there is any poi-son in Mr. de Brasto's luggage. And I should also like to know where he was last night during the hours when the body of Miss Smith disappeared.' He paused and regarded the captain as if expecting an immediate reply.

No one, however, had any answers to the doctor's questions. It occurred to Captain Mansfield that they might be obtained. He pressed a button on his desk.

While awaiting the response, he said slowly: 'I must confess again that none of this had occurred to me. I know nothing of the controversies between you and Dr. Hayvier, but your theory is certainly as plausible as his. While I am not convinced this time, as I was last, nevertheless, I feel it my duty to inquire at once into the points you raise.'

He was interrupted by the entrance of his steward, who opened the door and stood waiting beside it.

'Mann,' said the captain, 'I want you to find Lieutenant Lane and give him a note. He will write a reply on it which you are to bring back. Also I want you to find Detective Bone or Detective Heddes and give him another note, to which there will be no reply.' He hastily scribbled on two sheets of paper and handed them to the steward. The latter went out immediately, and the captain turned again to the others.

'We shall find out something from Lieutenant Lane. And I have instructed the detectives to make a quiet search of de Brasto's cabin, if they find it unoccupied. While we are waiting, I should like to have you tell us, Dr. Plechs, how you reconstruct the actual crime. How do you account for the bullets? And why did de Brasto have a gun to fire, if your theory is correct?'

'These questions I have considered,' answered Plechs at once. 'I suppose in the first place that de Brasto had found out where Smith would sit and took the table next him. He had brought his poison and awaited an opportunity to slip it into the drinks. He may have done this when Smith's steward passed his own table, although of course I was not there and I do not profess to know just how it was accomplished. It was done in some way, for the drinks *were* poisoned. De Brasto then awaited the result. But the result did not come. Perhaps Smith left his drink alone, appeared to have forgotten it. Not only did it not come, but the lights went out, occasioning an unusual situation. If Smith had not taken his drink before, it was unlikely now that he ever would; it was possible that the room would be cleared and the passengers sent out. The attempt, so carefully planned, was on the verge of failing and de Brasto, with a gun in his pocket, at the last moment found his courage with an uncongenial weapon that he would never have used in the first place. His will to power forced him, in the end, and at the last moment, to an actual shooting. The very fact of the darkness, while not really valuable in the case of a gun without a silencer, made the shooting resemble more closely a poisoning than would a man-to-man encounter in broad daylight. We must remember that all these considerations were unknown to de Brasto himself; they were in his unconscious mind. Why he found himself with a gun in his pocket I do not know; but I do not think he had it with him in the first place with the explicit intention of shooting anyone. Perhaps the nature of his law practice had accustomed him to go about armed.

'Thus I account for the fact of de Brasto's shot, but regarding the bullets that actually entered Mr. Smith's body I am forced to admit that I have no definite theory. The fact that he was shot at all is a most amazing coincidence. It may be of course, that Mr. Smith has another enemy on board whose attempt to kill him was forestalled by de Brasto. If so, this second enemy would be of a very different type from the poisoner.

'I must say that I do not have a great confidence in the story of the gunman who was said to have fired at de Brasto. At any rate it seems now that these shots, for whatever reason they were fired, constitute a different offence than the murder we are engaged at present in solving. About them I cannot offer an opinion.'

'I am afraid you did not take my meaning, Doctor,' said the captain. 'I mean regarding the bullets that killed, that is, I should say the bullets that entered the body. I did not mean to ask you who fired them. I wondered if you could explain how Mr. Smith, having already died from the effects of this poison and fallen forward on to the table, could still be shot from in front. That is a point we must consider.'

Dr. Pell as he listened to the captain's words, suddenly remembered something. He said, 'It sounds queer, the way you put it, sir. But if I recall correctly, that is the way it must have happened. Do you remember that Stymond testified that he had heard the fall of Mr. Smith's body *before* the report of de Brasto's gun? Dr. Hayvier caught him up on it at the time, but, I think, that was later proved truthful. Let us think, now; how could that have been?'

'I think I see how it *could* have happened,' contributed Dr. Schall. 'I think, yes, I remember distinctly, that Mr. Smith's chair had fallen over backwards when the lights came on. Is it possible that as the poison took effect, Mr. Smith got to his feet, knocking over the chair, and as he pitched forward, already dead, received the bullets? Of course, it is only a guess, a rather wild one, I fear; but it would account for what seems to have happened.'

'Yes,' cried Pell, 'that must be it. That accounts for the sequence, and we know nothing that would preclude such an effect; he may have risen to his feet with some notion of seeking assistance at the first moment.'

'But it doesn't account for it,' Captain Mansfield put it. 'You have yet to explain how Mr. Smith had already *fallen* before the shot went off. Oh, no, I forget. It wasn't that bullet that hit him, was it?'

'No,' said Dr. Pell in confirmation. 'And de Brasto said he saw the flash of the other gun before he fired himself. In fact, we know it must have been fired sooner, if Smith's body had already fallen with two bullets in it before de Brasto shot.'

The captain seemed impressed. 'Yes,' he admitted, 'I see that it could have happened that way. Now the question is, how can we finally determine the guilt of this man, if he is actually guilty? I am not optimistic about the search of his cabin; I am afraid he would have found plenty of time in which to have disposed of any remaining poison by now. What do you say, Dr. Plechs? Will you examine him as Stymond was examined, if Dr. Pons is willing to set up his apparatus again? If de Brasto is the type you describe, I should think our chances of obtaining a confession from him under those conditions were better than with a man like Stymond.'

'You may be right,' Plechs responded. 'I feel, however, that I have done all I really can in pointing out the man I suspect. Of course, I shall be glad to make an examination of him, if you wish.'

'But I thought all you scientists were never satisfied until you had completed your theories with an experiment?'

'Ah, Captain, perhaps we are not all just that kind of scientist. Personally, I have always received verification for my own theories from the results of my treatment as evidenced by my patients.'

'I see. Well, I'm sure I don't know much about it, Doctor, although I am trying hard to learn something of your science of psychology,' Mansfield observed with the suggestion of a smile.

'It is a little difficult because you don't seem entirely to agree with each other.'

'That is true. As for me, these tests of Dr. Pons's do not impress me greatly. I do not mean to imply that the technique is not scientific,' he hastened to add, 'or that it is not really excellent work. But for me they are too—well, too physiological. I do not see that they are actually psychological. I would not care to give the same kind of test as Stymond was given; I am not familiar with it. But if you wish, I will examine Mr. de Brasto with the free association method. It has often been very effective and it is a much better way of dealing directly with the mind of the subject.'

'Any way you like, Doctor. So long as it may lead either to a confession or to some further evidence.

'Will you examine him in the morning, then, Doctor?'

As Dr. Plechs expressed his agreement, there came a knock at the door. Heddes entered and saluted the captain.

'Did you find anything, Heddes?' the latter asked immediately.

'Well, no, sir, we didn't. They were out, and we had a good look around. Just the same, sir, I'm glad we're on this track again. That fellow de Brasto is the man we want. Bone and me have been sure of it all along.'

'But you found no sign of a poison or anything that might have contained it or by which it could have been administered, such as a hypodermic syringe?'

'No, sir. We looked for any capsules, too. The only thing in the luggage—it was all open—or in the cabin either, that was like it, was a bottle of Bell-Ans. I brought up a couple of tablets for analysis, but they look like the real thing to me.' He handed two small pellets to Dr. Pell.

The ship's doctor peered at them closely. 'They look all right to me,' he admitted, 'but of course, we can't tell. I'll have them analysed right away, to be on the safe side.'

'Oh, yes, sir, and here is a note from Lieutenant Lane.'

The detective drew from his pocket the crumpled piece of paper, spread it out and read, 'With B. all evening. Left him at his cabin about one-thirty. Said he was turning in. Heard him lock door and left. Met him again at cabin this morning nine-thirty before his breakfast.'

'Just as I thought,' Captain Mansfield commented. 'He had the opportunity, but that doesn't prove he used it. Well, we shall see.'

Coming out on the bridge-like projection of the deck in front of the captain's quarters, Pons took up a position at the forward rail and looked out over the brightening sea ahead. At Drake's suggestion he had risen early to observe a sunrise at sea. The leaden sky remained overcast but away in the east it was broken by several long horizontal and parallel cloud banks just above the horizon. Here a very light blue peeped through, and the lower edges of the banks began to be tinged a faint, rosy gold. Slowly the bow rose and fell, with the slightest of motions.

Everywhere was a symphony of grey, blue, blue-grey and all the possible shades and shadings of the two colours. The smooth water, the clouds overhead, the cloud banks, all contributed these tones. Slowly the banks ahead changed colour; by infinitesimal degrees they became purple, red lights shot through them in unexpected places; and finally the brilliant orb of the sun itself appeared, edging its way above the lowest bank.

Not until then did the doctor happen to glance to his left

along the platform on which he stood, and espy another solitary figure, leaning bareheaded and in evening clothes against the farthest limit of the rail.

'I'll be damned,' muttered Pons; and with involuntary friendliness walked over to the man whom he had recognized at once as Younghusband.

'Well, young man,' he cried cheerfully, as he came up, 'I see you are also out enjoying nature.'

Younghusband turned sharply at hearing himself addressed, and Dr. Pons was amazed at the startling change in his appearance. His dark hair, blown by the wind, had little resemblance to its usual neat aspect; one dank lock hung raggedly down over his left eye. His rather good-looking face bore deep lines, especially from the ends of his mouth to his nostrils, and his straight nose seemed unaccustomedly long, heightening the pinched expression of his features. His black eyes had retired into his head; under each of them depended great, dark circles. Altogether he reminded Pons forcibly of a worried and desperate fox. A gust of wind brought on overpowering smell of liquor to the doctor's nose.

'What's the matter, Younghusband? You look sick.'

'I'm not sick,' replied the other, a little thickly, and Pons noticed that he kept a tense hold with both hands on the rail. 'Drank too much; trying to sober up.'

'Oh.' Pons leaned up against the rail beside him, and again looked out ahead. 'Well, I can't blame you for drinking good liquor while you can. Still, I'd say you'd missed the pleasantest effects. All-night party? Why don't you go down now and sleep it off?'

'Hell, I can't sleep. I'm worried. Can't you see I'm worried?' Younghusband demanded jerkily. 'All damn gunmen around, shooting people. Letting 'em off with silly tests. Must get one of them. Dangerous; they'll get us. Who killed Smith?' he cried bitterly. 'One o' them. Ought to get him. Nobody safe till we get him!'

Abruptly he became calm. He faced Pons and said more quietly, 'I know I'm making a fool of myself, but I *am* worried about this thing. Not reassuring to sit at a table with a man and have him shot at your side. I can't doze off comfortably with things like this. Went up to the Ritz when everything else closed and stayed there till four, when *that* closed. Been walking around since then, trying to think how to get him.'

Dr. Pons considered him steadily for some moments before he spoke. Then he said, 'You're in no condition to do much thinking just now. Better take my advice and go down. Anyhow, Dr. Plechs believes he has solved the crime. He is going to examine his man before the captain this morning; maybe the criminal will be in a cell before you wake up.'

'Who is it?' Younghusband turned eagerly toward the doctor.

'Why, it's de Brasto again. So Plechs told me.'

'De Brasto?' Younghusband's face fell. 'But we finished with him before. He was let out.'

'Sure. But didn't you know? Smith was killed by poison. De Brasto was only let out of the—'

'*Poison!*'

Younghusband's face, already pale, went dead white; even his lips were blanched. He swayed slightly and caught at the rail. 'Who found that out? Why, it's not true. It isn't true, I tell you! He was shot, I saw the holes in him myself. He was shot.'

'I know he was shot,' said Pons soothingly. 'But he was already dead when he was shot. Anyhow, you're upset, no use your worrying about it now. Much better if you get your steward to bring you a bromo, and then get some sleep. Why, you look almost as bad as your friend Gnosens did a couple of days ago.'

Younghusband stood now with his face averted, gazing down over the side, shivering a little and mumbling. 'De Brasto, de Brasto, yes, I didn't like his looks. Poison; don't believe it. They've made a mistake, another silly mistake.' He looked up again and spoke more clearly. 'You're right, I ought to be in bed. Going now.'

He turned away and took a few steps, then staggered perceptibly. Pons caught his arm and assisted him along the deck. Younghusband was evidently drunker than he seemed. Pons helped him into his cabin, rang for the steward, and left him sitting somewhat dazedly on the berth. He closed the door upon the other's muttering, and proceeded back toward the elevators.

When he reached them, he saw that one, at least, was now in commission. Pons pulled out his watch. Nearly seven o'clock. He wasn't sure just when breakfast was obtainable, but his stomach demanded suddenly that he find out. He pressed the button of the elevator. The car was then at the boat deck; it descended, lingered some moments at A deck, and then came down. The doors opened. 'Good morning, sir,' said the operator.

'Good morning,' responded the doctor, stepping within. 'The dining-room, please. Well, everyone seems to be up early this morning! How are you to-day, Gnosens?'

'Fine and dandy, Dr. Pons, isn't it? Looks like a nice day. On your way to a bit of breakfast, Doctor?'

Gnosens's face was pink and freshly shaven, his hair carefully brushed; he wore a light golf suit, expensive-looking and becoming. His bearing was cheerful and altogether he presented the picture of a healthy young man, looking forward eagerly to a day filled with pleasant diversions. For the second time that morning Pons found himself astonished by a remarkable change.

He regarded his companion curiously. 'You surprise me,' he admitted. 'Oh, here we are. Will you join me? That is, if we can find anything to eat yet.'

'With the greatest pleasure, Doctor,' Gnosens answered, almost jubilantly. 'Perhaps we're a little early,' he ventured, as a steward appeared around a corner and approached.

'Good morning, sir. Breakfast? Will you sit over here, please? The full staff has not come on yet, so if you don't mind leaving your regular table? Thank you.' The ordering completed, Dr. Pons pursued his previous remark.

'Look here, young fellow,' he continued, 'I haven't seen you since day before yesterday, but I must say you seem to have recovered with remarkable speed. None of my business, of course, but really I've seldom seen so much of a change.'

Gnosens's expression changed slightly, but he proceeded as cheerfully as before. 'Ah, you see I have been favoured by the good Dr. Plechs. Let us give him the credit. A splendid chap, our Plechs.' The young man's eyes twinkled suspiciously.

Pons grinned in spite of himself. Then he said more seriously, 'But you can't fool me that way, Gnosens. Plechs is competent, and successful. He does a lot of people a lot of good. But not so rapidly. And you weren't fooling the other day; you were pretty miserable up in the cafe.'

Gnosens appraised the doctor closely and also seriously. But when he replied, his tone was still light. 'Yes, that's right, I was. . . . Well, I got over it, that's all.' He smiled brightly. 'I was suffering from a—well—an infatuation, I guess. Plechs has a different name for it, but that's what I'd call it. Anyhow, it's gone and there you are. Why not give the man some credit? He's worked hard. A complete cure; I shall send him a testimonial, a signed statement, or something. As I said, a great fellow, Plechs.'

Pons shook his head humorously but dubiously. 'Well, have it your own way. You've done it yourself somehow, though Plechs doubtless helped. Not that it matters, as long as you've recovered. I was worried about you, boy.'

'Don't think I don't appreciate it, Doctor; I do. If I haven't thanked you very well, it's only because I don't know how. I—'

'Oh, don't think about that,' Pons assured him. 'I didn't do much that I can remember. Don't think about it again. Are you going up to the trial this morning? I suppose you know Plechs is going to put de Brasto through it again?'

'Yes. That is, if they'll let me in.'

'They'll let you in. Of course Plechs has told you about the new matter of the poison?'

'Yes, sure. Oh, he told me all about it, all his dope on de Brasto, too. But if you ask me, I think he's wrong. I don't believe de Brasto did it at all.'

'You don't eh? Well, Plechs is a pretty shrewd judge of people. Still, he might be wrong. Who *do* you think did it?'

'How should I know who did it? I'm not much of a detective, you know.'

'But if de Brasto isn't guilty, I think you'd better be a detective. There aren't many who had the chance, if it was put in his drink, as they suppose. Only you and Younghusband, and his daughter, if de Brasto's party is ruled out. By the way, was there anyone close to you on the other side?'

'No, not near enough to reach across, if that's what you mean. One of those standing lights they have, was on that side, and then a little space, before the next table. Not much, but enough to prevent any reaching. That's the side I was sitting on with . . . with Coralie.'

'Well, how about her?' asked Pons. 'I suppose I can ask, now that you've got over your infatuation? Do you think she did it?'

'Coralie! Why, you're crazy, man! She couldn't have done; she was poisoned herself, wasn't she?'

'Might have made a mistake.'

'Now, look here. Get that right out of your head. Why, she—she wouldn't have poisoned anyone. She was a damn sweet girl, even if I'm not silly about her any longer. She wouldn't have poisoned her father!'

'All right, all right; no need to get excited. I haven't accused her yet. But after all, you didn't really know much about her, did you now? Was she actually his daughter?'

'Actually his daughter?' Gnosens's face was a study in astonishment. 'Who said she wasn't? Has that chap Younghusband been hinting around to you? He tried me and I told him to go to hell. But, my God, he didn't say she wasn't his daughter. Of course she was his daughter; I ought to know, oughtn't I? What did you think?'

'A cousin, maybe; I don't know. I saw them that night, and certainly they didn't look much alike. But then, I have no reason to think she wasn't; it was only a chance remark. Let's pass it. What about Younghusband, then? He had the opportunity.'

'I don't like that bird at all,' said Gnosens frankly. 'Something about him gets under my skin. But he seems all right. I don't think we've come to *him* yet, do you? And how could he have done it, anyway? I was sitting right there next to him all evening. I don't see how he could have done anything without my seeing him, and I didn't.'

'In the dark?'

'No, not in the dark, either. When the lights went, I put my hand out and touched him, unintentionally. He sat perfectly still right up to the shooting, I know he did. Couldn't have seen where the glasses were if he'd tried, anyhow. It was pitch black, and no one could have known it was coming.'

'Yes, well, it looks as if you were right. I haven't any reason to suspect him, either. And that only leaves you. You didn't do it, did you? On account of parental objections?' Pons looked quizzically across the table at his fellow breakfaster.

Gnosens smiled back. 'No,' he said, 'I didn't do it. And you forget there weren't any parental objections; there hadn't been time for anything to object to.'

'You were so sure she was his daughter, I only wondered if you had had an interview.'

'I see. But it hadn't got that far. I'm sure Coralie was Smith's daughter because it's so absurd to go imagining anything else. She said so, he said so, everyone said so. You don't usually suspect people because they don't show you a birth certificate.'

'You're right, of course, Gnosens. It was nothing but a chance idea; the only reason I've thought of it twice myself, is because you took me up on it so sharply. And now we've let everyone out, except de Brasto. Somehow his motive doesn't seem strong enough to me, but then what do we know about it? He may have had another connection with Smith that we know nothing about. He's the first, anyhow. I wouldn't be surprised if Plechs were right about him. It's a strong case, as he puts it.'

Pons wiped his mouth with his napkin. 'Are you through, Gnosens? There's nothing the matter with your appetite, I'll say that for you. You've eaten enough for two men. Let's go up on deck and have a cigarette.'

Gnosens also rose, and together they walked over to the elevators. 'I'll join you later, if I may,' he said. 'I want to go back to my cabin for a few minutes. But I'll go up to the captain's room with you, if it's all right.'

'Meet me up there,' the doctor answered, now in the car, which had arrived while they were talking. 'I have some more junk to fix up for them for this session. Just ask for me and they will let you in. The captain's office again. So long.'

Pons got out at the promenade deck, and the first person he saw when he came out on deck was Dr. Plechs. The latter was just mounting the enclosed stairway to the captain's quarters. He stopped and turned at Pons's call; then came down to the deck again and awaited him.

'I have been looking for you,' said Dr. Plechs. 'Your steward tells me you got up very early. You have arranged everything successfully for the key you were speaking of?'

'The voice-key? Oh, yes. I've fixed everything. It will be ready for you. I'm to meet the electrician in the office at eight-thirty, to connect the motor to the chronoscope and make any adjustments necessary. Don't worry, we'll have everything ready in time.'

'Ah, I am glad. It is very kind of you, Doctor, especially as I did not want the other apparatus. But you know, I am not familiar with those instruments, that is how it is. And I do not think they will be necessary this time, do you see; we will a confession ob—er—we will obtain a confession, I think, when the association test is over. And after I explain it to the subject; yes, after I explain it.'

'I hope you're right,' Pons responded. 'The captain will think we're all a set of duds, if we don't produce the goods. I certainly hope you can get a confession.'

'This time, I think, we are right. I have found out more. This de Brasto, he will eat no food that is red, the waiter tells me. No, not even pink; everything of those hues must have false colouring added, artificial, I think he said. If it is not possible, then he will not eat it. A most curious symptom; I have never met with it before. Of course it must have to do with the guiding fiction, but as yet I do not know about it. We shall see, perhaps it will come out in the test.'

'That's a funny one,' Dr. Pons acknowledged. 'Never heard of it, either. By the bye, I had breakfast with a patient of yours, Gnosens. You seem to have fixed him up all right. He was as chipper as a daisy. Bit of a change, that man.'

'Ah, that Mr. Gnosens.' Dr. Plechs looked far from happy over his success. 'I have failed badly there. I have made a mistake. But I still have hope. Don't you see,' he advanced a step and tapped upon Dr. Pons's broad chest with his finger for emphasis, 'the poor young man, his troubles have not been cured. They have not been brought out and calmly analysed. There has been no ab-reaction at all. No, he could not face them and they have disappeared into his unconscious; I fear they have gone very deep down. For the moment he presents a false happiness, but they will trouble him all his life unless something is done. He might become cynical and never be able to marry. But I am afraid it is even worse. He shows the clinical picture, what some call maniac-depressive. He goes from the fever of misery to the fever of joy, both unreal. He is now entering upon an elation, a most serious elation. Yesterday he was, as you say, flippant with me, and last night he would not admit me to his cabin.'

'Wouldn't, eh?' said Pons, as Dr. Plechs paused for breath.

'No, he would not. He forebade me to come again. It is most serious, that. But I shall try. I shall approach him gently, in the public rooms. Even yet, I may be able to succeed with him. Ah, but I must go. The captain awaits me. And I have not eaten yet. You will pardon me, Doctor?'

'Surely. Yes, go ahead. If you feel like I did, you must be starved. I'll see you later in the captain's office. Don't worry about the voice-key.'

Dr. Plechs once more mounted the steps. He was shaking his head doubtfully and as he vanished, Pons heard him repeat, 'A serious elation.' He himself lit a cigarette and continued his walk thoughtfully. A sudden idea had occurred to him.

When Gnosens was admitted to the captain's sitting-room, whither he was told the inquiry had been shifted, he found Dr. Pons still at work with the chief electrician. As he came in, they were engaged in stowing several apparently heavy boxes and coils under the centre table.

The room had been returned to its customary appearance. It was now arranged as it had been on the occasion of de Brasto's first examination. The table had been cleared, but before the end and one of the side chairs, reposed what looked like telephone instruments; and in front of another chair rested a circular dial, with a pointer pivoted in its centre and graduated markings around its circumference, the whole enclosed in a case with a glass facing and backed by the covered armature of a small motor. From all three instruments wires ran to the mysterious boxes underneath the table; other wires connected these objects on the floor with a side-light bracket.

'You've just come at the right moment, Gnosens,' Pons grunted, getting up from his knees and mopping off his brow. 'Everything's fixed and now we want to try it out and be sure it's working properly. Sit down at that phone beside the table, will you? And you at the end, if you will,' he added, indicating Holt, who had also risen to his feet. 'Now speak into them, Mr. Gnosens first, please.' He himself sat down before the dial, reaching into his portfolio on the table for some paper and pencils.

Gnosens sat down gingerly. He hesitated, then said, 'Hello,' into the receiver. The electrician hesitated still more, but finally answered, 'Hello.'

'Well, that's no good,' explained Pons good-naturedly. 'This is a fast machine. If you're going to wait ten seconds or so you'll run the pointer off. We're measuring in twelve-hundredths of a second here. Now try again, Gnosens first, then a quick answer, then Gnosens, and so on for a few times. All right?'

'Hello'—'Hello.' . . . 'Hello'—'Hello.'

'Wait a minute,' cried Pons. 'Stupid of me; I forgot to tell you. You'll find little catches on each of the receivers; just turn them over and start again. I had better not speak after you turn them, so begin again when I raise my hand.'

Obediently both men found and turned their switches. Dr. Pons raised his hand.

'Hello'—'Hello.' . . . 'Hello'—'Hello.' . . . 'Hello'—'Hello.'. . . 'Hello'—'Hello.'

Pons turned a switch on his dial and raised his hand again. 'All right,' he said. 'That's fine. Thank you. Everything is working O.K. But I'd like to have you stay, Holt, if you can. I'm afraid I'm not familiar enough with your transformers, to fix them up if they go wrong. Can you stay?'

The chief electrician acquiesced. 'I can stay all right, if you need me.' It was evident that his curiosity was aroused. 'That's a clever arrangement you've got there; I'd like very much to see it in real action.'

Drake and the captain appeared in the doorway. The latter bowed slightly. 'Ah, good morning, gentlemen. Glad to see you,

Mr. Gnosens; I hear you have been ill the last few days. I can see you are quite well again now, however.'

'You won't mind if I stay, sir,' Gnosens began. Captain Mansfield waved his hand.

'Not at all, not at all. Is Mr. Younghusband coming this morning?'

Pons answered, 'I don't believe so, Captain. I put him to bed not so long ago; he'd been sitting up all night, worrying about the murder.'

'Humph. It is beginning to worry me a little, too. But I didn't stay up all night.' The captain pulled out a large, gold watch. 'Nine-thirty,' he pronounced. 'Where are the rest, do you suppose?'

Hardly had he spoken when the door opened again, and Dr. Plechs entered, followed by de Brasto. His bodyguard, Lieutenant Lane, Detectives Bone and Heddes came next and Stander, recently released from his confinement, came in last, to all appearances as full of importance as ever.

Captain Mansfield looked rather surprised. 'I see you have brought Mr. Stander, Mr. de Brasto.'

Stander stepped forward. 'I am here as Mr. de Brasto's counsel. I intend to be a witness to this illegal examination. You will prevent me at your peril. I warn you.'

The captain seemed unimpressed. He motioned to the divan. 'Sit over there, Mr. Stander,' he said. 'You will find there is nothing illegal about these proceedings the moment you consult a competent Admiralty lawyer. Meanwhile, I have no objection to your presence, provided you refrain from interruption. At the least sign of it, you will go out again, and you will remain in confinement until this voyage is ended. Mark my words well, sir. And take a seat.'

Stander moved ponderously to the divan without another word, and sat down. De Brasto was seated at the end of the table and Dr. Plechs at the telephone instrument nearest the door. The others found various places around the room.

When they were all settled, the captain inquired: 'Perhaps you will explain, Dr. Pons, what these instruments are for, before we begin to-day? Unless there is some reason why you do not wish the accused to know about them.'

'None at all,' said Pons. 'This set-up is what is known as a Marston-Troland voice-key. It measures the interval between the stimulus word of the examiner and the response of the subject, what we call the reaction-time. The circuits are so arranged that the voice coming over the first telephone starts the pointer revolving on the dial, and the following voice over the second, or response, line, stops it. That's all there is to it, a simple measuring device. Dr. Plechs will tell you about the "free association" test he is going to make.' Dr. Pons sat down, arranging his records, and looked across the table at his confrere. 'Oh, and one more thing,' he added. 'The instruments are rather sensitive, so we should have silence during the test, except for the stimulus word, given by Dr. Plechs, and the response of the subject.'

The stenographer-clerk entered, chatting amiably with Dr. Hayvier, and Plechs in a few words instructed him in his duties for the examination. Then he turned back to the others.

'What I am about to conduct,' he explained, 'is sometimes called the "free association" test. It is used generally in my profession for diagnostic purposes and has also been found of value in criminal proceedings. The method is of the most simple. I will read off to the subject a list of words and he will respond to them verbally with the first word that occurs to him. He should not stop to think and arrange a reply; in case he should expect to outwit me by those means, I will say at once that such hesitation, even if so slight as to be unnoticed by us, will nevertheless be recorded on Dr. Pons's instruments and serve as a valuable guide to our conclusions. He should reply at once, as quickly as possible, as soon as he finds a word to speak. Regarding the detailed interpretation of the results, I should prefer to wait until the responses are recorded, when I shall explain the matter fully both to him and to the rest of you gentlemen.'

He turned about and faced de Brasto. 'Do you understand what is required?' he asked.

'Yes,' de Brasto answered tonelessly. He looked worn-out, almost ill. His short, black hair seemed to have lost its natural curl and was plastered back dankly from his pale forehead. 'But there is no use in this persecution. I am innocent; I have been proved innocent. I did not shoot Mr. Smith. I am in continual fear of further attack myself. I don't know why you wish to subject me to this again.' He ended rather piteously and sank back in his chair.

Dr. Plechs, secure in his correct belief that all knowledge of the autopsy had been kept from his victim, regarded him with satisfaction. 'It is not necessary,' he said, 'that you should know our motive at present. You must place yourself in our hands. You should co-operate and answer to the best of your ability. Are you ready to begin?'

De Brasto reached slowly for the instrument before him and responded listlessly: 'All right. I see you are set upon it. I suppose I have no choice.'

The doctor sat down, arranged his papers before him, glanced across the table. 'Are you all ready, Dr. Pons?' he inquired.

Dr. Pons nodded, as did also the stenographer, who had pulled up a chair next to him.

Plechs turned toward the end of the table, raised his telephone, and spoke into it clearly, so that his voice would also carry directly to the subject.

'Table,' he pronounced.

  'Cloth,' responded de Brasto.

'Dark.'

  'Light.'

'Music.'

  'Violin.'

'Sickness.'

  'Sickness? Health.'

Dr. Plechs glanced up sharply. Then went on without comment.

'Man.'

  'Woman.'

'Deep.'

  'Light.'

'Soft.'

  'Heavy.'

'Eating.'

  'Drinking.'

'Mountain.'

  'Hill.'

'House.'

  'Chair.'

'Poison.'

  'Rats.'

'Black.'

  'White.'

'Mutton.'

  'White.'

'Comfort.'

'Mutton.'

At the end of the first twenty-two words, Dr. Plechs stopped. 'We will rest a little,' he announced. Across the table Pons jotted down his last notation, reset his dial, and leaned back. The stenographer looked up.

In a few moments Plechs again took up the telephone. 'Are you ready? Let us begin.

'Sweet.'

'Bitter.'

'Whistle.'

'Engine.'

. . . Presently, with a hundred and ten words, the list was completed. To de Brasto it had seemed interminable, but actually the whole operation had consumed less than ten minutes.

'If you do not mind waiting a little, gentlemen?' said Plechs. 'We will proceed as fast as compatible with accuracy. I shall hope to have the preliminary results for you presently.'

Gradually the others drifted into conversations, as Pons and Plechs worked on. The time dragged on, conversations lapsed into silence again; it was fully half an hour before all the computations had been completed, and Dr. Plechs, with a sheaf of notes in his hand, rose to address the assembly. Hayvier and the chief electrician, deep in a discussion beside one of the windows, sought chairs and everyone became attentive.

'Gentlemen,' Dr. Plechs began in his best platform manner, 'I have just given our subject two different tests in combination. The first is a list of one hundred words, referred to in the Kent-Rosanoff monograph, which has been used extensively upon both normal and abnormal subjects. The responses of a thousand normal subjects have been collected and organized;

they form a standard, as it were, against which we can check the replies of any new person we wish to examine. Certain associations have been found prevalent in normal cases; when any word is responded to in a way different from any of the thousand response words already recorded, we call that an individual reaction. The Kent-Rosanoff manual tells us that in normal adults the individual responses will be about 6.8 per cent. of the whole, the great majority being common responses represented in the standard thousand, with a few doubtful instances. I may say now that this subject shows nearly 27 per cent. of individual responses. When the results vary as greatly as this from the normal expectation, they are to be more fully explored, and we may confidently expect that they will yield valuable data regarding various complexes and abnormalities of the subject.

'But such complexes, or sore spots, are revealed not only by the response word itself, but also by the reaction time, that is, the time between the hearing of the stimulus and the spoken answer of the subject. These times have usually been taken upon hand-manipulated stop-watches recording 1/10 seconds; I need hardly say that Dr. Pons's voice-key, which you have seen in operation, is a great improvement in accuracy, since it measures in 1/1200 seconds and also cuts out the individual variations introduced by the stop-watch operator. We may therefore have greater confidence in the results. It is agreed upon that a long reaction time almost always indicates that a complex has been touched.

'In these and further ways we may conclude much regarding the present subject. I will refer to some of these points in a moment. But I have also introduced at random into the Kent-Rosanoff words this morning, a list of crucial stimulus words bearing directly or indirectly upon the crime we are investigating.

'We know as well as you do, Mr. de Brasto,' said Plechs suddenly, looking across at the divan, 'that Mr. Smith was poisoned, not shot. I have plenty of evidence here to implicate you in his death.'

De Brasto, who had been slouching back on the divan with his hands in his pockets, in an attitude that might have been an assumed nonchalance, jerked up spasmodically. His mouth fell slightly open and to everyone except the psychologist he appeared typically amazed.

'P-p-poisoned!' he stammered. 'Why, you're crazy. I—I don't know anything about it. He was shot!' He looked around at the other faces, saw that with the exception of Stander's and the stenographer's they expressed no surprise at all; his own face took on a tinge of horror, and he broke down, commencing to whimper in a fashion extremely disturbing to everyone but Dr. Plechs.

'You're trying to railroad me,' he gasped, between sobs. 'There was—wasn't any poison at all. You're all in—ulg—a conspiracy against me. I didn't do it,' his voice rose shrilly, 'I didn't do it. *I didn't do it!*'

Dr. Plechs spoke calmly to the captain. 'You see,' he pointed out, 'how abnormal he is. The conspiracy delusion is a frequent occurrence with this type of inferiority complex.' He turned back to de Brasto. 'Will you admit your guilt now, or do you force me to go further?'

The Hebrew's outburst had spent itself. Now he lay back on the couch, his gasping breath hardly audible. He shook his head hopelessly and wiped his eyes with a handkerchief. 'I don't know anything about it,' he said again, in a voice so low as scarcely to be heard.

Plechs went on with his recital as if no interruption had occurred. 'To take up the first part of the test, the Kent-Rosanoff list; here we find many illuminating side-lights upon the subject's personality. In the first place, he is a fast reaction type. His average response followed the stimulus word in 1 1/600 seconds, whereas any average less than 1 1/2 seconds is to be considered unusually fast. His median time, perhaps a better measure than the average, is still considerably below 1 1/2 seconds. The pertinence of this finding will appear in a minute.

'The results here bear out my diagnosis of an unstable type with a serious organic inferiority, centring about the digestive apparatus. The responses to words suggesting food were uniformly unusual. I may cite the instance of "mutton", where the response was "white", a significant repetition of the preceding response to "black", where the disturbance was carried over to the next response; that to the word "comfort", the response being a repetition of the preceding stimulus, "mutton". There were enough similar instances throughout the list to confirm this finding. Then also, when the stimulus word was "sickness", we find a repetition of it in the response, namely "sickness? health", indicating that the subject has an unconscious recognition of the presence of a psychic malady within him.

'Now we come to a striking point. Of the fifteen words in the Kent-Rosanoff list referring in some way to food or to eating, the subject's reaction time to twelve of them was far below both his average and his median. Even the average for the whole fifteen is but 872/1200 second, or slightly more than 3/4 second.

'Now, gentlemen, what does this show?' demanded Dr. Plechs. 'It shows,' he continued solemnly, 'that this subject is of a relatively small type, discovered by Dr. Pons some years ago. He is a "negative liar", the type that lies faster than it tells the truth. Of course, this propensity is carried over to the responses, to words touching upon his abnormal complexes or the guiding fiction. Dr. Pons tells me that his researches lead him to believe that about one person out of eight or nine is of this extraordinary type. An exaggerated instance of this is to be found in the present subject's response to the word "shady", one of the crucial list. He replied with the word "hippopotamus", an unheard-of reply as concerns the Kent-Rosanoff control list of a thousand, in the record time of 313/1200 seconds, about 1/4 second. I take it that this stimulus word touched off certain complexes concerned with his business; being the type of "negative liar" that he is, he had, as it were, responses up his sleeve for such words, producing them with unusual speed when needed. But our instruments have revealed him just as readily as if he had taken an undue length of time to answer.

'This brings us to the "Crucial" list. The words, scattered through the longer list, together with the subject's responses, were as follows:

> poison .... rats
> shady .... hippopotamus
> glass .... drink
> enemy .... man, woman
> Smith.................... what? oh, Jones
> vial .... needle
> die .... born
> beverage .... stein
> auction .... out
> kill .... die.

From this we can see at once that the subject feels very inferior; both man and woman are his enemies; an extremely anti-social attitude. He hesitated badly over the name of his victim, "Smith", and asked "what?" before responding. His mind was also running upon drinking, the means he used to administer the poison, his response to "glass" not being "tumbler", the usual response, but "drink", and to "beverage" it was "stein", a container in which many drinks are served on board this boat. No doubt Mr. Smith drank his fatal dose from a stein.'

'No,' Gnosens put in, 'he did not. He was drinking absinthe, as a matter of fact.'

'Well,' Dr. Plechs went on, 'it is not important. Let it pass. It shows the trend of the thoughts. The response, "die", to "kill" is obvious, although in this case it must be admitted, not unusual. And when he answered "auction" with "out", we find a key to his actions that I have commented upon before.'

Captain Mansfield interrupted. 'Pardon me, Dr. Plechs,' he asked, 'but what was the average time for this list?'

'For the crucial words?'

'Yes, for the list you are now discussing.'

'Let me see,' said Dr. Plechs, referring to his notes. 'Oh, yes, here it is. The average times for these words, if we omit the response to "Smith" which was untypically long, was just 119/1200 seconds. Of course, including the "Smith" response it was somewhat longer, but in so short a list, the inclusion of one exception would be misleading. That is why we take the median; the median was almost precisely one second.'

'And what did you say the average and median was for the whole list?' the captain persevered.

'It was—. Ah, yes, the average was 1 2/1200 seconds and the median 1 23/1200 seconds.

'Then we may take it, since these measures are so close together in both cases, that Mr. de Brasto was not constrained to lie with regard to the crucial words?'

Dr. Plechs shrugged deprecatingly. 'You are a close critic,

Captain,' he admitted. 'But you are right. I do not think that we would be justified in any conclusion as to his guilt from the reaction times recorded upon the crucial words. But as to their content, that is a far different matter. There, I think, I have been successful in demonstrating, so far as my technique will enable me in this brief time, that the subject is seriously involved in this crime. I believe I am right, sir, and I should advise that he be held for trial upon our arrival on shore. Meanwhile I shall organize my data more fully and have ready a complete report for the examining judges.' He started to say more, then concluded not to, and sat down.

Captain Mansfield seemed sorely perplexed. He hesitated, looked doubtfully around, and finally said: 'I am sorry, Dr. Plechs, but I cannot find myself convinced by these arguments. It seems to me that there is something wrong with Mr. de Brasto; so much has been established, and it is plain that he is nervous and overwrought. But that is a very different thing from a confession of guilt, even an unconscious one, regarding the death of Mr. Smith. *That*, of course, is my first interest. I confess that I am puzzled.' Again he looked around the room and noted that at some time during the proceedings, Professor Mittle had come in and taken a seat near the door. 'I should like to ask the opinion of your associates on this question. How do you feel, Dr. Pons? Is this a clear demonstration in your view?'

Pons looked uneasy; it was evident that he did not care to express himself. Seeing no alternative, he finally answered: 'To tell you the truth, Captain, I am not a psychoanalyst like Dr. Plechs. I am familiar with these techniques, of course, but I have never employed them myself, and I should not care to give any professional opinion in this case. I am sorry, but I shall have to ask to be excused. And I would ask, if possible, that you take my remarks as having no bearing one way or the other upon your decision.'

The captain's appearance was one of disappointment. 'I am disappointed,' he acknowledged, and turned to Hayvier. 'Well, what do you say, Doctor?'

'I?' Hayvier answered at once. 'Oh, well, I don't like to drag our controversies into your office, Captain Mansfield, but Dr. Plechs and everyone else knows that I have no use for all this talk about the unconscious and all the rest of it. Don't believe in these "minds", conscious or unconscious. Sorry, but I can't recommend the present theories.' He looked over at Plechs with his frank smile, in time to see a slight frown of annoyance on the latter's face. However, the frown disappeared at once.

The captain turned to Professor Mittle. 'I come to you, Professor,' he said. 'Would you be so good as to let me have your opinion?'

'Ah,' said Mittle, placing his fingers together and observing the captain judicially. 'Like Dr. Pons, I do not care to have my snap-judgment taken too seriously. I may, however, say this: I take no part in the current controversies of modern psychology. I am neither upon the side of Dr. Plechs nor upon that of Dr. Hayvier. How can I take sides in these arguments, when both sides go to false extremes? To be sure, there is much to be recommended in both viewpoints.'

Captain Mansfield interrupted the discourse to put in: 'But about the test that has just been made, Professor?'

'Oh,' said Mittle, 'there I fail to see how I can help you. No more than Dr. Pons would I care to commit myself as to this point. Especially as I came in late and did not witness all the proceedings.'

'But you heard all of Dr. Plechs's summary, did you not?'

'Yes, well, yes I think I did. Practically all of it, at any rate. But I am afraid you will have to excuse me, too, Captain. I am afraid I shall have to be excused.' His look plainly indicated that in his opinion the decision rested with the ship's commander.

'Well, dammit,' complained the latter, 'I haven't enough information.' He looked to his detectives. 'Have you found anything at all incriminating in Mr. de Brasto's cabin or effects? Anything at all?' he asked.

Heddes answered for them both. 'No, sir. Just this morning we made another search when they were all down to breakfast. He's either thrown the poison away, or he's got it hid somewhere else now, sir.'

'But I haven't got any poison,' de Brasto broke in feverishly; then he caught his breath and halted abruptly.

Detective Bone looked at him suspiciously. 'Captain Mansfield, sir,' he spoke as with a sudden inspiration, 'can I see you outside just a moment, sir?'

Mansfield was surprised, but went immediately to the door. 'Only a moment, gentlemen; I'll be right back.' He went out with his detective. Within five minutes he was back.

'I have come to a decision,' he announced. 'We have not sufficient evidence on which to hold Mr. de Brasto in confinement, especially as he cannot possibly escape. Accordingly I order him released for the present, and his position will be just as it was before this examination took place. I am sorry, gentlemen, that I have to close this meeting so abruptly, but I must go back to my duties. If you will all leave except Dr. Plechs and Lieutenant Lane, I should like to see them for a few moments. I have some instructions for Lieutenant Lane in regard to his men. He has not had much time for them for the past several days. All right,

Mr. de Brasto, Lieutenant Lane will rejoin you in a few moments.' With a final nod he dismissed the others.

When they had left, he said to the doctor: 'I wanted you to stay, Dr. Plechs, so that I could explain to you that I have not over-ruled your case. I am still suspicious of de Brasto, even if I am not fully convinced. Meantime, Detective Bone has offered his advice. It is that we release Mr. de Brasto unconditionally, in the hope that he may incriminate himself, lead us to the poison, or commit some other act upon which we may fasten. I fear that it is too late for anything of the sort, but it seems our last chance. You will see yourself that you have not given us enough proof to go into court.'

'That is all right, Captain,' responded Plechs with complete good nature. 'I am used to the criticisms just brought against me, and I agree with you that we have not got all I could wish. In such complicated situations, involving the subtleties of the distorted ego, it is not to be expected that we should find everything plainly and openly exposed. I am convinced, nevertheless, that de Brasto is the man, and sooner or later we will get a confession from him.'

'Perhaps we shall do so, Doctor. Now, Mr. Lane, this is what I want to say to you: I want you to go about with Mr. de Brasto just as you have been doing. But every now and then, not too often, make some excuse and leave him alone for a time; in short, give him some opportunities. Naturally, I do not want you really to leave him; you must keep an eye on him, especially when he thinks himself unobserved. Leave him in this way in different parts of the boat, so that he may have as much chance as possible to reach anything he may have secreted. You have seen nothing of his alleged assailant, I suppose? My God, it sounds as childish as a nursery rhyme,' the captain finished up, 'but what else can we do?'

'Very well, sir,' the lieutenant answered. 'I will carry out your instructions carefully.' He grinned. 'No, we haven't seen anything of the mysterious gunman. I'm beginning to think there is something imaginary about him, myself. Hoped not, to begin with.'

Captain Mansfield said: 'I don't doubt it. You know, Dr. Plechs, this young man is our crack shot; that's why I put him in command of the ship's police and the emergency squad. How is your shooting, Lane?' he asked affectionately. 'Up to scratch?'

'Four-thirty out of five hundred this morning, sir,' grinned Lane, patting the revolver beneath the edge of his sack coat. 'I can stop them if they're around to be stopped.'

Captain Mansfield made a wry face, not so much over the bloodthirsty words as over the idea of weapons being discharged on board his boat. 'Don't be too anxious,' he admonished his subordinate. 'I mean it. I don't want any unnecessary violence, if it does come to an arrest. And certainly no firing. But I guess we needn't worry about that. The stewards have made a quiet search of the ship and I don't think you will ever find this strange gunman. What is important now is to watch de Brasto diligently. It's lucky we have the excuse for you to be with him. Keep your eye peeled and he may slip up on something.'

'Right, sir, I'll tend to it,' promised Lane, saluting.

With no less formality, Dr. Plechs extended his hand. 'Goodbye, Captain,' he said, 'I shall work up my results into a more complete form for you this afternoon. I shall have them ready for any new event.'

'That's fine. Thank you again.' Captain Mansfield opened his office door and passed within to his interrupted duties.

★ ★ ★

The night had come bringing with it a silvered sea, across whose wavelets the broad moon-path led to the transient *Meganaut*. The ship slipped rapidly and silently through the smooth water. In the many passageways where, side by side, the cabins aligned themselves geometrically down the body of the boat, the lights burned dimly; here and there a steward trod their lengths quietly, bearing on his tray a belated nightcap to one of his charges. Mostly they were empty; into the deserted distance stretched the rows of paired shoes outside the doors, mutely awaiting the attention of the 'Boots', and no figure stirred. The first hour's sleep enfolded the great vessel.

Only in the Ritz restaurant at the forward end of the sun deck was activity still in full swing. In fact, it had just opened, after the interval of recuperation following the exit of the last diners who had departed about ten o'clock, replete and content. Light streamed from the windows into the night outside; within was the babble of high-pitched laughter and repartee, the cheerful popping of corks, and (literally the first time to be successfully accomplished) one of the best dance orchestras on either side of the Atlantic.

To the two men who paced slowly around the sun deck through the mild evening the melodies came in snatches as brief and infrequent as their own remarks. De Brasto and Lieutenant Lane had almost reached the end of their conversational tether. And Lane was tired. I wish to God he'd go to bed, he thought, if all he wants to do is to walk around and around. But de Brasto had no idea of bed; he was suffering the reaction from the morning's grilling and never had he felt more wide awake.

Suddenly Lane pulled out his watch. 'My word,' he exclaimed, 'I must report up forward. I'm five minutes late now.

Will you excuse me a few moments? I'll be right back, say in ten minutes. Meet you here, where we are now, just outside the Ritz door.' Scarcely waiting for his companion's reply, he turned through the entrance and ran down the interior staircase on his fictitious errand.

Within the minute his head protruded the fraction of an inch around the housing of the outside steps from the deck below. For the third time since leaving the captain in the morning his efforts obtained for him nothing but disappointment. No more than twenty feet down the deck de Brasto was leaning negligently against the rail, lighting a cigarette. The minute flare of the match lit up his face as plainly as a thousand watt spot light. The lieutenant waited, stooping and bringing his face nearer to the surface of the deck to guard against any unexpected glance of de Brasto's in his direction, as he peered around the corner from his place of concealment. After what seemed an interminable period, the latter threw his cigarette in a wide arc toward the dark waters below and started slowly down the deck, walking aft. Lane straightened up, hazarded a further extrusion of his head, and prepared to follow as soon as his quarry was far enough ahead. He reflected that he could always say he had just come back and was looking for him.

The sun deck was furnished with at least fifteen modern and powerful lights borne aloft on standards resembling those to be seen on the best avenues of any large city. But at this time of night most of them had been extinguished; on Lane's side of the deck only two were functioning, one half-way down and the other at the farthest limit aft. As de Brasto passed under the first of these, the lieutenant saw a slight glow from the distant reaches of the deck; it looked as if someone had pressed the button on a flash-light whose batteries had been almost worn out.

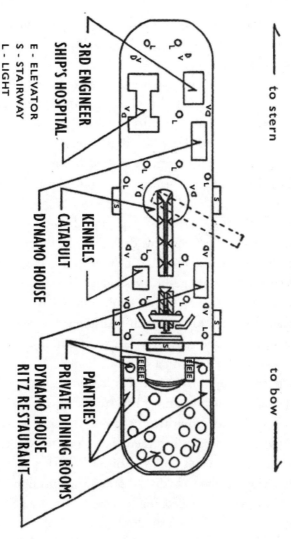

S.S.MEGANAUT

← to stern

to bow →

SUNDECK

3RD ENGINEER
SHIP'S HOSPITAL

E - ELEVATOR
S - STAIRWAY
L - LIGHT
V - VENTILATOR

DYNAMO HOUSE
CATAPULT
KENNELS

PANTRIES
PRIVATE DINING ROOMS
DYNAMO HOUSE
RITZ RESTAURANT

'Aiysh-ARRSH!' De Brasto's bubbling shriek rose in a wail, cut off as if by an axe. He pitched forward. It happened as quickly as that.

As Lane leaped out from the doorway, the moonlight flashed and glinted on the upward swing of his nickelled revolver. *C-rack! . . . Crack-crack!!*

He sprang down the open deck, every consideration of safety momentarily wiped out in his blinding, furious rage. The man he had been detailed to guard had been shot down before his eyes. By God! As he cleared de Brasto's prone body in a great bound, he saw something move in the shadows further down the deck. Increasing his mad dash, he brought up his gun and shot from the hip. *Crack!*

There had been no answering glow from his opponent's weapon as he hurtled along the deck. Now he dropped his own gun clattering on the planking behind him and sprang upon the deeper shadow prone in the shadows next a ventilator. By pure chance his gripping fingers found a throat. Before the slide engendered by his headlong rush had stopped, bracing himself on one elbow he had raised the head a foot from the deck and brought it down again with a shivering bump.

Lane scrambled to his feet. He looked searchingly for his enemy's hands, his foot drawn back to kick the weapon out of them. But his precaution was needless. The man was dead; a thick smear of red described their slide along the deck and the front of the lieutenant's best suit of mufti was splotched with scarlet where the other's body had pressed against him.

At the forward end a commotion arose. Twenty people were vainly endeavouring to push through the doorway which, at most, could accommodate three at a time. The lights from inside streamed down on the shoulders of women and the white faces of the men. Dr. Schall with the two men he had been sitting with, came out into the open space before the crowded doorway.

'Take him,' yelled Lane, pointing to where de Brasto still lay, under the centre light. Schall bent down over the recumbent figure.

Two sailors ran up the aft companionway behind Lane and approached him hurriedly. One of them, seeing the crimson stains, caught hold of him with apprehension.

'Not hurt at all. His blood,' gasped the lieutenant, yet somewhat dazed by the rapid succession of events. 'See to that man; dead I think, but better make sure.'

The two sailors leaned threateningly over the prostrate form, for Lieutenant Lane was a popular man with the crew. 'Dead as a smelt, sorr,' said one, a huge Irishman. 'And ripped up pretty, too. Did you get him, sorr, might I ask, sorr?'

'Yes—yes, I did, I guess.' Lane leaned up against the ventilator, drawing long breaths of air, for his final exertion had taken every ounce of strength he had. 'Stand guard here,' he directed a few moments later, and started up the deck toward the small crowd that had now gathered around de Brasto. As he approached, Captain Mansfield ran up the forward companionway, still buttoning the coat of his uniform.

'What is this disturbance?' cried the captain, hastily dropping his revolver into his pocket and keeping his hand there for a moment to mislead any chance glances that might have noticed the action.

Lane pushed his way through one side of the circle just as Captain Mansfield emerged from the other. 'It is my fault, sir,' he said, his face bitterly white. 'I left him for a few minutes, to follow our plan. He was shot while I was watching. How is he, Schall?' he asked, looking down.

One look was enough; he knew that de Brasto was dead before Dr. Schall stood up and said quietly, 'I'm afraid there is nothing I can do. He was shot through the heart. And if I'm not mistaken his wound is exactly the same as that inflicted upon Mr. Smith. The penetration is too large for one bullet; we shall find two I think, although there is only one wound.'

'Where is the man who fired these shots?' demanded the captain, his voice trembling with anger. 'Have you arrested him, Lieutenant?'

'I got him,' said Lane simply. 'He's dead. Further down the deck. I have two sailors on guard. O'Flaherty's one of them.'

The captain stood on tiptoe and looked over the heads of the throng. He espied his steward on the outskirts, who had just come up in some disarray. 'Mann,' he bellowed, 'call out the emergency squad. Instruct them I want this deck cleared immediately. And notify Dr. Pell. Tell him to come here at once; he'll want two stretchers. Come, Lieutenant, let us see what's at the other end of the deck. Tell me what happened.'

Lieutenant Lane told his superior in a few terse words the events of the last fifteen minutes. 'So de Brasto was innocent; his story was only too true,' he finished, his voice still tinged with bitterness. They approached the pair of sailors, standing above the sprawled-out object beside the ventilator.

The body was huddled stiffly, and a strange dead smile lifted the lips, showing a gold tooth. The features had a grim humour as if they had witnessed a last desperate joke. The strong jaws and the slightly bulging eyes were more prominent than in life.

One of the sailors stepped forward, saluting. 'Here, sir,' he said, 'here's his gun. We found it over there.'

Lane took the outstretched weapon and examined it curiously. 'I guess that's the answer, sir,' he commented, handing it over to Captain Mansfield.

The captain took it and held it up to the light. He saw a large, strange pistol, equipped with a long silencer. But the remarkable part about it was that it was double-barrelled, not in the usual way of a shot-gun, but with the barrels one above the other, separated only by a thin partition of steel. It could fire but two bullets without reloading; and both of them must be fired at once. A light of comprehension broke over Captain Mansfield's expression, as he felt for an empty pocket and slowly dropped the captured weapon into it.

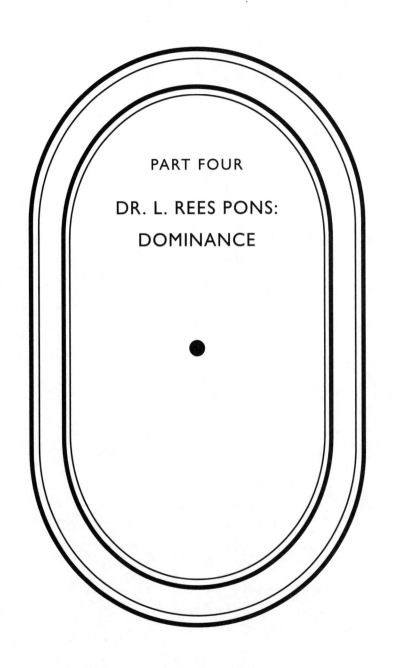

PART FOUR

DR. L. REES PONS:
DOMINANCE

PART FOUR

DR. L. REES PONS: DOMINANCE

Dr. Hayvier's prophecy was on the verge of fulfilment.

Although it was the breakfast rather than the dinner hour, Dr. Pons was turning his steps toward the boat deck forward, the recipient of an unprecedented invitation to a passenger to share a meal with Captain Mansfield in the latter's tiny but luxurious dining saloon. Overhead the clouds were sullen and unbroken; the sea, a slate-grey with here and there a few touches of white on the crests of the mounting rollers, stretched in all directions to a drab, colourless horizon. A rising wind, cool and bleak even if not bitterly cold, whistled past Pons's ears as he progressed with the landsman's uncertainty along the damp deck whose movements were becoming more and more unexpected. It must be admitted that the doctor's large and pleasant countenance did not exhibit its usual colour of complete health; in fact, it looked just a little pasty.

However, he reached the captain's room without mishap. Entering, he found the table laid for two, and Mansfield standing beside it with Lieutenant Lane. He had evidently interrupted them in an earnest conversation.

'Good morning, Dr. Pons,' said the captain, approaching to shake hands with his guest. 'Breakfast is about to come in, but Lieutenant Lane is just reporting to me about de Brasto's murderer. He's been up all night, keeping in touch with New York by radio. Go on, Lane. Dr. Pons will excuse us.'

'Is it right for me to hear it?' asked Pons, politely suggesting his own exclusion, although the keenness of his curiosity for the moment banished his growing physical qualms.

'Certainly, certainly; I'd like you to know. You were saying, Lane—about the last report?'

'It told us no more than the others, sir. The gang de Brasto went in fear of was the Videtti gang—well enough known, it seems, in Chicago. De Brasto and Stander were shady lawyers, and got several of these gangsters off—probably saved more than one from the chair. The gang turned against them after their defence of a man called Derringham. His name was the only new thing we learnt from the last radio. And Stander had told us that.'

'So de Brasto's story is confirmed, sir—except that he very likely did take a bribe from another gang to let this Derringham down. It's not likely that his clients would have turned murderous against him for an honest failure to get their man off. About that the police tell us nothing, and probably don't know much, either. They may be able to tell us something later about the man that I shot. But there's no reason to doubt that he was one of these Videtti gangsters.'

'Has Stander been troublesome?' asked the captain, frowning.

Lieutenant Lane gave a wry grin: 'Very, sir. Threatened and talked big, about criminal neglect of his partner's safety, and so on. I finally shut him up. He's a coward, anyway, and will do nothing. You can be sure enough, sir, that neither of those men was entitled to much police protection.'

'Then the whole de Brasto business is over,' put in Dr. Pons, 'and has nothing to do with the crime you are left to investigate?'

'That's clear, I think, sir,' said Lane.

'Yes,' said the captain. 'That's that.'

The Lieutenant shortly departed, as Mann entered balancing himself and two breakfast trays upon a floor that was beginning to heave and sink surprisingly. Still, Pons's sensations, as he seated himself at the table, were a little less disturbing than they had been on the deck without. Even so, he did not find himself able to regard the captain's very excellent fare with marked favour. The culinary display seemed slightly too lavish.

'No, thank you,' he earnestly assured the captain for the second time. 'Only coffee and a little toast. I eat very little for breakfast.'

Captain Mansfield had taken his role as host the more seriously since it was in sober truth the first time he had ever played it thus with one of his passengers. A full selection from the extensive breakfast menu of the ship had been ordered brought up in portable heaters by Mann, who had been forced to call two other stewards to his assistance.

Captain Mansfield, at any rate, was enjoying his own munificence. Now, having dispatched both his grapefruit and a generous helping of oatmeal and cream, there lay spread before him a large slice of appetizing ham upon which two fried eggs reposed side by side, an assortment of hot muffins, a dish of marmalade and, of course, a cup of coffee. Already there rose before his mind the prospect of a few buckwheat cakes, with perhaps a grilled frankfurter, to follow. From the midst of such delicious thoughts he once more urged the doctor to have anything he wanted.

'No, really,' Dr. Pons reiterated. 'I never eat anything at all for breakfast. Haven't for years.' He became unusually silent.

'Just as you say,' responded his host, munching contentedly. 'As for me, I can't understand that system at all. I've always eaten a good breakfast ever since I was a lad. I can go without it, of course, if I have to, but I never feel really up to scratch. Well, have another cup of coffee, anyhow.'

'Thank you, I will,' said Pons, deciding that this, at least, was within the bounds of possibility. An extraordinarily long dip, as the bow of the *Meganaut* fell forward, made him regret his acquiescence a moment afterward; but it was too late, already Mann was replenishing the cup.

The one-sided meal went on. . . .

At last—Pons felt certain that the time must now be well on toward noon—Captain Mansfield wiped his mouth, drank off his tumblerful of water, and leaned back in his chair. About to address himself to the real purpose of his invitation, he noticed his guest's pale features for the first time.

'My dear Dr. Pons,' he cried contritely. 'You're not feeling well. Good gracious, you must forgive me. All this food. I had no idea. It *is* blowing up a bit, but of course I'm so accustomed—'

Pons smiled somewhat wanly as he interrupted. 'Don't worry, Captain, I shall be all right. This is my first experience of rough weather, you know, I can't claim to feel fit as a fiddle. I've an idea you wanted to see me about something,' he went on, directly; 'I'm all right for that, so let's go ahead.'

'You're correct, of course,' Mansfield admitted. 'I did want to talk seriously with you and obtain your opinion. But perhaps it would be better if you lay down for a while in your cabin. The barometer has fallen sharply.'

'Not at all,' Dr. Pons insisted. 'The best thing in the world for me will be to give my attention to something besides the weather. I know what I'm talking about. Once I had to have six or eight teeth removed, and I made some interesting experiments in the dentist's chair; with the same apparatus on me that I used on Stymond, by the way. I don't mean to boast, but I really have developed a slight control over antagonistic stimuli. I'm quite sure there is no reason why we should not proceed, if you are willing to.'

The captain looked doubtful, but the last thing he wanted to do was to waste time. 'Very well; if you will promise to let me know the moment you don't feel like going on with it,' he provided.

Pons nodded, and Captain Mansfield began, 'I find myself in a damned awkward position. I am not a criminal investigator and I don't know the first thing about it. I have a pair of detectives who are supposed to take care of such matters; hitherto they have always been able to do so satisfactorily, but it is plain as day to me that the present situation is too much for them. All that will not excuse me, either in my own eyes or in those of the Line. This murder,' said the captain bitterly, 'must be solved. And I don't know where to turn for assistance. I am not too proud, I hope, to accept it, if I can find it.'

'And,' Pons put in, 'you haven't found it. You have already had the assistance of a pair of eminent psychologists, and found them eager and willing but no more satisfactory than your detectives. I should think you would be about through with that brand of help.'

'For heaven's sake,' Mansfield said hastily. 'Don't go away with the idea that I don't appreciate what these gentlemen have been kind enough to do for me. I am very grateful. Nevertheless, they have failed to solve this crime. You yourself have cleared the most likely suspect we had, and poor de Brasto, I am very much afraid, has paid with his life for the suspicions I harboured against him. Dr. Plechs's idea was so plausible that I found myself convinced for a time. Too much so, I guess. Never before have I made such a mistake in my life.'

Pons tried to reassure him. 'I wouldn't feel that way about it, if I were you. It wasn't your fault, nor Dr. Plechs's either, for that matter. The notion of leaving him alone occasionally came from one of the detectives. But I can't see that anyone is really to blame. That gunman would have got a shot at him sooner or later in any event. And the mystery of those three bullets is explained, at any rate.'

'Yes,' the captain agreed; he was too practical a man to spend overlong in vain regrets. 'That matter seems to be entirely cleared up now. But we are still left with the original problem. Who killed Smith and how are we to bring him to book? I won't feel safe until we have that fellow under lock and key. I don't want anything else to happen, that's certain.'

'Well, naturally, I see how you feel. I'll be glad to do anything I can. But what exactly do you want of me?'

Captain Mansfield was unaccustomedly vague. 'Why, really what I wanted to see you for, was to ask your advice. Without any reflections on the others, you strike me as a very competent man. You have already assisted your friends excellently in their own attempts; and you must have been thinking about the case yourself, and I thought you might be willing to give me your impressions. We might talk over the situation. . . . But perhaps,' he said suddenly, 'you yourself supported one of the previous theories.'

'No,' said Pons, 'I didn't. I don't like to criticize these men, both of whom I regard very highly. I hope you'll consider this confidential, but in my opinion their theories were examples of their particular weakness. Hayvier is really a very pragmatic fellow; his idea was too simple and obvious to suit me. The conditioned or unconditioned reflex on which he founds himself is no more than a verbal abstraction; in nature it doesn't exist. But then he is a doer, not a theorist, and that's why his theories are weak.

'Now Plechs, on the other hand, is strong on theory. His theories are involved and complicated, and also logical, provided you admit the premises. He suspected de Brasto, not for obvious but for subtle reasons. I thought in the first place that Plechs's idea was too cleverly subtle, just as Hayvier's was too simple. It is astonishing that the contributions of these two men, which no one can overlook, have been just the opposite of their own characters. Hayvier, the pragmatist, has done an inestimable service in clearing out a whole swamp of subjectivity and prejudice from psychological theory and method; and Plechs, the theorist, still indulges, it seems to me, in much muddled thinking, but has given practical help of untold value to hundreds of patients. It is strange. . . .'

'As you put it,' Captain Mansfield said, lighting another cigarette, 'it is very strange indeed.'

'It is. But I suppose you would rather we talked about the immediate problem?'

'I won't say I'm not interested in this rather complicated

world of your science,' admitted the captain, 'but of course the other matter *is* pressing. I should like to hear who you think might have committed the crime.'

Dr. Pons smiled. 'That's just the trouble, you see. I haven't any suspect in mind that I can introduce on the spot. Human responses are very complex things; but the ultimate criterion for understanding human behaviour is that it is integrated behaviour. When we come to a particular problem in this behaviour, a problem of a practical nature, there is one element that is overwhelmingly important, that, properly grasped, will give the clue. That element is *motive*. But I must explain to you what I mean by motive, if you care to have me go on. Perhaps you will feel that this isn't getting us anywhere?'

'On the contrary, Doctor. Go ahead, please.'

As Pons opened his mouth to continue, the captain's dining saloon, which in the past fifteen minutes had become more and more unsteady, described a definite arc to starboard and downward. The doctor gulped, and grasped hastily for a glass of water.

Captain Mansfield smiled involuntarily. 'Don't try to balance,' he advised his guest. 'Go with the motion, don't oppose it and you will feel much better. Shall I have the steward bring you a bromo? Might settle your stomach a bit.'

'I think so. Yes,' Pons accepted, still somewhat green. Mann, who had previously cleared off the table, much to the psychologist's relief, brought the order at once. Pons drank off the sharp, effervescing tumblerful and wiped the resulting tears out of his eyes.

'Let's see, where were we?' he continued. 'Oh, yes; motive. I never use the word, purpose, another subjective term that I hope we shall soon be rid of. Motive is very little like purpose, and it is still less like those simple crudities described in police courts and detective stories under the name. It is not just "here's a necklace, let's steal it" or the more vague, general situation of the criminally disposed in the face of a criminal opportunity.

'I believe human beings to be motivated by three fundamental "drives"; the appetitive, self-seeking drive which is based upon the hunger mechanisms of the body and develops from their operations, the love drive, originally based upon the genital system, and what I have called the procreative drive, arising in the first instance from the reproductive functions. All these constitute spontaneous drives of the organism toward specific types of behaviour, and each of them may be opposed or assisted by the external forces of the environment.'

'But surely,' put in the captain, 'these three drives will not account for all kinds of behaviour.'

'Yes, I think so,' Pons responded. 'You see, the connection-making functions of the correlation centres in the cerebrum allow these fundamental motivations to be transferred from their original objects to all sorts of other things, even to mental abstractions, so that the drive that in the first place served to relieve hunger-pangs can become directed later to the acquisition of preferment, or honours, or yachts, or almost anything under the sun.

'And here we have to take account of environmental influences, which act upon the individual in various ways. A human being is the centre of strong forces which he generates within himself. But of course the forces outside him are not negligible, and actual behaviour is the resultant of the balance of those two kinds of influence.

'Since we have two sets of forces, there result only four type possibilities in their integration. The outside forces may oppose the interior ones and be either weaker or stronger; or they may be in alliance with the organism and again either weaker or stronger. I have given to these four types of situation the names of Dominance, Compliance, Inducement, and Submission. Such responses may be either active or passive and there may be many gradations combining two or more of them in various proportions. I don't want to take your time to go into this too fully. I shall have to say a little about emotions, though. This is not so surprising when one reflects that emotional consciousness is motor consciousness, as I believe.'

Captain Mansfield interrupted again. 'Now there,' he said, 'you seem to me to base your conclusions as much upon the physical as Dr. Hayvier does; but you apparently do not agree with him about consciousness. Is not "consciousness" one of your literary terms?'

'Not with me,' answered Dr. Pons, and would have smiled, had not environmental forces too strongly opposed this spontaneous response. 'In my view, Captain, consciousness is a physical force generated within the body upon the "psychons" that are parts of the synapses in the central nervous system.

'Now we are confronted— By the way, Captain, what is that terrific booming I hear?' The doctor braced himself uneasily in his chair as he listened, then remembering his friend's advice, slumped back into it as the *Meganaut* heaved forward.

'Oh, that. That's only the fog-horn.'

'Are we in a fog? Perhaps you should leave?' Of all the perils of the sea Dr. Pons was least enthusiastic about fog.

'No, I guess not,' Mansfield smiled with reassurance. 'It won't be fog, anyhow. Just a squall, I imagine. Whenever the visibility drops to a few hundred yards, we blow; it's a rule. As soon as the squall goes over, it will stop.' And indeed the hoarse sound, tearing over their heads, had now suspended. 'Go ahead, Doctor, I am very much interested in your theories. Now just how are we to apply them to this crime?'

From the depths of his chair, Pons resumed. 'Well, the principles I should apply are these. The strongest of all human motives is love and it is usually to be found somewhere in any drastic behaviour. As it is typically called out by a person of the opposite sex, the old dictum, *"cherchez la femme"*, is frequently a sound one. I see you are surprised when I allude to love in connection with a murder, but I mean love in the abnormal relationship in which it is controlled or used by dominance. Of course, some crimes express almost pure dominance emotion unmixed with anything else, but they are usually of a direct, simple kind, the slayings of rival gangsters, for example. De Brasto's murder, for instance, I should be inclined to believe was an expression of dominance. Although even there we have some love elements coming in, if we believe that he was killed to avenge the member of some mob whom the others supposed he had betrayed.

'As regards the Smith murder, however, there was nothing straightforward about it at all. It wasn't a shooting, but a poisoning; and the appetitive type of person motivated by dominance alone, hardly ever uses poison. Moreover, if anything is plain about it, it is that the criminal is not obvious; to this extent the crime is a subtle one, carefully planned and carried out with attention to detail. The criminal is an intelligent person and I should say that the motivation is correspondingly complicated. I should guess that the crime was committed by a duplex type of personality, one in whom the appetitive and love responses are usually kept separate but in whom the abnormal control of the love element by the dominant interest might occur. I should look for such a person.'

'But this is so general,' the captain objected, 'it might be almost anyone, so far as we know. It might be either a man or a woman.'

'Yes, it might. And then— By George, I have an idea!' Pons cried, with a semblance of animation. 'I knew there was something, a sort of hint, floating around in my mind. Wait now, let me see. . . . Yes, that's worth thinking about.' In his excitement, Pons got up out of his chair, and started to walk about the tiny room.

'I—, ugh, ahr, arh—' said Pons.

'Here, Mann!' the captain called loudly, with sudden energy. The steward's surprised face appeared at the doorway. 'Here, take Dr. Pons—' He got no farther.

The steward's first glance told him all. As Pons buried his face in his enormous handkerchief, Mann took him by the arm and propelled the heaving bulk of the psychologist rapidly through the door to the captain's cabin. . . .

It was ten full minutes before Dr. Pons reappeared. When he did, he still looked pale but it was evident that he felt somewhat better.

'I'm very sorry, Captain. Not a nice way to reward your hospitality. I'm afraid I over-rated my endurance. Yes, thanks, I do feel much better now. But I'm still a little weak, and I think I'll go down and lie on my berth for a while.'

'Best thing you can do,' said his host. 'It's my fault; I should have insisted earlier. But just before the—er—catastrophe you said something about a hint; you seemed to have an idea. Can you tell me what it was before you go?'

'I can, but I don't think I will, if you don't mind. If you can let me work it out alone for an hour or so, I'll step in about four, say?'

'Better make it five, if you can,' the captain answered. 'I can give you more time. Naturally I'm curious.'

'Five will be better for me, too.' A recollection came abruptly to Pons. 'My God,' he groaned, 'I've an engagement at two-thirty myself. I wonder if I can keep it. It is with a most attractive lady.'

'Oh, you'll be all right long before then. There should be good weather just ahead of us now. Meanwhile—'

'Meanwhile, will you get some information for me over the radio, Captain? I want to know where Mr. Smith's daughter was born, who his wife was or is, and anything else that can be found out about his family. You have none of this already, have you?'

'No, I'm afraid not. But I'll try to get it for you right away. Funny, now that you mention it, there wasn't anything at all about his family in the résumé that was sent when I made my first request. Just his business career; I suppose that was the important thing about him, after all.'

'The other may be more important for us, though,' answered the doctor. 'I'll go along, then. Be sure to ask especially about his daughter, will you?'

'Surely you don't suspect his daughter?'

'No, I don't suspect his daughter,' said Pons, and nodded his adieux.

As Dr. Pons walked through the lounge, his step was firm and his eye clear. His complexion, furthermore, presented a much happier appearance than during his earlier visit to the *Meganaut's* captain. Secluded within his cabin, he had worked out a theory of the crime that had astonished even himself; at the end of his three hours' cogitation he had felt so gratified at his success that he had ventured to partake of a little nourishment. This had further aided his recovery until, when he emerged promptly at two-fifteen, he looked much as usual. There had followed his participation in the ship's ping-pong tournament with a certain, very attractive Madame Sudeau, a tournament which, chiefly through her efforts and much to his surprise, they had actually won.

As Dr. Pons, on his way to revisit the captain, pressed the signal button beside the elevators outside the lounge, he felt again the little thrill that he always experienced when, his theory painstakingly and elaborately constructed, he took his first glance at the experimental results that would either confirm or destroy it.

At his entrance Captain Mansfield looked over his shoulder and thrust the report he had been studying into the further reaches of his desk.

'Sit down, Dr. Pons,' he invited heartily. 'You look fully recovered, eh? Did you have to stay in your bunk long?'

'Only a couple of hours,' Pons assured him. 'I've been up and about all the afternoon. I even found it possible to win a ping-pong tournament.'

'And have you thought over that clue that occurred to you this morning, Doctor? Have you come to a conclusion?'

'Oh, yes,' Pons answered. 'I've been thinking about that. I have a theory of the crime entirely worked out. But before I go into that, I would like to hear what has been found out over the radio.'

The captain reached into one of his desk drawers and pulled out a large radio sheet. 'Yes,' he said, quizzically, 'and that's one reason I'm so glad to see you strong and healthy again. You are in for a shock, I'm afraid. If you have built up a theory based upon Smith's family relations, you may as well throw it out now. It seems—'

Pons interrupted quickly, almost with relief, it seemed. 'He never had a daughter, then? Is that what you found?'

'Well, I'm damned!' Mansfield's eyes opened widely in surprise. 'How in the name of heaven did you ever guess that?'

'Part of my theory,' grinned Pons.

'Not only that,' the captain continued, 'but he hasn't any family at all. He has been in the limelight for a good many years, too; I doubt whether it would have been possible to conceal any relatives of his, if he had had them.'

'Oh, I don't think we need contemplate an unknown relative with a grudge,' Pons added. 'I wasn't thinking of that. But I'm glad to hear my guess about the girl was right; otherwise my carefully built hypothesis *would* have gone smash.'

'I am more anxious than ever to hear about this hypothesis of yours now,' the captain declared. 'Wait a moment, will you have a cigarette? . . . All right, go ahead then, if you will.'

Dr. Pons nodded, lighting a cigarette of his own, and commenced his exposition forthwith.

'Nothing but pure chance put me on to it in the first place,' he admitted. 'A conversation I had with young Gnosens the other morning at breakfast. Simply by the way we happened to mention "Miss Smith", although it was natural enough, since he had been rather madly in love with her; got over it now, it appears. That started me thinking about the young woman, more or less casually, and the more I thought, the more curious I began to feel. She was such an entirely different type from her "father", one of the purest blonde types I have ever seen. Then there was something else about the girl that no one could possibly miss. I only saw her twice, I believe; once was that last night in the smoking-room. But her beauty was simply breath-taking. I'm not sure that she isn't the most beautiful woman I have ever looked at.'

'I didn't see her,' remarked Captain Mansfield gravely. 'I appear to have missed an opportunity.'

'You did,' Pons assured him. 'And I must tell you this,' he went on with the utmost seriousness, 'the beauty of women is the strongest stimulating force in the whole world. Why, if I could direct the influence exercised by the world's beautiful women for just one year, I could change the direction and the future history of the entire human race; I could re-make the social life of the planet. Some day perhaps we can educate them to use their power for themselves intelligently. . . .

'But I am getting off on a subject that I must admit fascinates me. In this present case we find a woman who represents in herself the most powerful forces conceivable for influencing her fellow creatures, both men and women, for women, too, if left to themselves, without a false education, worship the outstanding beauty of other women just as men do. Here are two points, then. First "Miss Smith" is very beautiful, and thus very powerful; and second, she is not "Miss Smith" at all. And I may add a third point. Although I saw her only twice, and each time for a very short period, I have no question in my mind but that she is a natural captivatress of men; she practised all the little tricks of beautiful women, not artificially but naturally, as is entirely normal; all the little, intriguing, captivating mannerisms that are so irresistible in inducing the submission of men to the love-spell.

'If you will add up these three points, Captain, you will get the answer at once as to who this young lady was. She was not Mr. Smith's daughter; she was his mistress. I hope you will not be shocked at the presence of such an affair on your boat, for I have no doubt there are several other ladies of the same kind among your passengers.'

'No,' said the captain, with a thoroughly worldly smile, 'no, I am not even greatly surprised. Of course we cannot countenance such proceedings if we know about them, but they happen, ah, in spite of our best efforts, frequently. And at the eastern end of our run, my dear Doctor, they do not cause anything like the excitement that appears to be felt over them in your own country. However, while I am no great moralist myself, I must say that I do not approve of the practice.'

'Nor do I,' Pons replied. 'But my objections certainly have nothing at all to do with morals, by which I suppose you mean Christian morals. In my view Christianity will have some day to answer the very serious charge of destroying and polluting true love-relationships by its self-assumed and moralistic restrictions. My own objection to mistresses is not that they are unconsecrated but that they are impermanent. A real love-relationship must stretch over many years in order to develop fully and properly, whereas these affairs usually last a few months, or at most a few years. And in by far the greatest number of instances, as in the one we are discussing, they are motivated entirely wrongly.

'But let me get back to my theory. This beautiful and captivating woman—. By the way, Captain, did you find out what her real name is, as a result of your inquiries?'

'Yes, it was in the reply. Let's see now, it was a peculiar name; quite gone out of my mind.' The captain rummaged about on the top of his desk for the radio sheet. 'Yes, here it is. Coralie R-e-a-k-e hyphen L-y-o-n-s,' he spelled out. 'One of those hyphenated names. Probably assumed. These women seldom go by their real names, anyway.'

'Yes. Well, we can't tell about that, of course,' the doctor considered. 'Coralie Reake-Lyons. Reake-Lyons. I don't find it so inappropriate, at all events. Now, to get back again. . . .

'We have this beautiful captivatress and her lover, a man old enough to pass himself off as her father. Her captivation is perfectly normal, as I said, but the fact that she was his temporary mistress is not normal at all. No matter how expensively you dress it up, it is an abnormal reversal of the harmonious emotional sequence, Inducement-Submission. The prostitute completely reverses the organically efficient combination; first she submits to the man, and subsequently she induces payment from him. Frequently, and especially often in these affairs with wealthy men, she does not even use Inducement, but extorts payment from her victim by dominating him with the threat of blackmail. The Submission is made in this case only for the purpose of and with a view toward the subsequent Dominance.

'You remember that I mentioned previously, and upon quite different grounds, that we should look about for a duplex type of personality in our search for the criminal. Most duplex types are quite normal, of course; their activities, both of the love and the appetitive varieties, are excellently organized but kept pretty well separated from each other in the behaviour pattern. But it can come about that the well-organized appetitive responses control the equally well-organized love responses.

'And that is the situation that I think we have to deal with at present. The young woman was certainly very successful in captivation, but she had equally strong appetitive interests. I think if we had known her, we should have found her extremely selfish and obstinate.

'Now what happened? She had no difficulty in captivating Smith, who was himself a strong appetitive personality. But where she ran up against an insurmountable obstacle, was in trying to exact payment from him. In moments of Submission he would probably have given her anything. But there is a self-regulating safety device in the love responses. It has been decided by nature that the love responses cannot really be misused: they can only be distorted, with the resulting disease of the distorter.

'At any rate, Coralie Reake-Lyons made the mistake of trying to dominate a more dominating personality than her own. Naturally she was defeated, and doubtless she was defeated many times. Finally, with her own Dominance responses worked up and called out to their full extent by Smith's probably brutal opposition, she yielded to their flouted clamour for expression and came under their complete control. Realizing in despair that she could never gain her original ends, for a man like Smith would laugh even at blackmail, she experienced a moment of full abnormality and decided to dominate him completely. The final domination, of course, is the death of one's opponent. Actually she selected a poison and administered it to her lover in the smoking-room that night. That, Captain, is what I think occurred.'

Dr. Pons paused, and sat back in his chair after his long speech. Again he mopped his brow.

For some time Captain Mansfield sat in silence also, while his forgotten cigarette added to the scars already burned into his desk.

Then he broke out with: 'My word, you psychologists are certainly the most plausible people I have ever met. Now here's the third suspect offered me, and once more I find myself convinced that this is the criminal. But wait! Now I think I have *you*, at any rate. The girl herself was poisoned, Doctor. How do you get around that? You won't ask me to believe that her Dominance went to such lengths that she even poisoned herself, I suppose?'

Dr. Pons was smiling. 'And what makes you think that she *was* poisoned, Captain?' he asked quietly.

'What makes me think—. Why, er, Pell said so, of course!'

'Did he?' asked Pons again. 'Now I didn't get that idea, myself. I thought he said that he hadn't been able to tell what was the matter with her, and that he merely presumed she had been the victim of the same weapon as her "father". What do you think yourself?'

'Why, well, why, yes, perhaps that's so,' the captain considered. 'But I can't believe that she could have feigned unconsciousness in such a way as to deceive an experienced physician like Pell.'

'No more do I,' said the psychologist at once. 'This girl was much too clever to try anything like that. No, I think she actually drugged herself with some harmless mixture that for a time would give her the appearance of having died. I don't know enough about drugs even to guess at the nature of the self-administered one, although I suppose it might have been some hemp or hasheesh derivative. Those drugs can cause suspended animation closely resembling death, I've been told. Undoubtedly she intended to revive later and, since it would seem that she had been poisoned also, she would avoid any suspicion being thrown upon her.'

'And then, Doctor? Why should her body have been stolen and disposed of?'

Pons smiled again. 'But you see I don't think it was. Who would have taken such risks as that? So far as I know, no one was ever suggested for the part except de Brasto. And we know he didn't do it, now.'

'You think she escaped herself?'

'I do. I think she climbed out the window. She might have been fully conscious for a half-day or even a whole day before she made the attempt.'

'But Doctor,' cried Mansfield, 'just think. You can't mean to tell me that a young girl, certainly accustomed to every luxury, could lie quietly in that little room in the hospital with a—with a corpse? For a whole day, or half a day, either?'

'Human beings have been known to do far worse things than that, Captain,' stated Pons calmly.

'But then what made her leave the hospital at all? Why didn't she just wait and appear to come to, as you first suggested?'

'Ah, that I'm afraid I can't answer.' The psychologist's face now reflected something of the captain's puzzlement.

'And where is she now?' asked Captain Mansfield.

'She is right aboard this boat, in hiding somewhere below,' answered Dr. Pons.

'*She is?*' the captain cried, the full and exasperating significance of this repeated flouting of his authority dawning upon him for the first time. 'Now, by damn, this is too much! I don't know whether you're right or wrong, but if that woman is hiding anywhere on board my ship, she shall be found at once.'

'And just how will we do that?' Pons inquired. 'This ship is so big I can hardly find my way around it yet. The problem of getting enough to eat to live on, should not be hard for a clever person; trays left in the passages, that sort of thing.'

'We will find her, if she is there to be found.'

'My dear Captain, I make no reflections against the boat, but

I remember that there was a careful search made, lasting over a day or two at least, for the man who finally killed de Brasto. He had no difficulty in keeping out of sight. No, I'm afraid the chances of finding her are pretty small.'

'You may think so but I don't,' answered Captain Mansfield. When it came to doing something definite, he was not a doubter. 'I'll go through this ship with a fine tooth-comb, sir! Don't you believe for a moment that, when I decide on it, there is anything aboard the *Meganaut* that I can't find out or deal with.'

The growing darkness in the office had finally caused Dr. Pons to pull out his watch during the captain's last determined statements. 'We've been talking longer than I had any idea of,' he said apologetically. 'It's nearly seven o'clock. I really had no intention of taking up so much of your time.'

'Don't worry about the time,' growled Mansfield. 'If you're right, it's been worth it.'

'And I hope,' added Pons, 'that you are right about finding that girl. If she knew what I've been saying, I wouldn't give much for my own chances. I haven't the slightest doubt that she'd seduce me first and murder me afterwards.'

'She would, eh?' said Captain Mansfield, by no means ready to take the matter lightly. As Pons went out the door he shook an admonitory finger after the psychologist. 'If she's on board, I'll have her,' he repeated.

In spite of the sensation caused in New York, and even upon the Bourses of the Continent, by the sudden death of Victor Timothy Smith, the routine of the *Meganaut's* voyage went forward much as usual for the large majority of her passengers. With the shooting of de Brasto and his assailant the excitement and the talking had flared up once more. But here the affair had been witnessed by a much smaller number. The general impression was that some desperado had been carelessly allowed to include himself in the ship's company, had shot and killed three of the passengers for certain dark reasons of his own, and had at last been slain in turn by the constituted authorities. As 99 per cent. of the travellers resided in America, and most of these either in New York, Chicago or Philadelphia, only the setting on a trans-Atlantic liner in mid-ocean made such events unusual.

The little wave of interest raised by the sinister doings at their doorsteps flattened out rapidly into the unruffled surface of forgetfulness. To say truly, his charges were much less disturbed than Captain Mansfield feared.

In spite of all that could be done by Chief Electrician Holt and his staff, the injured dynamos continued to give trouble and to force a reduced speed upon the ship. If this caused some minor changes in the future reservations of the passengers at their favourite hotels, it provided no further inconvenience, for there was so much entertainment to be found aboard the *Meganaut* that a few extra days in her luxurious quarters worked no hardship. Now, as the lights gleamed brightly on the evening throngs along the decks, in the lounge and the smoking-room and the ballroom, as the violins sang and the saxophones moaned, and the drinks were brought and the passengers danced and talked and flirted and played, the ship was the picture of careless and carefree enjoyment.

It was just at this untroubled moment that a dozen of the higher officers, with very serious faces indeed, walked out of Captain Mansfield's quarters, saluted him smartly, and watched him pass quickly to the bridge.

Brroom!—Brrroom!—Broo-ooom!

As the officers turned and scattered, running, the patter of their feet along the boat deck was echoed janglingly by the clangour of the big alarm gongs resounding simultaneously from all parts of the ship.

The engines were slowing. Slowing. They stopped, and the *Meganaut* drifted forward over the waves.

Brroom!—Brrroom!—Brroo-ooom! Again the deep-throated whistle, backed by all the steam in the boilers far below, hurled its thunderous note of alarm across the calm and quiet night.

The deep roar penetrated resonantly to the farthest passageways of the ship, a menacing undertone beneath the higher pitched clanging of the bells. Ten miles away, over the silence of the sea, it could still be heard. And it was heard. Where the lights of a westward liner twinkled in the distance, a lookout called sharply to another bridge-officer, and the latter spoke hurriedly through a tube to his radio man. Crackle, crack, crack; crackle, crackle, crack, crack, crackle, crack. The radio man was busy with his key.

Below decks on the *Meganaut* consternation reigned. In the ballroom the music stopped, as if the score had been abruptly cloven by a giant sword. One of the wind instruments wavered on for a further note or two, and petered out. The dancers hesitated, and stood still, many of the couples yet in each other's arms. The strongest native fear-stimulus of all, a loudly shattering noise, beat raucously at their ears. The colour drained from their faces, and they trembled like frightened sheep.

Stewards dropped their trays and sprang to their stations at the doorways; over-stewards jumped up on the nearest tables or chairs, exhorting those present to calmness and assuring them that there was no danger; ridiculous enough the assurances sounded, in competition with the alarm bells. Boat drills have been mostly abandoned on the larger vessels since the war, nor had there been the slightest warning to the crew that one was intended. Both passengers and stewards feared the worst. Here and there a more sturdy-hearted man met the crisis calmly and proved invaluable to those in his neighbourhood.

But Captain Mansfield's rigid discipline was telling now. At the first signal all of the eight passenger elevators smoothly rose or dropped to the promenade deck, their starting-point at this hour in case of danger; the doors clanged open, the operators stood at their posts, awaiting the first rush. The cars were filled, and dropped rapidly to the decks below; returned, were filled again, and repeated their trips until no more remained to be carried. Then they descended once more and came to rest at the level of D deck, in preparation for the reverse conveyance of the passengers to their boat stations after they had obtained the life-belts in their state-rooms.

Already small bands of sailors, under their petty officers, were scrambling up from below and running to their stations along the decks. Along the boat deck the covers were being ripped from the electric davit-motors and pulled back from the huge lifeboats; into each of these one man was hoisted by his comrades, and a series of popping explosions heralded the smooth purring that spread along both sides of the ship as the gasoline motors in her boats settled down to a steady drone.

Now most of the passengers were beginning to emerge from the cabins with their life-belts; many also clutched in their arms small bags or parcels containing the most easily salvaged of their valuables. Quickly by stair or elevator they made their way back to the promenade deck, where they were received by other stewards and guided to their proper boat stations. Fortunately the sea was calm and the slight breeze through the opened windows warm; but there was no mistaking the increasing slant of the deck. The list, already obvious, was growing greater.

At this time the lobby between the tiers of elevators just forward of the lounge was the focus of greatest activity. The ordinarily ample space soon resembled a major subway stop at the rush hour. At the height of the press it was necessary for several of the elevators to remain with opened doors for some minutes before the loads they carried could push their way out into the lobby at all. Those passengers who passed through this mill at the period of its greatest congestion, reached the deck in a bedraggled condition. By a miracle no one was seriously injured.

The deck outside began to fill with the mounting hundreds, and the jam in the lobby thinned; it became possible to distinguish separate individuals in the onward-pressing stream. Here a family party debouched from the stairway, father, mother, and three children, the youngest so little a chap that he was being carried protestingly in the arms of his nurse. For the thirtieth time the father, liberally draped with their six life-belts, counted them all over anxiously and hurried them around the corner of the passageway toward the deck. Behind them an old gentleman with a cane hobbled up the now momentarily empty steps, looking on all sides and even behind him in a bewildered fashion; his life-belt, hung rakishly around his neck, further impeded his feeble progress. As he hesitated just below the final steps, a pair of college boys, dashing up behind him, lifted him between them and deposited him gently in the middle of the lobby. 'Good luck, old sport,' they cried excitedly, and dashed toward the bar, some idea of seizing a last emergency ration before the ship sank, obsessing their minds. The old gentleman, more bewildered than ever, looked dazedly about, and staggered shakily toward the exit.

A door opened and out of an elevator came an assorted party of six or eight, among them a good-looking young man and his even better looking young wife. 'I won't go without you, John,' cried the latter, between overwrought laughter and sobs, 'I won't, I won't, *I won't!*' John put his arm around her white shoulders and pushed her rapidly ahead of him. 'You'll go where you're told, sweetheart: now please be—' They too passed through the outer doorway.

On the open sun deck, above, was much feverish, though disciplined, activity. Two hundred or more of the crew went about their carefully-planned tasks in small, efficient squads. In addition to the usual illumination of the arc lights on their high standards, four searchlights, each controlled by a petty officer, played brightly upon special points from fore and aft.

The great life-rafts, capable of carrying nearly a hundred persons each, were rapidly unlashed and pushed into their launching positions. A special crew of mechanics worked energetically to unfasten the two-seater open mail 'plane from its carriage behind the metal wind shields that guarded it just aft of the bridge. Now they had it unblocked and rolled it back along the track of the movable catapult in its rear. Other men sprang to the turntable levers and directed the catapult outboard over the ship's side, while one of the mechanics cranked over the 'plane's propeller and with a bright flash of flame from the exhausts the big motor began to warm itself up. As its deep roar, like a magnified machine-gun in action, leaped over the deck, the two leather-coated aviators climbed up on the catapult, hastily adjusting their goggled helmets on their heads. They slipped into their seats, opened up the gas and throttled it down several times, as they glanced sharply over their various instrument dials and the mechanics swarmed about the 'plane making a final test of the control wires to wings and tail. As the 'plane had cruising radius of only three hundred miles, the purpose of its launching was not to save the aviators; in an emergency it might prove of great assistance by guiding other ships to the point of disaster.

Last of all the captain's own boat was rolled out on its special carriage, a smart little mahogany tender holding no more than six, to be launched desperately from this very deck only at the last moment when the ship was about to go down. Its tiny engine buzzed angrily and minutely as the coxswain started it.

On the now abandoned 'plane carrier the officer commanding the deck stood overlooking the scene in his gleaming, white uniform. He blew a shrill blast on his whistle, and spoke briefly into his deck telephone.

'Sun deck prepared, sir!'

With a groan from the iron wheels of its carriage the first lifeboat swung out and down the *Meganaut's* side.

Hayvier and Pons found themselves together in the same group of forty or fifty about half-way down the starboard side of the promenade deck.

'What in God's name do you suppose is the matter?' Hayvier demanded, craning his head in all directions and seeing nothing but the crowded, inclined deck.

'How do I know?' Pons replied. 'I always thought they gave you some warning if it was just a drill. I'm worried about that Mrs. Sudeau, too, I can tell you; I wonder where she is.' He rose on tiptoe and peered over the heads of those around him.

'Oh, I know whom you mean,' said Hayvier. 'She's all right. I saw her down the deck there when I came up.' And indeed at the same moment, Pons himself caught sight of her. She felt his gaze apparently, for she turned and waved to him from the distance. Then calmly lit a cigarette and spoke to the woman beside her.

'Yes, she's all right,' said her previous partner, much relieved. 'Wonder how Plechs and Mittle are getting on. Well, they can take care of themselves as well as the rest of us, I guess.'

Hayvier agreed. 'Just the same there's nothing funny about this list we're getting. Look there!'

As he spoke, a white beam cut through the night outside and played blindingly over the side of the *Meganaut*. Around her bows another great boat glided to leeward and with reversed engine, came to rest several hundred yards away. After a moment's surprised silence a scattering cheer broke from the passengers on the promenade deck. A woman cried hysterically.

Down the deck Commander Drake was making a slow progress, stopping continually to harangue the groups in his path. All along the windows the lifeboats were falling and rising almost rhythmically, as they were lowered to within a few feet of the water and then pulled up again.

'There is no danger at all,' Drake assured his successive listeners. 'Absolutely none. In a short time I think you can go back to your cabins and take off your life-belts. I ask you only to wait as patiently as possible until you can be dismissed.'

He approached Pons's group, and catching sight of him, called, 'Dr. Pons.'

'Here,' answered the doctor, pushing his way to the front.

'Oh, Pons, Captain Mansfield wants to see you on the bridge. No, I don't know what he wants. Just wait a moment until I speak to these people, and I'll take you to the door.'

A moment later Dr. Pons perceived the significance of the

executive officer's remark. The entrance was firmly locked and not until Drake had produced and manipulated his key, could Pons proceed further. As soon as he had passed, the lock clicked shut behind him.

An hour later, twelve hundred passengers, released at last, were returning over the now level decks from their rather drastic experience, and the lights of the *Meganaut's* sister ship were rapidly dwindling in the westward distance.

In Captain Mansfield's office a small group was gathered, composed of Younghusband, Gnosens, Drake, Pons and the captain. The last sat slumped in his chair, drumming steadily with his fingers on the desk top. His expression was that of a discouraged man, and when he spoke a similar note appeared in his voice.

'That girl simply isn't on this boat,' he said, in a disgruntled tone. 'There isn't so much as a rat on board that hasn't been accounted for. Everybody on deck has been looked over by you, Pons, or by Gnosens or Younghusband; and while you were doing it Lieutenant Lane and his men made a thorough search through all the cabins and public rooms. Even the crew's quarters were gone through, and the only baggage hold that had been opened since her disappearance was searched earlier in the evening and then closed. I gave no one but Mr. Younghusband and Mr. Gnosens any warning at all, and I made it look as much like a realistic abandonment of the ship as possible, with the idea that the woman might be frightened into showing herself on deck, if she were really in hiding below. I even had all our oil pumped into the starboard tanks to produce that list. . . . Well,' he finished with a deep sigh, 'she's not on board. That's all we have succeeded in finding out.'

They looked into each other's faces, and if there was anyone there who was not completely puzzled, it was not apparent in their expressions. The captain's discouragement deepened; once again it appeared that modern psychology had misled him.

'I just can't believe it,' said Younghusband, in the tone of one denying the plain evidence of his senses. 'I was certain she was hiding somewhere on board, the moment I heard about it. But we *have* looked everywhere, there is no getting around that.'

His voice trailed off, and for some minutes no one broke the silence.

Finally Dr. Pons, despite his responsibility for the fiasco, found his curiosity undeniable. 'But what about that other ship?' he asked.

'Oh, that,' said the captain. 'Fellows must think I've lost my mind. I wanted to reassure my passengers, and luckily it was one of our own boats or I shouldn't have dared do it.' He handed a radio blank to the doctor.

Pons took it and read,

'S.S. *Meganaut* rad.   9:46p
to S.S. *Argonaut,* Fellowes commanding
Acknowledge message Request you proceed and lay to
alongside us No necessity transfer passengers or crew
Mansfield commanding.

The day after the boat-drill dawned clear and calm. There were few on deck; after their exciting experience of the previous night most of the passengers had found it necessary to compose their nerves, either in the saloons or in their own cabins, by sharing their adventure with friends and restoring themselves with liquid or more substantial refreshments. Now they were sleeping late.

Not so Captain Mansfield. As always, he had breakfasted at seven. At eight-forty-five, when his executive officer presented himself to accompany him on the morning inspection, the captain was still engaged in going over the time sheets of the boat-drill performance recorded under actual circumstances and comparing them with the planned and predicted periods. Drake had been waiting for twenty minutes before the captain finally finished and they started out on their tour of the ship.

On as admirably conducted a vessel as the *Meganaut,* the captain's daily inspection amounted to little more than a personal confirmation that everything was as it should be. Some time later, emerging from the extensive kitchens of the boat, Captain Mansfield and the executive officer entered the main dining saloon. As they passed through, the captain noticed Dr. Pons and Mr. Younghusband breakfasting together at one of the small side tables; with a word to Drake, he turned aside and stepped over to wish them a good morning.

'Good morning gentlemen,' he greeted them as he approached. 'No, don't get up, please. I only wanted to say, Dr. Pons, that I wouldn't like you to feel any responsibility for the unsuccessful test I made last night. We were all rather tired, I'm afraid, when we broke up, and I felt some fear that you might have received a wrong impression.'

'That's very kind of you,' Pons answered in some surprise. 'But I can't escape some of the responsibility; after all, it was my theory that served as a basis for the experiment. Younghusband

and I have been discussing it, and trying to define the possibilities that remain.'

'Is that so?' commented Mansfield. 'Well, I must complete my inspection, and as I usually end it at the smoking-room, perhaps we shall have a few minutes then. I should be glad to hear what you think of the matter now.'

Some time later the four met again in the smoking-room. After a cursory look about and a few words with the smoking-room steward, Captain Mansfield suggested that they sit down for a short discussion in the winter garden outside. He led them to a secluded table hidden behind a cluster of high palms in their green tubs, and they all sat down.

'I suppose you haven't very much time, Captain,' Pons commenced immediately, 'so I'll try to put what we have been saying in a nutshell. If we may take it that the Reake-Lyons girl is not aboard, I can see only three possibilities. Either her body was thrown overboard, living or dead, or she fell overboard unnoticed by anyone, or else she jumped off of her own accord. The first of these possibilities you and I dismissed during our earlier discussion. Nothing has happened since to change our view; we know of no one who would wish to dispose of her body any more than we did then, and although you may think me a little obstinate, I am still of the opinion that the main lines of my idea were correct.'

'You think the girl poisoned Smith intending to kill him?' Drake asked. 'I take it you still consider it probable.'

'Yes, I do,' Pons answered seriously.

Younghusband added, 'I think so too, gentlemen. I could not fail to notice during the first few days of the voyage that something was decidedly peculiar about their relationship. In fact, I was foolish enough to say as much to young Gnosens, who took it somewhat amiss. I suspected more or less what the actual situation was. But that's not the point; the point is that underneath their dealings with each other there was an undercurrent of tenseness. It is hard to point to definite instances; but I could feel it all along—well—a sort of enmity, almost. It would come out occasionally in their conversations. I am sensitive to things like that, and I felt it distinctly.'

Mansfield had listened carefully to all in turn. Now he said, 'Of course, Mr. Younghusband, that is corroboration of sorts. It may still be as Dr. Pons thought. But you mentioned three possibilities, I think, Doctor. What are your ideas about the last two?'

'Well, the second alternative was that she might have fallen overboard accidentally. It seems to me that we can dismiss that also. I don't quite see how anyone could very well fall off this boat unintentionally, even if in this case the victim were ill and groggy. Still, you know the boat better than I do, Captain; what do you think?'

Captain Mansfield thought for a moment. 'No, Doctor,' he then replied, 'I hardly think it possible. Assuming that she climbed out of the hospital window as you think, and found herself weak and dizzy on the deck outside, I still don't see how she could fall off the ship. The sun deck and the boat deck next below are the only open decks, and a fall from the sun deck, since it does not extend to the side of the ship, would bring her only to the boat deck. It might injure her seriously, but it could scarcely cause her to disappear.'

'Suppose,' ventured Drake, 'that she had tried to climb into one of the lifeboats to hide herself. If she had tried to do that from the boat deck, she would have had a ten-foot climb above the railings; a dip of the ship might have thrown her off, especially if she were dizzy as has been suggested. In the middle of the night, of course, it is quite possible that no one would have seen the accident.'

'Yes, I suppose there *is* a chance of that,' Dr. Pons admitted. 'Still, I hardly think so. In the first place, she couldn't get food in such a place of concealment, and she must have needed that desperately after a coma of forty to fifty hours.'

'Oh, but she could,' the executive answered. 'The boats are stocked with biscuits, water and brandy every second trip. Of course, she may not have known that.'

'I didn't know it,' said Pons. 'Let's leave it open and go on to the third point, which I had selected as the most probable.' He turned to the captain. 'You will remember that I had guessed this girl to be of a duplex type of personality. Now I suppose that under the pressure of circumstances the girl's dominance came into control of her love responses and caused her to murder her lover. Such a reversal of responses happens more often than might be supposed, but less frequently it occurs that after the crisis is past and the dominance appeased, the love responses resume their rightful place and a period of the bitterest remorse follows.

'Should such have been the case here, all the outward events were calculated to build up the remorse to an overwhelming degree. The drug itself that she took, may have had this sort of effect to begin with, for of course slight glandular changes can produce great effects emotionally. Then the girl recovered consciousness and found herself, drugged and weakened, in the same small room with the man whom she had murdered but who in certain respects had been her benefactor. Under such conditions her dominance would naturally have been at its lowest ebb, and it is quite possible that she was overcome with crushing sorrow and regret. I have treated unfortunate people who have experienced the same situation to a much less degree, and I know how overwrought they can become.'

He paused and Captain Mansfield asked, 'Then you now think she may have repented her action and thrown herself overboard in her grief?'

'Yes,' Pons agreed, 'that is the way it looks to me now. I can imagine her lying for some hours in that hospital room, as her guilt became clearer and clearer to her. Finally she could bear it no longer; she got up, managed to crawl through the window and threw herself overboard. It could easily happen with such a personality as hers and that's about what it seems to me must have occurred.'

'It sounds reasonable enough,' acknowledged Mansfield. 'Of course it all depends upon the accuracy of your diagnosis.'

'Yes, and ordinarily I shouldn't care to risk an opinion on such slight actual knowledge. If we could examine this Miss Reake-Lyons, we could come to a better founded conclusion, but it seems we can't do that. She may not, of course, be a duplex type at all; but if not, then I should suppose her to be a less organized, more unbalanced personality; and in that case her actions would be less predictable but it would be more likely than ever that she might jump into the sea after so drastic an experience as murder.'

To Captain Mansfield the outcome suggested by Pons was far from satisfactory. There was no evidence to prove it either true or untrue, and worse than that, there was no criminal who could be produced and tried at the end of the voyage. He was fair enough to admit that Pons's reasoning was rational, even convincing; the final objection was really that no means of testing it was presented, and in this Pons himself concurred. All of this attitude the captain expressed courteously and regretfully.

'Well,' the doctor suggested when he had finished, 'I must say I feel the same way. No doubt you are rather fed up on psychologists by this time, but there is one more of us who has not yet made an attempt to solve the mystery. Why not ask Professor Mittle?'

Captain Mansfield considered. 'No, I am not "fed up" as you say, although naturally I am disappointed that no one has managed a satisfactory solution. And it may all have happened just as you think, Doctor. But when all is said and done, I shall have to admit that I do not feel able to leave the matter as it stands. Yes, I should be glad to hear the Professor's opinion, if you think he will not mind giving us his time.'

'I doubt,' said Pons, 'if he will present us with a fourth suspect. But I'm sure he won't object to letting us have his advice. There can be nothing wrong in asking his views.'

'I am entirely agreeable,' the captain declared. 'Do you suppose we could find him now? Our trip is almost over and I am anxious to begin at once if there is a new trail to follow,' he explained, touching the bell in the middle of the table.

Dr. Pons supported the proposal and, a steward presenting himself in answer to the bell, Mansfield instructed him to find the Professor and request him to come up to the captain's quarters, if convenient.

'I think it will be better if we go above,' he said, after the steward had left. 'We are becoming a little too conspicuous here.'

For some little time more, however, the captain and his companions continued their conversation. Pons thought he would like to try a glass of light beer and they waited for him to finish it. Just as they were rising, about twenty minutes later, the steward who had been sent to find Mittle, returned. He came up to the table and saluted Captain Mansfield.

'I am sorry, sir,' announced this emissary, 'but I have not been able to find the gentleman on the boat.'

'*What?*' cried the captain. 'Where did you look, man?'

The steward answered respectfully, but it was plain that he had done everything he could. 'I have looked through all the saloons, sir; I have been to the gentleman's cabin and to the cabins of his friends. Then I went about all the decks, sir, paging him, but he is not about.'

Captain Mansfield shook his head in puzzled determination. He found it by no means congenial to be informed of the disappearance. Was it possible that yet another of his passengers had vanished?

'I am going above, gentlemen,' he said. 'Mr. Drake, will you be so good as to see the chief steward at once and direct him to make a thorough search of the boat. Professor Mittle must be found immediately.'

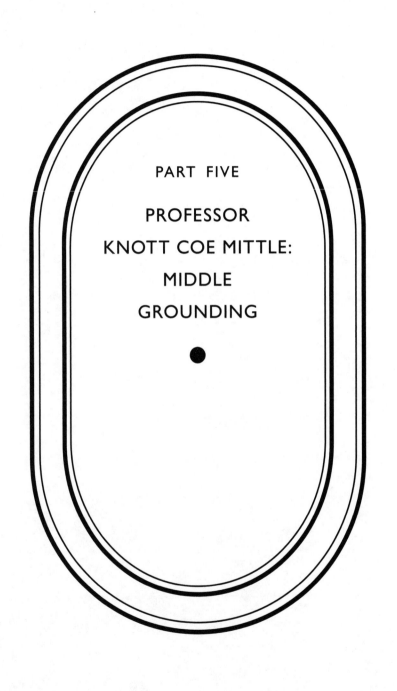

PART FIVE

PROFESSOR
KNOTT COE MITTLE:
MIDDLE
GROUNDING

PART FIVE

PROFESSOR KNOTT COE MITTLE: MIDDLE GROUNDING

'Yes, sir,' said Drake, 'if you'll believe it, sir, he was in the swimming pool all the time.'

'And why shouldn't he be?' the captain demanded. 'The man can't be expected to finish his swim in five minutes, after all.'

'But he wasn't swimming.'

'He wasn't swimming? Oh, I see; he was exercising in the gymnasium.'

'No, sir, nor that either. He was writing his address for the Convention.'

'Eh?' asked the startled captain. 'Writing his address, did you say? And where was he writing it, pray? On the walls? Or in the water?'

'No, sir,' grinned the executive officer. 'The chief steward and I found him sitting on a camp stool banging away at his typewriter, all got up in his bathing suit, right at the edge of the pool. Books piled up all around him in the wet.'

'He must be looney, Drake.'

'Not at all, sir. Trifle unconventional, perhaps. He explained to me that he bothered no one down there, and was undisturbed himself. He says he likes to get away from people when he composes his papers, and also for some reason, he is fond of looking out over water. I believe he tried the sun deck but found it too windy. Papers blew about or something. It all seemed reasonable enough when he explained it. He'll be up presently, when he's dressed.'

Captain Mansfield still appeared somewhat mystified when Mann opened the door and admitted Professor Mittle, but turned to other topics. 'Ah, Professor, there you are. I hope I didn't interrupt your address? I didn't mean you to come up at once if you were busy.'

'Not at all, Captain Mansfield. I had finished, in fact. And it wasn't my address; it was a short paper upon the word association test, as used recently by Dr. Plechs. There were some unusual features. I thought I would note them down, for the future.'

'Oh,' Drake put in, 'then I informed the captain incorrectly. But I'm glad to hear you are interested in our investigations. Captain Mansfield wants to obtain your opinion on them.'

Mansfield confirmed the executive's statement, but the professor's interest seemed to have been fully satisfied by his late notes. 'I am afraid,' he began, 'that it is useless to ask my opinion. While I should be happy to assist, very happy indeed, Captain, I do not quite see what I can do. The other gentlemen have tried their methods, but I judge that they have not succeeded, if the question is still undecided. And to tell you the truth, the matter seems to me to be outside our province. I would really not care to make any claims about it at all.'

'No, no, Professor, you have mistaken my intention.' Captain Mansfield smiled reassuringly. 'I do not expect you to say, "Here is your criminal," or to advocate anyone's immediate arrest. But, as we have not yet succeeded in solving this serious problem, despite everyone's efforts, I thought perhaps you would be willing to help us. Maybe regarding the methods we have so far employed. Would you think our methods have been correct?'

Professor Mittle considered the question gravely. He sat forward in his chair, his elbows resting in his lap and his hands joined between his knees. After some minutes he gave an opinion.

'Any methods,' he stated, 'that lead to a successful conclusion, are good methods for a problem. But if you are asking whether I approve specifically of the special methods employed by Dr. Hayvier, Dr. Plechs, or Dr. Pons, then I must say that I am not a disciple of any of them. There are many controversies in psychology to-day, as you are by now well aware, and most of them will some time be settled one way or the other as sufficient evidence accumulates. In all these controversies I hold a middle ground. I have often been criticized for straddling the issue, but I have asked in return how can I be expected to espouse either side when both sides are wrong and the dispute itself mistaken?

'I would not, however, have you misunderstand me,' the professor continued, uplifting a cautious hand. 'I am by no means opposed to all these contesting "schools" as we call them. Much very splendid work is being done. But while the extremists are nowadays making by far the most noise, 80 to 90 per cent. of all our qualified psychologists adhere to none of their specialized formulas. It is with these middle grounders, if I may so call them, that I would include myself.'

'I see,' the captain commented. 'I take it, then, that you would not recommend any of the special approaches that your colleagues have been employing so far?'

'Oh, yes. If you were to ask me about Dr. Hayvier's viewpoint, for example, I should have to say that I consider it extremist, but I would have no objection at all to his methods of investigation, provided they were suitable to the problem at hand. Dr. Plechs, of course, is a psychoanalyst; and this, I believe, is more a therapeutic than a pure science technique. In psychoanalysis practice has preceded theory; various techniques have been found to eventuate with success, and thereafter some theoretical explanation has been sought in order to account for what has happened. As a result psychoanalytic theory is not perhaps quite as strong as we could wish. But there is much to be admired in psycholanalysis.'

At this moment there was a knock at the door; Mr. Younghusband and Mr. Gnosens looked in enquiringly. Captain Mansfield, recognizing the friends of his murdered passenger, welcomed them silently and motioned them to seats. He then turned again to the professor.

'I see. And what do you think of Dr. Pons's theories, Professor?'

Mittle once more placed his hands gently together between his knees. 'Yes,' he said. 'Pons's theories. Well, Pons's theories are probably the newest of all. It is perhaps too soon to judge of them accurately. From what I know of them, however, I should be inclined to think that they are almost too perfected. All the possible responses and attitudes are carefully diagrammed out in a perfect, logical structure. Even consciousness is smoothly explained in physical terms. In my opinion all that is a little too good to be true. Life, I think, is more complicated than that, Captain; we cannot yet compress it into algebra. On the other hand, I believe of course that Dr. Pons has made some excellent contributions to psychology.

'To conclude what I was saying,' he finished. 'I would use any or all of these different techniques and outlooks whenever they seemed to be indicated by the difficulties to be overcome. My only objection to them in your own case is that they do not seem to have worked. Perhaps no one theory is sufficient by itself. In my own work, for instance, I often use a combination of several methods.'

Younghusband looked up hopefully. 'Well, it's an idea to combine the various theories. But of course each one has select- ed a different suspect. I wonder if we could combine them in some way? Now how could we do that?'

'Let me see, sir,' said Drake, turning to his superior. 'How could we do it? We might begin with the criminal, I think. We might pick a new suspect who combined all the points of each method.'

The captain fell in with Drake's notion without much en- thusiasm. He allowed himself to be carried along for want of any better proposal. 'Let me think,' he considered. 'If I'm right, Hayvier said he must be conditioned to crime, Dr. Plechs be- lieved that he was the sort who was convinced of his own infe- riority, and Pons said that in this case the appetites, no, the im- pulse to dominate, was in control of the love impulses. What we should call the altruistic attitude, I imagine, rather than what we usually mean by love. Well, there you are, Drake; what do you make of it?'

'What do you think, sir?' Gnosens turned to Mittle, while Drake remained in thought.

'Why,' said the latter unguardedly, 'I think it sounds like quite a comprehensive description of the man you are looking for. If you could find such a person, you would probably have him.'

'Dr. Pons believes the crime was committed by a woman,' the captain observed.

'But perhaps,' put in Gnosens, 'that is the part of his theory that is wrong.'

Drake asked, 'And who fits the bill? Why not that man Stander?'

'Stander? Stander?' For a moment the professor did not remember him. 'Oh, yes, now I recall whom you mean. The friend of the man Dr. Plechs examined. . . . No, I hardly think he appeared sufficiently neurotic. Now I should think the other man—Stymond I believe his name was—had more of these qualifications. He is a criminal and all criminals are more or less unbalanced and feel that the world is against them; some authorities maintain that they are people too weak, perhaps too inferior, to make their way in the world except by breaking the rules that bind their competitors. And his whole record is one of violence, if I am correctly—'

Younghusband interrupted eagerly. 'Then you think, Professor,' he cried, 'that Stymond is the criminal? Of course he was examined before we knew the truth; he was innocent of firing the bullets, but no one asked him anything about poison, because we didn't know about it ourselves. He certainly was surprised, too, when we let him off,' the young man went on enthusiastically. 'Do you know, Captain, I believe the professor is right. Stymond is our man. I think we should have him up again and let the professor examine his own suspect.'

'But—but—' spluttered the scientist.

'There may be something in it,' Captain Mansfield was saying. 'Certainly we can have him up again if you wish. Would you care to examine him, Professor? Your man, you know, this time.'

'But he isn't my man!' The professor protested energetically. 'I have not accused him at all. All this seems to me entirely premature. The suggestions have come from those gentlemen,' pointing to Drake and Younghusband. 'I only said it might be that Stymond had such qualifications; I did not say he did the murder.'

'But,' pursued the captain. 'There is some likelihood of it in your opinion, is there not?'

'It is possible, certainly,' Mittle admitted.

'And will you examine him?'

'No, no, my dear sir. Really. I shall have to think this over further. We must not jump to such hasty conclusions. Of course, if you wish, I will confer with the others. I will think the matter over. And I'm sorry, but I must be going, Captain. I have made a luncheon engagement, and I see it is already past one o'clock. You will excuse me, I'm sure?'

'Why, of course. I'm sorry.' Captain Mansfield was apologetic. 'I had no idea it was so late. But you will think about this new idea, won't you, Professor? I wish you would let me know as soon as possible.'

'Indeed, yes, I will.' Mittle got up and was already edging toward the door. 'I will let you know no later than this evening. Well, I really must go. Good-bye.'

'Thanks,' called the captain. 'Good-bye, sir. Don't forget.'

Drake lit a cigarette and inhaling deeply, asked, 'Well, what do you think, sir? Professor Mittle seems a great deal more cautious than the others. But that was a good point of his about the middle ground. He's more broad-minded, too, I guess.'

'As for me,' said the captain, 'I was never in favour of the middle of the road. You go on in supposed security, but sooner or later you get hit from behind. Well, we'll give him this afternoon, but if he doesn't make his mind up soon, I shall have Sty-mond up and question him myself.'

Down below the water line the sailor on guard duty sat sol-itary at his desk outside the steel grille shutting off the confine-ment cabins. An ancient pack of cards, spread out before him, was helping while away the hours of his trick. Occasional-ly he would gather them up, reshuffle them and deal them out once more into the little piles dictated by the game. Once he glanced at the clock on the opposite wall; ten-fifteen, another three-quarters of an hour before his relief would free him for the more congenial, if even deeper, quarters where his friends were doubtless now engaged in their evening round of poker. Behind him the polished rifle gleamed in its rack, not once so much as pressing against the leather guard that held it, so smooth had the sea become with nightfall.

Suddenly he raised his head. What was that? It had sounded almost like a groan. It was not repeated, and believing he had perhaps imagined it, the sailor bent again over the cards and went on with his game.

But no, surely that was some sort of a cry. Weak, but un-mistakable. He got up quickly and stepping to the grille, stood listening. As he strained his ears another groan came from the only occupied cabin within.

'Hey!' called the sailor. 'What's the matter in there? Any-thing wrong?'

The only answer was yet another moan, fainter than its pre-decessor, indeed nearly inaudible.

'Sure, he can't be sick in this weather,' the man muttered. But he unlocked the small steel-barred door, swung it clicking shut behind him and went down the passage to investigate. Approaching the cabin door, he reached for his key, unlocked it and thrust his head inside the darkened room.

'Say, what's the— UGH!'

There was the dull thud of a fall, followed, in a few seconds, by a series of light, rather stealthy noises. . . .

Five minutes later a man in a dinner suit, clean shaven, his hair sleeked back and his left arm supported in an improvised sling, stepped out into the passageway, carefully closing and locking the door behind him.

Before the steel grille Stymond hesitated a few moments, finally selecting the correct key after several mistrials. He walked calmly to the end of the passage, peered cautiously around the turn to the left, and without haste began mounting the right-hand stairway. Behind him he left a complete silence.

The Bridge Officer paced slowly up and down among his instruments. The night was fair, spangled with stars and soft in the haze of the moonlight. Far on the port beam glowed the two white mast-lights of another ship, with a green speck below and between them. Ahead and some points to starboard, the lights of a third ship indicated its gradual approach. The ship on the beam he knew to be the *Moordan,* a freighter for London, for he had just exchanged messages with her; he was not yet close enough to the one ahead for a blinker message.

From behind the officer, interrupting his reflections, came a subdued tinkling, and a tiny bulb spat intermittent flashes from the dark wall of the bridge. The officer stepped quickly over to the telephone.

'Bridge' . . . 'What!' . . . 'Escaped?' . . . 'Right.'

He clicked off the connection. In succession he pressed the little buttons marked respectively 'E.Squad' and 'P.Off.', speaking sharply and shortly into each. Last of all he pressed the larger knob, between the rows of little buttons.

In Captain Mansfield's office and cabin the phones began a shrill clamoring.

'Now, my Doctor,' Madame Sudeau murmured, settling herself comfortably in her chair, 'you will tell me all about those so charming love responses, yes?'

They had just selected a table at one side of the veranda café. A steward approached and they gave their orders. From the ballroom came the strains of the dance orchestra, and from across the café the whooping of an hilarious party of youngsters, all of whom seemed to be under the impression that Swedish punch, which they drank undiluted in highball glasses, was a mild and innocuous beverage. Except for this gathering which was rapidly approaching a state in which they could notice nothing, Dr. Pons and his companion had the room to themselves. Around the open side of the café aft peeped a glint of moonlight.

He leaned over her, lighting her cigarette; she *was* a fragrant girl, no doubt about it. From the tips of her little silver slippers to the top of her freshly waved hair she was a slender masterpiece of seductive, feminine curves. Pons, who could scarcely distinguish an evening dress from a hunting costume (and indeed, in Madame Sudeau's case, the one was, in a sense, the other), was aware to-night that her creamy, white gown gave the *coup de grâce* to every other dress displayed on board. It was very simple; made on full lines and yet it clung in exactly the right places; it was not really cut very low, either in front or in back, and nevertheless it certainly seemed to be. For no apparent reason it made one think inevitably of the very white and polished Madame Sudeau inside it. It achieved, in fact, the distinction of being part of her, in the sense in which a fine rider seems to be part of his horse; it was not just something draped over her, but it partook of her own life and when she moved, it was not carried along, but moved with her. A silvered Spanish shawl, falling off one of her shoulders, disclosed the circlet of pearls, her only jewels, lying against her soft throat, and the faintest whiff of *Nuit d'Amour* drifted from her lips and from behind the pink lobes of her ears.

As he leaned back, 'Don't you think we'd do better on the sun deck, Colette?' Pons suggested.

'No, no.' She smiled and patted his hand; had she been masculine, the pat would have been plainly avuncular. 'I do not think now, my Doctor. It is early yet; but now I weesh so much to learn from you. I 'ave heard you know all about the love. You will tell Colette, yes? I am what you call only the instincts; I know of love, but I do not know why I do—what I do. And I want to know. No, no, I do not play fooling. I mean it, my Doctor. You will tell me?'

'So, you're really in earnest?' said Pons. 'You know, you're always surprising me. What do you care about theories, anyhow? You're naturally captivating, and—'

'Yes,' Colette broke in, 'I know I am captivating. Yes, yes, but what is that, captivating? Really?'

'Why, if you must know, it's active inducement, passive submission.'

'Ah, now you see. But I know nothing of all this. You will tell me, please, what is all this inducement and—and submission?'

'Do you really want to know, Colette? I'm afraid you'll be bored to death.'

'But yes,' cried Colette. 'Of course I want to know.' She shook her dark head vigorously. 'You tell me.'

'From the beginning?'

'Yes, please, I like to hear it all.'

'Very well, then,' Pons said. He was not loath to inform his friend of what he felt was the only correct and normal attitude toward life; far from it, for this was in fact a very particular hobby of his, and Dr. Pons, at bottom, was something of a propagandist, as in fact all men must be who believe themselves in possession of a serious truth. Yet just because he was anxious to make himself fully understood, he hesitated, realizing the difficulty of explaining a complicated and fundamental viewpoint to one who knew nothing of his terms. In the outcome he started in, rather warily.

Briefly, he explained to her that human conduct is response to two sets of forces, those arising within the individual, and those arising without. He told her how this naturally gives rise to four types of response—Dominance, Compliance, Inducement and Submission. In Dominance the person destroys or removes the outside forces that are interfering with him, but in Compliance he is not strong enough to do that and so he has to modify his behaviour so as to yield to them, at any rate in part. In Inducement the inside forces, that is, the person himself, induces the outside forces to co-operate with him, although they are already turned in that direction. Last of all is Submission, the same case except that the outside forces are the stronger and thus the person submits to their more powerful influence.

'Yes,' said Colette, who had become very charmingly serious. 'About the Dominance and the Inducement, I see it. But I do not quite see the difference between what you call the Compliance and the Submission. To me they look like the same, yes? In both cases one must yield, *n'est ce pas?*'

'No,' Pons answered. 'No. This is the difficulty, this is what people do not see at once. The difference is this, perhaps. In Compliance you *must*, but in Submission you are glad to. They are entirely opposite; by Submission I mean *willing* Submission, but Compliance is always unwilling, because you have to. Now do you see it?'

'Yes, my Doctor, now I see.'

'Very good. Now the first two responses, Dominance and Compliance, should be used by the person toward things, but Inducement and Submission should be used toward other persons. This is not because there is anything moral or good about it, but just because human beings are made so that that is the way they function best and most healthfully for themselves. Of course in actual circumstances these four primary kinds of response do not occur in pure form but in various combinations with each other. We see this, for instance, in the love responses; Captivation, which is active Inducement, passive Submission; and the other combination, of passive Inducement, active Submission, that I call Passion. Captivation plus Passion equals love; the first is the typical feminine love response and Passion is typically male. The first is the active phase of love, the second the passive phase, and—'

'But wait,' cried Madame Sudeau, 'wait, wait, my Doctor. This is just what I want to hear, but do you really mean that in love the woman is the active one and the man the passive?'

Pons smiled. 'That is exactly what I mean, and I daresay you, for one, have always known it.'

'Oh, yes, but of course I know it, me. But,' the girl sighed, 'the men, they do not know this at all. And so they spoil everything because they think they should be the great pos—pos—possessors, is it? And all the time that is not what they want, no, not at all.'

'Of course they don't,' the doctor agreed. 'But they have been wrongly taught and they are trying to do what they think is expected of them, even though they make an awful botch of it. At the same time, although no doubt almost all women feel correctly about it, they too have been taught and had it hammered into them that for them to lead in matters of love, which is exactly what they should do, is "unwomanly".'

Colette shook her head. 'But, Doctor,' she ventured, 'I think you are right, but how can we be sure? It does seem that men are really more active than women, do you not think?'

'Toward things, yes, and rightly so. But not toward other people. That is the function of women, to lead in all relationships between persons, and especially between men and women, because they are equipped for that and men are not. Until they do fulfil their function and take the leadership that is theirs, we shall have the stupid, ignorant, wasteful, appetitive world that is making all of us sick. But the difficulty is to find women who possess the intelligence.'

'Oh, but I think we could learn to do it, if they would let us,' Colette said wistfully. 'But still I do not quite see how it is that women should be better for these relations than men.'

'Oh, that.' Pons began to get slightly red in the face. 'Well, you see, the love responses come really from the sexual organization of the body. Mind you, the love *emotions* are not a matter of sex at all; both Captivation and Submission are the same emotions for men and women, but the drive which produces them is far more powerful in women than in men, because of the feminine organism. A man, left to himself, has almost no love drive and very little Captivation; he is built to be always ready to respond with Passion, but absolutely not to be the initiator of a love relationship. Woman, on the other hand, has a periodic drive of a very powerful sort, urging her to exercise her natural Captivation upon the man. That is her function and if it is stultified, she must become in some part unnatural.

'I will tell you,' declared the doctor, 'what is the matter with marriage. The worst fault is not with marriage itself, although there may be some question about that, too, but with the people who enter into it. The courtship period is usually quite natural and normal. The woman captivates her man actively and he responds with fervent Passion. And then they get married, and the trouble begins. The wife is no longer captivatress; she has her man, and though she is not usually cynical about it at all, she has been taught that it is now "unbecoming" and "unwomanly" of her to be over-active in alluring him further. Ignorantly she leaves the active part of their love relationship to the man, who is totally unfitted for it. He can't captivate, but he is as ready as ever to be passionate.

'What happens? His wife no longer captivates him, but sooner or later some other woman does. And there is no use blaming him for responding to these extra-marital advances; he is quite willing to respond at home, but there is nothing, or very little, to respond to. Nature has had no hand in the marriage custom; if he is a healthy man, he will and must respond to Captivation with Passion, and if the Captivation comes from someone else than his own wife, then that is just too bad for his wife. It may not be her fault that she has been wrongly taught, but she will pay the price just as surely as if she inadvertently puts her hand into the fire in the stove. Of course, sensible women, too healthy to be fooled by moralistic propaganda, have always known this, and have held their men.'

Madame Sudeau put down the glass from which she had just been sipping her cognac, inhaled a deep breath from her cigarette and blew it out in a long streamer. 'You are wise, my Doctor. You do know about the love, I can see it. It is, then, that one should captivate and keep on captivating, and all would be well.'

'Ah, but there is more than that, Colette.' The doctor was now warming to his subject. 'There are emotional pitfalls, more fundamental than those of marriage. One of the commonest mistakes is to confuse desire with love; nothing could be worse, for desire is an appetitive emotion and an appetitive response, of an utterly different kind than the love responses. If a person desires to possess another person's wealth or position, or her entertaining company, or even that other person's physically beautiful and seductive body, that sort of thing is frequently called "love". But it is not love and it has nothing to do with love; it is just Desire, the same sort of Desire that one may feel toward jewels or a house, and Desire, when directed toward persons, is unhealthy and vicious.

'That is one error, to mistake Desire and Satisfaction, the appetitive responses, for a true Love response. A Love response is for the benefit of the other person, primarily and without equivocation or ulterior motive; the lover looks for nothing for himself or herself because what he is looking for is someone else's benefit. I am well aware that people are almost ashamed to acknowledge that simple fact and that hoggish, appetitive persons ridicule it as being a far-fetched and "noble" ideal. Cynicism, however, has never yet changed a chemical fact, and it will not now change a biological one; the penalty for ignorance is disease, and the hogs are diseased and unhappy.'

He paused for a moment, but as Colette said nothing and continued to sip her cognac thoughtfully, he went on. 'There are other distortions of the right responses, which I call reversals of the normal relations between the responses in a state of healthy functioning. One is the use of the love responses in order to get something else, usually some material object or else something like position or reflected prestige.

'"Social" marriages are effected upon this basis, but no matter how respectable and stuffy the surrounding circumstances may be, such responses arrange themselves inevitably into the prostitute pattern; in fact, that *is* the prostitute pattern. Possibly you have no idea how general that reversal is, Colette; we call women prostitutes when they take money, but most women take something that is frequently more of a drain upon men than money could ever be. Do you see what I mean by this?'

Madame Sudeau's voice was very low when she answered, and there was a little frown above her handsome eyes. 'Yes, my Doctor,' she replied, 'I know so well what you mean.'

She turned to him impulsively. 'You know, I am not what you call a moral woman, but I see you do not care about that. It is true I have given myself to men, but never, never, I swear it, to a man I did not like. In every affair I have ever had, there has been love, what I have thought was love. But it was not, I see it, so much as what you call the love. And you, I think, are right. Beside the love, there was always something else; and now I do not know, I am not sure—

'Oh, I should be fair!' she cried, almost savagely. 'What is my life? Me, I will say it. It is just a succession of loves, and always they are used for these other things, these other reasons. So it is not love, after all; and really I have always known it. But, but, what can I do?' She finished with the slightest of catches in the low tone of her voice.

'You can pick out the man you care for, or *a* man you care for, and make a success of your relation with him,' answered Pons. 'You have temporary affairs, and that is possibly the only real trouble. Tell me, do you know no man whom you care for enough for that?'

Madame Sudeau did not reply for so long that Pons wondered if she had heard his question. Finally she said softly, 'Yes, I know a boy. He is only a boy, he is five years younger than I am, but he is crazee about me and I, I am very fond of him. He is of Bordeaux and he wish to marry me, but I have thought that is foolish. I have been with him some weeks at Aix, and again at Carcasonne; he is a dear boy, really. But of course his family would, how do you say, throw him off; that did not seem to me sensible.'

'Could you manage to live, could he make a living if he was thrown off, as you fear?'

'Oh, yes, I think. He is *ingenieur*—engineer, and if I encourage him, he could do well, I am sure. He would be glad, he has begged me, often he has begged me. But for me, I love the beautiful things, the clothes, the lingerie, many things, and those I could not have. Nevertheless,' Colette added, 'I do not love those things so much as I care for Paul. No, not nearly.'

'Well,' asked Pons reasonably, 'then what's the matter with that?'

'But there is with that nothing the matter, as you say. It is what I should do. I have thought of it before, and now I am sure. But I am afraid I could never stay just with one man all my life, all alone, and never see the others. There are so many men, and I like so many.'

'Don't worry about that; you needn't be a female hermit. Of course you will flirt with lots of men, you couldn't help it. And there's no harm in it; you may even go further than flirting with some. I'm not a moralist by any means, but there is one thing you must always be careful of, very careful indeed, or you will lose a fortune for the sake of a dime. And that is that you must never have a new affair that will interfere with or injure the old and permanent one, for that one will be, should be, the final basis of your life. Surely you are clever enough for that.'

'But yes, I am clever,' she acknowledged. 'And now I see what you mean, you are right and I will do it. But this is all so different than I thought.' With a vague, but graceful movement of her bare arm she sought to indicate the preceding discussion. 'I came out here thinking to flirt, and now, now, why, everything seems to be changed. Me, I seem to be changed, too. Oh, I mean it, I am decided; I shall marry Paul. But it is all so funnee, this.'

After a moment she continued wistfully and somewhat irrelevantly, 'You and I, my Doctor, we could be very happy together for a little time, do you think?'

'Eh?' Pons jerked up in his seat and, after his first exclamation, fell silent. Then he said quietly, 'Yes, Colette, we could. Very happy. But it would only be temporary, and it wouldn't really count. And especially now. If you've really come to a decision. No, it—it wouldn't do, I'm afraid.'

Colette raised a very serious face to his, and now there was undoubtedly a catch in her voice, as she said so softly that he could hardly hear her, 'You are good. I know you would like to, and I know you do not because it is that you really care for me.

Oh, you are a man, and I—I—I have known only so very few who were men.' She ended with an unmistakable sob, much to the doctor's embarrassment.

'Now, now,' said he, endeavouring clumsily to pat her warm shoulder.

She had bent her head, but now she looked up, full into his face. Her brown eyes, holding the glistening suggestion of tears, were deep and soft, with the softness of rich velvet. The corners of her lips hinted at a coming smile.

'I am so foolish,' she murmured, half-way between a sigh and laughter. 'But you will kiss me, please—just once, yes—'

As Pons leaned over, her arms crept up around his neck. One hand, rumpling the back of his head, pressed his lips gently, but very firmly to hers. Across the cafe the noise of the Swedish punch drinkers continued, but whether they were observed and, if so, with what sentiments, to this neither Colette nor 'my Doctor' gave the slightest thought.

The problem of searching, at a moment's notice, any area as large as that covered by the *S.S. Meganaut*, an area, moreover, split up into hundreds of smaller divisions not only by the various decks but by the many public, semi-public and private apartments of which these decks were composed, presented no small difficulties to Lieutenant Lane and his men. By good fortune he ran into Dr. Hayvier in the ship's library and pressed the psychologist into service at once, as one of the few who were well acquainted with Stymond's appearance.

With his men, their numbers now reduced to half-a-dozen, Lane ascended to the boat deck. Having peered behind all the ventilators and under the canvas coverings of every lifeboat, the party gathered once more at the forward companionway. No sign of Stymond had been discovered, nothing in fact had been accomplished beyond the disturbance of not a few secluded couples who appeared to find the moonlit shadows behind the various structures on the highest deck the pleasantest places on board and to have not the slightest interest in Stymond, either confined or at large.

Now, as they began to descend the steps, Lane could not conceal his disappointment. 'There's nothing for it now but the cabins, I guess,' he muttered to the psychologist who still bore him company.

But just as Lane was calling in the two sailors he had left on guard, there came the shrill blast of a whistle from below.

'Come on,' called the officer, plunging down the next series of stairs. In a crowding mass his companions clambered down at his heels.

At the foot of the stairs stood the petty officer who had been left in charge of this entrance to the promenade deck. 'Down there, sir!' he cried loudly, as Lane tumbled down the steps. He pointed toward the aft limit of the deck. 'There was a man down there, sir; someone spoke to him, and he ran round the corner as fast as he could go.'

'Stay where you are,' cried the lieutenant, and dashed off, followed by the others. Far down the deck a solitary gentleman in one of the chairs looked up, perceived the approaching throng and throwing the rug off his knees, clambered to his feet. It was Professor Mittle, who, espying Hayvier in the forefront of the runners, stepped out to accost him.

'Pardon me,' exclaimed Lane to the surprised scientist. 'Did someone just run around the corner here toward the Veranda Café?'

'Why—er—I was reading,' Mittle replied. 'But I believe someone did just go round the corner. I didn't notice. Perhaps he *was* running. Whisked around quickly, anyhow.'

The entire party surged on, Lane in the lead. The Professor hesitated, then joined himself to the rear of the pursuit.

As they plunged around the corner of the wall that separated the Veranda Café from the outside deck, the lieutenant collided violently with the large bulk of Dr. Pons. His progress was abruptly stopped, and Pons too was severely shaken, and was thrown sharply against his companion. Madame Sudeau uttered a little scream; she clutched at the doctor's arm to save herself from falling, and her evening bag was flung to the deck where it crashed open, disgorging upon the planking a varied collection of small objects. With a quick apology Lane stepped past them and went quickly on into the café.

'Well,' gasped Pons. 'This is an exciting trip. Are you all right, Colette? Nothing broken?'

'I—oh—I—oh. But yes,' Colette also gasped, in very pretty confusion. Already one pink-tipped hand was busy tentatively exploring the state of her hair. 'But look,' she cried, pointing to her feet in consternation. 'It is what you call a mess.' She stooped down and began to gather her scattered belongings.

Both Pons and the professor sprang to her assistance. Lipstick, rouge, a handkerchief, and many other little objects lay about the deck. For some moments all three were busy grovelling.

Pons handed up the mirror. 'Ooh,' wailed the girl, 'but it is broken. That is the bad luck, veree bad.' She gazed in dismay at the surface, in which a diagonal crack had appeared.

'Too bad,' Pons agreed. 'Can't be helped now, though. I'll get you another when the shops open to-morrow. Is that the lot, do you think?'

'Yes,' said Colette. 'No.' She seemed slightly confused. Quickly she probed among the contents, now restored to their places within the silver bag. 'There is one more thing, my friends. We must find it.'

A glint near the wall of the cafe caught the professor's eye. He bent down and retrieved a small object from the floor; he looked at it closely as he picked it up and then unthinkingly handed it to Madame Sudeau.

'Oh, thank you,' said she, taking it in her out-stretched hand. Very calmly and without any hesitation, she walked over to the open end of the deck and threw it overboard. In a glistening orbit it left her hand and dropped down, down, down, into the waves below. Pons and the professor looked on in surprise, and too late the latter realized that, instead of handing it back to its owner, his proper course would have been to drop it into his own pocket.

Colette came back to them as calmly as she had left. 'It is something I wish to get rid of,' she explained. 'Will you be so good to present your friend, my doctor? I do not think I have yet the pleasure.'

As Pons began stammering his apologies, Lieutenant Lane across the café had finished interviewing a lone young man. He turned away in some chagrin, after being assured that this was the passenger who had hopped around the corner into the cafe some minutes previously. 'Saw an old dowager I didn't want to speak to,' the youth had explained, 'and I had to jump quick. She has two daughters and has dragged me up to the Ritz twice already. But not to-night. I'm in hiding. Sorry to have caused all the trouble, but there it is; you can see I'm not the man you're after, I guess.'

Lane could indeed see this, and only too well. Once more he offered his regrets for the disturbance, and prepared to make a round of the deck to see that all his men were still at the proper stairways, before proceeding below. Madame Sudeau and Dr. Pons were taking their leave of the professor, for Colette had decided to introduce the doctor to the restaurant on the sun deck. They disappeared around the corner, on their way forward.

Mittle accompanied them as far as his deck chair, into which he lowered himself and pulled his rug again over his legs. But his book, which had fallen to the deck, he did not recover. It lay disregarded while the professor appeared to enter into a succession of deep and serious reflections. For the best part of an hour he remained motionless, staring out of the windows into the night. At last he appeared to come to some decision; he got up, folded his rug, and started up the deck. His book, totally forgotten, lay abandoned to the mercies of the crew.

Gnosens burst unceremoniously into his cabin, to find a steward from the valet's department engaged in laying out one of his freshly pressed suits across the berth.

'What are you doing in here?' Gnosens demanded hotly. 'I have left instructions that no one, no one you understand, is to come into this cabin. You can give my suits to my steward; he'll bring them in to me when I want them.'

The valet's mouth dropped open at the newcomer's unexpected vehemence. He stared at the young passenger stupidly. 'Why, yes, sir; yes, sir,' he stammered. 'Very sorry, sir, I didn't know—'

'All right,' snapped Gnosens, 'all right. Remember what I said. And get out. You can get out, can't you?'

'Y—yes, sir.' The valet dropped the trousers he had been tastefully arranging on the berth, as if they had suddenly become red-hot, and backed out through the door. Gnosens followed him and clicked the latch over, almost before the door had been closed. Then he stepped quickly over to the wardrobe and tried its doors, his expression indicating relief when he found them to be still locked.

His subsequent actions might well have impressed an onlooker as those of a man who had abruptly taken leave of his senses. Working with obvious haste, Gnosens first unstrapped and opened his trunk. It was practically empty, most of his belongings having been previously transferred to the chest of drawers and the wardrobe; a tennis racket, several pairs of heavy shoes, and other miscellaneous articles were now rapidly transferred to one of the closets. Thereafter Gnosens hastily pulled out all the drawers from one side of the trunk, which was of the wardrobe variety, the other side containing only the empty hangers for his clothes. These drawers he piled in the centre of the floor, and stood looking from them to the porthole in momentary perplexity. It was plain that they were too large to pass through.

Suddenly his face cleared, and he darted to the closet, returning with the tennis racket in its heavy wooden press. With this he vigorously attacked the pile of drawers, swinging his club shoulder high and bringing it down upon them in a series of mighty crashes. Under his blows the thin wood splintered and collapsed at once; within a very few minutes the neat drawers had been reduced to a mass of broken and shivered chips. He conveyed them in handfuls to the open porthole, through which he consigned them speedily to the waves beneath. After a dozen trips they were all disposed of; the hangers from the wardrobe side of the trunk followed them into the ocean, and Gnosens set himself carefully to pick up the tinier pieces of debris.

Five minutes later the now ruined racket had been replaced in the closet, the trunk closed and strapped once more into its rack, and Gnosens, arrayed in his best dressing-gown, was lying on his berth, smoking a cigarette and apparently fully absorbed in the latest sensational novel. There came a rapping at the door.

'Come in,' called Gnosens. The handle of the door rattled, but nothing further occurred. 'Oh, sorry. I forgot it was locked.'

He got up and walking over, opened the entrance. Outside stood an embarrassed steward, accompanied by one of Lane's petty officers. 'I'm very sorry, sir,' began the former. 'We are looking for a man who has escaped from below. You haven't seen anything of him, sir?'

'Not a thing,' answered Gnosens. 'I don't see just how he could be in here, but you're welcome to look, if you want.'

Gnosens received the searchers good-naturedly. He even assisted with a certain eagerness, pulling back the curtains from the closets and swinging back the large doors of the built-in wardrobe. Nothing, however, was to be seen, and with voluble apologies the steward and the sailor left. Immediately they were to be heard knocking upon the door of the next cabin forward; there was no reply to their raps, and in a moment the sound of the steward's key became audible, as he unlocked the door and entered.

Gnosens, however, went back to his berth and became once more immersed in his novel.

★ ★ ★

The door of the darkened broker's office opened and a man stepped out into the small passage leading past it from the lobby to the deck outside. Stymond glanced quickly in both directions along the short alleyway and seeing no one on either side, bent quickly over the lock. For a moment he worked speedily but carefully; there was a slight click, and he returned the bent wire that served him as an improvised skeleton key, to his pocket.

He walked down the passage and stepped calmly out on deck. In his right hand he carried two wicked-looking revolvers, but as they both dangled by their guards from his middle finger, it seemed evident that he had no intention of using them. His next action made it perfectly plain, for he proceeded directly to the window opposite the doorway from which he had emerged, and lifting them through the opening, dropped them both overboard. Leaning out, he saw the two little splashes far below him, where the black water was racing past the side of the ship.

'Just a minute, my man.'

Stymond turned at the voice behind him and found himself confronting the very steady muzzle of Captain Mansfield's automatic.

'Hold your right arm out in front of you, straight out,' continued the captain, for the man's other arm was of course in its sling. 'No funny business now, or you stand an excellent chance of being killed. We shall take no more chances with you this trip, no chances of any kind at all. Find Lieutenant Lane and ask him to report here at once,' he added to the sailor who had run up from the forward stairway.

'I saw you throw those two guns overboard,' Mansfield went on to his prisoner. 'So that won't do you any good.'

Stymond grinned; he appeared to bear no grudge. 'So you saw it, eh?' he responded. 'I didn't get away with it after all?

Well, I tried, and that's that. I know you've got me for the beads and I thought I might get off easier if you couldn't prove I'd had any rods on me. I've never used 'em, though; my lawyer'll get that out of you all right.'

'Do you mean to say you broke loose just to get those guns and throw them overboard?' the captain demanded. 'I suppose you are aware that no one knew where they were.'

'Oh, sure. But you'da found 'em sooner or later. And they got my prints all over them. Sure; I thought I'd better drop them off while I had the chance.'

'And where had you hidden them, by the way? You might as well tell, now.'

'Sure thing, Cap. What do I care, since you seen 'em. I tucked them away behind the board in the office here. There's a little space behind it; you know, where they stick up the gyp prices for the stocks in there. The door was open the night when I wanted to lose them rods, and when I saw the windows was closed out on deck, I just dropped in there. Say, can I put my arm down now?'

'You cannot,' Mansfield advised him grimly. 'Keep it right where it is, if you want to keep a whole skin. I'm not at all concerned as to whether it hurts you or not. In fact I hope it gives you a touch of the headache you gave the poor fellow who was on duty when you got out.'

Stymond sighed and continued to hold out his right arm resignedly in front of him. Fortunately, from the captain's viewpoint, it was now considerably after midnight and only one or two very curious onlookers had gathered before Lieutenant Lane came hastily up from below decks where he had been superintending the search of the cabins.

'Here he is, Mr. Lane,' his superior greeted him with relief.

'Put the handcuffs on him and take him down. Also, I want him kept handcuffed for the rest of the trip. We'll keep him out of mischief from now on. Search him thoroughly, too, as soon as he is returned to his cabin; he has been loose for some time and he may have got something else beside his guns. He didn't throw anything else overboard, however; I'm sure of that. Watch him on the way down, Mr. Lane.'

'Yes, sir,' Lane replied, rather out of breath. He took Stymond's hand, still outstretched before him and brought it down next to its companion, which he pulled out none too gently from the edge of the sling. With his arms thus folded across the prisoner's chest, the handcuffs were clamped about his wrists.

And without further ado he was hustled off by Lane, who at the same time dispatched the men who were with him to reassemble and dismiss the emergency squad. Captain Mansfield walked slowly to the forward stairs and vanished in the direction of his quarters, consoling himself with the reflection that when a voyage had already been upset by so much inopportune excitement, a little more could scarcely do further harm. 'It's about enough, though,' he muttered savagely to himself, 'to do me, and the Line too, for the rest of my life.'

The captain, thought Mann as he served him his breakfast promptly at seven the following morning, was not sleeping well these nights. There was that slightest increase of formality in his voice, too, which was unnoticeable even to most of his officers but which the steward, from his long and close association, could always tell spoke of tenser nerves.

'An omelette, sir; a hot, jelly omelette?' Mann suggested enticingly, as he prepared to clear away the remains of the cereal.

'No,' said Mansfield. 'Oh, yes, all right. And see who's making that row at the door, Mann. There's someone knocking. I don't know who it can be, at this time of the morning. If it's one of those damn psychologists, I suppose you had better let him in right away. I'll speak to him now; I can't let them take up my time from the reports every day.'

The steward returned in a few moments leading Professor Mittle up the short passage to the captain's dining-room.

'Well, well, good morning, Professor,' cried Mansfield heartily, as the latter's face appeared in the doorway; his welcoming tones were more than courteous and to all appearances he was delighted to see his unexpected guest. 'Mann, bring a chair. Sit down; you'll join me? You haven't breakfasted yet?'

'Thank you, that's very kind of you,' Mittle responded, 'but I had a bite in my cabin before I came up.' He sat down beside the captain in the chair the steward was holding for him. 'A cup of coffee perhaps, thank you, but that will be all. I would not have ventured to intrude upon you, Captain, at such an hour, but I have made what I believe is a most important discovery.'

'A discovery, eh? What kind of a discovery?' For the first time Captain Mansfield began to feel that his visitor might not prove unwelcome, after all.

The professor nodded. 'Yes. Yes, indeed. You remember we were discussing the possibility that the man Stymond might turn out to be the criminal you were looking for. After I left you, I devoted some time to a serious consideration of that possibility, but I believe now that I have found a far more likely person against whom I think we would do well to entertain grave suspicions.'

'A new suspect?' asked the captain, now embarking upon the

omelette, while Mittle sipped gingerly at his steaming coffee. 'You mean someone we have not thought of at all, hitherto?'

'As to that, I can't say. You see,' the professor pointed out, 'you have no doubt had many conferences at which I have not been present. For all I know you may have held this person under suspicion for some time.'

'I see. Well, of course I can't tell as to that, until you let me know who the man is.'

'Ah, naturally. But you see, Captain, it is not a man; it is a woman, as I am told that Dr. Pons has already suggested. No, not the young lady who was travelling with Mr. Smith; this is another woman entirely. When I first became suspicious of her, I had the good fortune to encounter one of your detectives, Mr. Bone I think, and I asked him if he could give me any information concerning her.

'It appeared at once,' Mittle continued gravely, 'that this woman is a well-known gambler. Mr. Bone knew all about her and admitted that, except for the unusual circumstances of this trip, he would have been keeping her under closer watch. So here, you see, we have all the qualifications that have been indicated. I am assured by your own detective that these professional gamblers are minor criminals; they indulge, I am told, in sharp practices and have no hesitation in cheating the victims whom they succeed in inveigling into games of chance with them. Here, then, is a criminal, conditioned as Dr. Hayvier would say, to unlawful proceedings, undoubtedly calloused regarding the distinction between right and wrong; and as I have already pointed out, it is held by many qualified students that such people are in fact of the inferior type which Dr. Plechs has told us are to be suspected of the present crime. As to the appetitive predispositions of these gamblers I can see little doubt; I am sure that Dr. Pons himself would agree that they are largely motivated by what he terms Dominance. And in addition, this person is a woman, and for reasons about which I am not as yet entirely clear I am given to understand that there is great likelihood that a woman committed the murder. The other person, Stymond, whom we were thinking of before, is hardly the type to resort to poison, whereas a woman might well find it the most congenial weapon. *A priori* it seems to me that we find the conditions completely fulfilled in this instance.'

'Yes,' said Mansfield slowly. 'Yes, I see what you mean. As you say, it is evident that this woman sums up all the qualifications that have been put forward as applying to the criminal by your various colleagues. However, I am afraid that there are thousands of people in the world to whom such a description might apply equally well. I fear that the mere possession of the characteristics you have listed, is scarcely sufficient to permit us to take action. Or have you reason to suppose that there is some other element in the present case, connecting the woman with the crime? Is there a provable relation between her and Smith?'

A hint of a smile appeared on the professor's face, and it was plain that he was gratified, rather than otherwise, by the captain's objection.

'Quite so,' he answered gently, 'quite so. I should not have considered speaking so plainly, were it not for another piece of evidence that I was fortunate enough to run across late last night. While I know of no connection between the woman in question and Smith, it seemed to me that this evidence was so important as to justify me in laying it before you at the earliest opportunity. As to the other matter, her connection with the murdered man, her actual motive and so on, I suspect that that can be unearthed through the proper investigations. Personally I know little about such proceedings; but since you have consulted me, I felt that I should at least inform you at once of my thought on the subject.'

'You are entirely right about that, sir,' Mansfield declared at once. 'I am very glad you came to me immediately. Perhaps we are at last on the trail. Tell me just what this evidence is.'

The professor cocked his head slightly to one side. He did not, however, hesitate, but went on to say: 'All this happened, I must admit, quite by accident. You see, last night while your men were in pursuit of Stymond on the promenade deck, I chanced to be drawn into the chase and, to make a short story of it, as we came round the end of the deck we ran into this woman and almost upset her. In the confusion she dropped a small bag she was carrying and the contents were spilled out on the floor. Dr. Pons and I helped her to recover these trinkets, and the last one I picked up was of a most suspicious character. I was not looking for anything of the sort and without thinking I handed it back to her; before I could interfere in any way, she stepped to the rail and threw it overboard. I blame myself severely, Captain, for my lack of promptitude; it is possible that a most important piece of evidence has been destroyed in this way.'

The professor's portentous tone of voice, even more than his words, went far to impress his hearer. Leaning forward eagerly, the captain inquired urgently: 'Yes, yes, but what was it the woman threw overboard? It was something definitely connecting her with the crime? It was not—my God, it was not a vial of the poison?'

'It was,' Mittle assured him seriously, 'even more incriminating than a vial. It was a small hypodermic needle, and as I handed it back to her, I noticed that it was half full of some sort of liquid.'

'*What!*' cried the captain. 'And you let her dispose of this right under your nose? Well, it can't be helped now, I suppose; and after all you did see it. I presume you can swear to the character of the object, and that you saw her throw it away. Perhaps Dr. Pons saw it too?'

The professor was doubtful. 'I hardly think so,' he said. 'You see, I gave it to her as soon as I had picked it up and she walked at once to the side of the boat. I am afraid, too, that Dr. Pons would make a reluctant witness; he appears to have struck up a regrettable friendship with the woman, they seemed most friendly together when I saw them last. In fact, they left in each other's company and I believe that they were going to the restaurant on the top deck.'

'You surprise me,' Mansfield asserted, 'I should not have thought Pons the man to be ensnared by an adventuress. You must warn him, Professor,' he added with the suggestion of a smile. 'It would not do for one of you psychologists to be tricked in public. But leave Pons out of it for the present. Now tell me, please, who is this woman? What is her name? It appears to me that she should be questioned at the earliest opportunity.'

'Ah, yes, her name. To tell the truth, I am not certain as to that. Mr. Bone, I am sure, told me it was something like Dubois, but when Dr. Pons introduced me last night, what he said sounded more like Soodo. However, there will be no trouble in finding her; her appearance is striking in the extreme, and your detective already knows who she is.'

'Hm. Well, we shall soon find out.' Captain Mansfield pressed the button beside his plate, and the steward came in from his pantry. 'Mann, I want you to summon Mr. Bone; have him report to me here at once.'

In a surprisingly short time the detective appeared. 'Yes, sir,' he informed them, in response to Mansfield's questions, 'the woman you want is Colette Dubois, but this trip she is calling herself Madame Sudeau. You will remember her, sir; she is the one that that Mr. Rosenblatt complained about last winter. He said she had cheated him at bridge, but there was no evidence and we had to let her go. It seems to me you warned her off the boat.'

'That's right,' the captain admitted. 'I remember the lady very well indeed. So she's back again, is she? A regular spitfire she was, as I recall her. Now, Mr. Bone, I want you to go to her cabin and inform her that she is to come up here at once for some questioning. If she is asleep, wake her up. I want no excuses; I want her up just as soon as she can get here. You understand?'

When the detective had left, Mansfield turned back to the professor. 'Well, Professor,' he said cautiously, having learned that the latter's enthusiasm was easily damped, 'between us we shall put Miss Dubois, or Madame Sudeau, or whatever she wants to call herself, through a little grilling. Naturally the credit belongs to you, and no doubt you will want to ask her a few questions. Perhaps,' he added, endeavouring, almost successfully, to keep any hint of sarcasm out of his voice, 'you would like to subject her to some test, similar to those made upon the other suspects?' Captain Mansfield's interest in psychological examinations, it must be admitted, was becoming academic and theoretical rather than practical.

Somewhat to his relief, Mittle disclaimed any intention of taking blood pressure measurements or delving into reaction times. 'I do not think,' he responded, 'that these methods are particularly applicable to the present case. I think we may take a middle ground, without any special techniques. There is no question that she is a woman and engaged in unlawful pursuits; that covers two points. There remains, perhaps, some doubt as to whether she is unbalanced in Dr. Plechs's sense, and yes, I am willing to examine her on that point. I have,' the professor ventured, 'a small questionnaire; it is simple, just a few questions that will not take long to answer. And it is possible, by a method of scoring these answers, to decide whether the subject is definitely neurotic. If you wish,' he offered, 'I will see if I can find this questionnaire in my trunk.'

'By all means,' replied Mansfield generously. 'Why don't you step down now, while Mr. Bone is getting our suspect? And when you come back, go right into my sitting-room; we will do our questioning there.'

The captain turned back to his interrupted breakfast with renewed appetite, now that some kind of action was in sight, and spent the next fifteen minutes in pleasantly replenishing his physical reserves.

Toward the conclusion of this process certain doubts began to assail him. As usual he had acted at once and without hesitation, but upon second thought it occurred to him that there had been no very extensive grounds for his prompt measures. He remembered Colette Dubois, a professional gambler who had begun working the trans-Atlantic route some five years ago, so far as his information went. Rather more attractive than most of them, he recalled; she was still quite young, probably there had not yet been time for her occupation to stamp the hardened lines of her hand-to-mouth existence on her face and on her naturally friendly disposition. He had reason enough not to forget her indignant repudiation of trickery at cards, when the stout Rosenblatt had accused her of cheating him out of some four thousand dollars. But the man had been able to produce no evidence to support his charge, and another player in the same game, a lean Yankee named Sharp, had observed in disgust that those who couldn't take their losses ought to content themselves with a stake of a tenth of a cent. Sharp, who had easily identified himself as a well-known player at the New York clubs, had actually won a matter of two hundred dollars in the same game; his testimony that he could spot a card cheat at ten miles and that he had not spotted one on this occasion, had carried the day, and Madame Sudeau (then Miss Dubois) had been excused, after giving a short but forceful summary of the captain's character as that of an 'old fool who put the finger into affairs that are not to himself'. And apparently she had paid no attention to his suggestion that in the future she cross on some other ship.

The more he thought of it, with the less pleasure he looked forward to the coming interview. Captain Mansfield was undoubtedly more at home in dealing with men than with undeniably pretty and attractive women, especially when the latter became angry and assailed him with reflections upon his personality. And what had he against her now, he considered with increasing gloom. Only that he felt certain she really was a professional gambler, and that another of those psychologists had built up another more or less plausible case. The captain had to admit to himself that it was a far cry, just the same, from fleecing the wealthy passengers who travelled with him to introducing a deadly poison into one of their drinks. Nevertheless, it was very peculiar about that hypodermic, to say the least, especially when one reflected that its appearance had not initiated, but only confirmed, the professor's suspicions. The captain seemed to recall someone's statement, doubtless Dr. Pell's, that the poison could have been administered by a mere scratch of a hypodermic needle. It might, after all, be just as well to investigate.

On a sudden impulse he rang again for Mann, and sent the steward to summon Dr. Pell. If anything was disclosed concerning the contents of the hypodermic, it would be a good idea to have someone present who could at least guess whether there was any resemblance to the fatal dose administered to Smith.

At length Mansfield got up and went out to the sitting-room. He was none too soon, for Professor Mittle and Dr. Pell were already awaiting him, the former with a printed form in his hand which the captain conjectured, rightly, to be the questionnaire previously mentioned. Madame Sudeau had not hurried; in fact she had dressed in what Bone considered uncalled-for leisure and had insisted that she would not budge an inch until her steward had brought her the tiny, Continental breakfast to which she was addicted. Finally, however, she had declared herself ready, and the detective had found his seemingly endless vigil in the passage outside her door, ended.

At her entrance Captain Mansfield looked up with carefully concealed trepidation. Her appearance was even worse than he had feared. She was dressed in a striking black and white sports costume that set off her dark beauty to excellent advantage; her pleated skirt had vertical black stripes and was topped by a white silk blouse and an open coat of white over which black lightning flashes played in futuristic abandon. A closefitting little white hat, a bright green tie about the open neck of her blouse, white silken stockings and small black and white sport shoes completed her visible apparel. She sat down uninvited in the most comfortable unoccupied chair, and crossed her legs.

'Now,' she said calmly, 'what you want of me, my Captain?

You cause me much disturbance, to get up at the so early hour. But I come because I weesh to oblige. And now, what is it?'

The captain cleared his throat and began in gruff tones. 'In the first place Miss Dubois—'

'My name is Madame Sudeau, Captain,' the lady interrupted him, in perfect soberness. 'You make the mistake to call me by another name.'

'All right,' said Mansfield, 'all right. Madame Sudeau, then. In the first place, this is a very serious matter on which I have called you up here. This is no question of a game of cards, and in all fairness I must tell you that I have several witnesses present who will listen carefully to what you have to say and will therefore be in a position to give evidence concerning it, should that become necessary.'

'But I see that is so,' Madame Sudeau answered. 'I do not yet know, however, what is this so important business of which I should be question'. Perhaps now you will tell me, for it is true I have not played at the cards since, three, four days. And I think, my Captain, you have realize' before this that you have nothing to say to me about those cards. What is it, then, that you wish?'

Captain Mansfield said severely. 'There has been a murder committed on this ship, Madame Sudeau.'

'Well, but me, I know that. Everyone know' it, I think. And what has that to do with me?'

'We think you may know more of this than you indicate. Suppose you tell us where you met Mr. Smith and what you do know about it.'

'But I have never met this Mr. Smith. I know of him nothing at all.' The girl's eyes opened wide with surprise, and a slight flush of indignation began to mount to her cheeks. 'He who say' I know of this man, is the great liar. It is the lie, that. And you wish to put me into a so bad affair! Oh, you are the big fool, just like before,' cried Madame Sudeau. 'Only now,' she added, 'worse.'

'Now see here,' said Mansfield. 'There is no use in your getting excited and abusive. I can see you won't co-operate with us, and I didn't expect you would; but since that is the case, you will have to answer the questions that I intend to have put to you, under penalty of being confined and facing very serious charges when we land. I hope you will see the wisdom of answering properly. Before we go any further, Professor Mittle has a questionnaire to which he wants your replies. Let her have it, Professor, will you, please?'

'Oh,' said Colette, 'that funnee little man. I have met him last night. But let me see what it is, this questionnaire.' She held out her hand and Mittle, looking extremely uncomfortable, passed her the printed form and a pencil with which to fill in the required answers.

Madame Sudeau regarded the paper closely and, it seemed, with growing astonishment. As she read on, a puzzled frown appeared above her eyes, and before she had half finished her perusal, she jumped dramatically up from her seat with Gallic abruptness, crushing the sheet into a crumpled ball in her hand. Her eyes flashed angrily.

'You think I am the big fool,' she cried loudly, while one little foot stamped sharply twice on the captain's carpet. 'But it is you who are the fool. The moon, is it of green cheese? What direction is the North Pole from New York? Bah! I should answer a so silly questions!'

'But those are not the questions at all,' the professor found courage to protest. His face also had become flushed, but probably not from anger.

'No,' Madame Sudeau exclaimed, 'no, those are not the questions. The questions, they are more foolish than that! I would not answer them; they are for the idiots, imbeciles, *bah!*' With a sudden motion she flung the crumpled ball violently across the room, no more than missing the professor's scarlet countenance.

The captain himself picked the paper up from the floor. 'Shall we insist?' he inquired calmly. 'Or do you think this demonstration sufficient, Professor?'

In the short interval Mittle had become himself again. 'I hardly think it will be necessary to go farther with the questionnaire,' he considered. 'No replies could be more unbalanced than the exhibition we have just had. I think we may take it for granted that the purpose has been served already. In my opinion the subject is very neurotic indeed. In fact, I may say that I have never seen a serious questionnaire treated in so abnormal a fashion.' He leaned over and took his paper from the captain's hand, folded it neatly and put it away in his pocket.

'Just as you say,' Mansfield conceded, secretly quite content that the technical test had been finished with and that he could now get on with the straightforward questions.

He looked across at Madame Sudeau, who had resumed her seat; with the hurling of the questionnaire at the professor's head her excitement seemed to have been fully appeased, and she now appeared as calm and collected as when she had entered the sitting-room. She even had the audacity to summon up a smile and to murmur her apologies for having disturbed 'my Captain'.

Mansfield, at a loss as to how to treat these sentiments, passed over them completely and addressed himself to a further catechism. 'Now, Madame,' he continued gravely, 'there are one or two points I want to have cleared up. And first, last evening you were carrying in your bag a charged hypodermic needle; I should like to hear with what that needle was filled and why you were in such haste to throw it overboard after it had been observed by Professor Mittle. Ordinarily, I admit, I should possess no right to inquire into your private affairs, but under the circumstances that have arisen during this trip it becomes my duty to do so, and I must insist upon your answer.'

For a moment Colette hesitated; then she said with a shrug of her slim shoulders: 'Very well, my Captain; I tell you. It is, as you say, not of your affair, but it is nothing dreadful, after all. I have, it is since two year', a sickness of what you say the glands, and the Doctor Miquellet of Paris, he give me the medicine to take by the needle. It is nearly a year I must do this, and so I have a fine needle with silver guards, to carry about with me. But after the year is finished, I like what does the medicine to me, and although it is not that I must do it longer, yet I keep up to take this. *Eh bien*, but last night I have the long talk with the so excellent Dr. Pons, who give to me the good advice, and I decide to change over my life in many way. For other thing', no, *with* other thing' I decide that no more I will take this medicine which maybe begin to be with me the habit. With all that I am now finish' and so, *enfin*, I throw it away. That is all; this so watching *professeur*, he have nothing to do with it at all.' With another shrug Colette concluded her explanation and stared frankly at the captain.

During her remarks Dr. Pell had been leaning forward, observing her as closely as possible from his position on the other side of the room. Now, before the captain had an opportunity to make any comment, he asked quickly: 'What was this injection, or medicine, that you have been taking Madame—er—Sudeau?'

'A drug, do you think, Dr. Pell?' Mansfield put in.

The doctor rose and stepped across to where Colette sat. He

regarded her attentively, bending over to peer into her eyes. 'No,' he said, 'I shouldn't think so, from her appearance; but of course I cannot be sure without more than a superficial examination. Well, Madame, what do you say it was?' he repeated.

Madame Sudeau disclaimed the drug. 'But no, it was not the drug. It was *extrait*, extrac' you say? How do you call it, adren—adrenal?'

'Adrenalin?'

'But yes, that is it. Adrenalin, yes. It give me the good feeling, what you say pep, I think. That is why I take it longer than I need. But now all over.'

Captain Mansfield looked puzzled. 'Would that be anything like the poison that killed Smith, Dr. Pell?' he inquired.

'No, I should say not. Hydrocyanic acid has no resemblance to an adrenalin solution, except perhaps the superficial one that they may both be colourless. In fact, adrenalin is a heart stimulant, and would have quite the opposite effect to paralysing the heart muscles and thus causing death. It would have to be injected intravenously in very large quantity before it could affect a healthy heart; and I have great doubt that a single injection in any strength could kill. By the way,' he turned back to Colette, 'what was the strength of the solution you were using?'

'It was, I think, one twentieth grain in five *centimètres* of water.' She appeared considerably bewildered by the turn that the conversation was taking.

'Weak,' said Pell.

'But I suppose any liquid substance could be squirted from a hypodermic into a drink just as easily as it could be injected into the arm?' It was Drake who asked this.

Dr. Pell started to answer, but before he could get out a word, Madame Sudeau cried briskly: 'What do you think now? That

I poison the *Monsieur* Smith? But that, it is silly. It was not the poison, what I take; I take it since two years and it hurt me not at all. There was nothing else, only this adren—adrenalin. Oh, you are all the foolish ones. See, you look; you send this Mr. Noseymans to my cabin now, at once. There is still some of this medicine in my dressing table that I have not yet throw away. He will bring it and you will see; he will look also for something else while he is there, and he will not find it. Go ahead, you; go now.' She pointed imperiously to Detective Bone in the background.

The captain nodded. 'All right, go along, Mr. Bone. And have a good look around, don't hurry. Perhaps you had better let him have your keys, Madame Sudeau, if you have locked up your things.'

'No, it is all unlock' now, because I hurry to come up here,' Colette informed them. 'Now,' she said, when Bone had left, 'this is all the great nonsense. I do not know the Mr. Smith what is dead, and if I have all the poison in the world, yet I am nowhere near to him that night and I could not put it into his drink. He sit down the room near by the main door and me, I am by the other door, far away. So you see, all that, it is the foolishness.'

'Hm,' said Captain Mansfield, 'that is a point, of course. But did anyone see you there, Madame? Can you prove your statement?' He looked around the room, but no one present, except Dr. Pell, had been in the smoking-room on the night of the tragedy.

'Bone was there, of course,' Drake commented. 'Perhaps he can tell us when he returns.'

'But yes, he will tell you,' added the girl. 'He watch me much, that foolish man. And I make the high bid that night just as the light' go out; one thousand dollar' I bid for the number of Mr. de Brasto. He will remember that. But of course I do not get the number, for the pool, it is call' off, after all.'

'So you're the one that made that bid,' said Drake. 'Why did you make so high a bid?'

'Me, I will tell you,' Colette said earnestly. 'It is true I gamble much when I cross on these boats, and the people who know to gamble, they know very well that the luck, it is a real thing. For me, sometimes I have it and sometimes I do not have it. This I *feel*, very well. And so, when I do not have it, then I follow someone who always have it and never lose. Such person is the Mr. de Brasto, but only somewhat; for the real luck that never fail, it is the Mr. Smith that have that. Wherever he turn, there is the money for him. I see him in the pool since we leave New York, and always he win; if he did not win the pool, then he sell his number for much profit the next day.

'So that night,' she explained, 'I do not feel that the luck is with me, and I do not bid for the numbers. But at last both the Mr. de Brasto and the Mr. Smith they bid up very high for the same number. At once I have the hunch; I feel that this number, he will win. So I make the high bid to get it, and just then it become' dark. After all it make' no difference what I have to pay, because this number, it will win anyhow. Also,' she concluded calmly, 'the next day I look on the log, and of course there is the number. But *hélas,* it do me no good.'

'Well,' said Drake at last, 'what do you think of that?'

The professor found his voice for the first time since the catastrophe to his questionnaire. 'It is not at all improbable,' he informed the company. 'Her type often feel that way. Naturally it is mere superstition. The fact that the number did come out is only a lucky coincidence.'

'But of course,' cried Colette triumphantly. 'That is just what it is, the lucky one.'

At this point Bone re-entered, bearing two small bottles, both of which were properly labelled as adrenalin solutions. Having handed these to Dr. Pell, he acknowledged that he had searched thoroughly but had been unable to find anything else of a suspicious nature. The physician took them and gave it as his opinion that they appeared to be genuine, but added that he would have them analysed at once. There was no doubt, he added, that neither of them contained hydrocyanic acid. Thereupon Mann was dispatched with them to the hospital, with the corresponding instructions to the doctor's assistant.

'Now, you Mr. Detective,' said Madame Sudeau, 'you think well. You remember the night in the smoking-room when the Mr. Smith, he is kill'?'

'Sure,' admitted Bone with a grin.

'Yes. Well, you remember also about me, that I was there. But now you tell them where it was that I sit, and how I make the big bid of one thousand dollars when the light go out. Go on now, you tell.'

The detective looked surprised, and glanced around. 'All right, Mr. Bone, where was she, if you remember?' the captain encouraged him.

'Why—er—why, she was sitting off to one side from me, right by the port door. I remember spotting her when I came in. And she must have made that bid all right. I remember it now, but it had gone clean out of my head, what with all the other things that began to happen right afterwards. Yeah, I recall now, I meant to remember who made that bid, and then I forgot all about it. Sure, that's right, Captain.'

'You see,' cried Colette. 'I was there by the door when it become dark and I could not to run all the way across the room and do anything to the Mr. Smith at that so confuse' time. So now you see.'

Neither Captain Mansfield nor any of the others could very well fail to see the cogency of Madame Sudeau's assertion; and when Mann brought back, a few minutes later, the report that the two bottles did indeed contain nothing but a harmless adrenalin solution, he felt convinced that for the fourth time the investigation had been barking up the wrong tree.

With a wry smile he turned to Mittle. 'Well, Professor,' he considered, 'your suspect appears to have turned out no better than the others, after all.'

'But, Captain,' protested the professor, 'I must protest. This lady was never my suspect, as you call her. I have accused no-body of this serious crime, nor do I intend to. I only offered to help examine her, if you wished, as a possible suspect, and it seems unfair to me that I should now be alleged to have accused her. By no means, I assure you; on the other—'

'Never mind,' said Mansfield, 'it's of no importance, any-how.' With some difficulty he concealed his surprise, for he had certainly been under the impression that his present sus-pect had been proposed by the psychologist. 'At all events, I can see nothing to do now except to offer Madame Sudeau our apologies for the annoyance we have caused her, and to excuse her at once.'

Madame Sudeau rose immediately and took her leave with the brightest of smiles. 'It is all right, my Captain,' she assured Mansfield from the doorway. 'I see that you have troubles about this trip, and I do not mind. Once more you make the mistake about me, but I am quite happy now and I do not make the complaint. I say farewell then, and I wish you the better fortune for the future.' Professor Mittle followed her out, leaving the captain with Drake, Dr. Pell and the detective.

Mansfield, once the professor had departed, made no pretense of concealing his disappointment. 'Gentlemen,' he pronounced disgustedly, 'I have made a great mistake in relying upon these psychologists. I should never have handed it over to them to begin with. What have they done? Nothing at all, in the net result. We have had four different and separate suspects produced, and each proposal has come to nothing. Four days or more have been completely wasted, and we are no further forward than the morning after the murder.'

'But I thought, sir,' Drake put in, 'that you had become very much interested in the theories of these men. And you know, it is only fair to remember that they did not volunteer of themselves; in fact, if I am right, they all said that they did not feel able to promise any definite results.'

'Of course, of course,' repeated the captain, almost testily. 'I am really the one who is to blame in the whole matter. As you very properly point out, they have done their best, and even warned me beforehand. I was rather foolishly impressed by them, and I have no doubt that is what makes me angry. Well, there is no use in wasting further time in vain regrets. The fact remains that one of the most prominent men in America has been killed on board the *Meganaut* and that we still have no idea at all about who did it. Moreover, to-morrow morning we reach Cherbourg; we have wasted our time, that's all there is to it, and now at the last moment we must take counsel and see if there remains anything that we can do to retrieve our mistakes. I do not mind telling you gentlemen that I am extremely discouraged. If there is anything you can suggest, I should be very glad to hear it.'

Finally Drake ventured: 'Well, sir, I'm afraid I have nothing definite to propose this minute. As far as I can see, I think the best thing is to call a conference as soon as possible, get everyone together that you wish to include and see if among us we can hit upon something. It's getting rather desperate now, I think myself.'

Captain Mansfield listened to the executive officer's remarks, and then spoke with renewed decision. 'You're right, Drake. We have very little time left now. I shall call a conference to convene here immediately after luncheon. Let's see now; I want you and Dr. Pell and of course Mr. Bone and Mr. Heddes. I think we will dispense with outside assistance now, but it might be well to include Mr. Gnosens and Mr. Younghusband. I think that's all for the present, gentlemen. Come with me, Mr. Drake; after all, we must see to the *Meganaut* every now and then.'

He stood up in a gesture of dismissal and left the room immediately, accompanied by his executive officer.

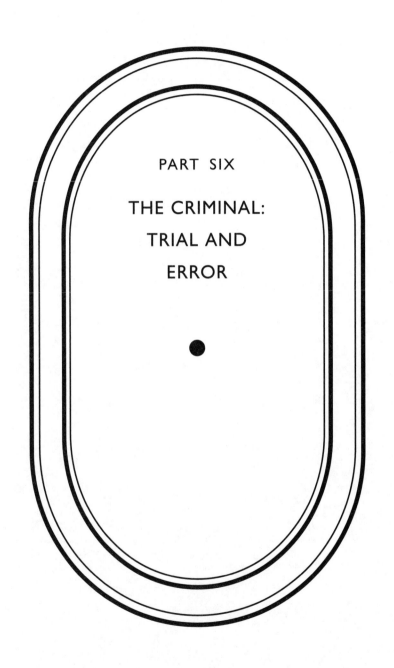

PART SIX

THE CRIMINAL:
TRIAL AND
ERROR

PART SIX

THE CRIMINAL: TRIAL AND ERROR

'DAMN IT, Drake,' Mansfield muttered, pacing up and down his sitting-room, with his hands clasped behind his back, 'to-morrow morning we'll be in. And nothing accomplished, absolutely nothing. We've succeeded in dismissing four different suspects and in getting one of them killed off, mainly by reason of our suspicions; not a record to be proud of.'

Drake understood his proper role in the circumstances well enough; he endeavoured to look upon the other side of the matter. 'Oh, I don't know, sir,' he contributed. 'It's not as bad as you think. After all, we have recovered a very valuable necklace, we have Stymond for the theft, and we will undoubtedly secure his conviction. Also we have disposed of the rabid criminal who murdered de Brasto. No one can say that crime exactly flourishes on the *Meganaut* or that we don't take prompt and effective measures against it.'

'Can't they, eh?' Mansfield growled. 'Just read that and see if they can't.' He fumbled in the pockets of his uniform and finally produced a radio sheet. 'Headlines from the New York and

London papers of the last several days,' he explained, handing it over to his companion.

Drake took the well-covered sheet and ran his eyes over a sufficiently disturbing assortment of titles. With more verve than accuracy they followed the recent course of events in mid-Atlantic.

NOTED FINANCIER SLAUGHTERED AT SEA

V. T. Smith Succumbs to Assassin's Bullet in Smoking-Room of *Meganaut.*

PSYCHOLOGISTS AS SLEUTHS

Take Field Against Murderer of American Crœsus. Promise Quick Results.
Coming to Convention Here.

NO PROGRESS IN SEA MYSTERY

Killer of Victor Timothy Smith Still at Large.
Market in Severe Break. Later Recovery.

OCEAN HORROR

Smith's Murderer Sought in Vain by Psychologists.

ANOTHER MURDER ON MEGANAUT!

New York Attorney Slain by Gunman's Bullet.
Quick Action by Ship's Officer Fells Assailant.
Passengers Frantic.

MEGANAUT MYSTERY

Further Deaths.
Gangster and Victim Die in Second Shooting Affray.

MEGANAUT MURDERS UNSOLVED: DEATH SHIP NEARS PORT

Psychologists and Special Investigators Completely Baffled.
Orgy of Death Ending in Escape of Bloodman.*
Authorities Refuse Comment.

* (Pictures of floating tomb and murdered prey will be found on page eight of this issue.)

There were other headlines in a similar vein, a particularly offensive one announcing the 'Panic of Passengers', but Drake felt he had seen enough. His expression as he looked up, was both angry and puzzled. 'But where could they have got it?' he asked. 'No one in authority would have given out such—such damned trash.'

'Of course not,' assented the captain. 'Some smart passenger did it, of course. A self-constituted reporter on the spot. People will do anything for a few dollars and a little notoriety. Needless to say, I have tried to locate the person responsible. And naturally the messages themselves bear little resemblance to what these newspaper writers have turned them into. Oh, well, let's forget it for the present.'

Captain Mansfield crammed the offending radio sheet back into his pocket and took several more turns about the room. 'I go over and over that list of suspects,' he confessed, 'and I always come to the conclusion that they must all be innocent. Except perhaps the Reake-Lyons girl, and we know she is no longer on the boat. I can't get over the feeling that we have the criminal right here somewhere, if we only knew where to put our hands on him.'

'You know, sir,' Drake considered, 'of all the people who had an opportunity to poison those drinks, it seems to me that we have paid singularly little attention to the two men at Smith's own table, that is, Mr. Gnosens and Mr. Younghusband.'

'But what more can we do?' The captain's objection seemed fully justified. 'You've seen the radio reports on them yourself. Younghusband does come from Chicago, just as his papers testify—has been known there for some years as a minor contributor to journals of opinion. Nothing very suspicious about that, and no hint that he ever saw Smith before the meeting he himself describes as taking place in Chicago only a few weeks back.'

'Didn't our report say he was married?'

'Yes, he is married. I asked him casually and he told me his wife had had a breakdown and was now recuperating in some sanatorium in the Middle West. I have no reason to doubt that, any more than the other items he has told us and which have proven true. As for the Gnosens boy, he comes from a family living on Long Island, apparently quite well known; he is a recent graduate of Harvard University and belongs to all those clubs in New York. He told us that and it was all corroborated. I must say I cannot see any grounds for suspecting either of them.'

'Still they did have the best opportunity of all,' Drake insisted.

'Perhaps they did,' replied the captain. 'But we can't arrest them for that.'

'Just the same, I think we ought to have their cabins searched; we could do that, at any rate.'

'I don't think it's the least use now, Drake. But if you want, we'll have it done while they are up here for our conference. I'll have Heddes do it.'

The captain hastily scribbled a note to his detective, rang for Mann and sent him off with it.

'You seem to have a hunch about this,' he remarked. 'But to me, I must confess, both those young men appear to be just what they claim. By the way, I don't suppose you object to having them at the conference?'

'No,' the executive replied, 'I don't. Besides, it will keep them both here while their state-rooms are being searched. After all, I have no more reason to connect them with the crime than you have. It only seemed to me that they had rather escaped attention, that's all.'

'I see. But that's only because there has been no reason to pay much attention to them.' Mansfield pulled out his watch. 'It's time they were getting here now. I—'

As he spoke, Dr. Pell knocked and came in; and while he was still selecting his seat, Younghusband and Gnosens entered together. A few minutes later Detective Bone put in his appearance, and the captain looked gratified.

'Gentlemen,' he greeted them, 'I'm glad you are all on time. Just sit anywhere that suits you and we will get right down to business, if you are willing.'

'Now,' he continued, when they were all seated, 'you know, of course, the purpose of this conference. We are still searching for the murderer. We have as yet no substantial clue to his or her identity, and our time draws to an end. To-morrow morning we reach Cherbourg, and for all we know the criminal will then make good a final escape. I have called this conference in the hope that we can hit upon some means of action before it is too late.

'You are all aware, I think, of the succession of accused persons. All those accused have either been cleared or are dead, and we have yet to find the actual criminal. I should be very glad, gentlemen, if among you any suggestion can be offered for proceeding further in our search.'

For some time after the captain had ceased, no one came forward with anything definite. They were desultory remarks, leading nowhere in particular, and only the vaguest of suggestions as to some unknown criminal among the passengers in the smoking-room on the fatal evening. Finally Captain Mansfield turned to the two passengers present.

'Will you two gentlemen please try to remember everything that happened at your table that night, either before or after Mr. Smith was killed, that was in any degree at all out of the ordinary?' he begged them. 'Never mind whether it has any evident bearing on the crime or not; was there anything at all that struck you as peculiar in any way?'

'If there was,' said Gnosens at once, 'I didn't notice it; I saw nothing at all out of the way. But,' he hesitated, 'there was something unusual that happened to me afterwards. But I don't see how it could be connected with the crime in any way at all; and I hardly think it's worth mentioning.'

'Never mind that,' Drake urged him. 'It happened afterwards, you say? What was it?'

'I found a rubber ball in my pocket that I had never seen before.'

'A rubber ball?' The captain's tone was one of disappointment.

'Well,' Gnosens smiled. 'I only mentioned it because you asked about anything unusual. It was nothing but a little rubber ball, like those that children bounce on an elastic; but the elastic had been broken off, leaving a little hole where it had been attached. I found it while Bone was searching me afterwards. It was unusual because I'm positive that I had never seen it before and I hadn't the slightest idea how it got there.' He turned to the detective. 'You remember, I told you about it at the time?'

Bone nodded his head. 'Sure,' he said, 'that's right. But it was nothing but one of them little hollow rubber balls like he said. I couldn't see anything to it then, and I can't now.'

'And what did you do with it?'

'I don't know,' Gnosens replied. 'I meant to throw it away, but I don't remember doing it, and now I don't know what became of the thing. I don't see, though, what it can have to do with what we are trying to find out here.'

'No, I don't either,' said Mansfield. 'And you're sure that that is the only unusual thing of any kind you can remember? And you, Mr. Younghusband?'

'No,' Younghusband answered, 'I can't remember a thing. What I want to say, Captain, is this. There has been no evidence of the innocence of the girl who was travelling with Mr. Smith. She has vanished, but that is not proof that she did not commit the crime. Rather the opposite, I should think. The fact is that she is the only suspect left out of all the original ones; and doesn't that in itself go a long way to show that she is the criminal? It seems to me that Dr. Pons's theory remains the only one against which no testimony nor any evidence has been brought. I must admit that I am afraid the girl did it.'

'I think that's the silliest theory of the lot,' began Gnosens, and then stopped suddenly, as a subdued roar broke out overhead. 'What's that?' he asked.

Drake answered him. 'That's the mail 'plane,' he said. 'Leaves at two-forty-five. Sounds like the final warming up; it will be off in a few minutes now.'

A curious expression of relief spread momentarily over Gnosens's face, but it vanished so rapidly that of all those present only Younghusband and Dr. Pell noticed it.

'To tell you the truth,' Gnosens went on at once, 'an idea has just occurred to me. If you will let me work it out for a few minutes, I think I can tell you something.'

For a space of some thirty seconds they sat in silence, while the roar of the mail 'plane rose and diminished and rose again overhead. Then—

'How long do you want?' snapped Younghusband suddenly. 'Till the 'plane goes? My God!' he cried. *'The 'plane!'* Without warning he sprang out of his chair and rushed for the door.

Gnosens lunged after him, but he was the fraction of a second too late; instead of seizing the other's coat as he intended, he brought up with a crash against the frame of the door. 'Stop him!' he yelled, and flung himself down the passage from which Younghusband had already disappeared.

For an instant the others sat stupefied in their chairs. Then Drake and Bone, the first to recover, jumped up and dashed after the fugitives.

'What gets me about this whole thing,' announced Hayvier disgustedly, 'is the ease with which it was accomplished. The plain fact is that this murderer is even now, while we discuss him, still within a couple of hundred yards of us. He picks out probably the most prominent man on board to kill, and he doesn't do it in a secluded state-room but actually in public, in full view of several hundred people. Some of us, Pons here for example, saw the thing done right under our noses, but none of us, nor anyone else, has an inkling either as to who did it or how. If you ask me, I call it humiliating.'

They were seated around one of the centre tables in the lounge after luncheon, while Dr. Plechs and the professor took their coffee. Pons had ordered a benedictine with which he toyed rather absently. The big room was fairly well filled and down at the end the orchestra provided the usual early after-noon concert.

'To me,' said Plechs, putting down his cup, 'it seems, as always, that you look too much to the exterior circumstances, Doctor. I agree with you that they were not of advantage to the man we seek, but it is not from them that his identity will be disclosed. All such things are a matter of the psyche. The criminal is as well hidden as if he were in New York or Berlin, because we know nothing of the interior histories involved.'

Pons took up the discussion next, after first sipping his benedictine and lighting a cigarette. 'To a certain extent I think you're both right, but it's still true that both your approaches were tried and that neither succeeded. Oh, I know,' he hastened to add, 'I'm in the same boat with you, except that my candidate has disappeared. But I may as well confess that I still think she was the central figure in the affair and that she really poisoned the man.'

'Much too complicated, that theory of yours,' Hayvier grunted. 'I think her body was thrown overboard. A highly conditioned criminal wouldn't balk at that for a moment.'

'Well, you failed, too, Professor,' continued Pons. 'What is your idea of the whole matter now?'

Professor Mittle, leaning back in his chair and having finished his coffee, regarded the others with an inclusive smile. He said: 'I didn't want to have anything to do with it in the first place, because I don't think we are yet able, as psychologists, to attack these problems off-hand. Nevertheless, I was finally persuaded to try to help, and I proceeded on a theory of my own as well as the idea that all of your attempted solutions were partly right and partly wrong. As you know, in my opinion we ought never to have allowed ourselves to be drawn into it. But we were, and although I do not think we have raised the prestige of our science especially as a result, I guess no very great harm has been done. We can do very little indeed as yet; for some time in the future we ought to work quietly and keep out of notoriety as much as possible. Naturally I hope that in the end we shall build a science capable of handling far more complex problems than the present one and at a moment's notice.'

The professor, whose throat had dried during his speech, stopped and poured himself another demi-tasse from the pot before him, as Dr. Hayvier glanced at his wrist-watch and suddenly exclaimed, 'You know, if Pons wants to see the airplane go off, we had better be getting up above. It's scheduled to leave in fifteen minutes now.'

Allowing Mittle no more than time to gulp down his second cup, they all got up and, proceeding outside, began their climb to the highest deck. On their arrival they found the sun deck already crowded with several hundred of their fellow-passengers. Ropes had been stretched, confining the onlookers to that part of deck away from the catapult mechanism, at whose rear the 'plane once more rested on its movable launching cradle. The propeller was turning over slowly with a series of popping explosions and as the four scientists came up the last steps to the deck level, the two aviators were just climbing into the cockpit. They settled the goggles over their eyes, inspected the dials on the panels in front of them and began testing the motor controls, while the mechanics swarmed over the catapult framework trying the control wires to the wings and tail.

One audacious youth balanced precariously on the rounded top of a ventilator; and the permanent carriage for the 'plane, at the forward end of the deck, was covered with spectators. When the psychologists finally emerged from the stairs, the crowd was so dense that they found it impossible to move further; after some manoeuvring they ended jammed against the after extremity of the restraining rope, facing the present position of the 'plane, with the outboard section of the catapult almost over their heads. And there they stayed.

The motor of the 'plane roared until the machine quivered and strained against the catch holding it to its carriage, like a leashed bird anxious to begin its flight; the noise sank, then increased once more, as the pilot eased the throttle down and again opened it.

One after another the mechanics completed their inspections and climbed down to the surface of the turntable. An officer blew a shrill whistle and motioned to the sailor in charge of the flag, who turned a small lever beside him. Down came the staff with its fluttering pennant, and the runway was clear.

It was just then, as the officer was raising his whistle for the final blast, that a commotion arose on the stairway behind the psychologists. Someone was dashing up madly from the deck below and crying in a frantic voice, 'Stop the 'plane!'

The roar of the now fully opened motor drowned his cry from all except those nearest to him, and when he reached the deck, he was still unheard by anyone in charge. Younghusband, without the slightest pause, sprang at the line against the rope and began clawing his way through. With a final push against Hayvier's hips, that sent the latter violently against Pons, who was next to him, he rolled under the rope and, scrambling to his feet, rushed across the open space toward the officer, before any of the surprised sailors within the enclosure could stop him.

Even as he ran, the officer's whistle cut through the noise of the motor, and he signalled to the men at the tanks. The 'plane slid smoothly forward, so smoothly that its acceleration to forty miles an hour in the distance of comparatively few feet was scarcely perceptible to the spectators, and it was launched into space.

Younghusband had despairingly caught hold of the shoulder of the astonished officer and was gasping into his ear. Meanwhile Gnosens had pushed his way into the space surrounding the catapult, closely followed by Bone and Commander Drake. They came up together to the two on the turntable. The officer turned at once, with evident relief, to Drake.

'He says there's a stowaway on the 'plane,' he explained incredulously. 'He got here just as it left.'

'There is,' gasped Younghusband.

'You're crazy,' cried Gnosens.

'We'll see,' said Drake.

It was a moment for quick decision, and the executive officer was equal to the occasion. A few strides took him to the side, where he glanced quickly at the sea; then he turned and ran for the engineer's office aft, into which he burst without ceremony and seizing the telephone on the wall, spoke hurriedly to the bridge.

Far astern, the 'plane was now circling, as Drake knew it would, to pass the *Meganaut* at a low altitude for the benefit of the passengers and to receive their final acclaim as it whirled past them on its flight ahead of the ship. Now it had turned and was rapidly speeding toward them from astern.

Hardly had Drake put up the receiver than the *Meganaut's* great whistle began emitting a series of short, staccato blasts. Broomp, broomp, broomp, broomp, broomp, broomp, broomp, broomp, the sharp sounds came tumbling across the deck. The aviators of course could hear nothing behind the thundering of their motor, but they could see the little, successive clouds of steam escaping from the whistle. Moreover, as they approached, two rockets, released simultaneously from either end of the bridge, soared upward and burst far overhead, throwing their tiny red lights into the sky.

The passengers, not yet realizing what was afoot, immediately perceived the effect of these phenomena upon the 'plane. As it swept past the stern, scarcely above the level of the sun deck, its nose tilted sharply upward and it began to climb. As it climbed, it turned, and at what might have been about a thousand feet, banking steeply, it continued to circle above the ship. At this moment two further rockets were fired, bursting in plain view of the aviators above.

At once the 'plane dived and straightened out again, began circling for a landing on the sea. At the same time the *Meganaut*, with engines reversed, came to a stop; and shortly afterwards the 'plane glided down, bounced off one wave and, in a shower of spray, settled on the water and taxied toward the ship. About fifty yards to leeward its motor went dead and the aviators, pulling off their helmets, stood up and gazed inquiringly toward the boat.

Commander Drake had already reached C deck, where he ordered the steel doors forming part of the side of the ship to be opened, as was done when the *Meganaut* received or discharged passengers. Standing in this opening, he called through a large megaphone to the airmen, 'We have information that you have a stowaway on board!'

After several repetitions it was plain that the aviators had understood. The man in the rear cockpit bent down and was opening the partition that separated his seat from the mail compartment behind it. He pulled out a few mail sacks, then bent down lower still and peered within. Further sacks followed the first, until his comrade in the front cockpit was entirely surrounded by them. Finally the aviator straightened up and proceeded to open the trap door in the top of the fuselage behind the cockpit. He remained with his head lowered through this aperture for what seemed a long time, but at last he wriggled out. And presently another head appeared in the opening. The owner of this head he assisted into his own cramped quarters, whereupon he commenced waving vigorously toward the *Meganaut*.

In a short time a small boat had been lowered and was putting out to the 'plane. But all this had taken time, and Pons with his companions had long since hurried down from the sun deck and joined the throng of passengers who were leaning out of the opened windows on the starboard promenade. They saw the boat reach the 'plane and they saw the very small man who had attempted to stow away with the mail, climb down into it.

As the boat pushed off and began its return journey, Pons persuaded the passenger next to him to lend him his glasses, which he immediately trained upon the disconsolate figure crouching in the stern of the small boat beside the petty officer. For some time he could make out nothing, but as the distance decreased, the figure of the detected one turned slightly and its face sprang sharply into focus.

'Well, by heavens!' Pons shouted suddenly to Hayvier and the others who were just behind him. 'That's not a man at all; it's a girl. And it's my suspect!'

They all craned forward, and the boat was now so close, almost beneath them, that its occupants were easily distinguishable. No one could mistake the figure in the stern for a man, despite the enormously oversize coat and trousers in which it was garbed. The blonde hair, disordered as it was, was unquestionably a girl's and the face that was looking reproachfully up at the towering side of the *Meganaut,* possessed the beauty that had focused all eyes upon it on the night of the murder in the smoking-room.

'But—but—but,' cried Dr. Plechs, while the professor contributed a pair of 'well, buts' and Pons, after his first exclamation, was speechless.

Dr. Hayvier was the first to comment rationally upon this totally unexpected discovery. 'So that's the answer,' he said briskly, as the others' exclamations ceased. 'Her body wasn't thrown overboard, she did recover, and she didn't fall overboard, either. She must have been in the 'plane all the time. When they had that boat-drill search the other night, too.'

'If she was,' Pons considered, 'she must have had quite a shock. That must have been more than she bargained for; probably thought she was in for a ride half-way across the ocean. I don't know whether you'll believe it or not,' he went on to assert, 'but I have never really believed that she left the boat. I will admit, though, that I never thought of the 'plane.'

'But how could this be?' Dr. Plechs queried. 'Surely this young woman could not find it possible to lie hidden in the 'plane three or four days without food or water. It could not be possible.'

'As far as I'm concerned,' declared Dr. Pons with decision, 'I am going up to the captain's quarters to see the end of this. And if you're wise, the rest of you will come along with me.'

The curiosity of the other three psychologists permitted none of them to oppose the suggestion, even the professor accompanying the rest as they started toward the forward stairway under the envious glances of the other, less fortunate, passengers. As they went, the 'plane, its mail sacks once more restored to their proper places, was being cranked by its pilot. Again the roar of its motor came, more faintly now, over the waves; it taxied away from the ship, its tail lifted, the spray scattered by its accelerating passage fell back in tiny cascades behind the pontoons, and with a final, graceful motion it lifted clear of the water and climbed away into the east.

The *Meganaut's* engines throbbed again, and the great ship moved off again upon its course. Captain Mansfield, who had gone at once to the bridge when the first signals to the 'plane had been sounded, had spent the last twenty minutes at his post of command. But with the finding of the stowaway and the return of the small boat that was now approaching the ship, he had turned over the direction of the *Meganaut* to the bridge officer and was making his way back to his quarters. Just outside he met Dr. Pell, who had been observing the unusual proceedings from a point of vantage on the boat deck, and together they went within.

As yet none of the other members of the interrupted conference had returned, but they had no sooner entered the sitting-room than Detective Heddes knocked on the door and came in. He saluted the captain and reported that his search of Younghusband's cabin had been fruitless.

'Mr. Younghusband's cabin?' responded Mansfield. 'Oh, yes, of course. You were to search both his and Mr. Gnosens's cabin while we were having our conference. And you found nothing, eh? Well, I never thought you would. Mr. Gnosens's cabin was the same, I suppose?'

'Yes, sir,' Heddes was forced to admit. 'I went through them both from door to port-hole and there's nothing in either of them to incriminate anyone. I did find a rubber ball though. He must have dropped it without knowing and it rolled into the corner under his dressing-table.' He held out the object in question for the captain's inspection.

Mansfield took it and looked at it absently; he was preoccupied with the stowaway on the 'plane. In these circumstances the appearance of a stray rubber ball seemed a trifle unimportant. After scarcely more than glancing at it, he laid it down on the long centre table beside which he was sitting.

From this position Dr. Pell presently rescued it, as the captain continued to drum abstractedly on the table-top with his fingers. Pell seemed to have little more interest in it than Mansfield, but there was an interval while they awaited the others and more, apparently, for something to do than anything else, he took up the ball and examined it with no great attention. It was hardly an inch in diameter. The rubber looked soft and from its weight one could tell at once that it was hollow. As he rolled it over on his hand he saw the little hole through which it had been suggested that an elastic had some time been attached, but this hole seemed to be now stopped up with dust.

Idly he raised the ball nearer his face and attempted to clear the tiny hole by blowing the dust away. The attempt was unsuccessful and, still with the ball only a few inches from his nose, he gave it a sharp pinch between his thumb and fore-finger. The resulting puff blew out the dust in a minute stream and Dr. Pell, after the usual facial contortions, gave voice to a loud sneeze. He looked distinctly surprised, regarded the inanimate ball as if it had suddenly addressed him in articulate speech and, again raising it to his nostrils, began sniffing at it eagerly.

'I think,' said Pell quietly, 'that we have found something.' He quickly produced a penknife, and slit the ball neatly into two halves. It was empty, but when he raised it once more to his nose, there was no mistaking the odour of bitter almonds that still clung to the interior surface. 'Yes,' the doctor added with more animation, 'that's it. This ball has contained hydrocyanic acid; fortunately it has been stopped up and the odour is still present. The criminal either carried it about with him in this container or— But surely! This is the means he used to squirt it into the drinks! A ball this size could easily be palmed and manipulated without the knowledge of anyone, even if he sat next the manipulator.'

'Eh!' cried Mansfield. 'What? What's that you say? The poison was carried about in this ball? You're positive, Pell? There can be no mistake about it?'

'None at all,' the doctor assured him excitedly, as the significance of his find became more apparent. 'Absolutely none! This ball has recently contained hydrocyanic acid. I'll swear to that in any court on earth.'

'But then,' began the captain, 'why, in that case—'

He was interrupted by the entrance of the four psychologists, who were crowding in at the door. Dr. Pons came first, and addressed himself to the ship's commander without preliminaries. 'Captain Mansfield,' he spoke, 'we have come to ask your permission to be present when the stowaway who has just been captured, is examined. As this person is the girl concerning whom

I gave you my ideas when I suggested a theory of the murder, I thought that you might not object to our presence.'

'It's quite all right,' Mansfield responded at once. 'I shall be pleased to have you here, I expect Mr. Drake to bring his prisoner up at any moment. Meanwhile, we have just made a most important discovery, the only real discovery so far in the whole case. Detective Heddes has found a rubber ball in Mr. Gnosens's cabin which Dr. Pell is willing to swear contained the poison used in killing Mr. Smith.'

'Ahah,' said Pons. 'In Gnosens's cabin. Yes, Gnosens is mixed up in this, sure enough. Since I recognized the girl they took off the 'plane, it has occurred to me with some force that his queer actions are now explicable. In my opinion there is little doubt that he has been her accomplice, certainly to the extent of keeping her hidden since she disappeared from the hospital. But we'll soon know more about it now. Here they come.'

Drake came through the entrance first, followed by the girl, with Younghusband and the detective bringing up the rear. 'Here she is, sir,' reported the executive. 'Through Mr. Younghusband's quick action we managed to apprehend this woman just in time.'

Coralie followed him into the centre of the room and hesitated before Captain Mansfield. From every direction the frank stares of those present were trained upon her, but of this she seemed scarcely aware. Her small figure, of less than average height, was bundled into the most incongruous of costumes; a grey flannel shirt, open at the neck and displaying the smooth whiteness of her girlish throat, was covered by an enormous hunting coat of rough material that hung down almost to her knees and whose sleeves it had been necessary to turn back in several folds in order that only the fingers of her small hands might peep through the ends. About her waist an equally over-size pair of trousers had been tightly belted and these hung in great folds down her legs, the tips of a pair of her own tiny slippers just appearing beneath their lower edges, which had also been rolled back. Her curly, yellow hair, rumpled into complete disorder by its recent misadventures, framed the face whose beauty Pons had praised so warmly to the captain. The little, determined chin, the full, naturally red lips, the long-lashed blue eyes, now turned to a deep aquamarine by excitement, and the straight little tilted nose affected the good doctor, now that he was confronted with them at close quarters, much more poignantly than had his earlier remembrance of them as seen across the smoking-room. For a moment he found it impossible to hold to his own theory of her guilt; he experienced an almost irrepressible impulse to gather her slight body into his arms and to comfort her as he would a frightened child. She was trembling ever so little, and she did look undeniably frightened. 'No jury,' he consoled himself, as Mansfield commenced speaking, 'will ever convict that lovely girl.'

The captain, it appeared, was suffering no such qualms. He was saying in a distinctly hard voice, 'Now, Miss Reake-Lyons, this is a very pretty attempt you have made. I suppose you know that there are severe penalties for hiding away on a mail 'plane under government charter. You have imperilled the lives of my two aviators, and furthermore you have remained hidden on this ship for the past several days while the most extensive search has been made for you. And after we have had some explanation of these actions of yours, one of which, I again remind you, is a serious offence, there will be an even more serious matter to be gone into. Now, Miss Reake-Lyons, what have you to say?'

After a moment's silence the girl asked in a small voice,

'Why do you call me Miss Reake-Lyons. That is not my name. I am Mrs. ——, I am married and that is not my name.'

'I don't care what your name is, just now,' said Mansfield. 'I want you to answer to the points I have raised.'

'I have only done what I had to do,' Coralie answered slowly, still trying to bring her voice under complete control. 'I have been trying to save my life.'

'And what about Smith's life?' Younghusband burst in. 'You killed him, didn't you? Dr. Pons here knows all about it.' He turned toward the scientist, who was sitting on the opposite side of the table, breathing rather heavily. 'She did it, Dr. Pons, didn't she?'

'Ah,' said Pons.

'Perhaps,' was Mansfield's comment, 'we might better begin with that, after all. Undoubtedly, all that has occurred since, has followed from the occasion of the murder itself. Now, Dr. Pons, you were the first to bring this young woman to my attention in that connection; perhaps it would be best if you examined her to begin with as regards your theory of the crime. I must say,' he added generously, 'that circumstances are beginning to point increasingly to your solution.'

Pons pulled himself together. He had no desire at all to try, by dominant methods, to wring from the lips of the beautiful girl before him a damning confession of the hideous crime of murder. He had a fleeting wish that he had gone and hidden himself under his berth at once, upon recognizing her in the small boat, rather than pushed himself into the torture chamber of an inquisition. However, it was too late now; he had no choice but to proceed as he had begun. If she were just a little less beautiful, it would be so much easier.

'She should have advice,' said Pons abruptly. 'It is not only unfair, it is plainly illegal, for her to be examined regarding a capital crime in this fashion.'

Younghusband snorted, the captain looked somewhat impressed, but Coralie said quickly, 'I don't want advice. I didn't want to tell anything aboard this boat, but now I shall have to, because I have been caught. I don't need advice, I don't want it; I will answer your questions, if there is something I can tell you.'

Since Pons's last speech her whole appearance had changed. She knew perfectly well that she had found a friend in the large doctor, and even if he turned out to be her chief accuser, she felt an inner assurance that he would be prejudiced in her favour and that she would succeed in convincing him of the story she told. She ceased entirely to tremble and her voice, also, took on a new fullness and confidence. She turned and looked directly at him and her eyes alone smiled.

Pons's attitude then underwent a sudden change. It became mixed. Her prompt recognition of his first attitude of assistance and her response to it, intensified his feeling, but he also became aware at once of the further element in her response, the belief that he could be prejudiced and that she could take advantage of his reaction to her beauty. He resented that, and his willingness to question her increased. It was not the first time, he reflected, that beautiful women had committed murder. And murder was murder. He was forcibly reminded of his duty to assist in disclosing the perpetrator of the crime. If she thought she could fool him out of finding the truth, she was sadly mistaken; he worshipped beauty emotionally, as was proper, but he was quite competent to prevent that beauty from taking him in intellectually, as was also proper. She will be right though, he thought, when it comes to the jury; and addressed himself forthwith to the task of a conscientious examination.

'Very well,' said Dr. Pons. 'If you volunteer to answer my questions, I will put them to you. At the same time it is my duty to warn you that you are under grave suspicion of having played a leading part, the leading part in fact, in the murder of Mr. V. T. Smith. I am not a police officer and I have no police powers; Captain Mansfield possesses those powers while we are at sea, and if an examination bears out the present suspicions, he will undoubtedly turn you over to the police authorities when we land to-morrow. The point is, that while the present proceedings are rather informal, they may be used as the basis for preferring formal charges against you. Do you fully understand all this?'

'I know what you mean,' she replied to Pons, and accepted from Drake the chair which he brought forward for her. After seating herself, she remarked, again to the psychologist, 'But I will not be the one who is arrested; that will be someone else. Please go ahead with your questions.'

Pons shrugged. 'In the first place,' he began, 'it is my belief that you are not Mr. Smith's daughter at all: you were travelling as his daughter, but the real truth of the matter is that you were his, well, his "friend". Is that true?'

'I was his mistress,' said Coralie, with her eyes appropriately lowered.

'Exactly. And more than that, you plotted to make use of your position for the purpose of forcing Mr. Smith to accede to certain of your demands, under threat of publicly disclosing your relations with him. It was for that reason that you accompanied him on this trip, where records would be made and evidence accumulated that would be undeniable.'

As he paused, the girl looked up at him. 'That is close to the truth,' she admitted, with surprising frankness. 'There was such a plot made against Mr. Smith and that was the primary reason for my coming with him on the ship.'

'I thought so,' said the psychologist. He nodded to himself with a trace of satisfaction. 'I also think that you found Smith a harder nut to crack than you had expected. When you threatened him, he probably only laughed at you and paraphrased the correct retort, to "publish and be damned". In short, your game couldn't be played on Smith and it collapsed at the very outset. Will you admit that, too?'

'Why,' Coralie looked puzzled, 'how could you guess so well about him? Did you know him? I never heard him speak of you, but you seem to know the kind of man he was. What you say is what I think *would have happened*; only it didn't. You see, what you call the plot against him had not got nearly as far as you think, when he was killed. He had no idea of it then; I was still procuring the evidence, as you said, and he had not yet heard a word about it.'

'You had not threatened him with exposure? Come now, I think you had probably threatened him many times.'

'No,' she asserted calmly, 'I hadn't. Up to this point you have been right, but now you're wrong about it. I had never said a word to him of that kind, nor had anyone else. And besides, I didn't intend to.'

'You didn't intend to? But you have just admitted that that was your real intention. What do you mean now? Are you denying your first statement?'

'No, I'm not. It may seem queer, but it's true. I intended to once, and then I didn't intend to. I—'

'Then,' said Pons, 'you deny that you threatened him?'

'I do.'

'And I suppose you also deny,' the psychologist went on, 'that Gnosens was your accomplice in this affair?'

For a moment Coralie hesitated, and it seemed to Pons, who was watching her closely, that the pulse in her throat began to flutter more rapidly. Then she replied quietly, 'I am answering your questions, but as long as I am doing that, you will have to confine them to me. I will not answer any of your questions that refer to other people than myself. There will be no use wrangling about that, because I mean it.'

'Is that so?' the captain broke in abruptly, in a tone that held both sarcasm and more than a hint of threat.

The girl turned directly toward him and regarded him as calmly as ever. 'Yes,' she said, as if replying to a quite ordinary question, 'that is so.' She nodded her head ever so slightly.

Mansfield, somewhat taken aback, glanced about his sitting-room. 'Where is the young man?' he demanded. 'He's not here, eh? Well, Mr. Heddes, I want you to find him and bring him here as soon as possible. If necessary, put him under arrest. This time we are going to find out just what has been going on behind our backs for the last few days. Go along, Mr. Heddes; I want him found at once.'

As the detective left the room, Dr. Pons turned back to the girl. 'You have admitted,' he continued, 'that you were Mr. Smith's mistress and that you formed a plot of what is to all intents blackmail against him. You deny that this plot was ever put into execution and you refuse to say anything about Gnosens, who we happen to know was at one time very much in love with you, and probably still is, although he has been at some pains to conceal it recently. We will let this point go for the moment; now I want to ask you about something else. I suggest that when Smith was poisoned, you took a drug which was intended to produce a state of coma resembling death, for some indeterminate period. Naturally, you knew nothing about the shooting that took place by coincidence just when he died, and you wished it to be thought that you also had been poisoned. Is this admitted?'

'I—, well you have just said a good deal. You are right that I knew nothing about any shooting; I did not expect it, and I was unconscious when it happened, and I only found out about it a good deal later. Nor did I know anything about my necklace being stolen until later. But I don't know what you mean about taking a drug. I had no drug and I certainly didn't take one of my own accord, nor did I expect at all to be drugged. I was poisoned when Vic—when Mr. Smith was poisoned; I don't know why it killed him and I recovered, but I think the poison was put in our drinks and that I must have taken much less than he did. The last thing I remember is taking a sip from my glass just before the lights went out. I had a funny feeling, I got weaker and weaker, and then everything went black. I didn't know anything else until I came to afterwards up on the top deck in that awful room.'

'And when you recovered, you at once escaped from the hospital?'

'I had to,' said Coralie. She began to tremble again and her voice went a full octave higher. 'It—I—it was awful. I couldn't stay, I couldn't bear it, I—oh—' Her voice dwindled off as she fought to control it.

'All right, all right,' Pons interposed hastily. 'Never mind about that now. As I understand it, you claim that you took no drug yourself, but that you were poisoned by the same means that killed Smith. And that you subsequently recovered and then escaped from the hospital. Is that right?'

Coralie nodded wordlessly. There were tears in her eyes and once more she looked very appealing as she sat there shaken by the recollection of her experience in the *Meganaut's* hospital. Pons, seeking to avoid the full effect of this picture, looked away from her and his eye caught that of the ship's doctor.

'We have heard Miss Reake-Lyons's assertion,' he stated, 'and I think first of all, before we either accept it or dispute it, that we should decide whether her story of what happened is physiologically possible. Do you think she could have taken any of the hydrocyanic acid with the results she describes?'

'Are you asking me?' said Dr. Pell; and upon Pons's confirmation, went on, 'I doubt it. In the case of hydrocyanic acid so small a dose is fatal, and especially in the case of a woman, that I seriously doubt whether she could have taken any of it into the alimentary tract and eventually recovered. Her symptoms were compatible with the idea, both before and after I took her to the hospital, but after all that doesn't mean much; the same symptoms, as we know only too well, can indicate many diverse conditions. No, I don't think so.'

'Just the same,' the psychologist continued, 'I think we should canvass the possibility thoroughly. The question as to whether both Smith's condition and hers resulted from the same or from different agents, seems to me to be extremely important; it bears upon the whole theory of the crime. Now I am still of the opinion that she drugged herself intentionally, but I am not so sure you are right in saying the other possibility is out of the question. What do the rest of you think?' He turned in his chair and looked around at the others.

They had all been absorbed in the proceedings, but more as spectators than participants. Dr. Hayvier was the first to find his voice. He said, 'I don't think there is much use in asking us.

As far as I am concerned, I don't know the first thing about the detailed effects of this poison. It is a question of fact; there is nothing to do except to take the doctor's word for it. He knows more about it than the rest of us.'

Plechs and Mittle disclaimed any knowledge that might be of assistance, and the captain voiced his agreement with Dr. Hayvier. 'Pell knows about these things,' he added; 'I can see no reason for doubting what he says.'

'No,' spoke the physician fairly, 'I think now that you are going too far. I do not know all the effects of hydrocyanic acid on the human organism; and to tell you the truth, I do not believe that medical science could categorically answer the question. What I gave was only my opinion, and I should most certainly not swear to it as being unquestionably correct.'

Pons turned back to the last speaker. 'That encourages me,' he confessed, 'to say what I have in mind. I am not a physician, as you know, but I have had occasion to investigate physiology to some extent, and Miss Reake-Lyons's assertion does not seem to me entirely impossible. That is, not on physiological grounds.

'I believe I am right in saying, that in the case of many poisons like hydrocyanic acid, the effect upon the human system is remarkably different, it may even be contradictory, when doses of different sizes are taken. Now in this case the poison is soluble in alcohol. Miss Reake-Lyons took but a "sip" of hers, it may easily be that she received a dose much too small to measure, if by chance the poison had not yet penetrated to the part she sipped. It may have been less than one molecule, it may have been no more than a single atom.

'She then developed symptoms corresponding to this poison; she went into a state of partial coma, which was mistaken for a faint, and soon lapsed into a coma so complete, with such shallow respiration, that it was mistaken for death.

'Such mistakes, of course, have been made thousands of times; in the present state of our physiological knowledge it is impossible to avoid them. It is true that if the victim survives the immediate effects, he is supposed to recover, due to the throwing off of the poison through lung action; but here the breathing was so shallow that little, if any, was so got rid of; and further organic conditions may well have prevented it. The result is a deep coma, with recovery long delayed. Now what do you think, Doctor? Is it not possible that physiological phenomena such as I have outlined, took place?'

Dr. Pell had listened attentively, and now he said, 'The only possible way I can answer that frankly is to say I don't know. And I suppose that is the same as saying that, as far as my own knowledge goes, it is possible. Yes,' he finished, turning to Captain Mansfield, 'so far as I can truthfully say, the situation just outlined by Dr. Pons may well have been the actual one.'

'Well, we will have to leave it that way. But I'll tell you this,' Mansfield complained, 'I'm getting very tired of these technical discussions. Every time they arise, the same thing happens. What was plain enough at first, becomes clouded over, then it becomes reversed, then there is more and more doubt on both sides of the proposition, whatever it may be, and finally we always come to the same conclusion; we don't know. Is nothing whatsoever known about these things, some of which appear to me to be certainly important?'

Dr. Pell smiled and spread out his hands in good-natured deprecation. 'From what I have gathered during this trip on the subject of psychology it seems plain to me that very little is known or certain in that realm. As to my own profession, I will tell you in confidence the truth as I see it; it will certainly be many years, and maybe it will be centuries, before the real problems of medical science are finally solved.'

These lugubrious reflections on the present state of mankind's understanding were rudely interrupted by the return of Detective Heddes. Gnosens came with him, and as everyone looked around at their entrance, the detective embarked at once on his report.

'Captain Mansfield, sir,' he related, 'I had a lot of trouble finding this man but I finally located him in the last place I thought of. He was in Mr. Younghusband's cabin tearing his things to pieces and when I caught him, all he would say was that he was looking for something. I stopped him all right, and brought him along; and here he is, sir.'

Gnosens, meanwhile, had walked directly over to the seated girl. 'I'm sorry,' he said to her, without any attempt at concealment, 'I'm damned sorry. I tried to stop them, but they were too quick for me. I was stupid; I ought to have been on the look-out until you got away.'

She smiled up at him, but before she could say anything, Pons put in 'So you were her accomplice all the time, were you, Gnosens? I've thought so for some little time, and this is tantamount to a confession. You surely won't try to conceal it any longer, Miss Reake-Lyons; suppose you tell us just how Gnosens has been aiding you in your plot against Smith.'

For the first time since she had been brought in, Coralie pulled herself together and with more activity than she had yet shown, turned to Captain Mansfield. 'You have been questioning me ever since I came in here,' she declared, 'and as you don't know what has happened at all, most of your questions have been a good way off the point. Now I am through answering any further questions at all. If you wish, I will tell you all that I know and what I believe about the death of Mr. Smith; but I will do it my own way, I will not be interrupted in what I want to say by questions from anyone. Do you want me to do this? At the same time, I will tell you this, anyhow; my life has been threatened, and it is still threatened. Whatever you decide to do, I beg you to protect me until we reach shore again.'

The captain thought a moment before replying. Then he answered, 'Young woman, as to the protection you demand, I assure you that every means at my disposal will be used to that end. There is going to be no more violence of any nature on the *Meganaut*. If you really believe that anyone is seriously threatening you, you have only to name him and I will put him in confinement on your mere word, until we have succeeded in unravelling this case further.'

As Coralie shook her head decidedly in the negative, he squared his shoulders and, unluckily remembering de Brasto at this very moment, went on. 'Very well; then I shall say this to all present. I am sick and tired of the flouting of authority that has been taking place on my ship. Here and now it stops; from now on the penalty for violence of a serious kind is death. I intend to instruct my police officer and his men at once that any person responsible for further violence is not to be arrested but killed immediately. I am not often aroused, gentlemen, to this pitch, but I tell you that I will stake my future and my career on ending the turbulence on board my ship.'

The captain, whose voice had remained low and even during the whole of his menacing speech, stopped; and a dead silence reigned throughout the room.

It was a full half-minute before anyone spoke; and then Hayvier said seriously, 'I consider you entirely justified, Captain.

You may be assured of my full support both now and in anything that may result from your decision.'

Captain Mansfield looked across at him and answered, 'I trust that my plan will not need to be carried out, but if necessary, it will be. At any rate, Dr. Hayvier, I want to thank you for your expression.' Then he turned back to Coralie again. 'I am sorry, young woman, that you will not answer Dr. Pons's questions, which seem to me to be very much to the point; but if you wish to make a statement of your own, you have a right to be heard and I will undertake that you will not be interrupted.'

'Thank you,' said Coralie. 'I want to tell you what I know about Mr. Smith's death, and if you will let me do it my own way, I should like to say what I think is surely the truth as to who killed him. But you must let me do it my own way; you must not insist upon my answering questions when you do not know what effect my answers might have. Is that all right?'

Upon the captain's acquiescence she proceeded immediately, 'I have already told you that I was married, and it is true that my husband and I originally formed a plot against Mr. Smith. There is no reason why you should believe that this is the first of the sort that I have ever done, although that is true. I have been married only a short time and I was married under peculiar circumstances, and—well, I am not going into all that. It is necessary, though, for me to admit that I did allow my husband to persuade me to join him in the attempt against Mr. Smith. He arranged the means for me to meet him; I was successful with him, that is Mr. Smith, and he consented to bring me to Europe with him. It was arranged that I should pass as his daughter; I thought he was too well known for that, but he had no difficulty in getting our connecting cabins, and I suppose he was so rich that he could do about what he pleased as long as he was willing to make the mere concession to appearance. Anyhow, that was what he did. The scheme was just what you have guessed; it was to compromise Mr. Smith and to make him pay for my silence.

'I am not trying to excuse myself when I say that my husband was the one who planned the attempt and was to direct its working out. That was why he crossed with us, and is now on the boat. Of course Mr. Smith didn't even suspect that I was married, and my husband arranged that he and Mr. Smith should meet under the most natural conditions only after the boat had sailed. He thought it best, however, that he and I should not appear totally unacquainted, since he wanted to confer with me from time to time and he could thus find ordinary opportunities to do so.'

At this point Dr. Pons found it impossible to refrain from interrupting. 'If you don't mind,' he inquired, 'who is this precious husband of yours? He is on the boat, you say?'

'He is on the boat,' the girl admitted. 'But I am not going to tell you who he is; if you are at all clever, you will see why in a minute.'

'You must see, young lady, that that is very unsatisfactory,' Mansfield observed.

'Of course I do, from your point of view. Just the same, you agreed that I could tell what I have to tell in my own way, didn't you? . . . All right. I have told you what the situation was when we left New York. I don't know if you will believe the next part, but it ought to be plain enough to anyone from what has happened. I became too fond of Mr. Smith to carry out my part of the plan.

'I did not expect the kind of treatment I received. At first I had thought of Mr. Smith as a hard, grasping kind of man who had practically robbed people of all the money he had. I had no feeling for him at all; he was not physically repugnant to me, but I was not fond of him, either.

'As I went on living with him, all that changed. I found that he was not hard and grasping at all; at least he never was with me, however he may have been toward other people. He was always very affectionate and tender with me and he put himself out in all sorts of little ways in order to please me.

'And then there was something else, too, something that I never expected at all. He had no use for what are called the "conventions" himself, and he was very anxious for me to understand that he thought no less of me because I was flouting them with him. He seemed to have a real fear that I should think he considered me as something he had bought, and he did everything he could think of to overcome any such idea of mine. His position, he told me so, was that he was living with me because he loved me and, as long as I was willing to live with him, he would provide me with everything I wanted. Perhaps I don't make this very clear; do you see what I mean?'

She glanced across the table at Dr. Pons, but it was Plechs who answered. 'Yes, yes,' he said, bending forward with his eyes fastened upon the girl in an interested stare, 'we are psychologists, we understand all this. But it is unusual, most unusual, for such a man to behave so, like you have said. Most unusual, yes.'

'I thought so, too,' Coralie nodded, 'and I was surprised. But it affected me just the same. The truth is that I became very, very fond of him; I wasn't in love with him exactly, I sort of felt about him as I used to feel about my father, although that's silly, of course, for our relations weren't anything like that. I don't know how to express it at all. He was thirty-five years older than I am, you know, and I often thought that he sometimes loved me just as if I had really been his daughter. Other times, of course, it wasn't like that. I, well, I just don't know how to tell you about it.' Coralie paused and looked both bewildered and slightly uncomfortable.

Dr. Plechs nodded his head vigorously and at the same time contrived to add a rather sage impression to his gesture. 'Yes,' he pronounced, 'yes indeed. It is true we all possess the suppressed desire for incest. I would not wish to embarrass you, so that you could not continue, but in science we must speak frankly.'

'You do not embarrass me,' replied Coralie, looking frankly at the psychoanalyst, 'because I do not believe you. I have read a good deal of psychoanalysis,' she added casually, 'and it always gives me a rather dirty feeling. There was nothing furtive about Mr. Smith; he was very clean, even at his most fatherly moments.'

'But, but,' cried Plechs, astonished, 'You do not understand, you do not know ab—'

Captain Mansfield interrupted peremptorily, 'Never mind. What difference does it make? Surely it is not necessary, Dr. Plechs, for you to argue your position here and now. Let us get on with this statement.'

Dr. Plechs collapsed like a punctured tyre, Hayvier's pleasure just escaped becoming audible, and Coralie sent the captain a grateful look.

She carried on at once.

'As I began feeling more and more as I have told you about Mr. Smith, it became more and more impossible for me to go ahead with the plan my husband and I had formed against him. I found I couldn't do it.

'All this time you must not think that I had lost all my feeling for my husband, either. I had a real affection for him, or I would never have married him in the first place, although it is true that I was practically forced into that. Also, he had entirely persuaded me that while our actions were illegal, there was nothing morally wrong about them; we were only taking by another kind of force what had already been brutally acquired by a ruthless millionaire. Because of all this, I immediately arranged to meet him privately when I had come to my new decision, and I told him frankly why I would not consent to go on with our plot. At first he refused to believe me, but I soon managed to convince him that I was fully in earnest and meant just what I said.

'He did not take my decision well. After he saw that he could not shake me by arguments, he became very angry. He is rather temperamental anyway and he worked himself up into a rage against both of us, myself and Mr. Smith. He was jealous, too, when he found out that I was really fond of the man we had planned to attack, and he said some pretty nasty things; enough to make me almost as mad as he was.

'I walked away from him then, but soon afterwards, the next morning, he got me alone again and demanded that I retract what I had said. I told him I would not go on with it under any conditions; and we ended up with another scene. Fortunately, there was no one to witness it. This time I got as angry as I have ever been in my life. I told him that I was through with him; that if he persisted I would disclose the whole thing to Mr. Smith, and that in any case, as soon as we reached Europe, I intended to go to Paris and procure a divorce. At this he became furious; he reviled me in worse terms than I had ever heard before, and when he saw that I was determined in my stand, he threatened both me and Mr. Smith and went away muttering violently to himself.

'After I had calmed down somewhat, I took all this with a grain of salt. I knew he was clever, and I was sure he would injure us if he could; but it seemed to me that whatever happened, I would always have the upper hand, and that there was nothing really to fear from him. I decided not to give him away, unless he himself might force me to do so for my own protection. And so I said nothing at all to Mr. Smith. If I only had, it might all have been so different. But I had not the remotest idea that my husband would go to the lengths he did, that very night.

'I had no inkling of what was to happen, but you all know what did happen in the smoking-room that evening. Mr. Smith and I were poisoned by some means that I do not yet know about for certain. He was killed and by some chance or other I just escaped.

'The next thing that I remember is coming to in a small room, which you say was in the hospital. For a long time I was sick and only half conscious; there was a terrific ache in the back of my head, and I could only lie there and groan a little, but it was so feeble that no one could have heard me ten feet away. I had no idea what had happened, but I got my first shock when, later, I realized that I was only wrapped up in a sheet. Then I think I fainted again, or went to sleep; when I recovered a second time, it was dark and I felt quite a bit stronger. I finally managed to sit up; there was a light shining through the window from outside and by this I could see dimly around the room. I was puzzled because it was not my own cabin. And then I saw something lying on another bed, all covered up by the same kind of sheet that was around me. I went over and pulled the sheet, and, and, and I—and there was—and—'

For a moment it seemed as if Coralie was going to break down completely. Drake quickly got her a glass of water and

304 · C. DALY KING

in another moment the captain procured a brandy bottle, from which he poured a liberal drink.

Gnosens began to protest angrily. 'Why do you make her go through this now?' he demanded. 'Can't you see she's worn out? For God's sake wait until she's more fit, at least.'

'No,' said Coralie. She coughed a little as the stinging brandy burned her throat. 'No; I'm all right. I will tell it now. . . . So,' she continued, after a short pause, during which no one spoke, 'when I realized that it was Mr. Smith and that he was dead, it suddenly burst on me that I, too, had been thought dead, and I guess I fainted again. It could only have been for a moment though, for there was only a little interval before I found myself looking at him again. I must have become hysterical then, for I remember trying to scream and being unable to, and everything else is a sort of haze. I think I finally crawled through the window, I was frantic to get away, anywhere, and I found myself on one of the decks. I hardly knew at all what I was doing, but I had an idea I must find someone who would protect me, someone who would not believe I was dead and insist on burying me. I kept thinking I must find Mr. Smith's cabin and then remembering that he was dead and couldn't help me. Then it occurred to me that there was someone else I could go to; all the time I was going lower, toward the cabins, and I met no one at all, although I don't think I followed a very straight route. Anyhow, I finally remembered where I could go and I managed to get there. For a long time I knocked on the door as hard as I could, and at last it was opened. I fell inside and collapsed completely; but I had been right, for the one I had gone to, took care of me.'

'Was it your husband's cabin you went to?' Pons demanded suddenly.

'I didn't say so,' replied Coralie quickly, alert at once. 'I didn't say it was and I didn't say it wasn't.'

'At any rate it was Gnosens's cabin, I'm sure of that.'

'It certainly was.' Gnosens himself spoke up defiantly. 'Her story is perfectly true. I was awakened by her knocking in the middle of the night, and when I opened the door, she fell in, just as she said. I put her in bed and did what I could for her. She wanted to be hidden and I hid her. I got food for her by having meals brought to my cabin, supposedly for me, and then having my own meals in the dining saloon. The boat is so big that I had no trouble in finding places to spend the night; once or twice I slept in the lounge, and one morning I was almost caught there when Dr. Pons suddenly looked in the door very early, before anyone was about. Then the captain kindly told me of his plan to search the boat for her, and I succeeded in getting her into the 'plane. We found that from the rear cockpit she could crawl into the mail compartment, and she was there when we had the boat drill. Afterwards I got her back to my cabin again; of course she was always dressed in my clothes, for her own had been taken by the captain after the murder. We were seen coming back from the 'plane that night, but only at a distance and no one bothered us.'

'And you got her back to the 'plane the same way?' Drake asked, rather incredulously.

'I did. I got her back there last night, or rather very early this morning. Of course there were tarpaulins over the cockpits, but I fastened those again after she had got in. She told me that there were some mail sacks already loaded and that she would pull those around in front of her, so that she would be hidden in case any more were loaded in later.

'The only real scare I had was when you were looking for

Stymond the other night. I was in the ballroom when I first noticed another search and of course I thought it was for her again. So I ran down to my cabin, where she usually stayed in a big wardrobe that could be locked whenever I was out of the cabin. I knew that wouldn't do, if anyone really searched the cabin, so I broke up the drawers of my trunk and she just squeezed in there until the search was over.'

'But why did she want to hide away like this, if she was perfectly innocent?' Captain Mansfield was puzzled. 'Why did she not come to me immediately with her story?'

'Because,' said Gnosens, 'she wanted—'

'Stop,' cried the girl. 'I will tell you why I did this,' she went on, turning to the captain. 'What he has said is true, as far as it goes, I had two reasons for doing it, and he doesn't know what they are. First of all I did not believe you could protect me from my husband if I told you that I thought he had murdered Mr. Smith. Somehow he would have found a way to kill me. That was the first reason; even if he knew I had recovered, I preferred him to think that he was safe from my accusation. And the second reason was that, while he still didn't know whether I was going to accuse him or not, I wanted to try and see if I couldn't secure some concrete evidence against him by searching his cabin on the quiet. I knew that I could easily have access to his cabin at certain times, and I thought it absolutely necessary that I find some tangible evidence, which I was sure he had. What I was looking for was the poison. I have looked carefully twice; I have looked everywhere I could think of, and there isn't a sign of it. Just the same I am positive he has it somewhere, but I have failed. He must carry it with him, that's the only possibility, and of course I haven't had any chance to search his clothes when he was asleep.'

'But he won't have it now,' the captain broke in. 'He would be crazy to keep it with him.'

Coralie shook her head with decision. 'Never mind,' she said. 'I'm sure he has it. But let me finish what I want to say. When I saw that I couldn't find this proof, I decided that I must get to shore ahead of him and have him arrested there. I knew the 'plane would go to Cherbourg, and when I saw how easily I could hide on it, I planned to go that way.

'However, my plan has failed, as you know. You have arrested me, and here I am. I have told you now what I know and what I suspect. But I have failed to get the proof I needed; I don't know what to do, and I don't see how I can do anything else.'

Coralie's voice ceased. Gnosens's and Younghusband's faces were both set and expressionless, the others were all more or less puzzled to decide how much of the girl's story to believe, or whether it should all be dismissed as a clever defence. As far as could be judged by their expressions, Hayvier, Drake and Pell seemed impressed, Plechs and Pons sceptical, while the professor, the captain and the two detectives remained noncommittal.

Mansfield leaned forward and said impressively, 'Now see here, young woman, you must tell us who this husband of yours is. We will try to obtain the evidence which you have failed to find, but in any case, if your story is true, it is my opinion that he will not escape his punishment. It is your duty to assist us; I am sure, if you *have* been telling us the truth, that you must be as anxious as the rest of us to bring him to justice.'

'I am,' acknowledged Coralie, 'but I cannot see that my own death will benefit anyone. It will not bring Mr. Smith back if I tell who he is, and I have made up my mind not to take the chance. Oh, you don't understand,' she cried in an urgent voice.

'If I were to accuse him now, you wouldn't believe me. I might be able to convince you in the end, but before I had, he would certainly have found the chance to kill me, while you were investigating my story. Probably you wouldn't believe me at all. I will not identify him until after he has left this boat.'

'And how do you expect him to know that?' the executive officer demanded. 'He undoubtedly knows you have been up here, and he will suppose of course that you have given him away.'

Coralie smiled. 'No,' she said, 'he will know just what I have said.'

'Of course,' Dr. Pons assured them. 'Of course he knows what she has said. It is perfectly obvious that, if her story is true, either Younghusband or Gnosens is the man she is married to. Come, Miss Reake-Lyons, or Mrs. Question-Mark, why not tell us? We are all here, and we are certainly able to protect you. Captain Mansfield will take any measures you wish, I am sure, until we land to-morrow morning. Why not tell us and get it over?'

But the girl only shook her head obstinately.

'That only leaves us one thing to do,' Pons replied. 'Without endorsing the story we have just heard, it seems to me that we may be able, provisionally, to determine which of these two men is the one referred to. With your permission, Captain, I should like to go into that question.'

Mansfield assented at once. Dr. Pons glanced round the room and he began slowly. 'I have always thought,' he declared, 'that the young woman found on the 'plane played a central role in the murder of Smith. My theory that she was his mistress and that she was engaged upon a blackmail plot against him, has been borne out by her own confession. But from this point on, her story, if it is true, destroys my own theory almost entirely, leaving only valid the point that she was intimately involved in the circumstances of the murder. It does much more than that, however; it definitely alleges that the criminal is her husband and that he is now not only on the *Meganaut* but *actually in this room with us*. For it is plain that, unless she is trying to deceive us, the man we want is either Mr. Younghusband or Mr. Gnosens. If I were to place any faith in names,' the doctor smiled broadly, 'I should at once pick the man called Younghusband; but I rather think that our problem is not to be solved quite so easily.'

'Excuse me, Doctor,' Drake put in, his fancy caught by the last remark. 'It occurs to me that the other man's name is John I. Gnosens. It would not be hard to make John Innocence out of that.'

'That's right,' admitted the psychologist. 'I had forgotten that. But I think it will be more difficult to establish his innocence from the facts about him than from the name he goes by. Naturally, I am only attempting a feeble joke; their names are of no more use to us than their expressions, and I don't think we can tell much from those.'

Dr. Pons, as well as the others in the captain's room, turned and regarded, with various degrees of concentration, the two young men who were under suspicion. It did not seem to anyone that the moment was one for politeness. But, as Pons had said, there was little to be gathered from the inspection. Both appeared to be as much at ease as could be expected under the circumstances; Gnosens had lighted a cigarette which he was leisurely smoking and Younghusband returned them a grim smile in exchange for their glances.

'No,' continued the doctor, 'I don't think we shall progress far that way. Let me try to tell you the items that occur to me against both our suspects. While the young lady was talking, I took occasion to note down on an envelope the points against them both. First I should like to take the case against Mr. Younghusband.'

'Excellent,' murmured Captain Mansfield. 'Go ahead, Dr. Pons.'

Thus adjured, Pons picked up from the table a large envelope with a closely scribbled surface, to which he continued to refer from time to time as his exposition progressed.

'The first thing against Younghusband is that it was to him that Gnosens appealed for an introduction to the girl, on the first day out, if I am not mistaken. It is therefore obvious that Younghusband was acquainted with her. If we may believe Gnosens, who himself claimed to be greatly astonished when he recognized "Miss Smith" on the *Meganaut*, it is thus possible that Younghusband knew beforehand that the girl would be on the boat, arranged his own passage and met her there to renew what would appear to be a casual acquaintance.

'My second point is that the girl has kept herself carefully concealed from Younghusband ever since her escape from the hospital. This is surely compatible with the idea that she considers him a dangerous enemy. Also, Younghusband seemed greatly surprised when she was not found as a result of the boat drill search; he appeared to be convinced that she was on board and that the criminal had not disposed of her body as had been suggested. Naturally, if he were the criminal himself, he would have definite knowledge on this point.

'The third point is that Gnosens had no hesitancy in sustaining the girl's story and admitting that it was he who had hidden her. It scarcely seems to me that he would have gone out of his way to do this, had he been the criminal; and of course anything tending to suggest his innocence automatically throws suspicion upon the other man.

'Point four. That Younghusband, even though the search for the girl had proven fruitless, was still on the look-out for her and at the very last moment, due to his continuing suspicions, realized that she might be on the 'plane. This again would indicate that he knew the criminal had not disposed of her body. And his drastic action in insisting that the 'plane be stopped, shows that he was prepared to go a long way to prevent her escape from the ship.

'The fifth point is simple. Younghusband was sitting at the table when the drinks were poisoned; thus he had the opportunity to poison them. It is now established that this was done by means of a small rubber ball that could be concealed in the hand and from which the poison could be squirted into the glasses as the hand passed over them.

'The last item I have is really not very incriminating, although it may be significant. I have noticed all along that Younghusband has been so eager to find the murderer that he has successively backed all the various theories as they have been proposed. This may be accounted for, of course, by his natural eagerness to see the death of his friend, Smith, avenged; but it may also be due to the fact that if someone else is convicted of the crime, he himself becomes safe.

'Now,' said Dr. Pons, 'that is all I have noted down against Younghusband. So I come to Gnosens. We have nothing beyond his own word that he did not take passage on the *Meganaut* because he already knew that she and Smith would travel on it. In this case he may have decided to meet both Smith and the girl, the first actually and the second artificially, by means of a shipboard introduction.

'In the second place we have the fact that she selected his cabin for a place of refuge. This point may be as telling against

Gnosens as against Younghusband. Even if we accept that she was in considerable fear of him, she has herself admitted that she was hysterical and confused when she sought help; and it would certainly be more natural for her to go to her husband's cabin than to that of a man who was almost a stranger, although to be sure Gnosens has alleged that he was deeply in love with her and this she must have known, if it was true. We must remember what the girl has told us, that despite her growing affection for Smith, she still retained a feeling for the man she had married. To a psychologist all this does not seem at all as unlikely as it may sound. There is no doubt that he must once have been greatly influenced by her or he would not have married her. She may well have felt, that though he had tried to kill her, she could now win him back by deceiving him with her assurance of aid.

'The third point that I have, has a bearing upon this last. When he thought she had died, Gnosens exhibited a very deep depression. Although we may concede that some of this may have been an attitude assumed intentionally to divert suspicion from him, nevertheless, once adopted, it grew and became in large degree sincere. Both Dr. Plechs and myself observed Gnosens in this condition; in our professional activities we have seen many similar cases and I would seriously challenge the idea that both of us were misled. And if this were so, she read his character correctly when she sought his cabin, for in this state of remorse he would have done anything possible to assist her.

'The next point fits in again with the preceding. As soon as she had reached his cabin and he was assured that she was still alive, Gnosens's attitude underwent one of the most abrupt changes I have ever seen. From the deepest depression he reacted to a state of the highest elation; I happened to breakfast with him the morning after she had come to his cabin, and he was overflowing with happiness. The change was in fact so great that Dr. Plechs was not to be blamed for supposing the young man to be the victim of a maniac-depressive condition and, from the psychoanalytic viewpoint, to have repressed a serious complex into the unconscious.

'The fifth point is that he fell in at once with her proposal of concealment. If he were overjoyed to find that she was alive, he would do anything she asked; and if he were the criminal, it would obviously be to his advantage that she should disappear completely.

'That he did his best to accomplish her final escape from the ship, has a significance identical with that of the point above.

'Point number seven is that he had the same opportunity to administer the poison that I have referred to in connection with Younghusband.

'The eighth point is that the rubber ball by means of which the poison was squirted into the drinks, was found in his cabin where, according to him, he must have lost it. Also, this ball was in his pocket just after the crime and was seen by one of the detectives.

'And the ninth and last point is that he has just been found in Younghusband's cabin, searching, as he says, for incriminating evidence but, for all we know, engaged in planting there some evidence of his own which may later be found and used against the other man.

'Well,' Dr. Pons drew a long breath and paused momentarily, 'those are all the items that I managed to note down. There are my notes, Captain. Numbered and fairly legible, I think.'

POINTS AGAINST

YOUNGHUSBAND	GNOSENS
1. Y. introduced G. to girl.	1. Introduction perhaps fake.
2. She has kept herself concealed from Y. since escape.	2. She might select husband's cabin for refuge.
3. G. frankly admits he helped her.	3. G. manifested depression (remorse?) when he thought her dead.
4. Y. was on lookout for girl and eventually discovered her.	4. G. greatly elated when he found she had not died.
5. Y. had opportunity to administer poison.	5. G. at once agreed to conceal her.
6. Y. has been actively backing every theory proposed.	6. G. tried to aid her escape from ship.
	7. G. had opportunity to administer poison.
	8. Rubber ball found in G.'s cabin.
	9. G. was arrested in Y.'s cabin.

The document, which Pons laid before the captain, was now handed gravely around the room and everyone present scanned it in turn. It was even handed to the two suspected men, both of whom looked it over with an interest at least as great as that of the others.

Dr. Hayvier, when his turn came, took the paper and went over each of the noted points with considerable care. 'There seems to me,' he remarked, as he passed it on to his neighbour, 'to be one thing in connection with these points that has escaped attention.'

Everyone looked up quickly, and the captain asked: 'Yes, Dr. Hayvier, and what is that?'

'Why,' said Hayvier, 'no one seems to have recalled what the young woman has told us about her own attempts to find the poison. She said that she had twice searched her husband's cabin and she also said that she was unable to reach him when he slept and to search his clothes then. That might give us a line. . . . No,' he added, after a moment's thought, 'I guess not, after all. I suppose the conditions would apply to either of them. Gnosens has just been discovered in Younghusband's cabin; and that means either that the door is left unlocked or that he has a key or some other means of opening it. And if he has, so had she; whereas at night it would be almost impossible for her to get in while Younghusband was asleep and to make her search without awakening him. At the same time, she obviously had access to Gnosens' cabin when he was away from it but would have been unable to find him asleep, because he has been spending the nights in different parts of the boat. No, I guess that was a false alarm.'

'Yes,' agreed Pell, who had leaned forward eagerly when Hayvier had first spoken. 'I thought you had something, too, but you're right; it might apply to either. You can't think of anything else, I suppose?'

'No, nothing more.' Then Dr. Hayvier grinned slyly. 'I notice, though, that one of these men is a blond and the other a brunette. Pons made a great investigation of blonds and brunettes a few years ago; we might ask him to tell us which is the original criminal on that basis.'

Dr. Pons grinned back at him. 'I guess Hayvier knows the answer to that as well as I do,' he answered. 'Seriously, if the murder has been repeated a hundred thousand times, with a blond and a brunette as the suspects, I should say that in the majority of cases the criminal would be the brunette. No such prediction could be made in a single case, however. Only a sufficiently detailed study of the two individual character patterns could indicate which of these two men is the most likely to have done murder.

'And besides,' he continued, 'I don't want you to forget that the theory that either of them is guilty remains no more than provisional. The whole story we have heard may be a fake, for I don't see that we have any evidence for it except the girl's word. It may still be that she never had a husband, that she committed the murder herself according to my original theory and that Gnosens hid her and did all the rest of it simply because she had captivated him and he was really in love with her. Nevertheless, I must say in all fairness that the story we have heard from the girl is psychologically possible in my opinion. We just haven't found any proof as yet to support one theory or the other.'

Captain Mansfield, upon whose face a frown had been growing during the last few minutes, appeared to have come to some decision. 'I don't see that at all,' he objected to Pons's conclusion. 'It seems to me this is all getting much too theoretical. We have two men here under suspicion, and the ball that contained the poison has been found in the cabin of one of them. I can't see what more proof we need than that; many a man has been hanged on less direct evidence.'

'Just a minute,' Gnosens interrupted. 'I haven't said anything because I know I'm innocent and I won't have any trouble proving it eventually. As for this ball that seems so important to you, I think you have forgotten that it was found in my pocket when we were all searched for the missing necklace in the smoking-room. I spoke about it at the time to Bone here, and told him I didn't know where it had come from. And I want to remind you that all this happened before we knew anything about the poison and thought that Mr. Smith had been shot to death. I would hardly have called the ball especially to a detective's attention, if I had just used it for murder. I didn't know where it could have come from then, but it is plain enough now that it was planted in my pocket during the darkness or in the excitement afterwards.' He paused and looked at Younghusband with every appearance of hostility.

'That is perhaps so,' Dr. Plechs offered, 'and perhaps it is not so. It is to me possible that all this mentioning of the ball may have been a safety in case, I mean a safety measure to be taken just in view of so distant an occasion as this one now. The human mind, when clever, is capable of much more complicated thoughts than this.'

Mansfield passed his hand wearily across his head. 'It always comes to the same thing,' he sighed; 'we don't know and we have no actual proof. The idea of trying to look for a supply of poison itself appears to me to be merely senseless. There is no chance whatsoever that the criminal would not have thrown it into the ocean long ago. In my opinion Miss Reake—this young woman—was wasting her time in ever searching for it.'

'No,' said Coralie. She had been following the various arguments closely. 'I was not. It was not like him to hurry to get rid of it when everything had gone so well and Mr. Smith was thought to have been shot. Until he was completely sure what I would do, he could not afford to part with a supply of something so quick and so certain. He might need it to use on me again; and as long as he had the least suspicion that this might happen, he would keep it. He is that sort of man, I know.'

'But my dear young lady,' the captain answered in some exasperation, 'the cabins and the effects of these men have been searched thoroughly only this afternoon by my detectives. And you yourself say that you have made not one, but two, similar searches. The poison is not there to be found.'

'Well?' said Coralie.

Younghusband now made his first speech. He said: 'I know what you think; you think that if it isn't in his cabin, this lunatic husband of yours must be carrying it around with him actually on his person. Well, as far as I'm concerned, I am entirely willing that one of the detectives should now search my clothes. I am anxious to help you in any way I can, but up to now there has been no chance for me to do so, especially as I have evidently been one of the chief suspects ever since I came in here. However, I'm willing to help. Not that I think you'll find any murderer carrying his poison around in his pocket.'

'Suits me, too,' Gnosens spoke up. 'I'd like to be searched right away.'

'All right.' But Mansfield was still dubious. 'I suppose we may as well get that out of the way, at any rate. It will at least take one point out of the field of theory.' He directed Heddes and Bone to take the two men into his own cabin and conduct the searches there.

While they were absent, there was little conversation. The strain of the long conference was commencing to tell and except for slight shiftings of position there was an oppressive silence.

Then the captain remarked suddenly. 'By the way, what makes anyone think there *is* a supply of this poison. The man, whoever he is, probably didn't have an inexhaustible supply; and what he had, he carried in the ball that we have already found. Why not?'

'But the ball had a hole in it,' Drake replied. 'No, he wouldn't have done that, I'm certain. It would leak in his pocket or in his trunk or wherever he left it. And the odour is strong and also distinctive. I don't believe the ball was ever used except for a short time preceding the murder itself. Originally there must have been some other container from which the ball was filled.'

'Oh, all right,' Mansfield acquiesced testily. 'Have it your own way. But it won't be found on either of those men now.'

A few minutes later the two detectives came back with their charges and reported complete failure. 'Nothing at all,' said Bone, speaking for both. 'We had 'em strip and went over everything they have. There's no poison on either of them boys nor anything like it.'

'That's right,' said Heddes.

'But there must be,' Coralie cried; '*there must* be! Did you look everywhere?'

'Lady,' said Bone, 'we sure looked everywhere. You'd be surprised.'

'You can't be right. I *know* he has it,' insisted the girl.

'So,' Pons said abruptly. 'One of these men is your husband. *Which one is it?*'

'I won't tell you.'

'Unless her whole attitude is false,' Pons informed the company. 'It is now certain that either Gnosens or Younghusband is the man. And if we accept that much we might as well accept everything she says. In spite of the searches one of these men probably is carrying the poison; the only alternative is that she herself is the criminal.'

'It is not at all impossible that one of them has it.' Professor Mittle's totally unexpected speech startled everyone. As they all shifted in their chairs to look in his direction, he pursued: 'It is almost banal to say that the best place to hide anything is where it is sure to be seen—and mistaken. Either mistaken for something else or passed over as too commonplace to be worthy of attention. It occurs to me, in view of the young woman's insistence, that such may be the case here.'

The two detectives looked uncomfortable, and Heddes went so far as to scowl. But Plechs added: 'That is so, Professor Mittle. Among the publications of the *Wiener Polizei* there is found a long monograph upon this very subject. Once, for a research, I have read it.'

'Why not search them yourself, Professor?' suggested Hayvier. 'With this idea you might find something the detectives have missed.'

Mittle demurred. 'No, no, I should not care to make a search myself. But it may be possible to discover the hiding place without that. You see, it will not be anywhere out of the ordinary, if this idea should be right; that is, it will be somewhere that is not in any sense individual with the person, somewhere where anyone might carry it. Of course,' he turned and addressed the captain, 'all this has nothing to do with my profession. This sort of thing is very often called psychology, but it has nothing to do with the psychology that is a technical science.'

'In that case,' Drake observed sarcastically, 'we can all guess. A special education is not necessary.'

'You can all guess,' Mittle admitted, 'but I shall have a certain advantage, I think. Though not because I am a psychologist. You see, I have always been interested in modifying all sorts of ordinary implements; in an amateur way and on a small scale I am an inventor by hobby. You yourself, Mr. Drake, have seen the equipment I have invented for setting up my typewriter and working in unusual places. And if I am not mistaken you also manifested the customary surprise. All this, of course, is not exactly the same as what I am trying to do now, but the trend of thought is very similar in both cases. The truth is that I should much prefer someone else to discover this poison before I do, but I shall do my best nevertheless.'

There was a pause while everyone tried to imagine where he would himself attempt to conceal on his person a supply of poison. All round the room foreheads became furrowed as their owners pursued the elusive, shrewd guess that, Mittle alleged, had nothing to do with psychology. Dr. Hayvier began turning out his pockets.

But at the end of several minutes no suggestion had been offered except that of a hollow ring; which was useless because neither of the men wore rings. The professor sighed audibly. 'I can think of nothing,' he confessed. 'A watch-fob? No. I have been over everything I can think of and there is nothing. I don't want to ask you to give any more time to this idea of mine, for I am afraid it has been wrong all along. Another idea has occurred to me, though, of an entirely different kind.'

'What is that?' Mansfield asked him quickly. 'I must admit that I can't get anywhere with your first suggestion. It's the sort of thing they do in detective stories, I suppose,' he added rather sententiously, 'but in real life those things don't seem to work.'

'No,' the professor assured him, 'this is an entirely different idea; it has nothing to do with a hiding place or with the poison either, directly. I should like to have,' he went on, 'a sample of the handwriting of each of these men. I think that it may provide us with a clue as to which is the guilty one.'

'What?' cried Hayvier involuntarily. He looked amazed and disgusted. Pons's appearance, too, was one of incredulity, and the others exhibited their surprise in various fashions. Only Dr. Plechs seemed, to judge from his expression, to feel that the interpretation of handwriting might have a possible bearing on the problem.

'But Professor,' it was Captain Mansfield who voiced the general scepticism, 'I have always thought that modern science denied the claims of so-called "handwriting experts", I thought they were considered to be quacks.'

'That was certainly the case until very recently,' Mittle admitted. 'But much very good work has been done no longer ago than last year. I was reading the reports just before I left New York. If there is any other suggestion, I shall be glad to withdraw mine, but I really have hopes that something might come of it this time.'

'It is true,' Dr. Plechs added, 'that the unconscious is undoubtedly manifested through the idiosyncrasies of handwriting. Repressed elements sometimes secure a partial release.'

'We're about at the end of our tether,' said Mansfield. 'And there don't seem to be any other suggestions. Go ahead, if you want to.'

'Very well. If you will please both come over here?' The professor approached the centre table and indicated an empty chair. Dr. Hayvier, whose seat was next, rose with an expression that plainly disclosed his belief that the atmosphere had become mediæval; and Gnosens and Younghusband sat down next each other. 'You will write, please,' the professor directed them. '"Now is the time for all good men." Just that; no more please.'

They both took out their pens, and Gnosens, who was the first to finish the short line, handed his paper to the professor, behind his seat. The latter took it and glanced curiously at

Younghusband, who had not yet begun to write upon the blank paper lying before him.

'And where is your specimen, sir?' Mittle demanded pleasantly.

'I was thinking,' said Younghusband absently. 'And—oh, yes, I see. I see!' His face broke into a smile for the first time that afternoon.

'By gad, Professor,' he acknowledged, 'that was clever. I'm only sorry it isn't going to work. Just the same it's an idea.'

With the utmost calmness he unscrewed the cap from his fountain pen and wrote off the few words requested. As he handed the paper up with a quizzical grin, he added, 'Too bad. The incriminating symptoms aren't there; no, they're not there, are they, Professor?'

Mittle, whose face had become very slightly flushed, accepted the second paper and without replying to Younghusband's observations, sat down at the table and commenced comparing the two samples. For a minute or two there was no sound except a suppressed snort from where Dr. Hayvier was leaning against the wall.

'How does it go, Professor?' asked Younghusband softly.

The professor looked up. 'No,' he admitted, 'you are right. It is impossible to come to a conclusion from this comparison. At least it is impossible for me, but of course I am only an amateur at this. As there is no expert present, however, it comes to the same thing. I am sorry, Captain Mansfield; I have done my best, but I regret to say that I can give you no opinion as a result of this test. These two handwritings are distinct and individual, but I find it impossible to tell which of them discloses criminal tendencies. I'm afraid we have failed again.'

'I was afraid you would, too,' Younghusband put in, before the captain could reply. He rose from his seat with a quick movement and turned to face Mansfield.

In the instant his appearance had changed so radically that everyone present stared at him with amazement, and yet it would have been difficult to enumerate the detailed changes that underlay the entire alteration of his presence. One could only have ventured that instead of looking rather sly, he now appeared shrewd and intelligent and that a certain measure of authority had suddenly replaced his former impression of wily defensiveness.

'Captain Mansfield,' said Younghusband clearly, 'it is necessary that I disclose myself. I have been playing for time, but my time is at an end. I dare not wait longer; events have marched beyond my control, and from what I have already heard here this afternoon, it is plain that I must speak and I even hope that I may speak to some purpose. I am throwing down my cards. I was not a casual acquaintance of Mr. Smith's as I claimed to be. I am a detective who was assigned to guard his interests. I carry no credentials on such duty as this, but if you will radio the New York Police Department requesting identification of BL 3F, you will receive all the assurance you need. I must ask you to do this at once, sir, as a formal re—'

He stopped and spun round on his heel with another of those swift movements of which no one had suspected him. As he was talking, his ear had caught a low sigh from behind him.

Even as he turned, the girl slid forward from her chair and her body collapsed on the floor. There she lay in a crumpled heap, white and motionless, in her incongruous costume, her tousled blonde hair pressing into the captain's thick rug.

Younghusband was the first to reach her, after a quick glance to assure himself as to the identity of her neighbours, before they could change their positions. Nearest her he saw Drake, whose chair was a little behind hers; on the other side was Plechs and beyond him Dr. Pell. There was no one else in her immediate vicinity.

As Younghusband knelt beside her, Gnosens reached the girl's side and gathered her body into his arms. Her head fell back against his elbow. By this time Pell had reached them, and the detective crouched back, his attitude one of intense watchfulness. He did not seem nearly so much concerned about the girl's condition as about what would happen next. His eyes darted rapidly from the girl to Pell and to Gnosens and not a gesture of those near him escaped his attention.

Now the physician and Gnosens raised her body and carried it to the divan across the room, Younghusband following closely. Drake hastened to arrange a pillow for her head. 'Only a faint, I think,' said Dr. Pell. 'She's worn out with all she's been through. Will you get me some water and brandy, please, Mr. Younghusband?'

'No,' said Younghusband. 'From now on I'm not leaving her. Not for an instant.' Pell looked genuinely surprised at the response, but before he could ask anyone else, Drake had brought the desired articles. The doctor administered the homely restoratives, and within a few moments the colour began to creep back to the girl's white cheeks and she gave another faint sigh.

Dr. Pell spoke to her quietly. 'You're all right,' he said. 'You have just fainted and now you are coming to. Everything is all right; we will take care of you, don't be frightened. In a few minutes you can go down to your cabin and rest.'

Coralie looked up dazedly at the circle of faces above her. She began to weep feebly, and turned her face away, into the pillow. 'Don't let him get—get me,' she murmured. 'He'll kill—k-kill me.'

'It's all right,' Pell reiterated soothingly. 'We will see that nothing happens to you. Here now, just sit up; let me help you.' Gently he assisted her to an upright position and, as she leaned back against the divan, poured out another small drink of brandy. 'Here,' he said, 'take this.'

Coralie covered her face with her hands. 'No,' she moaned, 'no, no. Take it away.' She seemed thoroughly terror-stricken.

Dr. Pell looked around helplessly, and Younghusband came to his assistance. 'Go ahead,' he told the girl, 'take it; it won't hurt you. We will protect you; do as the doctor says.'

Thus admonished, Coralie took the proffered glass in a shaky hand and drank of its contents. She gasped, choked, then sat up straighter and began to wipe the tears out of her eyes with one of Gnosens's large handkerchiefs. 'Oh, oh, I'm all right now, I guess,' she managed, with the beginnings of an attempted smile.

'Of course you are,' the physician confirmed. 'It was only a faint, and primarily due to exhaustion. What you need is rest. I'll send for Miss Jenkins from the hospital and she can go down with you. I'll step in later and give you a sedative, if you need it; but I think you'll be asleep five minutes after the nurse tucks you in.' He stepped over to the telephone in the corner of the room and called the hospital at once.

'No,' cried Coralie, while he was yet speaking into the receiver. All her terror seemed to have returned and she stretched out an imploring hand toward the captain. 'Don't let them take me away. I'm fri-frightened. Let me stay here; please let me stay here. I'm safe here. If they take me away, he'll kill me. He will. I, oh, *please*—'

'But my dear young woman,' Mansfield replied in some confusion, 'you are worn out, really. Dr. Pell is only trying to take care of you. I'm sure you will be better off in bed, as he says. I think you should do as the doctor says.'

'I cannot be responsible for the consequences,' Pell assured the captain, 'unless my instructions are followed. This lady is on the verge of a very serious breakdown. She must be put to bed at once.'

'Don't leave me alone,' Coralie sobbed.

Younghusband, who had watched the situation develop with close attention, once more supported the ship's doctor. He turned to the girl and said with one of his friendliest smiles, 'I think you should go below, as Dr. Pell advises. We won't leave you alone, though. I would go with you myself, but I must remain here; I have something that I must say to the captain and to these gentlemen. One of them will go with you, however.'

'I'll go,' said Gnosens immediately, getting up from beside the divan.

Younghusband looked over at him. 'No,' he said. 'I don't think so. I think one of the psychological gentlemen would be better. Let me see; will you go down, Dr. Hayvier?' He turned back to the girl. 'You will go with Dr. Hayvier, won't you?'

Coralie nodded. She had become much calmer under Younghusband's comforting words, and she looked at Hayvier's supple figure and competent face with reassurance. For his part Dr. Hayvier agreed at once, although it was evident from his tone that he was far from appreciating the necessity for Younghusband's suggestion.

As the latter began to speak again, a trim nurse knocked at the captain's door and was admitted. At a word from Dr. Pell she went across the room and helped Coralie to her feet; then stood waiting with her arm around the girl's waist, half supporting her.

'All right,' said Younghusband. 'Now, Dr. Hayvier, you have accepted my suggestion, and I must impress upon you that you have undertaken a most serious duty.'

'Do you really take these fears of hers seriously?' Captain Mansfield interrupted. 'I think the young lady is exhausted and a little hysterical.'

Younghusband answered: 'I take them very seriously indeed, Captain. I only wish it were possible for me to spend the next few hours in her cabin myself. As I cannot do that, I have selected Dr. Hayvier for the task and she has accepted him. Now,' he continued, 'I have only one thing to say to you, Hayvier, and I exhort you to follow this out without any exception whatsoever. You are to allow *no one*, no one at all upon any excuse whatsoever, to have access to this young woman until I myself come to the cabin and relieve you. I will come at the very first moment I can. Meanwhile—*no one*.'

Dr. Hayvier shrugged his shoulders. 'I see you are very much in earnest,' he assured the other. 'Although it seems exaggerated to me, I shall do as you say. No strange man will get in while I am there.'

'And no familiar man,' added Younghusband. 'And no woman. Nobody. Except the nurse,' he added.

'Of course,' Hayvier agreed. 'All right. Nobody at all.'

'Very well. Go ahead now. And remember.' Younghusband motioned to the nurse and she and Coralie proceeded slowly out of the room, with the psychologist close upon their heels. Coralie was once again on the verge of tears; even as she went through the door, she was protesting, 'I don't want to go, I don't want—'

'Now,' said Younghusband, when they had disappeared. He turned back to the captain, drew a long breath and wiped the small beads of perspiration off his forehead. 'I am taking a risk,' he declared, 'a terrible risk. But it is plain that I am the only one who knows anything about this case, and I can see no alternative. I must stay here some time longer. If Dr. Hayvier will only do exactly as I told him, it will be all right. Now, Captain, it is absolutely necessary that I establish myself. Will you please send that radio?'

'I have done so,' Mansfield replied. 'I dispatched it while you were all reviving Miss Reake-Lyons from her faint. It should be well on its way by now. I had it marked "Urgent"; we should have the reply in an hour at most. Meanwhile—'

'Meanwhile,' said Younghusband, 'I will assure you as best I can. First, I call your attention to the fact that the girl has done as I told her to; she took the brandy at my suggestion and she consented to go below when I urged her to do so. She knows that I am a detective; she found it out the first day after we came aboard, because Mr. Smith reposed the most complete confidence in her. In the second place, you doubtless inquired about me from the New York Police long ago. If so, their reply confirmed what I had told you about myself; and this despite the fact that it is all false. My name is not Younghusband and I have never been in Chicago in my life. My name, in fact, is Michael Lord. I am, however, a member of the Department; and unless your inquiry contained the essential code, which it does now, they would only confirm my present *alias*. That they did so, should furnish you with some proof that I am what I now claim to be. What do you say, Captain Mansfield? Are you prepared to accept me provisionally, until you get your reply back?'

'I don't know.' Mansfield had commenced drumming on the

arm of his chair and was in a deep study. 'Events seem to be coming to some sort of a climax,' he considered. 'I am still in the dark, I confess, but—yes, up to a certain point I am willing to accept your statement and to hear what you have to say. Beyond that I don't know. I will certainly not delegate any authority to you or allow you to act in any drastic fashion, until I am sure. What you have pointed out impresses me but it does not convince me by any means. I have been misled too often up to now. From now on I may go slowly, but I shall make certain. Let us hear, Mr. Younghusband, what your role has been in this case, according to your own story.'

'All right,' Younghusband acknowledged. 'Perhaps that is the best I can expect. I hope to God your inquiry is not delayed, however. I have little time and if I am to discharge my duty, I cannot afford to be hampered in any way at all. If I were sure of the criminal, I would insist that you arrest him now and hold him until you hear from New York. But I am not sure. . . . And any mistake would be disastrous. . . . And I don't know how far I can trust Dr. Hayvier. . . .

'. . . Captain,' added Younghusband suddenly, 'can I speak to your steward alone?'

'To my steward?' Mansfield was frankly astonished. 'No, Mr. Younghusband, you cannot. And certainly not alone.'

'With you, then. This is important, Captain! I cannot tell you how important it is. I am perfectly serious; a life may well depend upon it.'

The captain was impressed in spite of himself. 'If you put it that way,' he admitted, 'I cannot very well refuse.' He rang for Mann. 'I shall step outside with you myself, sir, and hear what you say to him.'

He got up and Younghusband followed him outside, carefully closing the door. Not content with this, when Mann appeared, he led the way down to the end of the passage. The captain went with them.

'This steward of yours is trustworthy, Captain?' Younghusband asked.

'Absolutely,' said Mansfield. 'He has been with me for years. I will vouch for him in every respect.'

'Good. Now, Steward, I have something I want you to do. It is extremely important. Don't think about it, just do it. I want you to go down to the cabin that was occupied by Miss Smith before the murder in the smoking-room. You know where that is?'

'Yes, sir,' answered Mann in complete bewilderment.

'I want you to stand at the end of the passage or in some other position from which you will have a clear view of the door to that cabin and also of the door to the cabin next it, the one that was occupied by Mr. Smith. If you see anyone go into either of those doors and not come out immediately, that is within five seconds, I want you to come as fast as you can to the captain's room, where we are all in conference, and tell me at once. Do you understand?'

'Yes, sir.'

'Do you understand that you are to do this if anyone at all enters either of those doors? Anyone, a steward, a radio boy, a woman, or anyone else?'

'Yes, sir.'

'And do you understand that you are to come fast? To run, and to run hard?'

'Yes, sir, I understand.'

'Very well. Go ahead. And stay there until someone goes in or until I personally relieve you.'

'Yes, sir.' At a nod from the captain, Mann turned and made his way out on deck. Mansfield looked at his companion in astonishment.

'You really believe it, don't you?' he asked.

'I should say I do. I've dealt with criminals like this before. Clever ones.' Younghusband was walking back toward the sitting-room. 'I know it, Captain. Unless I can circumvent this murderer, his wife will be dead before that message from New York ever arrives. But I believe Dr. Pell when he says that she must be put to bed and furthermore I cannot leave your conference where I hope to reach a final conclusion. Time; time is the thing now. Let us go in.'

They found the others talking excitedly when they entered, but the noise subsided abruptly when Younghusband again took the floor. He addressed them all.

'I will tell you my real position as quickly as I can,' he began. 'Mr. Smith's trip to Europe was not entirely one of pleasure. He had business interests of his own to attend to; and as he was always receiving threats, most very wealthy men usually are receiving them, I was assigned to accompany him. He himself made the request, and as he has aided the New York Department in many ways in the past, it was granted at once. Exactly what he wanted me for he never told me. But he has had affairs with women in the past, and they have ended in blackmail attempts more than once. It may have been just to help him in dealing with such an eventuality that he wanted me along, or it may have been some more definite danger that he feared. Anyhow, he informed me that he had no special apprehension about the trip across and that I need not take my duties too seriously until we had landed. So of course I was totally unprepared for what happened. I am sure neither he nor the girl had any suspicion of danger; that is one of the points in favour of what she has told us.

'Naturally my duty was obvious after he had been killed. It was to discover and capture his murderer. For this purpose I have done my best, without giving up the role in which I originally came aboard, to get someone, anyone, accused and confined for the crime. I had no notion at all as to who had committed it, but I hoped that some innocent person could be held, for it is my experience that the chances against the real criminal are greatly increased whenever that happens.

'I have, of course, attended all the examinations except one, and I have been busy also on my own account. The one examination I missed was the second accusation of de Brasto. When he was accused of the poisoning by Dr. Plechs. I already knew that he could not be guilty; I convinced Dr. Pons on that occasion that I was drunk in my berth and I used the opportunity to go very carefully through not only his cabin but those of the other scientific gentlemen as well. But I discovered nothing for my pains.'

'Just a moment,' Drake interrupted him. 'I don't remember that you were present when we had Madame Sudeau up here.'

'When was that?' Younghusband asked in surprise. 'Madame Sudeau, you say? No, I didn't know she had been examined. It just happens that I know whom you mean, but why on earth was she suspected? I have never considered her seriously. Why didn't you tell me, Captain? And why did you suspect her?'

'Why should I have told you?' Mansfield inquired, while Professor Mittle seemed undecided whether to squirm a little in his seat or to suspect that he might have been right after all. 'I would have admitted you, had you asked, but I had no idea who you were, remember, and I must still remind you that even now I have not yet received proof of your identity.'

'Of course,' said Younghusband. 'But I think you had better tell me about that examination now. Please try to give me everything that was brought out,' he requested earnestly. 'And if any of the rest of you were there, I would ask you to follow closely and add anything that Captain Mansfield may omit.'

'I see no harm in that,' the captain admitted, and forthwith detailed the account of the construction and dismissal of the charge against Madame Sudeau. He added what he himself knew of her and Drake confirmed the recital.

'There's one thing that hasn't been brought out,' Pell remarked, as the others finished. 'I was there when we examined her, and I recall that one of the reasons for dismissing the idea that she might be guilty was the fact that she was sitting far away from the Smith table all evening and so could not have had an opportunity of poisoning the drinks. It did not occur to me then, but I have remembered since, that just before the lights went out, I saw a steward go to her table with a loaded tray of glasses, one of which he set down for her. What I remember especially is that she kept him in conversation for some time, it must have been one or two minutes easily. It has occurred to me that she might have found the opportunity to doctor the Smith drinks then, if they were on that tray and she knew which they were. Of course, those are two large-sized "ifs" and I have no knowledge bearing upon them at all.'

'What do you say to that, Captain Mansfield?' Younghusband looked interested.

'Why, well, why, yes, I suppose it's just possible. But no,' Mansfield was decided. 'I just do not believe that that woman had anything to do with it.'

'You can never judge by your impressions in cases like this,' Younghusband answered seriously. 'I wish I had been there when she was under examination. And by the way,' he turned back suddenly to Dr. Pell, 'I didn't know you were in the smoking-room that night.'

'Certainly,' said Pell, 'I was there. I thought you knew that.'

'But you didn't get to our table until long after Dr. Schall arrived. I always thought you had come in after the lights went up.'

'No,' the doctor assured him. 'I was there all the time. It took me so long to reach your table only because I was away down at the other end of the room, and of course it was slow going through the crowd.'

'I see,' Younghusband was going to continue, but he stopped as the telephone instrument began to jingle. Mansfield walked over to it.

'Captain Mansfield speaking. . . . Yes, he is. . . . Yes. . . . Yes, I see. . . . All right, Doctor, right away. I'll tell him.' He turned and addressed Pell. 'Dr. Schall has just called to find out where you are, Dr. Pell. He says you were to meet him for a consultation at the hospital. He is waiting for you now.'

Pell jumped to his feet and pulled out his watch. 'My word,' he cried, 'I had no idea what time it's getting to be. Will you excuse me, Captain? I must go at once. My patient up there has got steadily worse, and I have felt that a consultation is absolutely necessary. Will you excuse me?'

'Of course, Doctor, by all means.'

As Pell opened the door to go out, he almost collided with a page from the radio office. He stepped around him and the boy entered the room.

'Thank God,' Younghusband cried. 'Here's your answer.'

But Captain Mansfield handed over the envelope to Younghusband. 'No,' he said, 'this isn't mine. It's for you.'

'Where has Drake gone?' Younghusband wanted to know a moment later, having spread out his radio and regarded it with an expression of intense disappointment.

'Mr. Drake has gone to take over his duties,' the captain told him. 'Has your message any bearing on our matter?'

'No. It's from the Department, but it's in code, and I haven't any time to work it out now. I am not expecting anything from them on this case. Something else, I suppose. It will have to wait.' His expression had grown more worried in the past few minutes and again the tiny beads were gathering on his brow. He handed the paper to the captain.

The latter took it and read:

Younghusband
Meganaut   r.504p.
 dtsdapbvodps,laiZsdpp-slfDo,knahbs3200d
                        Cadmus

'Means nothing to me,' commented Mansfield, handing it back. 'Are you sure you had better leave it for the present? Who is Cadmus?'

'I'll have to leave it. Haven't any time to work it out now. Cadmus is a code word meaning that the message is an inquiry, that's all. Incidentally, that isn't in any of the ordinary commercial codes, the only ones that the companies will accept from unauthorized persons. So you can take it as a corroboration of my claims.'

'Perhaps,' Mansfield answered him. 'But I want my own reply before I'll be certain.'

'All right, all right. It will come—I only hope in time. Now I am almost through, but what I am going to say now is important. I have so far been able to obtain only one clue to the identity of the murderer aboard this boat; and I am going to ask all of you who are left to consider this clue with me and to see if you can add the necessary detail—'

'Look here,' said the captain. 'What's the matter with you, man? You look frightfully upset.' Mansfield was not accustomed to nervous detectives, and showed it.

'I am upset. There are too many people who have left here. There's Hayvier, whom I sent down myself, and Pell and Drake. And where is this Madame Sudeau now? No one knows. You're right, I'm worried.'

'I'm going down to that cabin,' declared Gnosens and rose in a determined way.

'You are not,' Younghusband was as determined as the other. 'No one else is to leave this room until I am through.'

'All right.' Gnosens sat down again. 'Then hurry up, will you? You're getting me as nervous as you are.'

'I'll hurry. Will you please all listen carefully. My clue is—'

'I don't care what your clue is.' It was Gnosens again. 'I thought I'd do what you asked at first, but I'm damned if I'm going to. Are you prepared to charge me with anything now? No? Well, all right then. You have no right to tell me what I shall do. I'm going down to Coralie's cabin.'

Younghusband regarded him appraisingly. 'Very well,' he answered. 'I can't stop you, as things are. But don't go inside; you heard what I told Dr. Hayvier. He won't let you in, anyhow.'

'I'm not going in; I'm going to wait outside. But if anyone else goes in, I'll be right after him, I can tell you that.'

'As you will,' Younghusband agreed, with new-found carelessness. 'Go along then.'

'I'm going,' Gnosens assured him from the doorway. He went out and closed the door. Hardly had he shut it than it opened again and the little radio page was disclosed in the aperture.

Captain Mansfield stood up. 'What is it now?' he asked.

'For you, sir,' the boy replied, saluting.

The others waited while the captain read through the message. At its conclusion he turned to Younghusband. 'That's my reply. You are right,' he acknowledged, 'this is full confirmation of what you say. It reads, "Younghusband our operative stop request you co-operate with him in any way he asks." That's conclusive enough for me, sir. Have you any request to make, now that you are established?'

'Only one at the moment, Captain,' was the prompt response. 'In the role I have been playing it has been impossible for me to go about armed. I would ask you to supply me with a revolver at once, if you can do so.'

'Why, I guess I can do that, Mr. Younghusband. Just a moment and I will let you have one of mine.'

Mansfield went out, and in a short time his footsteps were heard returning along the passage. But as he was about to enter, he turned, in the doorway itself, and looked sharply behind him. There was a clatter in the passage and, as the captain stepped aside, Mann's flushed and gasping face appeared at his shoulder. The steward was trembling from his exertions and for the moment was unable to speak.

Younghusband sprang instantly to Mansfield's side and seized the weapon out of his hand. His nervousness and hesitation disappeared as if by magic. As he clicked open the magazine and saw that it was filled, he cried sharply, 'Dr. Pons come with me! You too, Bone! Never mind, Steward; it doesn't matter who it was. We'll know soon enough.'

He was out of the door and half-way down the passage before Pons, galvanized as he had been by the urgency in the other's voice, could get to the door. With Younghusband well ahead and running at top speed, the three dashed out on deck. Pons saw the New York detective's shoulders just disappearing down the companionway, as he rounded the corner.

'Which way is it?' he asked Bone, who ran beside him.

'"A" 310,' replied the other, conserving his breath.

When they had tumbled down the companionway and on to the promenade deck, Younghusband was already out of sight. 'This way!' cried Bone and dashed for the entrance to the lobby. Pons, sprinting close behind him, just managed to escape colliding with an elderly couple who staggered back and stood rooted to the spot, looking after the chase with mouths agape.

Bone tore open the great, swinging doors and they were in the lobby. They flung themselves down the stairs. Bone turned right, then left, and they found themselves in one of the long passageways extending down the boat, with the lines of cabins on either side. Fifty yards ahead of them Younghusband was just pulling himself up beside the place where Gnosens was leaning negligently against a cabin door.

Pons and his companion, with a final sprint, came up just as Younghusband demanded, 'Who—who has gone in?'

Gnosens had straightened up as abruptly as the elderly couple on the promenade deck; also he appeared as astonished as they. 'Why,' he ejaculated in a surprised voice, 'no one's gone in. That is, no one but—'

'No one but,' Younghusband mimicked him in exasperation.

'No one but. Thank God the steward didn't pull that "No one but".' He took two further steps and quietly opened the door to cabin 310.

A peaceful enough scene met their eyes. Coralie lay on the berth under the porthole opposite the door, apparently fast asleep. Dr. Hayvier sat in a chair near the berth and the nurse was arranging a coverlet at its foot. Beside the sleeping girl the ship's doctor was stirring a glass of medicine and regarding her thoughtfully.

'What are you doing?' Younghusband cried in a sharp voice. The doctor looked around in surprise and withdrawing the instrument with which he had been stirring the mixture, slipped it into his pocket.

'I am giving my patient a sedative,' Pell said calmly and, raising the girl's head, placed the glass to her lips. With a single motion Younghusband's revolver came up and he fired.

The crash of the report in the confined space of the cabin was terrific. Dr. Hayvier leaped half out of his chair, the girl on the berth stiffened, cried out, and relapsed into unconsciousness again. The others stood momentarily paralysed by the shock, as the ship's doctor swayed, recovered and fell across the berth. A little trickle of red appeared at the edge of the coverlet and began to drip down on to the carpet.

Younghusband sprang across the room, and before touching the man he had shot, rescued the glass of medicine from where it had fallen on the berth. There was half-an-inch of the fluid still unspilled at the bottom. He turned to the others, who had now recovered sufficiently to gather around him, uncertain as to how to treat his act of violence.

'There is your murderer,' said Younghusband, pointing to Pell's motionless body. 'He was in the act of killing his wife when I shot him.' He turned reproachfully to Hayvier. 'I warned you to let no one in here. *No one.*'

'But the doctor,' Hayvier protested. 'I couldn't keep the doctor out.'

'The doctor? Of course it would be someone like the doctor. Someone who could come in on such a legitimate errand that you would all say no one had come in. It's lucky I found one man who could obey without thinking.

'Now, Bone, take this glass, and be careful you don't spill any of what's left in it. We'll have Dr. Schall analyse it; it's full of hydrocyanic acid, I'll stake my case on that. Pell was stirring it with his fountain pen. That's where he keeps his poison.'

Younghusband leaned down and turned over the body on the berth. It was plain that the shattering wound in the head had caused instantaneous death. He reached into Pell's vest pocket and brought out the pen. It was upside down and the partly loosened cap was full of a colourless liquid. As Younghusband raised it to his nose and sniffed at it gingerly, the odour of bitter almonds spread pungently about the circle of heads around him.

The Ritz restaurant on the sun deck boasted two private rooms just off its main dining saloon, and one of these had been reserved for Dr. Hayvier, who wished to celebrate the last evening aboard by a dinner tendered to his friends and colleagues. At the last moment he had decided to invite Commander Drake also, and the latter, who had struck up quite a friendship with the psychologists, had expressed his satisfaction when he found that he was able to accept.

The five men were now settling back comfortably in their chairs. Except for the ashtrays and glasses their waiter had cleared the table, gathered up his paraphernalia from the service stand and departed, closing the entrance behind him.

'So,' said Drake, stretching luxuriously, 'it ends. And the outcome is just like one of those detective stories that, if I remember rightly, our friend Hayvier denounced as being written by authors who had neglected their study of psychology. Surprise criminal and everything.' He grinned across the board at the scientist opposite. 'What have you to say now, my friend?' he inquired.

Dr. Hayvier bit off the end of his cigar before replying. 'What have I to say,' he considered. 'Well, what can I say? I shall have to admit what I have already admitted, that the man I selected for the criminal certainly did not commit the crime and that I never had the slightest suspicion of Pell. I accepted Pell all along as what he claimed to be, a physician, a man conditioned to save lives, not to take them. Just the same I think I may be able to derive some satisfaction from the final outcome. The man who murdered Smith turned out to be, not a physician, but a criminal of the first water, as I now understand it. He was not an amateur, but a professional; in other words he was conditioned by a long course of outside training and external pressure to his act. I may have been wrong about the actual man, but my principle, if I may be pardoned for saying so, was right.' Hayvier leaned back in his chair with the expression of one who has done slightly better than he had expected.

'It looks to me,' Drake admitted, 'as if we must grant your point. I understand from Younghusband that the man was a seasoned criminal, with at least two murders and several known blackmailings to his credit. I must say that he possessed the attributes that you predicted.'

Drake looked round the table and a rather bantering smile

had crept into his eyes. 'So Hayvier is satisfied, partially at any rate. But what about the rest of you? It would be most unfortunate, I think, if you were to arrive at your Convention with your feelings wounded and your theories undermined. I'm afraid that we can't make out that any of you solved the murder and caught the murderer, but it is just possible that we can conclude that everyone either contributed something to the correct solution or at least that his view was correct in some important respect. For example, what do you think we can do to assuage Dr. Plechs?'

'Too bad,' said Pons, grinding out his cigarette, 'but I'm afraid we can't do much. He was wrong this time and that's an end of it.'

'No, no,' Drake objected. 'I'm sure you are much too hasty. Now it has just occurred to me that Plechs was right in a most important matter. Indeed, had we but taken his idea more seriously, we should at least not have been so surprised by the identity of the criminal. We might even have been more likely to look in the right direction ourselves.'

Said Plechs, 'This is most kind of you, Mr. Drake. But I think you trouble yourself in vain. Before I have been right many times, but this time it is true that I was wrong. It is not so very important; I do not experience a harmful feeling of inferiority.'

'Not consciously perhaps,' the executive suggested slyly, 'but just think, my dear sir, what may be going on subconsciously. No, I insist; you were really right in a most important detail, and I feel compelled to say so. It was you who told us that in human behaviour we could not look for the obvious; you explained not once, but many times, that human beings are complicated and devious. Or it was their psyches that you told us were devious; as for me, it comes to the same thing. Well, you were no nearer picking the right suspect than anyone else, but it appears to me that this principle of yours was as correct as Dr. Hayvier's. In my opinion we should have done well to apply the principle you espoused, Dr. Plechs, and to have regarded with suspicion the unlikely person.'

'I have heard the captain, or somebody,' Professor Mittle interjected, 'express astonishment that there was so little agreement among us psychologists. But how could it be that so important a member of your staff as your physician could be so great an impostor? Surely you would discover his deceit within twenty-four hours.'

'Ah. Perhaps you didn't know this, Professor. Ordinarily, of course, it couldn't possibly happen. But our own doctor retired at the end of our last trip, and going west to New York we carried a temporary man who left us there. Meanwhile Dr. Pell, who had served in the past with another line than ours, had been engaged to fill this post regularly and was to join us at New York. None of us knew him and when this fellow came aboard and introduced himself to us as Dr. Pell, whose credentials he had somehow obtained, there was no cause for us to suspect any trickery at all. And think what an advantageous position he occupied for his own purposes. It was worth a good deal of risk to him; with the ship's doctor as a witness against him, Smith would have very little choice but to yield. What has happened to the real Dr. Pell I don't know; no doubt we shall learn when we land. This much must be true, that he has been robbed, for his papers were certainly presented to Captain Mansfield in dock at New York. And by the way, I have been so bold as to ask Younghusband to step in here after he gets through with Captain Mansfield; perhaps he can tell us more about Pell. Hope you don't object, Hayvier, to my inviting someone to your party?'

'Not a bit,' Hayvier assured him. 'I most certainly hope he comes in.'

'I think he will. As he isn't here yet, however, I am still concerned to rehabilitate Dr. Pons and the professor. I shall not be satisfied until you are all accounted for.'

'Don't you worry about me.' Pons poured himself another cup of black coffee. 'I know I was right without any outside assistance. I got hold of the key to the whole situation when I discovered that it all revolved around the girl. She was really the crux of it. She was engaged upon a blackmail plot just as I thought, and it was her change of heart about Smith that precipitated the murder and all the rest of it. That ought to let me out pretty nicely, don't you think so?'

'Yes,' Drake acknowledged, 'that was my idea. But what about the professor?'

'I may have spoken out of turn about Dr. Plechs,' admitted Pons, 'but I must say that I don't see how we can take care of Mittle in this affair. I don't believe he even accused anyone and so—'

The entrance of Younghusband interrupted him for the moment. Hayvier got up from his seat and welcomed the detective heartily and the latter drew up a chair at the end of the table. 'I think it's about time for some highballs,' Hayvier continued. He rang for the waiter. 'What will you have, gentlemen?'

The waiter having brought their selections and left several bottles and syphons comfortably grouped in the centre of the table, Drake turned at once to the newcomer.

'We have been trying,' he announced, 'to determine what

these various gentlemen have contributed to the case. So far, we have succeeded in fixing everyone up except the professor. I wonder if, from your point of view, you can tell us what he contributed, if anything.'

'If anything?' responded Younghusband, with a broad grin. 'Why, he contributed more than anyone else. He saved a life.'

'He did?' cried Pons; and the professor himself looked vastly astonished.

'Yes, he did,' Younghusband repeated, and went on with a good-natured smile. 'Of course I know why you have asked me to your party. You want to know what I can tell you about the final solution of the case you have all been interested in. Well, I'm not sure that even now I can tell you everything, but the case is closed and I have not objection to telling you as much as I know myself.'

'First of all,' Dr. Pons proposed, 'I should like to know what that mysterious message was, that you received up in the captain's room this afternoon. And why didn't you de-code it; could you read it right off, as it was?'

'No, I couldn't.' The detective looked ever so slightly chagrined. 'As a matter of fact, I should have de-coded it at once, but at the time I had no idea that it even referred to this case. It was signed "Cadmus", you remember, which meant merely a routine inquiry from the Department. But here it is; take a look at it.' He pulled the crumpled sheet from his pocket and Hayvier smoothed it out on the table. He saw the meaningless jumble of letters that the captain had observed earlier in the day:

dtsdapbvodps,laiZsdpp-slfDo,knahbs3200d

Beneath this there now appeared another line in pencil:

ddbd,id-f,astavplZpsDkhosposasplonbod

And this line had again been divided, as follows:

dd bd, id-f, as ta v pl Zps Dk ho s pos as pl on bod

Hayvier regarded the sheet with a puzzled frown. 'It's Greek to me,' he confessed. 'What does it mean?'

Younghusband got up and joined the others who were bending over their host's shoulder. 'It's one of the simpler codes,' he told them, 'so I guess there will be no harm if I explain it to such respectable citizens as you. In fact, I'm surprised they used such a simple one for a message of this importance. But of course they did not know how significant it would prove. If I had translated it when it first came, it would have solved the whole problem and the criminal would have been arrested and hanged, instead of shot.

'You see the figure, 32, in the original,' he went on. 'The 3 means that you take every third letter, beginning with the first and coming back to the beginning of the line whenever you reach the end, until all the letters have been transposed. And the 2 means that the last two letters are really the last two of the message and are to be dropped off and disregarded so far as concerns the transposition process indicated by the 3. When this is done you get the second line, my first pencilled line. The third line is simply the division of the second into words. There is no more decoding to be done; the last line is now a straightforward sentence, or rather two sentences, in a well-known system of shorthand called "Speedwriting".'

'Fine,' was Pons' comment. 'But we'd still like to know what it means.'

'Why, I should think you could almost read it for yourselves. Here it is, then: 'Dead body identified as that of Pell, ship's doctor. Who is posing as Pell on board?'

'Knowing I was on the *Meganaut* for this crossing, the Department communicated with me, rather than the captain, as soon as they had identified the body of the man they had found dead. As to the circumstances of this discovery in New York I know no more than you do; but I very greatly suspect that the real Pell was murdered in New York, at some time prior to our departure, by the man who took his place. From the fact that so much time has passed since then, I should also guess that he probably disposed of the body by dropping it either into the North or the East River. Several days might thus pass before it was discovered. The rest of the time before the message was sent is to be accounted for by the effecting of the identification. Now, what else can I tell you that you would like to know?'

It was Pons who asked the next question. 'Up in the captain's room this afternoon,' he reminded the detective, 'just before the chase down to the cabin began, you were saying that you had found one clue to the identity of the murderer. But you never said what it was. I should like to hear about that.'

'That I'm afraid I can't tell you,' Younghusband answered. 'And the reason is very simple. I never had a clue at all. I was only stalling for time.

'But I guess,' he went on, 'that I had better answer all your questions at once by telling you what I know about the case from beginning to end and how I finally managed to be sure that the criminal was in fact Pell.'

He paused and round the table several of the men poured themselves drinks and lit cigars and cigarettes. Younghusband waited until they were all settled, and began.

'There is little to tell up to the time we gathered in the captain's room this afternoon. You heard me tell Captain Mansfield about my position in connection with Mr. Smith and how I came to be aboard the *Meganaut* in the first place. I knew, of course, from the first the real relations between Smith and the girl he was travelling with, but I did not know either that she was married or that her husband was aboard. And incidentally, if the criminal is the man I suspect he is, she never was legally married to him, because he already has at least two other wives that we know of. It is my opinion that he simply saw the opportunity of using her for his own purposes and completely took her in. Her name, apparently, really is Coralie Reake-Lyons.

'When we came to the captain's conference this afternoon, I had done everything I could think of, and my role as a casual acquaintance of Smith's was still furnishing me with so good a means of private investigation that I had not yet abandoned it. But, together with Dr. Pons, I was still very sceptical about the disappearance of the girl. My own view was that she was still hiding somewhere aboard this boat, despite the failure of our elaborate search. So when Gnosens began his suspicious behaviour just prior to the 'plane's departure, and especially when I happened to catch his expression of relief at Mr. Drake's remark that it would have left in a minute or so, it suddenly clicked in my brain that, unlikely as it might seem, she was probably on that 'plane. So I took a chance and we found her. After all it was not much risk for me, for I could always disclose myself to Captain Mansfield and explain what I had done. As it turned out, I didn't have to.

'Then she was brought in and told us the story about her husband. It sounded reasonable to me as soon as I heard it, and I accepted it as a provisional hypothesis. It explained what I had been unable to account for all along, the presence of some random enemy of Smith's on the *Meganaut*. If the girl's story were true, his enemy was not a random one but a perfectly natural one. I must also say that I never agreed with Dr. Pons's idea that the girl herself had done the murder, although I supported that suggestion of his along with all the others for the purpose I explained this afternoon, namely, that of confusing the trail and making the real criminal suppose that all suspicion was fastened upon someone else.

'Then came the endurance contest between Gnosens and myself. I may say that I was not at all satisfied about Gnosens in my own mind up to the very last. Of course, when I saw him *outside* the girl's cabin, I knew he couldn't be our man. But his appearance was so ingenuous and frank all along that I had long ago suspected him of having a hand in concealing Miss Reake-Lyons, and I was not at all sure that he wasn't her husband.'

'Now just here,' it was Dr. Plechs who broke in, 'there is a thing I do not comprehend. When you and Mr. Gnosens were both searched for the poison, Miss Reake-Lyons insisted that nevertheless on one of you the poison must be. Still she must know that Pell is her husband all the time, and of course that it was not upon either of you. Why, then, does she say that?'

'I asked her that myself,' Younghusband returned, 'when I spoke with her some time ago. Her explanation was that, in her state of terror regarding Pell's intentions toward her, she took that means of trying to assure him that she would do her very best to avert suspicion from him in every possible way. She knew, she said, that there could be nothing found on us really, and so there was no actual harm in insisting. I've no doubt myself that that was her reason.

'Now we come to the professor's handwriting test. That puzzled me a great deal, for I was sure he didn't really expect to discover the criminal by such a means. It wasn't until I had sat down to write that the idea flashed across me; he suspected the poison was in someone's pen and he wanted to see if there was ink in ours.'

They all turned and looked at the professor, who sat calmly smoking.

'That's right, Professor, isn't it?' Younghusband asked.

'Such,' pronounced Mittle, 'was my notion.'

'Well, I'm damn' glad to hear it,' Hayvier declared. 'At the time I thought you had gone goofy. My apologies.'

'So,' the detective continued, 'when I had caught the idea, I was nearly ready to disclose myself and insist on a search of everyone present. But I didn't, for several reasons. I wasn't sure the professor's idea was correct, I wasn't sure that the story of the husband was true, and worst of all, I wasn't absolutely convinced that the criminal was necessarily in the room with us, although that was certainly my guess.

'At the same time I formed another plan. I didn't want the conference to break up, as it seemed to me it would, so I did announce who I was. And when the girl fainted, I saw an opportunity. I urged that she go below, and my plan was to give the criminal an opportunity to get at her and do away with her, as I was certain he would, now that he knew her attitude was definitely hostile to him. That was my chance, the only chance I could see, to trap him, as long as she herself refused to identify him. I was so sure that he would make the attempt that I was very seriously concerned for her safety, and fortunately I not only sent Dr. Hayvier down with her, but I established a less obvious guard to watch her door. Captain Mansfield's steward did much to save her life. I was afraid that Dr. Hayvier would not prove a real obstacle because I believed that whoever came in would have a very reasonable and innocent excuse for his or her presence.

'From then on it became a question of waiting until the criminal could see his chance and take it. And meanwhile of convincing him, if he were present, that it was impossible for me to leave the captain's room myself. That is why I had to stall along for time, while maintaining to everyone that I was really in a great hurry and only kept there against my will. My nervousness, however, was by no means assumed; what I was terribly afraid of was that the criminal was not with us at all and could therefore approach the cabin without my receiving any preliminary hint that he was doing so. When Pell, Drake and Gnosens had all left the room, I was prepared for action any minute. But I still had no notion as to which of them it might be, for they all had what seemed to be perfectly legitimate reasons for going. Gnosens's excuse, of course, was the weakest, and if he had not himself insisted after my first refusal to let him go, I should have had to supply him with another opportunity. He was still the only one I had any reason to suspect seriously.'

'But how did Dr. Pell get down to the cabin?' Plechs inquired. 'Surely the call that summoned him was from Dr. Schall; he was not the accomplice, was he?'

'Oh, no, Schall is all right. That was just a bit of luck for Pell. While he had a smattering of medical knowledge, enough for him to pass himself off as a doctor for one trip, he was not a qualified doctor by any means. And so, when his patient really began to get worse, he had to call in Dr. Schall and take a chance that the latter would not find him out. The consultation was not faked at all. But I don't think Pell had forgotten about it, as he made it appear; he only waited for Schall to call him from the hospital because he thought that in that way it would be clear to all of us that he had a perfectly legitimate reason to leave. He did actually go to the hospital, too. But when he got there, he made an excuse to his consultant about having to go below and see the girl at once, and assured him that he would be right back. Dr. Schall agreed to wait, and he did wait for him for about an hour, before he found out what had happened. Incidentally, he tells me that Pell had a good working knowledge of surgery, quite enough to have conducted the autopsies without creating any suspicion in Schall's mind, although it is true that he left most of the work to Schall.

'Well, there's not much else, I guess, except that I might explain how I was ready to fire at once, as soon as we got to the cabin. That was due to the professor here and that's why I say he saved the girl's life. When I first looked in, Pell was just finishing stirring up the dose he was about to administer. I was positive that whoever I found in the cabin would be the criminal, but what put the final stamp of certainty on it, was that I noticed he was stirring the liquid *with his fountain pen.* No proper doctor would do that. And furthermore it was in a fountain pen that the professor suspected the poison was carried. By the way, Hayvier, didn't you suspect anything when you saw that?'

'But I didn't see it,' Hayvier answered. 'He carefully turned away from me when he mixed up the stuff. I could only see his back.'

'That's right. Yes, I remember that was so, when I first looked in. I saw the pen clearly myself when he turned around and slipped it into his pocket, but then I was almost looking for it. The professor's trick had made a great impression upon me. So I was sure then. And when, even though he must have guessed the game was up, he made the final gesture of trying to kill his wife even at the last moment, I had no recourse but to fire across the room. It was the only way I could stop him; a couple of drops of that poison in her mouth and she was done for. And so,' Younghusband spread out his hands and at the same time took up his glass, 'I guess that's all.' He took a long drink and looked around at his hearers.

'I can't understand that,' Hayvier objected. 'I mean his daring to poison his wife at all when it would be perfectly obvious afterwards that he was the only one who could have done it.'

Younghusband shrugged. 'Consider his situation,' he suggested. 'As far as I can see, it was his only chance, even if it was a tremendous risk. At the least he would silence the only real witness against him, and only an immediate autopsy, conducted by Dr. Schall, could establish that her death was murder. He would have insisted upon heart failure, of course. Meanwhile, he had the slim chance of escaping from the boat, now that we are almost in. That he tried to kill her even at the last moment, I am inclined to attribute to pure animosity, although even then I don't see what other alternative was open to him. He was right, I think, in not trusting her to maintain her silence. She would have given him away in the end, if only to save Gnosens, whom I planned to arrest if all else failed.'

'Just one thing more,' Dr. Pons added. 'Who is this fellow who has been masquerading as Dr. Pell?'

'As I said,' was Younghusband's reply, 'I'm not sure as yet. I rather think he will turn out to have been a very slippery and desperate blackmailer whom we have been tracking for nearly six years now. If this really is he, it will be a feather in my cap when I get back home.'

'I hope it is,' said Pons. 'You deserve it. And by the way, have you heard anything further about the young lady? I'm somewhat worried about her. That shot of yours must nearly have killed her, as well as Pell, considering the condition she was in.'

'Don't worry,' Younghusband advised him. 'Dr. Schall was with the captain, when I left, and he told us that she recovered remarkably well from the shock. Pell took me in completely when he insisted that she go to bed. I thought she was seriously ill, but she wasn't. Even he probably knew that, but he had a reason for insisting and—'

There was a rap at the door and the waiter appeared apologetically in the entrance. 'I am sorry, gentlemen,' he announced as they all looked up. 'It is time we close.'

'All right,' said Hayvier in some surprise. He pulled out his watch. 'We'll adjourn down to the smoking-room, if you care to, gentlemen.'

One by one the six got out of their chairs and gathered round the doorway. 'You know,' Mittle commented to Younghusband, 'there is another point that is not clear to me. How is it that Pell managed to poison Mr. Smith? He was not at the table with Smith, I believe, and I thought it had been decided that the poison was slipped into the drinks by someone at the table?'

'So far as I know,' was Younghusband's reply, 'Pell never went near the Smith table. Of course we shall never know now for certain just how the poisoning of the drinks was done, but Pell was at the bar, probably at the service end of it, when Smith and his party came into the smoking-room. And naturally he was acquainted with the fact that both Smith and the girl were addicted to drinking absinthe. I don't mean that they were addicts, merely that they were both very fond of it and usually ordered it, when they drank at all, which was seldom. It is an unusual drink, especially after dinner, and when he saw them give their order and their steward came up to the bar next to him, he could be sure that the two absinthe glasses on that tray would go to Smith and the girl. Of course, he got the poison into the two glasses by means of the hollow, rubber ball, no doubt while the steward was collecting the remainder of the order, and afterwards disposed of the ball by slipping it into Gnosens's pocket. I remember his stopping and coming back to speak with him, but I didn't notice it particularly at the time.'

As Younghusband finished his explanation, Hayvier came up and the whole party sauntered out and down the broad steps leading to the small lobby and the elevators just before the restaurant's entrance. 'Yes,' Mittle considered, 'it certainly could have been accomplished as you say. I've no doubt you are right.' As they receded, their voices became less distinct in the distance, until only a confused murmur floated back toward the empty dining saloon.

Outside the night was quiet, a night through which an illusory moon sailed high with deceptive slowness. The reaches of the sun deck were hazy under the drifting light that filtered down from far above and covered them like a flood of ultra-microscopic snowflakes. Unimaginably distant, but seemingly as close as the moon, the stars glowed brightly, rather than sparkled, in the dark blue canopy overhead. On the deck a few confined circles of yellower light, widely separated from each other, attested that the troublesome dynamos were still functioning.

It was just past midnight. The hum of a ventilating motor merged with the low noises that never cease at sea. From forward, around the series of shields and superstructures whose purpose was so obscure, now that the 'plane had quitted their snug protection, came the hint of a song that faded out even as it wandered across the deck. 'I'm tellin' you what bliss is, and what. . . .'

Coralie, from where her freshly waved and curly head nestled against the comfortable shoulder behind, could see the after-mast with its skeleton rigging towering into the spangled sky; at its tip glowed a single light, a slightly larger star, weaving its way among its companions of the night. The air was balmy, soft; they were entering the Channel over a sea as placid as an inland pond. She stretched out her slim, lovely legs to their fullest extent along the foot-rest of the chair and sighed contentedly.

'I am *not* sorry he is dead,' said the girl in a low murmur. 'Why should I pretend that I am? He was hateful, and I think he was a little crazy. . . .'

Her voice drifted into silence; Gnosens's arm pressed her slender beauty closer.

'And I do love you. I'm a fool to say so.' She twisted around and searched his face anxiously, almost imploringly. Her lips were slightly parted. 'But I don't care. I do; I do love you. . . . Kiss me.'

'Darling!' . . .

'Oh,' said the girl suddenly, freeing herself, but only somewhat. 'Look! Over there, way over. It's a lighthouse; we're across.'

'Thank God,' said the man fervently. 'We're across.'

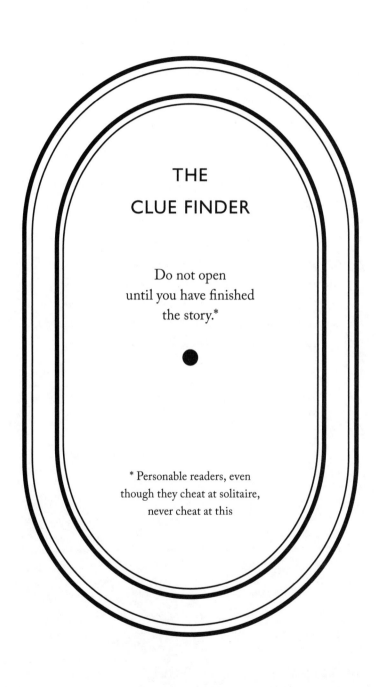

THE
CLUE FINDER

Do not open
until you have finished
the story.*

●

* Personable readers, even
though they cheat at solitaire,
never cheat at this

Without

reflection upon the judicious reader, who unquestionably has seen through the small pretenses hereinbefore employed, it will be well for the author, especially be he a prudent fellow, to indicate in no vague way wherein the criminal has been disclosed throughout the preceding leaves. Therefore, if only to spare the clever the embarrassment (and labour) of exposing to their less judicious friends both why and how their own acute conclusions were reached, it would seem best to propose that the outlaw has been revealed

----

As to the Opportunity to commit
    the crime:

(his presence on the scene)	*Page 12,*	*Par. 2,*	*Line 12.*
	Page 335	*Par. 2.*	
	Page 26	*Par. 3,*	*Line 10.*

(a Method he, too, might
    have used)

	Page 334,	*Par. 4,*	*Line 6.*
As to the apparatus he employed:	*Page 283,*	*Par. 5.*	

As to a Peculiar Circumstance
    about him:

	Page 115,	*Par. 4.*
	Page 116,	*Par. 4.*

As to his possible Anonymity on board:	*Page 116,*	*Par. 6.*

As to a Suspicious Reluctance that
    he evidenced:

	Page 49,	*Par. 4.*	
	Page 115,	*Par. 2*	
	Page 117,	*Par. 2.*	
	Page 117,	*Par. 3,*	*Line 4.*
	Page 118,	*Par. 4.*	
	Page 118,	*Par. 7.*	

As to an Excitement he overdid:	*Page 122,*	*Par. 3.*	
	Page 122,	*Par. 7,*	*Line 3.*
	Page 123,	*Par. 6.*	
	Page 123,	*Par. 8.*	

As to a Strange Uncertainty upon
    his part:

	Page 293,	*Par. 2,*	*Line 1.*
	Page 294,	*Par. 3,*	*Line 1.*
	Page 295,	*Par. 2,*	*Line 7.*
	Page 295,	*Par. 3,*	*Line 1.*

As to his Knowledge of an
   Impending Crisis: *Page 272,*   *Par. 7.*

As to his Attempt to implicate
   the Innocent: *Page 33,*   *Par. 2.*

                                         Page 283,   *Par. 5.*

                                         Page 272,   *Par. 5.*

                                         Page 273,   *Par. 1*

                                         Page 317,   *Par. 1,*   *Line 8.*

As to his Victim's Fear of him: *Page 303,*   *Par. 4.*

                                         Page 325,   *Par. 3,*   *Line 3.*

                                         Page 325,   *Par. 6.*

                                         Page 326,   *Par. 3.*

                                         Page 326,   *Par. 7.*

                                         Page 327,   *Par. 2.*

                                         Page 329,   *Par. 3.*

As to his Naming, on a list otherwise composed of Those
   Already Eliminated: *Page 337,*   *Par. 3.*

DISCUSSION QUESTIONS

- Were you able to predict any part of the solution to the case?

- After learning the solution, were there any clues you realized you had missed?

- Would the story be different if it were set in the present day? If so, how?

- Did the social context of the time play a role in the narrative? If so, how?

- How did the boat setting influence the narrative?

- If you were one of the main characters, would you have acted differently at any point in the story?

- Did you identify with any of the characters? If so, which?

- Did this story remind you of any other books you've read?

Erle Stanley Gardner, *The Case of the Baited Hook*
Erle Stanley Gardner, *The Case of the Careless Kitten*
Erle Stanley Gardner, *The Case of the Borrowed Brunette*
Erle Stanley Gardner, *The Case of the Shoplifter's Shoe*
Erle Stanley Gardner, *The Bigger They Come*

Frances Noyes Hart, *The Bellamy Trial*
Introduced by Hank Phillippi Ryan

H.F. Heard, *A Taste for Honey*

Dolores Hitchens, *The Cat Saw Murder*
Introduced by Joyce Carol Oates

Dorothy B. Hughes, *Dread Journey*
Introduced by Sarah Weinman
Dorothy B. Hughes, *Ride the Pink Horse*
Introduced by Sara Paretsky
Dorothy B. Hughes, *The So Blue Marble*

W. Bolingbroke Johnson, *The Widening Stain*
Introduced by Nicholas A. Basbanes

Baynard Kendrick, *The Odor of Violets*

Frances and Richard Lockridge, *Death on the Aisle*

John P. Marquand, *Your Turn, Mr. Moto*
Introduced by Lawrence Block